Memories
In Technicolor

Memories
In Technicolor

A Novel

Yamilé Stitt

Logan Masterworks
Miami, FL

Copyright © 2019 Yamilé Stitt
Published by Logan Masterworks

Cover Design:Al Esper Graphic Design
Interior Layout & Design: Roberto Nunez

Translation: Yamilé Stitt
Nadège Chérubin-K.I.T

Edited by Logan Masterworks, an imprint of Lominy Books

memoriesintechnicolor@gmail.com

ISBN: 978-0-578-52986-8
Library of Congress Control Number: 2019944552
BISAC Category Code: SOCIAL SCIENCE / Emigration & Immigration, SOCIAL SCIENCE / Minority Studies, TRAVEL / Caribbean & West Indies, TRAVEL / Europe / General, TRAVEL / Europe / France, TRAVEL / United States / General, HISTORY / Europe / France, FICTION / General, FICTION / Women, FICTION / Coming of Age

Printed in the United States of America

Originally published in French by Educa Vision (2016)
"Les Chemins de Lumière"

We are all travelers,
on a journey
at the heart of life

~ * ~

In memory of my husband and my parents, gone too soon

~ * ~

To my children and grandchildren, my reason for living

~ * ~

To these unforgettable pilgrims who have shared my path
for one brief moment
at the crossroads of life

These pages saw the light because you believed in them

Yamilé Stitt

~ * ~

PART I

Departure

~1~

Paris, France – September 1966

"Wake up, darling. We are flying over Paris!"

A little dazed, and sore after a six-hour flight over the Atlantic, I peek through the window. Yvette, usually reserved, can hardly contain her joy. Hanging between clouds and land, the Air France craft begins its aerial dance that precedes landing. The City of Light reveals itself in the daytime. A shy September sun greets us on French territory. Orly Airport is swarming with people, and sounds burst from everywhere. For the first time, I step on Parisian soil, suddenly self-conscious of my slow islander drawl. I answer, in shy whispers, the questions of the immigration agent.

Our taxi rushes through the heart of the city. We drive along the Champs-Elysées, as if I'm in a dream, but with my eyes wide open. My childhood storybooks come to life, as I feel catapulted right into the heart of a novel. Our pension-hotel is nestled in a residential area of the 17th Arrondissement. Ms. Levesque, the owner, offers us her most spacious room, with a private bath and a view. Exhausted by the jet lag, we fall into a deep sleep.

Hours later, we're awoken by a discreet knock at the door and an invitation to join the other guests in the large dining room by the lobby. The room has small, individual round tables, white tablecloths, and bud vases. Residents are quietly absorbed in the habitual gesture of spoon to soup bowl, to mouth. A young waitress in uniform escorts us to our table in the hushed room.

At dinner, I discover how much easier it is to order a bottle of wine than be served a glass of mineral water. I learn too, dumbfounded, that the best camembert cheese is one that is "oozing out…" The other boarders, year-round residents, gaze curiously at our arrival. We are, obviously, foreigners. A handsome man with jet-black hair sits alone next to our table. He nods in our direction, with a wink. Did I find him handsome because he is the only guest who does not seem to be of retirement age? This thought makes me smile.

Yvette hugs me when I wake up the next morning. I am celebrating, on foreign soil, my fifteenth birthday today. Breakfast is served in the room: crisp baguettes, whipped butter, raspberry jam, and a large steaming bowl of café au lait. Afterward, the race through the streets of Paris begins, in order to buy my boarding-school supplies. A list was provided by Saint Joseph with my admission letter. We mingle with the crowd at Galeries Lafayette and sip coffee at a terrace after our shopping spree. We are Parisians for a day. Sounds of "Oui, Oui" and "Ooh lala" come from the surrounding bistro tables. I inspect, curious, the thermal underwear Yvette selected, a mandatory purchase in anticipation of very cold months ahead. I am already dreaming of winter's first snowflakes.

~ * ~

The taxi drives deep into the heart of Val-de-Seine's enchanting woods, already adorned in fall's rich garments. The tires make a muffled sound as they slide on a thick carpet of dead leaves, sparkling with glints of fiery gold. We remain silent, overwhelmed with emotion at the imminent separation ahead. Suddenly, at the turn of the narrow road lined by centuries-old trees and shrubs adorned in autumn colors, a huge clearing reveals, to our stunned gaze, the majestic castle of Saint Joseph. Cracked stone walls wrapped in a blanket of ivy, towers and crenellated structures, and massive carved wooden doors bring to this eighteenth-century décor the element of dream so often evoked in fairytale books. The young and naïve Haitian girl with an unbridled imagination remains speechless, in the face of such splendor. We have just crossed the threshold of the stage in which I will experience the richest year of my adolescence.

Yvette Tyler, dressed in an elegant mustard-color suit that flatters her dark olive complexion, strides in her high heels toward the tall, brick staircase leading to the visitors' parlor. Impressed by the majesty of the place, I just stand there, paralyzed with shyness, in my navy-blue blazer and my long schoolgirl socks. The taxi driver has been kind enough to carry the heavy suitcase filled with the contents of my life. My guitar rests in a corner at the entrance hall. A nun referred to as the sœur messagère, the receptionist, escorts us to the parents' meeting room. A quick glance around me offers the reassurance I was seeking. Yvette, as always, handled things impeccably. My uniform is an exact replica of the one worn by these young boarding school girls.

A faint smile. A wink. Can they guess my anxiety?

After two enchanting weeks basking in Paris's magical charm, and preparing my trousseau for boarding school, Yvette has reached, today, the last phase of her mission. She smiles discreetly, aware of the wrenching waves of my heart, of the panic that settles, in letters of fire, in my eyes. In the silence we share, wrapped around us like a thick fog, I have never felt so close to her.

A graceful silhouette in long black veils approaches us and breaks the somber mood that engulfed us.

~2~

Port-au-Prince, Haiti

Marguerite held me close to her heart, her cheeks, wet with tears, pressed against mine, her eyes swollen with grief. I had her protective presence next to me during the wonderful journey of childhood. She already hated the country of France, about to rob her of "her" little girl. She had advised that I dress warm, as it gets so cold there, and to eat well to keep my strength. Marguerite had my future all mapped out: the height of bliss would crystallize in an early marriage to a young man from a "good family," one day, who would give me a baby every year, according to Caribbean tradition. It would then be my turn to rest, like Yvette, on a lounge chair by a beautiful flower-filled porch.

I might not have realized it then, but my heart did not want any trodden paths with familiar turns. A brand-new road awaited on the horizon. Leaving the only world I had ever known on that Caribbean island of my birth, I would cross, at the fragile age of adolescence, a huge ocean, to land in a new, scary world: Europe!

I wished, for a precious moment, to stop time, and recapture, for one brief instant, my childhood, in the arms of Marguerite. My tears met hers, as her fingers ran through my hair, repeating the gestures of the past. Was she going to sing "Dodo titit," the lullaby she favored when she used to tuck me in at night?

Charles and Leilah, my grandparents, flanked by my younger brothers Bobby, Freddy, and Junior, waved their arms enthusiastically at the travelers heading for François Duvalier Airport. These familiar faces disappeared onto the porch hidden by the pink laurel hedges, as our Peugeot, driven by my father, crossed the steel gate and made the turn for the street. Grandma and Grandpa had agreed to move in for a few weeks and lend a hand during Yvette's absence: their daughter was taking me to boarding school in France.

Nothing would be the same when I returned the following year. Time can never be reversed, I pondered philosophically. Charles and Leilah would have more "salt" than "pepper" in their hair, perhaps. My younger brothers would, for the first time, blow out their birthday candles without me.

But it was vital for my survival in a foreign land that the memory of James and Yvette remain immutable, sculpted in stone. My home, my family, my country were my world. They were my anchor, the place where one always comes back to, even from the most distant shores.

The familiar images of Port-au-Prince were parading, one last time, before my eyes, through the car window. I sat on the back seat of our grey Peugeot, as it fended its way through the motley crowd of pedestrians and cars; as I looked over my father's thick neck and Yvette's classic bun, my tears had, that day, a bittersweet taste.

On the runway, the Air France craft was already waiting.

~3~

Saint Joseph

"Madame Tyler? Allow me to introduce myself: Sister Marie Laurence, in charge of the 10th graders. Ladies, welcome to Saint Joseph!"

I look furtively at her as she speaks with Yvette. She has bright eyes behind silver-rimmed glasses. Will she be a strict teacher? Sister Marie Laurence, after the usual formalities, escorts us to the principal's office to complete the last details of admission. Reverend Mother Elizabeth, slightly corpulent behind her long black veils, a rosary resting in the folds of her habit, stands up as we come in and stretches out her hand. I do not notice the wrinkles of experience or the weight of years on that young, pleasant face. Like the Sisters of Sainte Thérèse, in Haiti, these French nuns wear a wedding band, a reminder that they are the brides of Christ, and that their life is devoted to the Lord.

During the interview with Mother Superior, an unexpected topic arises: the need for me to be assigned "correspondents"—a family who will host me on weekends, in Paris. We do not know anyone in France. Taken aback, Yvette confesses, "Myriam, your father will not consent to you staying in the home of strangers."

When a vast ocean severs a fifteen-year-old from her family, the fear of the unknown can cast scary shadows in her heart. We keep a cautious silence. Reverend Mother generously offers to let the school have charge of me on weekends, until a solution desirable for all is found. I am too upset to measure the magnitude of such a decision upon my life. Yvette wisely reminds me that the issue will pertain to Saturdays only because students return on Sundays.

Parents are offered a guided tour of the premises: classrooms, study and dining room, laboratory, library, chapel, and dormitory. The size of our small cubicles, cleverly dubbed "boxes," baffles me a second. It turns out our strictly regimented lives as boarders will mostly unfold in the classroom and the study-room, not in the dorm that should only be considered a refuge after an exhausting school day.

We remain intertwined in a long embrace at the foot of the grand brick staircase, shattered by the intensity of the moment. The taxi disappears with Yvette afterwards, taking away a little bit of my heart. Tomorrow, she will start her journey back to Haiti. At the thought of it, I cannot control the flow of tears.

In the crowded refectory, I have trouble swallowing a bite of food, the new foreign student lost among clusters of friends who chatter cheerfully, happy to meet up again after summer vacation. Generous servings of mashed potatoes, ham and green beans are passed around. The depth of my emotional void engulfs me, like an endless body of water stretching far into the horizon, a cruel ocean, a deep abyss. A knot feels stuck in the back of my throat, and I whisper inaudible answers to my classmates' friendly questions at the dinner table.

After supper, we are invited to return to our respective "box" in the dormitory. A narrow bed, tiny desk, chest of drawers and sink make up the rest of the area. My clothes have been neatly put away in the drawers by the housekeeper. My suitcase has been stored under the bed. I retrieve my toiletry case and, like a lost sheep, blindly follow my classmates who have already lined up for the showers. It is cold already, so early in the season.

I abandon, with regret, the warm, soothing water of the shower, to put on a long flannel nightgown. Bundled up under my covers, holding the picture frame of my happy family to my heart, I can finally unleash my grief. I am *freezing*. September's weather pierces me, penetrates, to the bones, my body still tan from the sunny climate of the tropics. At the entrance to the box, a thick curtain allows us some privacy. But the thinness of the wooden panels dividing our small cubicles betrays me. Did my classmates hear my muffled sobs? Did one of them warn the sister on duty? The shadow of a sudden presence startles me. Sister Marie Laurence has entered my box quietly, carefully closing the curtain behind her. Surprised, I quickly sit on my bed, and try awkwardly to hide my tears.

"Myriam," she says in a whisper, "I am guessing the reason for such grief, my daughter. But we are here to surround you, and become your new family, in France."

She takes a seat at the edge of the bed, and I hide my tears against her shoulder. Patiently, she finds the appropriate words that console, the gestures that bring comfort, but I have only one, desperate wish: to return to my family, my home, my country.

~ * ~

"Get up, young lady! Time to wake up and dress quickly."

Sister Angèle shakes me vigorously. It is still dark outside. A happy bustle can be heard in the large dormitory composed of double rows of residents' cubicles: water flows from the sinks; students quickly brush their teeth and grab their uniforms. Accustomed to showering in both the morning and night in Haiti, I have to adapt to the basic morning sponge bath, and follow, with a towel and toiletry case, the line of students for the evening showers. A blonde head peeks inside my box, from the corner of the curtain: "Myriam, I am Agnès Renaud. Our boxes are next to each other. Hurry up, we must rush to breakfast in the dining hall, and meet afterward at study-room for school-books distribution."

Agnès becomes a life preserver. I never leave her sight that day. Did she hear snippets of the scene last night, when I turned into a weeping willow tree? I will find out, days later, that she was instrumental in Sister Marie Laurence's presence by my side on that first night at Saint Joseph: that night, by solicitude for her classmate who was crying uncontrollably in the next room, she warned the sister on dormitory guard duty, who was none other than our homeroom teacher.

"Please, stay a while longer," I begged, in the throes of grief.

Turning back, Sister Marie Laurence flipped the nightlight switch on, to tuck me in, maternally, under the thick covers. I do not recall when I fell asleep.

~ * ~

The week passes at the speed of light. I must struggle to adapt to this new pace of life where everything is timed: be on a race for the bathroom, the refectory, in study hall and in class. The languid Caribbean girl exhausts all her energy to comply with the grueling schedule of interns. A friendship is forged with my dorm neighbors: Agnès, a young Parisian, and Ishtar, a Muslim of Middle Eastern origin. Passionate about her country and her culture, Ishtar welcomes my Lebanese heritage which, she says, brings us closer. A stranger in France, too, Ishtar stays on weekends with correspondents, a host family from her homeland.

Discreet, Sister Marie Laurence made no mention of the melodrama during my first night at Saint Joseph. I approached the podium at the end of her physics class to whisper a hasty "thank you," the next morning. She winked. I nodded. Words are useless. Strange…I no longer feel lost on a desert island.

Am I already adapting to my new life?

~ * ~

My first Saturday at boarding school.

The students left in a big brouhaha, swapping their uniforms for casual city clothes, happy to return home to their families. The 1:00 p.m. school bus disappears toward Paris. I find myself suddenly, desperately alone. The magnitude of my situation as a foreign student on foreign land without regular friends stabs me in the heart. I, too, will change clothes and pretend to be thousands of miles away from Saint Joseph, back to my island and the warm caress of the tropics. My eyelids have a hard time keeping the tears at bay. I am homesick for Haiti, my family, my friends, my home.

My uniforms and bedding will be sent to the laundry room, announces Sister Angèle, who brings me some detergent for my undergarments. A few minutes later, kindred sister to Cinderella, I find myself on all fours, sponging soapy water that has overflowed from my narrow sink and spread everywhere on the ground. Spicy words emerge from my Creole vocabulary at my clumsiness. The nun returns with fresh towels and sheets, and hears my litany of curses. Fortunately, she does not understand a word of Creole. I give her the biggest grin of my life. If Sister Angèle only knew what horrors came out of my mouth!

Delving into a thick romance novel would have distracted an avid reader like me from my loneliness. Unfortunately, the school library closes its doors on weekends. As I sit at my desk, a long letter to my parents begins to take shape. I paint a rosy picture of my life in boarding school, keeping my grief bottled up, not wanting to make them sad. I will purchase a book of stamps at the school's commissary office on Monday. Then my letter will begin its long journey to Haiti. My watch shows that it is still early for supper. Too cold for a walk in the park, I retrieve, from their refuge under the bed, my black leather journal and Parker pens collection. I have neglected them since my arrival in France. The words will flow through the pages, without fear of censorship. My journal does not have to please, nor protect the feelings of others. It is the confidante that welcomes the emotional outpouring of my heart, listens in silence and never, ever judges me.

Sunday morning, breakfast is a treat: a bowl of steaming hot chocolate and a croissant, a welcome change from the café au lait and mini baguette, butter and jam that students are served on weekdays. The large, empty refectory chills my lonely heart. Sister Angèle stopped by my "box" in the dormitory last night, to invite me to Sunday Mass, scheduled for 9 o'clock at the chapel this morning. Without a shadow of doubt, my peculiar presence must intrigue the retired nuns whose advanced age and limited mobility keep them secluded in their close-knit community, away from the busy student life teeming at Saint Joseph during the week.

After Mass, I hear brisk footsteps behind me. "Myriam, shall we go for a little walk in Chateaubriand's Park?"

Sister Marie Laurence has joined me under the arches. She must pity the solitude of her cloistered student, I suppose. We walk in silence for a long time, enjoying the splendor of the park. Autumn has colored the trees and shrubs with a thousand strokes of an invisible artist's paintbrush. Accustomed to the green of eternal summers in Haiti, I marvel at the rich and voluptuous colors of the season, amazed by such display of beauty. "Nature sings the wonders of the Creator," recalls Sister Marie Laurence.

Standing on a carpet of autumn leaves, towered by gigantic old trees, I learn, through this simple, poetic phrase, the beauty of the prayer of praise, when nature captures us in complete awe.

We have reached an old stone bench which seems to defy time. The towers of Saint Joseph have disappeared from the horizon, hidden in the thickness of the undergrowth. The air feels cool, with a timid sun. Shivering, I imagine the morning of Creation: tall, majestic trees, stretching as far as eyes can see, in the Garden of Eden; man, tiny, insignificant, and lost in the great vastness of nature. I close my eyes, overwhelmed by the majesty of my surroundings. Time stands still, frozen in space.

That Sunday, Sister Marie Laurence shares the legend of Chateaubriand Park: In the eighteenth century, Saint Joseph was the residence of a French noble family. The hardwood stairs, the archway doors, the old entry of the horses, and the fountain covered in moss, have all survived the ravages of time. According to legend, François-René de Chateaubriand, the famous poet of Romanticism, would take refuge in the park, seeking, in the solitude of the woods, inspiration from the muse. The cracked bench held, probably, the birth of immortal literary works.

The spirit of Chateaubriand will forever haunt me now. Pen and paper will collect the disorder of a capricious muse, who has awakened from her torpor. The extraordinary will arise from the ordinary. I feel, in my heart, that an incredible year is about to unfold, at this phase of my journey.

~4~

In Haiti, during the 1960s, the hope of many parents was to see their offspring pursue their studies overseas. A stay abroad would give the student a special halo and help open the doors to a brighter future, they firmly believed.

Political instability at the time had been the decisive factor that led to my departure for France. Papa Doc "t'ap fè chou e rav" –he was causing havoc in families where too many had suffered an untimely loss, through tragic or mysterious circumstances: a son, whose idealistic enthusiasm displeased the dictator; a careless uncle, who could not bridle his tongue or his temper; an air-head who talked too much in the presence of the gardener; and the culprit would land behind bars in the cells of the much feared penitentiary, Fort Dimanche. Sometimes, the writer who failed to restrain his pen had to take the path of exile to spare his life.

Spontaneity was punished, and dreams were stifled by the power in place. Survival had become the ultimate goal for fearful citizens. That was "life in Haiti," as peace of mind and heart was a luxury forbidden by the president's emissaries.

My family, and my teachers at Sainte Thérèse, had moved heaven and earth for my transfer to France. It would be my honor to make them proud. Getting my French baccalauréat would crown the end of my classical studies and symbolize my official entry into the adult world.

Cathy and I were inseparable at Sainte Thérèse. To leave her meant losing my childhood best friend. I did not dare ask her why her parents were not sending her abroad, like me, like so many youths of our generation. Discretion prevailed. During lunch recess, under the shadow of the big mahogany tree, we shared our souls, not the daily routine of our respective households. My friend was wiser than

I was, and she would often curb my wild imagination or whimsical moments. We complemented each other.

In my journal, I would express our deep aspirations in allegorical terms: "I am a flower, the ornament of homes. I sing the beauty of the Creator, and exhale His fragrance," Cathy would chant. I would echo in the wind: "They call me kite. I fly, light and free, in the ethereal azure, tossed by the breeze, caressed by the clouds."

"We will write often," we promised each other, after a long embrace. Our friendship, without the shadow of a doubt, would stand the test of time and distance.

In the fever of my imminent departure, I wrote a free verse poem, my farewell gift to Sister Nicole, our literature teacher. I still remember the ending lines:

"In the dull and grey of daily routine,
When she catches, from afar, a promise, a glow,
She marvels, fulfilled:
To mold a soul is beautiful!"

She is the one who planted in me the seed of creative writing. My Parker pens collection and my journal, faithful companions, headed to France with me.

~5~

I have been called to Sister Marie Laurence's office. Intrigued, yet a bit apprehensive, I step into her sanctuary for the first time. Religious and scientific books line the shelves. Her desk is piled with students' notebooks. The nun stays up late in her refuge, long after the students have completed their evening sessions in study hall. The ray of light under the door never fails to shine, as we pass by her office on our way to the dormitory.

Agnès's parents have been granted their request to invite me to their home this weekend, my teacher informs me with a smile. She hands me the permission slip, signed by Reverend Mother, like it's a trophy. The bird will finally get to fly out of her cage. I struggle to keep my excitement under control.

"The Renauds are a respectable family. Reverend Mother and I have agreed for you to be their guest, and you will be taking the coach to Paris Saturday with Agnès and your classmates."

Packed in the crowded bus on our way to Paris, we chat excitedly at the prospect of freedom. At the bus station, Mr. Renaud grabs my suitcase and places it in the trunk of his Citroën. We are driving at a brisk pace in the busy streets of Paris. Madame Renaud, frail like her daughters, has prepared a feast to welcome Agnès's friend. I am touched by such kindness. Wearing a little white apron, she is creating a culinary masterpiece in the kitchen.

At supper, the exotic guest who comes from *Haiti*, not Tahiti, cheerfully complies with Annette's intense interrogation. The elder sister is preparing her baccalauréat, the culmination of years of classical studies. I paint a colorful picture of my Caribbean life, to Mathieu's delight. He is twelve and bubbling with curiosity. "Bobby's age," I ponder. Mr. Renaud would like to understand, in one evening, the aberrant concept of Duvalier's dictatorship. How can one explain the unexplainable?

Sailing on the nostalgic shores of exile, so far from my family, I am grateful to my hosts for their hospitality. I will share the girls' room with Agnès, and Annette will sleep on the couch tonight.

It is 10:00 p.m., the time for sharing confidences. The topic of Saint Joseph naturally comes up. Agnès, who's been attending our school since she started the Secondary cycle, warns, "No breach of discipline."

Our teacher's reputation for intransigence is, apparently, legendary. The image of Sister Marie Laurence, praising God in the splendor of Chateaubriand' s park, overlaps the one painted by my classmate, of the stern and rigid professor. I find it challenging to reconcile these two portraits that seem to contradict themselves. I quietly hope to remain in her good graces.

~6~

The dictator François Duvalier was ruling as lord and master when I left Haiti for France. Our family made a point to remain outside the margins of politics, which was a forbidden topic of discussion for my brothers and me. By keeping a low profile, we hoped our lives would not be threatened. We endured the dictatorship regime with wisdom, a dose of fatalism and cautious reserve. I learned, very young, to be wary of my shadow and to hold my tongue.

I will never forget the visit of the president's emissary to our school, one memorable day in the annals of Sainte Thérèse, when the top student of each class received a copy of the book, Éléments d'une Doctrine, a gift from the author himself, Doctor Duvalier. I can still recall peering, fascinated, at this present from the "first citizen" of the nation. Here was a man of small stature, with shifty eyes behind his thick glasses, who sowed terror in the hearts of the people. Those who dared to defy the regime were publicly executed or mysteriously disappeared in the dungeons of Fort Dimanche.

Duvalier, self-proclaimed "Chief for Life" of the first Black Republic in the world, would endorse the victory of our courageous heroes of independence as his very own, appropriating the pride of an entire people. Building on the notion of a supreme and all-powerful leader, he decided one day to change our national blue-and-red flag for a black-and-red version. The image of the palm tree, topped by the Phrygian cap was replaced by the image of a guinea fowl, the subsequent symbol of Duvaliérisme, the Duvalier regime.

Every year, on May 18, the schools of the capital city of Port-au-Prince and of the province towns would send a delegation of students to march on the grounds of the National Palace on Flag Day and pay tribute to the president. One year, my class represented the delegation of Sainte Thérèse. In short, pleaded skirts and sneakers, we marched under a blazing sun until we stopped at the foot of the official tribune to pay homage to the head of state. There he stood, surrounded by his dignitaries. In a fraction of a second which, in the intensity of the moment, felt like a thousand years, the earth stopped turning, the sun froze still, and all ambient noise faded away.

With my heart pounding inside my chest, I kept my eyes on the one who held, in the palm of his hands, the fate of an entire nation. The image of an all-powerful despot did not suit this small frame of flesh and bone, this elusive figure in a dark hat and in somber clothes, whose strange, nasal voice seemed the very antithesis of eloquence and grandeur. Plunging my gaze into his, as if to capture the very soul of the one who had the right of life and death over his subjects, I tried to pierce, in a flash, the mystery of dictatorship in its essence, when power makes one forget the sacredness of life.

~ * ~

Port-au-Prince was suffocating in the shadow of a cruel dictatorship. The Macoutes, who roamed the capital city, were on the lookout for the slightest flaw, ready to act at the first sign of trouble. The dusty, pot-holed streets were their fiefdom, and the unfortunate citizens who were unlucky enough to be in their path humbly stepped aside, to quickly vanish out of their sight. Figures with uniforms made of dark jeans material, red scarf around the neck and dark glasses, worn in broad daylight as well as pitch dark nights, the Tonton Macoutes, or National Security Volunteers (VSN), executed the orders of the Chief for Life. Bearing belts, guns and sticks, they sowed terror in their path. Challenging one of them was considered an act of defiance toward the dictatorship itself.

Nights were laden with uncertainty, homes inhabited by anxiety. Extended power outages entertained a psychosis of fear. In the twilight moments preceding the darkness of night, one's shadow became one's own enemy. One morning, Sylvie was absent in school. Despite the teachers' silence, word of mouth—called *teledyòl*—spread like wild fire in town: during a home invasion incident the night before, my classmate's father was arrested and reported missing. Was he sent to rot in one of Fort Dimanche's damp cells, or was he executed and buried in Titanyen's mass grave? The hard part, for the bereaved family, is to have never known: Where?...Why?

We subsequently learned that Sylvie, her mother, and her brother sought refuge at an embassy and took the path to a long exile. The grandmother, following the tragic loss of her son, died of a broken heart. Life had lost all meaning and value for her. The country she had loved so much had become a land of sorrow, of blood and tears. She had no regret when her final hour came.

Even more than the fear of dying, the prospect of torture dominated people's fears. Those in power would delight in terrorizing their potential victims. No one was immune to the constant dangers that threatened young and old, men and women, employers and servants. Sometimes, there were muffled rumors circulating, of heroism in the heart of the dark dungeons. Public executions were the price to pay, for those who dared to be brave and had made their voice of rebellion heard.

I have often wondered if the cause was worth the ultimate sacrifice of life, plunging the bereaved family in painful despair.

One day, my grandparents' cook found one of her daughter's suitors standing by her bungalow door. The young man was proudly wearing the VSN uniform of Papa Doc's henchmen. Horrified and trembling with fear, Dieudonne prepared a dish of rice and beans for the visitor, imploring Jesus, Mary, Joseph and all the saints of the church for him to go away.

After his departure, Ti Sò, sixteen, endured the most humiliating lashing of her life from her mother. At each strike of the whip, Dieudonne, furious, would select a different synonym of the word slut, *from our Creole vocabulary: "Bouzen! Jenès!" She hit her daughter with rage, deaf to Ti Sò's cries of terror. The daughter, on her knees, was begging for her mother's forgiveness between her screams. The providential arrival of Grandfather in the courtyard magically calmed Dieudonne down. Wiping her forehead as if to clear her mind of a bad dream, she quietly returned to her charcoal burners.*

Another tragicomic incident remains etched in my memory. A respectable lady from the hills of Pétion-Ville's upper class, feeling suddenly ill, was returning home one night with her husband from their vacation home in Fermathe. Summoned to stop at a check point on the road, she endured the supreme humiliation of a body search by the Tonton Macoutes, in the middle of the road. It was the only time in her life when she took the chance to ride in a car wearing her nightgown and bathrobe.

This was the era of the Macoutes, and the streets were their turf.

~7~

Sitting by the window, eyes glued to the evening sky, I feel myself drowning in self-pity. Sadness has engulfed me since the plane took off from Haiti. We are flying over the Atlantic after a brief stop in Martinique. Christmas went by so fast! A young compatriot is returning to Paris too, after the holidays. Jean-Pierre lives with his cousins, in France. Disappointed by my lack of enthusiasm at sharing a friendly conversation, my travel companion has stopped his chatter to doze off, unaware of his head resting on my shoulder. I replied, slightly annoyed at his insistence earlier, "Rules are strict at Saint Joseph. Only parents are allowed to call." Overwhelmed by a splitting headache, I seek the refuge of sleep too, hoping to kill time until landing. I refuse to let my mind wander into the life I left behind a few hours ago. I must be brave: Haiti was a nice interlude. Boarding school is my new reality.

Air France's craft executes a bumpy landing at Orly airport. My nerves are on edge, but I dare not let fear betray me. Jean-Pierre is kind enough to help me recover my luggage and entrust it to the porter. We exchange addresses. I vaguely promise to answer his letters. This return to France brings me back to familiar horizons. I feel no anxiety. If only my headache could stop. I was thrilled, at Christmas, to wear my cotton outfits again. I am returning, perfectly tanned, from the Caribbean, to plunge in the heart of a pale European winter. At the entrance of Saint Joseph, the taxi stops at the foot of the brick staircase. I pay, without a blink, a small fortune. My sole preoccupation: to seek the refuge of my narrow bed, the warmth of my down comforter.

In the visitors' parlor, the sœur messagère, who fulfills the duties of a concierge, greets me with joyful and surprised exclamations. Sister Marie Laurence makes her appearance a few minutes later.

My teacher's face reflects sincere joy as she says, "Welcome back, Myriam! Your beautiful island tan suits you well. How are you?"

I smile faintly, responding in monosyllables. Headache. Bumpy landing. Nausea. Sensing I am feeling down, she invites me to go rest a few hours. Sister Angèle has been instructed to have a light dinner and an analgesic brought to my room. I wake up, burning with fever, bleary-eyed the next day. I must have slept nearly 20 hours. It is Sunday. Sister Clara, the school nurse, keeping vigil at my bedside, feels my pulse and places a thermometer under my tongue. "You must stay in bed and watch the fever."

What a gloomy day! I have an upset stomach and dare not violate Sister Clara's orders. She puts me on a clear liquid diet: Evian water; apple juice; clear soup. Anti-fever tablets are administered at every spike of fever. Sister Angèle and Sister Marie Laurence alternate their visits. My family, who called the day before to inquire about my trip, has been informed of my health condition. Dr. Leroux, the school physician, is expecting me at his clinic tomorrow morning.

What misfortune to have waited for my return to France to get sick. I miss my family, my home, my country. Yvette, methodical, would administer the proper medications; my father would splurge and buy me fresh grapes from Au Lincoln Market. Grandmother would pamper me, and Grandfather would spoil me with magazines purchased at the bookstore. He would also order my younger brothers to stop their incessant chatter. At this thought, I smile, as I even miss his "stiff upper lip" attitude. My mind continues to return to the comforts of my pampered childhood. At this stage, the fever has spiked again and consumes me. I wish Marguerite were here. She would call me "pitit mwen," her little girl, and would prepare me one of her miracle infusions.

On Sunday evening, the boarders arrive with great commotion. Students joyfully embrace after the Christmas holidays. Two heads peek out from the corner of the curtain: Agnès and Ishtar. I feel better already at the sight of those familiar faces. Tomorrow, this fever will only be a bad dream. The routine of our daily lives at Saint Joseph will resume its course.

~ * ~

I am cold, despite my thick comforter. Yet, I also feel sweaty. All my limbs tremble. My bones are sore. Inconvenienced by this feeling of dampness caused by profuse sweating during the night, I open my eyes and jump out of bed. A hazy glow seeps through the glass windows of the large dormitory: It's the lamps of the courtyard splitting the darkness of pre-dawn on that cold morning in early January. The students are still asleep. With the wet nightgown stuck to my skin, messy hair glued to my sweaty temples, dizzy, and barefoot on the cold floor, I try to find my way to the bathroom. What's happening? The double row of cubicles is blurry. My head is about to explode. The ground wobbles under my feet. The restroom seems to disappear, becoming a little dark spot on the horizon. A strange noise follows.

I learn that I lost consciousness at the entrance of the restroom. The thud of my body, sliding on the polished floor, woke up Astrid. My classmate ran to my rescue. Her screams alerted Sister Angèle, who was sleeping in the narrow warden room across from the dormitory's bathroom. Like a lightning bolt, Sister Angèle disappeared and came back with Sister Marie Laurence and the school nurse, Sister Clara, who made me inhale strong alcohol and placed a pillow under my neck.

Obviously shaken up, Astrid asked, "She is not going to die, is she?"

"Astrid, it is silly of you to speak that way," Sister Marie Laurence replied. "Myriam had a slight fainting spell. Everything will be fine."

The entire dormitory is up now. Panic has spread among students at the drama unfolding on the ground. Several pairs of arms lift me up. I find myself lying on my bed, shivering, floating in a daze, between unconsciousness and reality. What if I am at the threshold of death? I have no strength to react to this thought. Sister Angèle claps her hands and orders, "Go back to your rooms, young ladies. Get ready for class."

Dr. Leroux, with silver hair and a compassionate gaze behind his thick-rimmed glasses, leans toward me. In the presence of Sister Clara, he does a complete physical exam and expresses great interest at the news of my recent trip to the tropics, which he recalls as an "infectious fever's paradise." He adds, "Mademoiselle, it is safer to run some tests in a hospital environment and find the cause of this fever."

The tone might be reassuring, but I am not fooled. The word *hospital* sounds like a death sentence to my ears. In a sheer panic, I beg the doctor to let me go back to my country. "You are not fit to travel," he replies.

Shivering under the wool blanket wrapped around me like a large shawl, I sit in the back seat of the Sisters' vehicle as we head for Paris. Dr. Hoffmann, an infectious diseases specialist, is expecting our arrival at Hospital Sainte Anne. Reverend Mother and Sister Marie Laurence, my legal guardians in France, will handle the complicated hospital admission procedures of a minor in a foreign country, and keep my family posted in Haiti.

Sister Jean, in charge of the graduating class, the "Terminales," will lend a hand with our class of "Secondes" as well, until the return of her colleague. I have no strength to protest, or to offer any resistance to my hospitalization. I feel too weak to react to the absurdity of such an ironic turn of event. Fate will take its course.

Will I die alone, far from the country I left two days ago?

~8~

James Tyler, star athlete of his school's basketball team in the United States, thanks to his height (six feet four inches) and extreme agility, had been the idol of the female student body of his class. After university, he moved heaven and earth to land a federal job. Such a position would guarantee him financial stability without the headaches associated with the responsibilities of managing one's own business. He could, if he so wished, opt to retire with a comfortable government pension after twenty-five years of public service. He would still be in his prime to fulfill his lifelong dream of traveling around the world.

James chose to embrace a career in diplomacy. When his first overseas post led him to the U.S. embassy in Haiti, he could hardly contain his excitement. He had studied French in college, but his accent definitely needed polishing. He held Louise, his mother, one last time in his arms, and exchanged a big bear hug with his father Ross before boarding the Pan Am aircraft, en route for the adventure of a lifetime.

James's desire had always been to live on an island in the tropics, feeling the caress of the breeze on his skin and the taste of the ocean salt on his lips. He imagined a hammock suspended between two coconut trees, where he would devour books on weekends, sipping coconut water.

Haiti symbolized the earthly paradise he had envisioned, using his imagination and his books. But Port-au-Prince, James discovered, was not so accessible to the beaches of Montrouis and Jacmel. Poverty, present on every street corner, bothered him as much as the country's lack of infrastructure.

He did not know it yet, but, a few years later, a ruthless dictatorship would alter the entire landscape and heart of a nation.

The traditional Marine ball, held on the lawns of the American ambassador's private residence, changed the course of destiny for him.

Embassy staff, American nationals and a few local personalities of the Haitian political and business scenes were on the guest list. The breeze was soft, and the sky adorned with thousands of glittering stars. Alcohol poured generously from the open bar, and the food tables, artistically decorated, rivaled each other with their splendor.

A distinguished looking man with graying temples, escorted by two pretty young women, occupied one of the tables reserved for guests and their families. Charles Deveaux, born into one of the oldest families in Port-au-Prince, and whose insurance agency, located downtown on Rue Pavée, was well known to the public, had responded to the ambassador's invitation. Leilah, his wife, had become sedentary over the years, and avoided the social obligations of Charles' life. Their daughters, Yvette and Claire, therefore, often accompanied their father to these regular events.

Live musical entertainment, alternating Haitian and American music for this multicultural soirée, kept the dance floor packed. The Marines, elegant in their gala uniforms, made heads turn. James and his colleague, Rob, both dressed in dark suit and tie, were making their way around the guest tables to get to the bar. They noticed a refined looking elderly man, flanked by two lovely young brunettes, who were smiling at their escort. Their demeanor revealed they shared a special bond.

These young women looked alike, with long, jet-black hair covering the low-cut backs of their emerald green and bright red evening gowns, respectively.

The young men approached the table and introduced themselves. Cordial handshakes were exchanged with Charles Deveaux and his daughters. Gallantly, they invited the ladies to dance. Rob escorted Yvette to the dance floor. It was, like a thunder bolt, love at first sight for James, who discovered that night that Love had a face and a name: Claire Deveaux, the pretty brunette in the red evening gown.

Charles, who had strictly raised his two daughters, watched with suspicion a romance take shape between his younger child and this foreigner whose family origin remained shrouded in mystery. Over the months, however, James became a regular visitor to the Deveaux's family home in Bois Verna. Soon, he won Leilah's confidence...and Claire's heart. Charles decided he would no longer stand in the way of his daughter's happiness. In fact, without openly admitting to the fact, Claire's fiancé had won his approval by his total devotion to his daughter, his good manners, his work ethics, and also the great sense of humor that sparkled in his eyes. Charles' wedding gift to his future son-in-law, offered the day of their engagement, was a property in Bourdon, where James began frantically, day after day, stone by stone, to build a comfortable nest for his future wife.

Claire and James' marriage, celebrated at Sacred Heart Church where both Deveaux sisters had been baptized, was the happiest day of the couple's lives. The union was celebrated in strict privacy: James, though non-practicing, belonged to the Protestant faith, and his parents were notably absent. Charles and Leilah would not give the evil tongues in town the opportunity to gossip, while drinking their champagne.

The couple was basking in perfect happiness and the honeymoon would be eternal, thought the young husband. His wedding gift to his wife was the key to their brand-new house, constructed in reinforced concrete, capable of challenging the destructing forces of hurricanes and tropical storms.

Claire intended to live her married life in the reassuring shadow of her parents, in the country of her birth. A devoted husband, James opted for a salary in Gourdes and the status of "local hire" to avoid the mandatory and periodic transfer required of his American colleagues. No sacrifice was too great for the serenity of Claire, and the child she was carrying.

Yvette rejoiced at the happiness of her younger sister, without jealousy or envy. She was, moreover, dating the son of friends of her parents, who had returned to Haiti after his studies in France. But she seemed in no hurry to pursue a serious romance. Having attended classes at a commercial school after her classical studies, Yvette sometimes helped her father at the office. Her affable manners had earned her the respect of senior employees at the insurance agency.

At the same time, Claire was discovering Haiti's culinary secrets, alongside her mother and Dieudonne, her parents' cook. She meant to become an accomplished hostess.

The world collapsed for James in the middle of a violent storm, one September night.

~9~

Stuck in the hospital bed, I watch the nurse feel my pulse, take my temperature, and check my blood pressure. She then places an IV drip with rehydrating fluid. Struck down by the fever, I have no strength to react to the pain of blood being drawn by a lab technician in white coat. Dr. Hoffmann ordered a full range of laboratory tests. A quiet strength emanates from Reverend Mother. After her departure, I feel a pinch in the heart. My parents are away. The Atlantic separates us.

In the evening, my fever skyrockets and incoherent words come out of my burning lips. Very agitated, I pull the I.V. drip from my stiff left arm. The nurse on duty rushes into the room to immobilize my arm. In sheer panic, I start screaming from the top of my lungs. Dr. Hoffmann, alerted by the nursing staff of the urgent situation, decides to start a broad spectrum intravenous antibiotic treatment before the final laboratory tests results come in. But at the oral administration of quinine to treat a potential malaria infection, violent bouts of nausea shake my entire body. I seem to dive into a dark tunnel, where all notion of reality disappears, and I am floating in the heart of a dense fog. Strange faces appear and disappear in the confusion of my brain. Night's shadow slowly enters the room. I yell, desperate for my parents' presence: "Papa...Maman!"

A luminous creature has appeared before me. Am I in the presence of an angel? Claire, my mother, has emerged from the depths of time, wrapped in a soft, golden glow. She whispers in an angelic voice, "Do not worry. Everything will be fine."

And I beg, clutching her hand, "Please, do not leave me."

In the pale light of dawn, I recognize, stunned, the night angel: Sister Marie Laurence, exhausted after a sleepless night by my side, asleep on a chair at the foot of my bed. She was my lifeline on that first night in a Parisian hospital.

Two days later, at the clinical microbiology lab, the bacterial agent of typhoid fever is isolated: Salmonella typhi. In Haiti, people still die of typhoid. Am I going to die alone, in a foreign land?

"Sickness often reminds us of the frailty of life," my teacher wisely reminds me.

Although the daughter of a dictatorial regime where life is depreciated daily, I feel the personal threat of death for the first time in my young existence. I am not ready for this up-close encounter that awaits us all, at the end of life.

But, are we ever ready?

~10~

Why? *Why these awful tragedies, that suddenly hit a family, when only happiness was on the horizon, in a cloudless sky? One single question, repeated so many times in my mind, and always left unanswered. I had been able to reconstruct, over the years, the scenario of this terrible night of September by gleaning snippets of information from Yvette, Leilah, and Marguerite, but rarely from James, my father. My grandmother and her daughter were reticent on details, in their awkward desire to protect me. But it concerned **my** birth, and the loss of **my** mother! I was entitled to the truth. Even if it hurt. Marguerite secretly revealed the connecting dots, the missing parts, the small, seemingly insignificant details that allowed me to feel, for a brief instant, my mother's humanity.*

Claire had decided to spend her last month of pregnancy at her family home in Bois Verna, surrounded by her parents and older sister. They all looked forward to pampering her and satisfying her every need and desire. James welcomed this arrangement. It gave him peace of mind, knowing that guardian angels were watching over his wife while he was at work.

Even Marguerite, who had moved to Bourdon to manage the young couple's household, joined the team in Bois Verna. Yvette and Claire were like her daughters. She still remembered the day they let out their first cry, within the walls of the gingerbread-style family home. Mister Charles was pacing nervously in the hallway. Tears of joy had followed Mrs. Charles's groans of pain. And each new arrival had cemented Marguerite and Leilah's friendship even deeper. Marguerite's place was by Claire's side, in anticipation of the big event.

Claire, in her eighth month of pregnancy, was a radiant picture of health. In anticipation of a possible hurricane threat, James and Charles had returned home early from work. A dusty wind had started to blow, tearing the leaves off the trees already. The cook, Dieudonne, and Celia, the housekeeper, had followed Leilah's orders to the letter: the gas lamps were filled with kerosene, in case of power failure. André, the gardener, had returned from Peters' bakery with extra bread for the household, and gallons of water were filled and set along the walls of the indoor kitchen. The exterior charcoal kitchen temporarily closed its doors. Dinner, cooked on the gas stove, was served earlier than usual, and Dieudonne retired to the bungalow she shared with Ti Sò, her four-year old, for the evening. Celia, originally from the Southern town of Jérémie, like Dieudonne and their employer, Mr. Charles, kept an eye on the little girl when her mother was busy with Leilah.

Mrs. Charles spoiled Ti Sò. The girl's wardrobe, a collection of little dresses in pastel shades of pink, green and yellow, was the envy of all the young mothers at the five o'clock mass at Sacred Heart Church, where Dieudonne proudly paraded her daughter on Sunday afternoons. Ti Sò's schooling costs, the cook had no doubt, would be covered by Mr. Charles, a strict, but kind-hearted employer.

Dieudonne had lived through many hurricanes. Port-au-Prince was spread out at the foot of the mountain ranges that surrounded and protected her. The wind would blow hard, but would surely spare the capital city from destruction, to cause havoc, perhaps, in the Southern towns of Cayes, Jacmel and Jérémie, as it was often the case. The cook had declined Leilah's offer to spend the night in the main house with her daughter. She preferred the comfort and familiarity of her bungalow, where her minor treasures and belongings were gathered. Marguerite had not left Claire's sight since their return to Bois Verna. A cot had been placed for her in Charles's small office. Up at dawn, she had taken over the morning coffee ritual, to allow Dieudonne an extra hour of sleep, and Ti Sò the gift of more time in the arms of her mother.

~ * ~

A heart-wrenching cry split the night, louder than the howling of the wind, and the cracking sound of wooden shutters. The corridors of the house were pitch black, due to power failure. Marguerite, in her nightgown, was already climbing the long staircase of polished planks, a kerosene lamp in her hand. Her "little one" needed her. Leilah and Charles had also heard the harrowing scream and jumped to Claire's rescue: in the twilight of the room, their younger daughter was writhing in pain, a big pool of blood soiling the sheets of the bed. Leilah threw herself on her child, wrapping her in her arms. Charles attempted, without success, a telephone call to Dr. Toussaint, his friend and family doctor. James, in sheer panic, put on his clothes without bothering to remove his pajamas. He had to take Claire to the nearest hospital, Asile Français, located in the heart of downtown. He would defy the fury of the storm, which was raging outside.

Yvette and Marguerite had the presence of mind to examine Claire, with a flashlight. A baby, with a full head of thick, black hair, was emerging from the mysterious tunnel of life. But that fateful night, what should have been a miracle had become a nightmare. At the risk of breaking her neck, Marguerite tumbled down the stairs with the flashlight, safer to handle than a kerosene lamp. She boiled water on the gas stove and disinfected a pair of scissors.

Yvette who, in the midst of total panic and chaos, had struggled to keep her cool, managed, alongside Marguerite, to deliver the small whining baby. Mixing her screams with Claire's, a baby girl howled her surprise at the first breath of life. The umbilical cord cut, Yvette gently placed the bewildered infant against her mother's heart. Sublime silence enveloped them, for a fraction of a second. The young mother smiled and then closed her eyes, exhausted.

Claire was shivering. The bleeding would not stop and drained her of all strength. In a split-second decision, in a race against time and death, James and his father-in-law wrapped a feeble Claire in a blanket, before exposing her to the night air. Braving the storm at the risk of their lives, they climbed into Charles's spacious Ford, and he took the wheel. James sat in the back seat of the vehicle, his wife's head resting on his lap. Leilah, who had guided the men with a flashlight in the dark of the night, sat next to her husband in the front passenger seat, drowning her "Hail, Mary" into her tears, which flowed.

Fallen branches of trees crowded the dark streets, slowing down their already perilous journey. When the walls of the Asile Français Hospital finally appeared in the vehicle's headlight beams, her husband did not know it yet, but Claire was already deceased. She had slipped, silently, into this invisible world where the soul, set free, takes flight. James had, throughout the trip, caressed Claire's face, whispering tender words of love and hope.

~ * ~

At dawn on September 4, the Ford pulled into the front gate and parked under the arbor that served as a garage. Three passengers emerged, with haggard faces and disheveled clothes. Silence spoke louder than words. Dieudonne and Celia held Marguerite firmly: she was doubled-over, arms crossed over her abdomen as a woman in the throes of labor pain; strange grunting noises escaped from her throat. Consumed with grief at the news of such terrible tragedy that had just struck the family, the entire household plunged into a state of frenzy. Screams followed moments of silent stupor: delusion and reality became closely intertwined, deeply felt by family and servants, united in sorrow.

Leilah, inconsolable, howled her pain in Yvette's arms: unable to remain strong any longer, the older daughter let loose her grief, too. All night, Yvette had rocked the screaming infant who, in her innocence, was claiming her mother's breast. In desperation, Marguerite had fed her sugar water, which the baby devoured. Dieudonne had walked the deserted streets of Port-au-Prince at dawn, the next morning, looking for infant formula but had come back empty-handed, stores closed on the destructive aftermath of the hurricane.

Overcome, James and Charles were sitting on the sofa, speechless, looking dazed, in complete denial of Claire's departure. These two men, who had loved her so much, were plunged into their own silence, deaf to all the commotion around them, blocking the horror of reality.

André, caught in the total emotional upheaval that disrupted the immutable order of things, did not know which way to turn. In his sincere desire to be helpful and console Leilah, his long-time employer, the gardener alerted the neighborhood. Visitors soon lined up to show their support to the bereaved family.

"Hurry, Dieudonne! Hurry, Marguerite! Prepare the coffee."

The gardener was giving orders, since the mourning family members were unable to. André felt compelled to take charge. He traded his work clothes for a nice white shirt, put on his Sunday shoes and pulled out, from under his mattress, a small bundle of Gourdes to purchase croissants and patties from the bakery in Champ de Mars town square. In the midst of adversity, André understood it was imperative he kept his composure. He would not allow anyone to misjudge the Deveaux, a family known for their gracious hospitality towards visitors. The devoted employee would defend the honor of the household. That day, André went above the call of duty.

Mr. Lambert and his wife Clarisse, dressed in black as a sign of respect for the recent loss that had struck their neighbors, were already crossing the gate. Marguerite and Dieudonne magically regained their senses. Leilah, forced to calm down also, led the visitors to the formal living room, better suited for the magnitude of the recent tragedy. The silver coffeepot, used only on special occasions, sparkled. The news had spread like wild fire, and the porch was already packed with well-wishers.

*Yvette had, once again, kept a strong head, despite the collective grief. Just before the Lambert's arrival, she took the wheels of the Ford with James on the passenger seat, holding, for the first time, Claire's legacy: the baby she had given birth to before she died. The tiny infant whose arrival had caused such turmoil had stopped crying. Instinctively, Yvette sensed the urgency of the situation: the newborn had to be taken to the hospital, or there would not be one but two deaths in the family that day. She looked at her brother-in-law whose shoulders slumped while he held the motionless baby cradled in his arms. He wept inconsolably, shedding all the tears of his big man's body. James was staring, for the first time, at Claire's child…**his** child! The little girl had not asked to be born, nor wished for her mother to die. This tiny face was not that of a culprit, but rather reflected pure innocence. And now he risked losing the only link to his late wife, the infant daughter who had emerged from Claire's womb: her last gift to him.*

~ * ~

The birth certificate reveals that I was born on September 3rd. My mother's death certificate bears the date of September 4, but it is still that same fateful night, when the storm was raging, when my arrival into the world deprived me, forever, of a mother. My birthdays will always have a bittersweet taste: My mother died to give me life. My aunt Yvette and Marguerite, my dear nanny, heard my first cry. I am breathing today because, at the heart of grief, they remained strong, even when every fiber of their bodies and souls shouted their grief, in the face of a dying Claire. Sugar water was my welcome meal in a cruel, unfavorable world.

My mother gazed at me, for a split second. Were my eyes open? Did we exchange a poignant look, before being forever separated? Yvette placed me on her chest. Will I remember, one day, this beating heart, already departing from this world? I tried, unsuccessfully, to revive the memory of this precious moment, from the hidden depths of memory…I cannot.

My father acknowledged my existence when Yvette placed me in his arms...when he accepted the reality of Claire's departure. I existed for him when my mother stopped to exist. Yvette became my mother: a truth that resonates in the depth of my heart since I owe her my life too. Her arms have rocked me, and her heart beat against mine since the day I was born. Marguerite has, literally, seen me come into this life...a real miracle born of a great tragedy. I will always be her "baby." Leilah got attached to the flesh of her flesh and blood. I am the living symbol of her daughter, the evidence of Claire's short time on earth.

Charles never accepted the death of his daughter. He blamed the storm which delayed their arrival at the hospital. But I sense, by his eloquent silences, that I am, in his eyes, the guilty one.

~11~

Darkness has fallen a long time ago. The night light offers a soft, diffuse glow, conducive to sharing confidences. Earlier, Dr. Hoffmann signed papers for my discharge, which is scheduled for the morning. Time stopped at Sainte Anne. Tomorrow I will plunge back into the reality of Saint Joseph, to begin my recovery. I throw a furtive look at the sparse furniture and severe decor around my bed: the wall panel where a tube is hooked to an oxygen source; a moveable side table with a simple pitcher of water and a glass. This austere setting will be etched in my memory forever. Tonight, in the privacy of this Parisian hospital room, I reveal the secret of my birth to Sister Marie Laurence, the pilgrim whose path has crossed mine.

Claire died giving me life. I never recovered from the emotional void created by her absence and, since, my life has been the silent quest for her impossible presence. In my delirium, in the heart of pain, I dreamt I saw her face. Today, I yearn to feel my mother's gaze on me. Claire never had the chance to hold the baby she gave birth to, and I will never know the sweetness of her embrace. The radiant smile of a dark-haired beauty in a red evening gown is the image I will always carry of my mother. She will forever be twenty, in my mind, frozen in time, her framed picture towering on Grandfather's old piano.

I sometimes imagine the sound of her voice. Did she whisper words of love, her hand on her rounded belly, when I was only a little seed germinating? They say fetuses hear and remember their mother's voice. I have tried to recapture, so many times in the spirit, the journey of my birth, this hectic passage from the tunnel towards the light. My secret, I keep it buried in my heart, since the world capsized for me, at seven, the proverbial "age of reason." In mentally blocking reality, I gave myself the illusion of having, like my schoolmates, a "real" mother and a "real" father. In concealing my grief, I did not allow anyone to consider me motherless. Claire's death propelled Yvette into the role of motherhood, salvaging for me the appearance of a normal childhood. For this, I am grateful to her. If Claire is the dream, Yvette is the reassuring reality. In my efforts to forget, I try to erase the silent remorse I feel for my role in the death of my mother. But it always comes up. I dream of what might have been but will never be. This is my punishment, I guess, the price I will forever pay for the gift of my life…the heavy burden I will carry for the rest of my life.

~ * ~

The navy-blue skirt and blazer are now loose on me. This uniform symbolizes my imminent return to the real world at Saint Joseph. My eyes linger on the empty hospital bed, an inert witness of the dark hours I just endured. Sister Marie Laurence's gift has been her constant presence at my bedside. In the throes of suffering, we have bonded. In the revelation of the secret of my birth, I negotiate a fragile peace with fate and destiny.

I keep silent. I have come back from a long and painful journey, and it will take time for me to be able to describe it, put it into words, and meditate on its lessons. Lulled by the steady motion of the vehicle, I fall asleep on the back seat of the automobile, until our arrival at Val-de-Seine. I stand still at the entrance of our classroom: Sister Jean is substituting for her colleague, Sister Marie Laurence. Twenty pairs of eyes stare at me, smiling. Joyful exclamations of surprise follow. Emotions run amok. I suddenly turn around and flee this brutal return to reality, rushing to seek the refuge of my bed.

Sister Angèle draws the curtain at the entrance of my box. "Rest, young lady," she orders me, before leaving. In this big empty dorm, sleep will be my refuge and my salvation; clear soup and toast will find their way to my room. "No greasy food," the doctor advised.

The long-awaited telephone call from Haiti comes through at 2:00 p.m. and ends up causing distress in the visitor's parlor. It is 8:00 a.m. in my country; people already had coffee, and life and its noises invade the streets of Port-au-Prince. Holding the receiver, tears run down my face, but I can't utter a sound. I am paralyzed with emotion. Familiar voices take turn at the other end of the line but only my sobs echo.

Puzzled, the sœur messagère leaves the parlor to return with Reverend Mother. In a calm voice, she offers a detailed account of my hospital stay to my parents, and reassures them of Saint Joseph's devotion toward me. I finally manage to regain control of myself and talk to my loved ones: my father, Yvette, my grandparents and my little brothers offer me their get-well wishes. When Marguerite holds the receiver, it is she who remains silent at the end of the line, and I who console her.

Lying on my bed, in the darkness of a quiet dormitory, the final scene of the movie *Gone with the Wind* comes to my mind: the main character, Scarlett, a survivor of tragedy, stands firm on her beloved land, Tara, to declare, with strength and determination, "Tomorrow is another day." Tomorrow holds so many promises. Today, I am just a weeping willow, moved by the wonderful gift of life and my newfound health.

~12~

The horrific tragedy, triggered one stormy night, would turn out, over the months, to have a happy ending. According to Yvette, Leilah and Marguerite, the hospital kept me in an incubator for two weeks. While I was gaining strength to face a life that had started with a terrible loss, Charles and Leilah had the painful task of planning their daughter's funeral. I can only imagine the horror of this act against nature. It must be the most difficult ordeal any parent would have to endure. My mother's funeral service was held in Turgeau, at the Sacred Heart parish, in the church where she was baptized, and where the bells had made a joyful noise on her wedding day. Her life had come full circle with the sound of the knell, on the day of her funeral.

Claire would be laid to rest at Port-au-Prince's main cemetery, next to her paternal ancestors and her older brother Robert, who died from gastroenteritis when he was six months old. The Deveaux family mausoleum, built of black marble, harbored a truncated column, symbol of loved ones' lives cut short. Friends and relatives, stirred by the tragedy, had come in force to show their support to the bereaved family.

Numerous flower arrangements surrounded the coffin at the viewing. One could read, on the silk ribbon adorning the flowers, messages from well-wishers: "Deepest Sympathies" or "Sincere Condolences." Leilah had decided to keep one of these satin ribbons as a talisman of Claire's brief passage on Earth. The marble tombstone would be buried under the abundance of flowers, which symbolized, in a way, the fragility and ephemeral nature of life, as they would dry up and be tossed to the ground a few days later.

Flanked by her husband and her only living daughter, drained from shedding so many tears, Leilah sat motionless on a chair, like a pillar of salt. Yvette pressed her mother's hand silently; a second embroidered handkerchief was quickly passed from daughter's to mother's hand. But nothing could dry Leilah's tears. Destiny was forcing her to bury a second child. Why was life so cruel? What did she do wrong to receive such punishment? Charles stood stoically to receive the handshakes of the long line of mourners. Stiff as a board, he was consumed with grief but determined to remain the refined gentleman who had won Leilah's heart so long ago. The employees at his insurance agency had all come to express their sympathies to their boss.

James, like a robot, shook hands with those who had come to pay their respects. Claire looked as beautiful in death as she had in life, sleeping eternally on the white satin of the upholstered coffin, made of precious wood. How could the grieving widower remain strong and brave, when the earth had capsized under his feet, in the midst of a stormy night, one week ago? Sitting next to Claire, at the head of the casket, he sobbed inconsolably in the arms of his colleagues who had come to share his grief. With his spouse gone, his world was crumbling. In his adopted country, drowning in a culture so different than his, lost in a human tide of people he had never met before, James felt, at its core, the painful solitude of the foreigner transplanted in foreign soil.

At the foot of the coffin, Kimbram and Zahiye Habdoul, wrinkled with age, seemed like two mummies frozen in time by the absurd pain of having to bury their granddaughter. Leilah's parents, a haggard look on their faces, watched a steady stream of well-wishers arrive from the Levantine community of Port-au-Prince's Bord-de-Mer business section. This close-knit ethnic group had come to join the bereaved family in a touching show of support at the viewing. Farid, Leilah's younger brother, had flown in the night before from New York to be by his sister's side in her hour of need. He stood for a long time by the open casket, eyes fixed on his young niece, a true sleeping beauty at rest in an eternal sleep.

In the first row of seats reserved for the public, sat Marguerite, escorted by Dieudonne, Celia and André. Leilah had insisted on their close proximity at the funeral. Her gesture proclaimed her attachment toward these devoted employees who had shared, for years, her daily life in Bois Verna.

During the viewing and the parade of mourners who had come to pay their respect, Leilah had kept her composure with a herculean effort. But, as the funeral director and pall bearers approached to close the casket, the grieving mother leaned, for the last time, toward the child she would never get to see again. A raucous, heart-wrenching cry escaped from the depth of her womb, violent, raw, ignoring all measure or censorship. Marguerite's cry echoed hers. Charles glared at Leilah in disbelief. Yvette wrapped her arms around the woman who had given her life but wished, in that very instant when grief submerges all, that she would just let herself drown in sorrow. Dieudonne held Marguerite tight, for fear she would collapse.

As they exited the cemetery's gates, nearly a hundred mourners followed the grieving family to Bois Verna in their vehicles, causing a terrible traffic jam in the narrow streets of Port-au-Prince. Clarisse Lambert had made plans to accommodate the crowd's arrival. Her dear friend and neighbor Leilah, in the throes of grief, was unable to fulfill her role as hostess. The Buteau heirs, owners of the Aux Cosaques restaurant on nearby Chemin des Dalles street, and whose reputation had crossed international borders, had promised to provide the service of their famous consommé maison, the best soup in all of Port-au-Prince. After the funeral service, the warm, comforting beverage would be served by trained waiters in bow ties and long-sleeved shirts.

The funeral home had provided folding chairs to accommodate the guests. They had been placed around the veranda, the living room, and a few were even scattered on the front lawn. A beautiful picture of Claire, smiling in her red evening gown, was displayed on the old piano next to a huge bouquet of red roses, her favorite flowers. When the last visitor left, a sense of loss drained the bereaved family of all energy, and everyone fell into a deep, heavy sleep in the large, yellow-trimmed gingerbread house.

James, his heart broken into pieces, had endured two weeks of total agony. He received a call from the embassy a few days later and packed his bags to return to Bourdon. He had survived these last days suspended between hazy, surreal moments of denial, and the brutal pain that would suddenly engulf him and cause a knot in his stomach. Unable to face the reality of Claire's absence, James had contemplated a move back to his country. Leilah almost lost her mind at the prospect. She would not survive the loss of her daughter and her granddaughter.

Yvette, Leilah, and Marguerite followed James to Bourdon. A baby, who had not asked to be born, desperately needed their care and nurturing. The three women would help the young father regain his senses, until he found a capable nanny to take over babysitting duties while he was at work. Days, however, turned into weeks. Charles, disoriented by Leilah's prolonged absence, requested her return to Bois Verna to resume normalcy in his household. While Leilah, the obedient wife, returned to her husband, Yvette stayed behind. James and Claire's daughter, who was finally granted the name Myriam, still needed her.

Concerned about criticism and people's gossips, prevalent in Haitian society at the time, Charles frowned. But his eldest daughter, usually submissive to parental authority, ignored, for the first time in her life, her father's orders to return to Bois Verna. James' house in Bourdon was spacious enough to guarantee everyone's independence and privacy. In the Bible, a widow is encouraged to marry her brother-in-law if he is single. Why should not the widower marry the sister-in-law? A year after Claire's death, little Myriam would receive a precious gift: an official mother.

~ * ~

Slim, elegant, distinguished, with jet-black hair like Leilah in her youth, Yvette had inherited her father's character traits that defined him as a "good and decent man": measured, discreet, with an acute sense of duty and honor, refined in gestures and speech. Claire had definitely been an Habdoul, with the same inexhaustible verve, spontaneity and cheerfulness as Leilah; on the other hand, without the shadow of a doubt, Yvette was a Deveaux. The two sisters looked alike but Yvette would always hear people say, about her, "She is her father's daughter." I never understood the meaning of such comment that evoked the obvious: one is clearly the child of one's parent. In that optic, Claire had been her mother's daughter, governed by her heart and emotions. Yvette was the wise, older sister who always kept her younger sibling on the straight and narrow and protected her from their father's admonitions.

When did love replace a strong sense of duty in Yvette's heart? I will never know. Marguerite, the source of details that helped weave the mysterious tapestry of my childhood, would suddenly remain silent. A romance must have bloomed discreetly under her eyes, in Bourdon. Did she remain blind to the warning signs her emotional radar would usually detect? Yvette, the epitome of discretion, did not let anyone pick up any vibes about what was happening. When James returned home from work, she would retire to her bedroom, to allow father and daughter to share bonding times alone. On the mahogany rocking chair built to accommodate his height, James would cradle the little live doll in his arms, humming softly the nursery rhymes his mother would sing to him as a little boy. Marguerite swears I was a sweet and pleasant baby, who cooed and smiled at the sight of familiar faces around her.

Dinner, punctually served at six o'clock according to American customs, brought sister and brother-in-law around the same table in the evening. They would make small talk and share tidbits of information about my progresses as a baby. They would burst into an occasional laughter, followed by a guilty silence. Did they fear they were betraying Claire's memory?

I was three months old when Yvette returned to her parents' home in Bois Verna. She had hired a capable young woman, Simone, to assist Marguerite in her babysitting duties. Simone had stopped her studies as a nurse assistant to help support her ailing mother. She brought new life into my care while respecting, to the letter, Marguerite's orders, the final authority in matters pertaining to me. Upon his arrival, James would receive daily reports from Marguerite, who fulfilled the role of governess but was loved as a member of the family. With Yvette gone, James blindly depended on Marguerite, who managed the household budget, planned menus and took all appropriate decisions in the smooth unfolding of the Tyler's household. But Yvette's absence was sorely felt by James who had gotten accustomed to her serene and discreet presence under his roof. He was missing the pensive face of the young brunette.

~ * ~

Invited to share Sunday lunches with the family in Bois Verna, a serene, if not happy young father would watch his daughter go from Leilah's to Yvette's arms. Both women beamed with joy in the baby's presence. A beautiful pink cradle, adorned with a mosquito net, had been placed in the dining room, airier than the living room, but protected from the veranda's drafts. Dieudonne's cooking talents would exceed expectations on these Sunday lunches, a delight for James's palate, as he relished Creole cuisine: griot de porc (fried pork) or tassot de dinde (turkey in cubes), pikliz (hot pepper and raw cabbage mix), rice and beans, fried plantains, avocado and watercress salad. A savory pain patate (sweet potato pudding) would conclude these culinary feasts. James started a routine of weekday visits to the Deveaux, after work, on his way to Bourdon. Soon, Charles and Leilah sensed a budding romance between Yvette and her brother-in-law—through the silence they shared, and in the glances they exchanged in each other's presence.

A heart-to-heart discussion took place with their eldest daughter. Her trustworthiness, rectitude and determination won. In fact, this solution would prove to be providential for all. Leilah, whose feminine intuition rarely faltered, had realized long ago that the delights of her table would be another asset to James' happiness, as it had been for Charles, the man of her life. Faithful to her Lebanese culture, she would prepare, for her son-in-law's weekday visits, dishes of kibbeh nayeh, grounded beef consumed raw with olive oil and onions, served with a tabbouleh salad seasoned with fresh parsley and mint and a basket of flat, pita bread. James would leave Bois Verna for Bourdon, with a jar of homemade hummus (blended chick peas, tahini, cumin, garlic, lemon juice and sprinkled with olive oil) or baba ghanoush, an eggplant puree.

~ * ~

I had blown out my first birthday candle when my father James put a ring on my aunt's finger. The elder sibling wanted to keep intact the memory of her sister's wedding at Sacred Heart, where the bells had rung with joy and elation. Without fanfare or trumpet, after a private religious ceremony celebrated in the chapel, invisible from the main road of Christ-Roi in Bourdon, Yvette Deveaux became Mrs. James Tyler.

The mechanism of Yvette's biological clock fascinated me over the years: she offered me a little brother the year of my third birthday and named him Robert in memory of the baby her parents had lost; I fell in love with my little brother, nicknamed Bobby, at first glance. Three years later, Freddy joined the Tyler ranks. Like clockwork, three years after Freddy, my godson James Junior was born. I have no recollection of any favoritism on Yvette's part toward my little brothers at my expense.

We shared the same mother, calm, collected, full of grace and measure. She rarely laughed, but was devoted to us and the family's well-being, orchestrating, with the touch of her magic wand, the activities of the gardener, the cook and the housekeeper. Marguerite made sure her orders were executed to the letter by the household staff. Yvette, self-proclaimed cook for a day, sometimes offered her husband the surprise of a typically American meal: Turkey, gravy and canned cranberry sauce, mashed potatoes, green peas and apple pie. My father was pampered by his wife and basked in quiet happiness.

~ * ~

I savor the idea of having been the instrument of my father and my aunt's union. I am the one who put them on the same path, at any rate. Yvette's biological clock allowed her to give her husband a son every three years, and perhaps redeem me of my unforgivable fault on the day of my birth. Life will always transcend death. Claire is avenged from the clutches of Death with each son that came out of Yvette's womb, with each cry that welcomed, for the first time, the light.

~13~

The foreign student that I am is determined to excel in France. I often stay up late, reviewing lessons with a flashlight hidden under the covers, after nine o'clock. I must reprogram my working method: make a study plan, strip the essential from a text, memorize its basics points and apply them intelligently. Teaching methods in Haitian schools rely heavily on text memorization. Therefore, we have excellent memory ability. I could not help but smile, thinking about the absurd history phrase all Haitian students had to memorize: "our ancestors the Gallic." Our textbooks came from France, of course.

The 10th through 12th grade classes visited the Career Orientation Center last week. The advisor's report states that I have excellent abilities for the literary field. The irony is that my father expects me to pursue a field in science. Sister Marie Laurence's comment is full of positive wisdom: "Literature can also have its place in your life. It will be your special hobby. What matters is to reach your full potential."

~ * ~

Thursday afternoons' extracurricular activities offer a welcome diversion to our strict schedules as boarders. Those who, like me, selected swimming, travel by coach to the town of Tassy on Thursday evenings, chaperoned by Sister Jean, our literature professor and homeroom teacher for the 12th graders, the "Terminales." Our swimming instructor, Loic, is a young man with a perfect muscular torso. As he emerges from the water to demonstrate a dive, several pairs of adoring eyes follow his performance. Swimming caps are mandatory in Tassy's heated pool, which smells of bleach. I recall, nostalgic, the warm beaches of my childhood and the girl with long dark braids, barefoot in the sand and feeling the caress of the sea breeze on her bare shoulders.

Ishtar, Gisèle and Johanna have chosen horseback riding with all the fancy gears: high and shiny black boots, dark blazer, helmet and whip.

Isabella di Rossi, Sophie de Maisonrouge, and Astrid de Panière have, apparently, been practicing fencing for years in the spacious gym, which was, once upon a time, the castle's ceremonial room. The instructor, a slender man with graying temples, teaches this art to a handful of students who, coincidentally, use a nobiliary particle in their names. Fist on hip, sword in the right hand, my comrades scream, "en garde," to their teacher. All that's missing is the big feathered hat and the coat of arms of the Three Musketeers, I conclude with a chuckle, as I follow their antics of this antiquated sport. But more than a nobiliary particle in the name or talented fencing skills, real nobility remains a quality of the heart. I learned it in France, with classmates who did not hesitate to open the doors of their homes and extend their friendship to the lonely foreign student from Haiti...

~ * ~

Our lives as boarders are unfolding smoothly, over the months and the seasons, punctuated by minor incidents which, outside of Saint Joseph's perimeters, would seem insignificant. But, for us who share a tailor-made daily routine, the slightest change that could affect the smooth sailing of boarding school life can take on gigantic proportions.

Agnès, who has been a student at Saint Joseph for years, is organizing a mass in honor of Sister Marie Laurence's birthday. The theme will be Unity: "If all nations joined hands, the world would be a better place." Our class is known for its high percentage of foreign students. Noah will showcase the delicacy of Asia in the floral arrangements at the chapel. Ishtar will head the foreign delegation which, in folkloric costume of their respective countries, will offer our pièce de resistance, the Unity scene. Agnès, president of the organization committee, will choose the appropriate liturgical texts with the priest.

Astrid, Sister Marie Laurence's legendary tormentor, won over by the widespread excitement, volunteers to play the role of hostess. She wears a festive outfit: navy blue skirt, white buttoned up blouse, wool beret with the school logo embroidered in gold letters, nylon stockings and black patent leather shoes. I conclude that adolescence is a reservoir of generosity that surprises, sometimes. Astrid and her acolytes will escort guests to their respective church benches. Agnès, eyes fixed on me, announces, "Myriam, we are counting on you to deliver the message."

A sudden, illogical panic seizes me. I had kept the unspoken hope of remaining silent in my corner. I refuse to be in the hot seat and face a potential public audience. Agnès insists. Beatrice d'Ardompre, a high school senior known for her talent as an orator, offers a compromise: she will read the text of the message, if I agree to write it. Relieved, I throw myself into the project, night after night with a flashlight, when everyone is asleep. Silence and my muse are my sole companions.

On D-day, the excitement is at a fever pitch. Beatrice's tone marvelously captures the essence of the message. Then Ishtar, a beautiful veiled incarnation from the Middle East, appears on stage, leading the steps for the foreign delegation, which stands at the foot of the altar: Yuko, Japan's ambassador, Rada of Ivory Coast, and Lea, from the West Indies. Agnès, in stylish Parisian attire, has joined hands with the group to offer, in a silence laden with emotion, the moving Unity scene to a mesmerized public. Electricity is in the air, and a surprising thunder of applause burst within the walls of the chapel. The service ends with the choir's performance of our teacher's favorite oratorio: Handel's "Hallelujah." This day will live forever in our adolescent hearts and minds and remain engraved in the annals of Saint Joseph. Sister Marie Laurence thanked me for my text the next day. Agnès had revealed the author's name to her.

~ * ~

Our Catechism classes often turn into platforms for heated debates, where our brilliant speaker always manages to give new life to dry or sensitive topics. It is also an opportunity for Astrid to cause a ruckus, with the sadistic hope that our teacher will one day lose her superb self-control. Topics of discussion always arouse our teenage interest: religion, family, society at large. Ishtar loves theoretical debates that stretch out, when she is given the floor. She will make an excellent lawyer, some day, and will defend the cause of Muslim women in her country. Agnès always lets herself be guided by her heart.

Unlike my classmates who welcome, with passion, these group discussions, I always keep a low profile and prudent silence during Catechism. To speak my mind in public would mean venturing outside of my comfort zone and exposing myself to the scrutiny of others. I grew up in Haiti at a time where free speech and exchanges were silenced by the sacred rules of "hearsay" and the fear of political reprisals from the dictatorial regime. I prefer to remain invisible, a discrete presence who keeps a personal chronicle of people, events and places that cross my path.

On the day of "The youth and sexuality" debate, I predict the class will be offered an epic performance. The subject is a double treat for our group of curious adolescents. The topic itself will spark our excitement. We can also expect a theatrical spectacle from our two protagonists: Astrid, the forked tongue, and her favorite victim, Sister Marie Laurence. The floor is given to the student who, raising her hand, appears to be about to lose her patience. "Sister, having taken a vow of chastity, what can you teach us about sex?"

"Excellent question, Astrid. My knowledge on the subject is, I will admit, theoretical. But I possess solid credentials: I am a trained

Youth Advisor and Family Educator. I have also been teaching the senior classes for years. Today's topic could have been addressed in the light of my scientific and religious knowledge. The class is, obviously, not mature enough for such a debate. You might find it incredible, but I was sixteen too, once upon a time…Today's youth concerns are just the repetition of those of previous generations."

Astrid, ridiculed, lowers her gaze. The debate will not take place. Sister Marie Laurence, giving her a furious glare that could kill, is merciless in her sharp irony. She reminds us of those legendary heroes in universal times, who, through the ages, seek to be heard rather than be loved. Their journey is often a lonely one. But they stand tall, steadfast, as beacons of light. Our teacher concludes with these prophetic words, "Early sexuality will lead to drift. Freedom of choice becomes irremediably lost. We cannot turn back the clock, in life. I wish for you that, in times of big decisions, you have a choice."

~14~

At the end of the grading period, each month, my parents would reward me with a weekend at my grandparents' house located in Bois Verna, one of Port-au-Prince's oldest neighborhoods. Their home was an ancient wooden structure of "gingerbread" style, with carved balconies highly perched around the entire building. The intricate carvings were reminiscent of delicate embroidery and fine needlework, crafts taught at the renowned Center Elie Dubois. Our family home had witnessed the birth and death of several Deveaux generations. I was also born between these walls, one stormy night. My umbilical cord is buried in the backyard, Marguerite told me.

Every year, my grandparents would hire the best carpenters in town to maintain the elegant look of their home, despite its advanced age. The hardwood floors and curved staircase leading to the second story always sparkled, thanks to André's muscles and brushes. An open, flower-filled porch, tiled with mosaic of a remarkable brilliance, encircled the perimeters of the house. The veranda was airy and exposed to the elements: the soft, December breeze as well as the brutal gushes of wind during rainy season. Two rocking chairs kept each other company on the porch, and never parted, like their occupants, my grandparents.

Grandfather would boast about his ancestors who had served their country before the dictatorship. A portrait of his father, General Deveaux, a proud, military man with a bushy moustache, covered an entire panel of the living room wall. This large, ceremonial room, austere and dark like my grandfather, opened its doors only on holidays, when Limoges dishes and polished Christofle silverware gleamed under the crystal chandelier, which would lose its coat of dust in preparation of the festivities. I loved poking around my grandfather's narrow office, and caress the leather-bound books in red and black jacket, aligned on the shelves. I did not read yet, but found great pleasure in brushing my fingers on the gold letters embossed on the books' spines. I would be brave on occasions and, as if succumbing to the temptation of a forbidden fruit, dare to glance through the pages of one of these treasures of knowledge.

Regular visitors, neighbors, and longtime friends were usually entertained on the flowery veranda, where the light scent of jasmine perfumed the cool, late afternoon breeze. Charles Deveaux, immersed in the reading of Le Nouvelliste, *the daily local newspaper, would answer in monosyllables to Leilah's babbling. True to her Lebanese roots, my grandmother would sip, with obvious delight, a fresh cup of strong coffee served every afternoon at four o'clock when Grandfather returned home from the office. "Despite doctor's orders," she liked to remind us, sniffing the warm beverage with evident pleasure, before swallowing the first sip. Fresh coffee beans were roasted in a large boiler in the backyard and grinded in a pilon, a long wooden pestle, to preserve the aroma and freshness of this rich black powder. Leilah's coffee was the delight of visitors and had earned a solid reputation among neighbors, over the years.*

This ritual of my grandparents on their porch was as important to them as it was for me: It meant the continuity of things and of life. Their rocking chairs almost touched. One could guess the great love that bound them but would not be shown publicly, according to rules of etiquette governing the customs of their generation. At my grandparents' house, "children do not speak at the table" and are ordered to "go play outside." Awake at dawn on Saturday, I would open the high louvers which, from the second floor, offered me a panoramic view of the city and a timid glance at the Bay of Port-au-Prince. I could hear the familiar cry of street vendors, the noise of traffic jam. Port-au-Prince's cycle of life had started anew, at the sound of the rooster. The aroma of coffee and toast was already floating from the kitchen.

~ * ~

I invariably associate the smell of charcoal burning with Bois Verna, where a charcoal burner was perpetually lit in my grandparents' backyard. I would watch curiously as Dieudonne prepared huge boilers of rice and beans to feed the entire household, their unexpected guests and the staff: Dieudonne, the cook, and her daughter, Ti Sò; André, the gardener; and Celia, my grandmother's housekeeper.

Dieudonne, whose important role as cook gave her a special aura, ruled the backyard like a respected sovereign. No one would dare thwart her orders. Her daughter Ti Sò, a splendid teenager with copper tone skin and very popular among men, would help her mother out after school. By sheer coincidence, or perhaps perfectly orchestrated, Dieudonne's visitors and Ti Sò's steady admirers always arrived in the yard at mealtimes and politeness required an invitation to eat that was courteously accepted. They enjoyed the generous dish offered to them, of rice and beans topped by a spoonful of toufe, a vegetable stew flavored by sparse chunks of beef.

Ti Sò, sixteen, shared with her mother the cozy bungalow nestled in the backyard, under the shadow of an old mango tree. I would save my old magazines subscriptions for her, and she would patiently cut out the color illustrations and line the inner walls of the bungalow with photos of international stars. Ti Sò also loved old calendars' landscape illustrations. The snowy slopes of the Mont Blanc would share the display walls with Switzerland's mirror lakes or the Caribbean sandy beaches, under Johnny Hallyday and Elvis Presley's surprised gaze. This eclectic collage, carefully executed, was a true work of art.

Every Saturday, Dieudonne would bring her daughter two fresh eggs from her weekly shopping at the Iron Market. Located in the business section of downtown Port-au-Prince, this huge, intricate metal structure, towered by two minarets, was said to have been initially fabricated for the Muslim country of Egypt. Constant traffic jams and pedestrian congestion reigned in its vicinity. The market was always swarming with people: vegetable, goat, chicken, spices and craft vendors, all arguing for the right to survival. The buyers would become human preys that had to be wooed and seduced at all cost with the most attractive prices.

Ti Sò would swallow the egg yolks beaten with sugar, cinnamon and lemon peel. But her great joy came from the egg white, which she poured carefully into a clear, water-filled glass jar, and exposed to the sun. The egg whites, cooked by the sun rays, would solidify in the water, and take bizarre forms of stalagmites and stalactites. With the wisdom of age and unbridle imagination, Ti Sò would spot a church steeple, an omen that she would marry. Sometimes the egg white formed horizontal bands, symbol that a large ship would carry her away from Haiti someday. I would stare, fascinated, at this glass jar, convinced I was contemplating the silhouette of a majestic ship or the reproduction of a miniature cathedral.

Curious, I asked Ti Sò, "Would you choose marriage or travel abroad?"

Her reply was a cry from the heart: "Travel abroad!"

Years later, a large "bird" made of steel would take Ti Sò toward Montreal's skyscrapers.

~15~

Ishtar, who usually keeps silent on details of her private life outside of Saint Joseph, has invited me to join her for the weekend at her correspondents' Parisian abode. Sister Marie Laurence, at Reverend Mother's request, signs, with a puzzled look, the authorization slip. A driver in cap and uniform, with a broad black moustache covering half of his face, picks us up at the bus station and gallantly opens the rear door of the vehicle with tinted windows. A luxurious building greets me in the heart of Paris. Ishtar's correspondents, an elderly couple with a thick foreign accent, welcome us upon arrival and disappear. An elegant olive-skinned woman, dressed in a royal blue suit, offers me a polite handshake with a smile. "I am Najlah," she says. "My daughter has spoken highly of you."

She is wearing splendid gold jewelry around her wrists and neck. My friend seems in awe of her mother, in transit in Paris to attend an international conference on human rights. At supper, we are served skewered goat and couscous by a young man in a white shirt. He does not speak a word of French. Najlah, a patron of the arts, bids us farewell for a business meeting near the Louvre Museum. I never see her again until our departure. I bought a turquoise chiffon dress on sale that will be suited for Ishtar's evening with friends, at the restaurant La Coupe d'Or. Exhilarated by the delicious feeling of freedom after our week at boarding school, we are just two adolescents happy to play "les grandes dames" (grown women) and try out new make-up in front of the mirror. No one would guess our age. Ishtar's guests and compatriots join us at the entrance of the restaurant: exotic faces and names, dark hair cascading over their shoulders, gold bangles and sparkling earrings. I regret my costume jewelry for a second.

Waiters in livery keep busy around us. Ishtar, slender and tall in a cherry red dress that accentuates her olive-skinned complexion, is radiant tonight. She places our orders, with ease and grace, to the maître d' who recognizes Ishtar as a regular patron of the restaurant. Between two flights, Najlah enjoys taking her daughter to La Coupe d'Or, reserving a corner alcove conducive to intimate mother-daughter time and the pleasure of gastronomy.

Ishtar's menu choices are borderline extravagant. For appetizers she selects varied crustaceans and artichoke hearts, followed, for the main course, by the house specialty, the Chateaubriand, a cut of meat so tender that it melts in the mouth. A variety of tempting cheeses, fruits and desserts served with light, fruity wines conclude the scrumptious meal. Without blinking an eye, my friend signs the long tab. Broad smile and slight bow from the maître d'. I imagine the tip received must be very generous.

"Who are you, Ishtar?" I will not formulate this thought out loud, observing a cautious silence as I sit next to my friend on the back padded seat of the car. The black sedan cuts through the illuminated streets of Paris, driven silently by the mustached chauffer with a blue kepi on his head. I would need so many questions answered, to satisfy my curiosity. Ishtar reads my mind like an open book. "You are my best friend at Saint Joseph," she says. "Someday, you will know everything. Because you are special."

Sunday afternoon, I regretfully leave the opulence of Ishtar's Parisian foothold to sink back into the reality of our lives as boarders. We are the first to arrive at the station. I follow Ishtar as she selects a seat at the back of the bus. The mustached driver and car with tinted windows disappear on the horizon. Dressed in faded jeans, plain shirt and a coat so big it could swallow her, my friend intrigues me totally: such a contrast with her lavish lifestyle at her correspondents' Parisian home. Is Ishtar staying, incognito, at Saint Joseph?

~ * ~

"Your conduct borders on dementia, childishness to excess!" Sister Marie Laurence says, pacing nervously across the small space between her desk and our two chairs that brush against each other. Her eyes are blazing. Jaws tense, gaze reflecting the color of sharp grey metal, the nun seems like a proud warrior getting ready for battle.

The culprits, caught red-handed, are now facing their judge. My penchant for the extraordinary, mixed with a deepening friendship with my Muslim classmate, has plunged me into an incredible adventure with disastrous consequences. The movie of the recent events rolls in my brain: lights are out in the dormitory, and a pleasant slumber, prelude to sleep, has slowly taken over my body at rest. A sudden presence in the darkness of my room makes me jump: Ishtar.

"Myriam, my brother Saied is in Paris for the night. I must leave Saint Joseph tonight and go see him. He is fighting for the safeguard of our country. Should something happen to him, I would not forgive myself. Mustapha is waiting for me at the entrance of the park."

My night light is off, not to alert the nun on duty. My friend's folly scares me. But I picture a brave Saied lying in his own blood, a political martyr for his country, and his young sister inconsolable at his side. In a flash, I imagine Ishtar crossing, alone and terrified, the entire park of Saint Joseph, in the darkness of the night. Torn between heart and reason, I whisper these words, to regret them one second later, "I will go with you." But now it is too late to take them back. This unselfish gesture is exactly what Ishtar secretly hoped for. She advises, feverish with excitement, "Bring your flashlight."

Seduced by the extraordinary adventure unfolding before my eyes, I join ranks with the heroic characters that enchanted my childhood summer readings and fueled my imagination: *Le Club des Cinq* and *Le Clan des Sept* come to life. Our comforters are folded to mimic a human form at rest in our narrow beds, just as I've seen done in countless movie projections at the Rex Theater on Sunday afternoons in Haiti. Shoes in hand, to avoid any cracking of the wooden floor that could awaken Sister Angèle, we tiptoe through the dorm until we reach the spiral staircase that will lead to the corridors, balconies and visitors' parlor. A heavy wooden door separates us from the terrace that connects to the brick staircase at the entrance of the school. Once outside, we anticipate the frigid night air will brutally hit us. Instinctively, we adjust our long woolen scarves around our necks and allow ourselves one second of hesitation, before taking the last step.

"I command you to stop. Have you both lost your mind?"

Ishtar, frozen in a total state of panic, sees a veiled form emerge from obscurity and violently grab her by the wrist. Fear consumes my whole being; I am about to faint. Herculean force emanates from the fragile silhouette. Sister Marie Laurence, who often spends long hours in her office, working late at her desk by the window, followed, from her strategic point, the trajectory of our flashlights, the moment we crossed the balcony. Intrigued, she left her office to wait for the culprits in the visitor's parlor and catch them red-handed.

I am shivering under the wool sweater I accidentally wore inside out, in my haste to join Ishtar in the adventure of a lifetime. I am now torn between friendship and fear, terrified of potential reprisals that might follow. Tears run, shameless, abundant, and pathetic. Ishtar, wearing one black and one brown moccasin, sits immobile, eyes glued to her mismatched shoes. Our ridiculous attires would seem comical, but the solemnity of the hour does not allow for humor. Our teacher tersely reminds us that Reverend Mother must be informed of tonight's incident and decide of our fate.

"Myriam is not guilty. I have planned this crazy idea and should be the only one punished," Ishtar says in tears before confessing her plan to reach Paris tonight and join Saied, the military leader of forces fighting a feared rebel movement in their country. My friend is desperate at the thought of her brother going into harm's way before she gets to say goodbye.

Our teacher, stirred, offers her a consoling shoulder. "Ishtar, I understand your predicament, my child, but blinded by your pain, you have lost all sense of objectivity." The nun adds, in a tone more maternal than accusatory, "Myriam, loyalty in friendship is beautiful and honorable. But your lack of maturity has put you in the heart of a drama with serious consequences."

Lenient, she offers Ishtar the joy of a call to Saied, in the solitary parlor, before returning to the dorm. Reverend Mother opts against our expulsion, the next day, at Sister Marie Laurence's request. She has become our defense counsel. But every act carries consequences. Punished the entire weekend and unable to leave the school premises, Ishtar and I are ordered to write a lengthy dissertation on the importance of obedience to the Disciplinary Code. We are forbidden to exchange a single word until our classmates' return on Sunday evening. But our secret will be preserved. I conclude that the vow of silence must be the most difficult exercise in stoicism for human beings.

~16~

How does one choose "the right time" to inform a naïve little girl that her mother is actually her Aunt Yvette, and that her Aunt Claire, who died so young, is her mother? This moment when everything collapsed and the ground fell under my feet, I remember it as if it was yesterday. Noel was fast approaching, and millions of stars twinkled like glittering diamonds in the December night sky. I would spot the most brilliant, l'étoile des Rois Mages, the one that guided the Magi to baby Jesus two thousand years ago, a sign that Christmas was near. Happiness floated in the air.

I had celebrated, three months earlier, my seventh birthday, the proverbial "age of reason." I had recently lost my first baby front tooth and my odd, new smile gave me an air of superiority in my younger brothers' eyes. I would accept, complacent, Bobby's close inspection of my grinning open mouth. He did not hide his impatience at the prospect of losing a tooth as well and would shake his small incisor all day long. He even managed to convince me that his front tooth was indeed moving. After the candles were blown out, my best friend Cathy and our few guests shared the traditional slice of cake and glass of Cola Couronne on the veranda, in celebration of my birthday.

Everyone left before nightfall at the first rumbling sound of the thunder, under a grey blanket of menacing clouds ready to burst into torrential downpour. September is nested in the heart of hurricane season with its array of harrowing rains, violent lightening and destructive force winds.

School would start the first week of October and Catechism classes would prepare us, this year, for the Sacrament of First Communion. I looked forward to go downtown with my mother and grandmother and visit the fabric stores at Bord-de-Mer. Yvette and Leilah would choose the best fabric, of the purest white color, for my Communion dress. I would also be wearing a crown of white, woven flowers and carry a pearl rosary for the ceremony. Conscious of the occasion's solemnity, I already apprehended the sacrament of Confession, and the daunting encounter with the priest, who would absolve me of all sin, in the shadow of the confessional.

December was at our doorstep, with its cool breezes and starry nights. The last month of the year also brought back our family tradition of Sunday breakfasts served in the garden at my grandparents' home, after mass. In summer months and excruciating heat, these outdoor meals would lose their appeal. Wearing their "Sunday best," Grandma and Grandpa would walk back, arm in arm, from Sacred Heart. I loved watching these rare moments of physical intimacy between them, when our arrival in the garden preceded theirs. Their daughter had made it her duty to visit them after church, armed with a large box of hot pâtés and croissants purchased at the local bakery. My father fared well through these weekly rituals, aware that his union with Yvette married him also to the entire Deveaux family and their traditions.

Every detail of that ill-fated Sunday remains deeply engraved in my memory: the grease spots on the empty pastry box, the patties and croissants, placed in orderly fashion on the silver dish sculpted in the same pattern as the steaming silver coffee pot; the story, so often told, of Grandmother Deveaux's century-old silverware, which would belong to Yvette someday and subsequently to me; the aroma of velvety hot chocolate, served in our porcelain cups. At seven, I was finally entitled to a real, breakable cup, whereas my younger brothers had to contend with their plastic tumbler. It would be inconceivable to break one of these fragile porcelain objects finely designed with delicate red roses on both cup and saucer. I daydreamed I was one of the "model little girls" from the Comtesse de Ségur's novel, elegant with pink umbrella and crinoline skirt, a porcelain cup gracefully held to my lips.

The moment of truth came for me, at my grandparents' table, on this breezy December day, as three generations, bonded by blood and surrounded by laurel hedges and bougainvillea bushes, were sipping hot chocolate. Contrary to my usual polite and quiet ways in presence of my elders, I was talkative on that Sunday morning. I felt a new affinity with the "grown up" clan: the porcelain cup, perhaps, or the "age of reason"? With innocent, childish curiosity, I asked aloud why Aunt Claire had died.

This topic, taboo for the family, intrigued me. Grandfather, furious, leapt out of his chair, and dropped, at the risk of breaking it into a million pieces, his porcelain cup. Chocolate spilled on the white tablecloth, as he called me a nosy chatterbox and ordered me to shut up about Claire. I looked, in disbelief, at my grandmother's gaping mouth: Leilah, horrified, had become temporarily mute. Yvette stared, flabbergasted, at her father, the patriarch and supreme authority. She hugged one-year-old baby Freddy, as he started screaming, terrified by the sudden noise and commotion. Glued to my chair, I believed, for a fraction of second, that I would faint. Face flushed with anger, James glared at Charles.

Rising quickly and nimbly from the table, my father gently grabbed my small trembling palm and kept it in his. I followed him to the living room and took refuge in the paternal arms. Tears trickled down my cheeks and wetted the collar of his shirt. The veins in his neck were pounding. Inconsolable, stunned by my grandfather's unexpected outburst, I kept my head buried against my father's shoulder, my body nested against his chest, never wanting to let go of my refuge, of my rock. I still remember his discreet scent of aftershave that day.

Claire, the elegant young woman in a red evening gown, seemed to smile at us from the silver picture frame displayed on the piano. Using the photography, my father found simple, loving words to finally lift the curtain on a family secret kept too long in the shadows. It was a rare moment of intimacy that no one else would ever share: this cosmic encounter between three loved ones, which transcended the frontiers of life and death. I never forgot that day, marked all at once *by the discovery and the loss of the mother who gave me life. It created in my heart a void that will never be filled.*

That day I also felt I was losing the only mother I knew: Yvette. Weighing the different circumstances of my brothers' arrival into the world, I understood, with the wisdom of my seven years, that Yvette was their "real" mother. With me, it was an act, as she offered me the alms of her motherhood. Finally, I concluded I had lost a grandfather, whose withering stare and accusatory tone would always remind me of my unforgivable fault: Claire died one September night, in the heart of a storm, to give me life.

That painfully memorable year, Christmas would be the very first spent away from Leilah, my adoring grandmother. To Yvette's dismay, my father declined my grandparents' traditional invitation to Christmas brunch. On New Year, Charles Deveaux, a proud and uncompromising man, came to Bourdon to make amends with his son-in-law. The two men exchanged, relieved, the symbolic handshake of peace. Time heals wounds, I am told. I believe rather that they get placed on the back burner. Life seemed to return to normal, and I pretended to forget.

~ * ~

From that day on, the woman I had always called Mother became "Yvette" for me. Unconsciously perhaps, I resented my aunt for being alive, whereas my real mother did not get this chance at life. The stubborn girl I had become remained blind to Yvette's silent pain. Ironically, she stood up to my father, who had taken umbrage to this state of affairs, and pleaded on my behalf. "James, it will take time for Myriam to recover from such revelation about her birth. We should not rush her. She will process everything at her own rhythm."

The unfulfilled quest for an impossible dream dominated my child's heart. I was looking everywhere for Claire's image, her illusory presence, wishing to see the face and feel the touch of the one who gave me life. Yvette, the only mother I had known, kept her calm and composure despite my mood swings and aggressiveness towards my younger brothers. I envied my siblings for the privilege of having their "real" mother in their lives, whereas I had to settle for the crumbs I was offered. Yvette never showed any favoritism towards her own children. I wished she would, sometimes, and thus justify the secret resentment she inspired me. To ease my conscience, I convinced myself that by depriving Yvette of the title of "mother," I honored Claire's memory. I never shared my secret with my schoolmates, however, evoking "Mother and Father" when we were chatting informally about our respective families at recess. In public places I always managed a face-to-face with Yvette when engaging in conversation with her.

Over time, the family grew accustomed to the status quo. Yvette resigned herself to her new name calling, my grandmother dared not protest, and my father, loathing all confrontation, said nothing either. I believe Charles, my grandfather, appreciated in silence this bizarre tribute to the daughter he had lost. My younger brothers, too young for psychoanalysis, remained totally indifferent. Marguerite, whose privileged role within the family gave her all the rights, was the only one bold enough to scold me. She called me ungrateful towards Yvette, but her words landed on deaf ears. Discouraged, she eventually abandoned the fight.

When at age twelve, I discovered the truth about the intimate nature of marriage, my resentment redoubled towards Yvette who had usurped my mother's place in my father's heart and replaced her in his bed. How could James have had marital relations with two sisters who had grown up together under one roof? This thought disturbed me beyond measure. More than once, I sobbed with rage, in darkness's complicity and the solitude of my bedroom.

I was thirteen when I packed my bags one day and decided I would go live with my grandmother, after a rebuke from my father about a trifle. My parents pretended to go along with my plans, offered to drive me to Bois Verna and played the game until the very end. Leaving my younger brothers under the watchful care of Marguerite, James placed my suitcase in the trunk of the Peugeot, and sat at the wheels, Yvette by his side. As I opened the rear door of the vehicle, seized by sudden panic, I silently changed my mind. Head down, defeated, furious at myself for putting such an embarrassing show, I stepped out of the car, without a word, to go seek the refuge of my bedroom.

How could I even imagine leaving the people and things that shaped my daily life? James and Yvette would remain my firm assurance, my rock, despite myself, my tantrums, or the circumstances of my birth… despite what could have been in the perfect world of dreams, but would never be…despite, alas, the wishes of a tender girl who, at the age of adolescence, still dreamed of an angel's visit in the heart of the night.

*"Claire," my grandmother would whisper, "has become that sweet angel who will **always** watch over you."*

~17~

With the school's permission, I take the local bus to Paris today, right after mass. Madame Levesque has invited me for Sunday lunch at the hotel-pension where Yvette and I stayed upon our arrival in France. I love this quaint neighborhood, its older buildings and sober elegance. Everything exudes the owner's good taste. She took us, the foreigners in Paris, under her wings last September and gave Yvette precious advice in the purchase of my trousseau. Her luncheon invitation is a pleasant diversion to my routine at boarding school and an otherwise lonely Sunday in an empty dorm while my classmates are visiting their families.

Entering the spacious dining room with its cozy individual tables, I am surprised to find Romeo sitting at his usual place, as if the past several months have remained frozen in time. He smiles at me just like he did in September, with a wink from his sparkling brown eyes. Today, I do not blush. The young Haitian who had freshly landed from the Caribbean a few months ago has learned to dress elegantly like a young Parisian. After desert, I thank Madame Levesque for her kindness and leave to catch a taxi that will drop me at the Metro and on to the Val-de-Seine bus station.

Romeo suddenly pops up before me and puts a hand on my arm: "I hope, this time, to be luckier."

Ms. Levesque formally introduced us in September. Yvette was courteous but distant. She had a mission to accomplish in France, and little time to devote to mundane exchanges with a young man who, obviously, showed too much interest in the comings and goings of a shy teenager busy preparing her trousseau for boarding school. What demon pushes me to accept Romeo's invitation today? The one of curiosity, I presume. Sweeping all scruple aside, I agree to join him "for a pleasant afternoon" at the Longchamp race track, he promises, as he stops the first taxi in sight.

Torn between his caressing gaze, the warmth of his arm around my shoulder and the creeping guilt invading my conscience, I remain silent. When he approaches his lips toward mine, I snap out of my dangerous numbness to seek refuge against the car door. An indifferent taxi driver pretends to be deaf and blind to the commotion on the back seat. Romeo's frown fortunately gives way to a smile, as he gallantly helps me out of the car. A sure guide, he clears his way through the noisy crowd, his imposing height offering a welcome advantage. His hand holds mine tightly.

I am witnessing, for the first time in my life, the amazing spectacle of horses out of control on a race track. In a flash, I imagine myself transported back in time, a spectator at the Olympic Games of Greece, where the same explosive atmosphere must have reigned. My companion introduces me to his friends, men with hard features, who stare at me curiously. Faces contracted, harsh voices, they discuss winning and losing numbers with Romeo who seems, in the intensity of the moment, to have forgotten my presence by his side. I cannot help but notice the oddity of the scene and silently wonder what I am doing here.

The light of revelation suddenly blinds me: Romeo is a gambler in connection with shady individuals and my naivety has brought me into murky waters. How can I escape a precarious situation I voluntarily stepped into? Romeo's size will make a mouthful out of me if he wants to attack me. At this stage of my thoughts, panic has totally engulfed me. Beside Romeo's obsolete first name, and his address as a year-round client at Madame Levesque' pension-hotel, I realize I know nothing of him.

I beg. "I want to go. Please!"

We leave the premises under the mocking gaze of his friends. Romeo hails a taxi and I ask to be dropped at the nearest subway station. Once on the back seat, he swiftly wraps his left arm around my shoulders and takes my lips with authority. Prisoner of his firm embrace, he leaves me no chance to seek refuge against the door. Romeo's smile is gone. He is running his fingers on me in an intrusive way. Defeated by his physical strength, eyelids fogged up with tears, I endure in silence his lascivious game, embarrassed by the unflappable taxi driver. But when his hand grabs mine and directs it to this hard, quivering point who claims life under his garment, a desperate gasp escapes from my lips. "No!"

At the entrance of the Metro station, Romeo opens the taxi door and I can feel his mocking gaze on my back as I quickly step onto the curve. He must be laughing at the naïve, infantile boarding school girl who was ill prepared for these sorts of games. Too agitated by the recent turn of events, and worried about the time element and my return to Saint Joseph, I stop the first taxi in sight to drive me back to Val-de-Seine. My sole focus: find the shelter of my cubicle, under my comforter, shut my mind off and pretend it was all a crazy dream. But, at the astronomical cost claimed by the taxi driver, my eyes open wide in disbelief. My monthly allowance is insufficient to cover the taxi fare.

The only recourse available to me: my parents' emergency school fund account kept in reserve by the school administration. To disturb Sister Francis, the accountant, on a Sunday is an omen of tragedy. She joins me in the parlor, flanked by Sister Marie Laurence. Once the taxi driver leaves, I am summoned to follow my teacher in her office.

Not a single detail escapes my observing gaze: the modest dimensions of the crowded office, the monumental pile of science and religion manuals, students' homework papers, a collection of pens and pencils in a silver timbale. A tired-looking missal, bound in black leather, reveals its frequent use. On the wall, a picture of Christ stands above a wooden shelf on which rests a cassette player, unique modern twist in this ageless setting—an austere, obscure space that harbors a life of self-denial. The sole feminine note on her desk: a single silk rose in a crystal bud vase, so delicate that one would think it had been freshly cut from the garden. On the corner of the desk, an aspirin bottle seems to wink and silently remind us that Sister Marie Laurence is also subject to headaches and monthly events.

I confess everything, in one single burst, to clear my conscience of a heavy load. This first encounter with an older man's troubling sexual advances has upset me. Relieved by my voluntary confession, Sister Marie Laurence reveals that Madame Levesque had called the school earlier to inquire about my safe return. My teacher, confident of the trust the school had placed in me, pleaded in my favor. The superior agreed to wait for the arrival of the school bus, bringing the students back from Paris, before taking any disciplinary measures against me. Saint Joseph had taken on a great responsibility by authorizing this Sunday leave. If I had kept the school from the truth, I might have been expelled from Saint Joseph. God was watching over me, I silently conclude.

~18~

"We are descendants of Phoenicians," would repeat Leilah sometimes, evoking these merchant people of ancient times who crisscrossed the Mediterranean, dominated maritime trade, settled on land that has become Lebanon today, founded Tyre and Byblos, and bequeathed their alphabet to the world.

In the sixteenth century, Lebanon and Syria, like so many others, fell under the yoke of the Ottoman Turkish Empire. They would have to wait centuries to be granted the official status of autonomous countries. France, whose influence became significant in the region in the nineteenth century, would play a role in the future in their history as a people.

In Northern Lebanon, in the heights of Bcharre, lie vast forests of cedars, majestic millennial trees celebrated in the Bible by King Salomon, that sparkle in winter months under their cloak of snow. At the entrance to Tripoli, major port city in the area which spreads out on the shores of the Mediterranean, is Minieh, a quiet village located north of the Lebanese city, pleasant with its greenery, its water sources and flowery fields.

Towards the end of the nineteenth century, a young couple from Minieh had built their nest in the shadow of their two families: Zahiye Khalil, sixteen, had accepted her parents' choice to marry Kimbram Habdoul, her second cousin. They would age quietly, in their hometown and their parents' footstep, surrounded by their children and their children's children. But life is always full of surprises. The twentieth century was at their gates when Kimbram and Zahiye, like so many other immigrants of the time, left the land of their ancestors.

They abandoned their home and material possessions, taking only gold and precious-gem jewelry, money and some clothing. Christians of the Greek Orthodox denomination, they fled persecution by the Turkish

Islamic Empire. The difficult economic situation, raging towards the end of a reign whose heavy yoke would last for centuries, also contributed to this mass exodus of people seeking a better quality of life.

My ancestors set sail towards the new world and its promises of hope. The long journey on the high seas proved harmful to my grandmother who could not keep any food down. Farid and Leilah, two and three years old, clung, terrified, to their mother's skirts and watched her, powerless, in the throes of suffering. The family finally landed in Cuba, where Zahiye gave birth to a stillborn son.

For reasons unclear to Leilah, my grandmother, her parents left Cuba for the Dominican Republic. After a brief stay in the neighboring Caribbean island, they packed their bags again. Hispaniola's western side became their host country and the place where their children would grow up. Kimbram and Zahiye had left Lebanon, to settle in Haiti, a French-speaking country. They died, speaking only Arabic and a much-accented Creole.

~ * ~

My memories remain sketchy, of a patriarch with thick white hair, his speech impossible to decipher, who stared at me behind thick, opaque glasses and called me Habibi. Yvette would approach Giddy (Grandfather) and plant a light kiss on his forehead, when we visited him at his halle (store) in Grand-Rue. He smoked like a chimney, his face wrapped in an eternal veil of white wispy cloud. Giddy ate little, but swallowed cup after cup of a strong, black coffee he invited me to share once, a mischievous smile painted on his wrinkled face. Leilah tore the tiny blue cup away from my hand and glared at her father, grumbling a spicy reproach in Arabic.

Giddy loved to count his fluus, the worn and grimy banknotes his clients would give him, the resellers who often traveled from distant provinces of rural Haiti, and who hid their nest egg in a small cloth bag tucked between their heavy breasts, for the journey. The heaven-sent chair and the cold drink that welcomed them upon arrival reminded them that at Habdoul's store, the customer is king. His cashbox filled at the end of the day, Giddy methodically tied the banknotes in small piles with a string. He stacked them afterwards in orderly fashion and stored them in a large metal safe hidden inside a wooden chest protected by a padlock and a key he never parted from.

Here I am, walking down memory lane, back to my great-grandparents' store in downtown Port-au-Prince. Scents of exotic spices perfume the high ceiling room. The pungent aroma of fresh garlic fills the air, lingering forever in my childhood memories. Sweet cinnamon and bitter cloves are put in little brown bags for resellers to travel to distant markets with. I hold, fascinated, a star anise, imagining a fragrant wooden star has fallen from the sky to rest in the palm of my hand.

An elderly woman of modest height, wearing a long white braid, arises also from mists of the past. Leilah is a younger version of this foggy vision. Yvette wraps her arms around her, in a gesture full of tenderness. She towers over her grandmother, whom she calls Sitto. My aunt is Deveaux, by her tall, slender figure and elegant poise. But her thick black hair is her mother's legacy.

Sitting on a small wooden and woven straw chair, Zahiye negotiates a delicate transaction with the fruits vendor: oval shaped "ti jocelyne" tomatoes and golden tangerines change owners. The tangerine is then peeled by my great-grandmother and offered to me on a blue dish that matches the coffee cup my great-grandfather handed me earlier.

It was in Grand-Rue, years ago, but this snapshot of the past remains engraved in my memory: in the big, dark hall, fresh as an oasis and scents of exotic spices floating in the air, four generations of Habdoul women, united by blood, are sharing a special moment, frozen in time, with the savor of eternity.

I understood already, in my child's heart, the importance of family roots. Fate had bonded me to this couple wrinkled by age. Kimbram and Zahiye Habdoul did not speak my language, but their blood flowed through my veins. Their country was an ancestral homeland, and their culture, a legacy to behold.

Would I set foot on Lebanon soil, some day?

~ * ~

"Keefek?" inquired Mr. Fahoul in Arabic, a wide, friendly smile painted on his face, when my grandmother would visit his fabric shop, flanked by her daughter and granddaughter. His store was next to ours in Grand-Rue. Like my Habdoul ancestors, his parents had fled their native Lebanon to emigrate in Haiti and establish a small commerce in Port-au-Prince's Bord-de-Mer business section.

Young Mr. Fahoul had taken over his parents' business and their commerce in fabrics flourished. The man with the thick white mustache always treated us as distinguished guests, offering us the best seats in the store as the delicious aroma of coffee filled the air. Faithful to the sacred tradition of proverbial hospitality of the Middle East, the good neighbor relationship between the Habdoul and the Fahoul had endured through the years.

Yvette would stroke the different fabrics, feel their weight, admire their colors, a pensive look on her face, before the final selection. Her seamstress would be tasked to create masterpieces to hang in her closet. A curious child, I took obvious pleasure in absorbing everything around me: the ambulatory resellers, fabrics merchants who crisscrossed the streets of Port-au-Prince, yards of bright, colored cloth piled on a wooden slab over their heads, who were given the royal treatment, the comfortable chair, the fresh caress of the fan, the tall glass of ice water. This halt "kay Fahoul" (at the Fahoul store) symbolized an oasis for these women, after their journey under the scorching midday sun, in downtown Port-au-Prince.

Trade was an art. I was discovering its intricate nuances from my vantage point, in a first-row seat in busy Grand-Rue, Bord-de-Mer's business section. In the dusty streets of town, packed with pedestrians, peddlers would fend off the crowds, their wares perfectly balanced on their head. The sidewalks were always congested with resellers' merchandise displays, a situation store owners were powerless to control, as access to their shop would become increasingly difficult for potential clients.

Sometimes a fight broke out, the protagonists arguing over a few square inches of cement sidewalk that was, in truth, property of the State, detail that the instinct for survival often made street vendors forget. I have often wished to be a painter and capture, with a stroke of the brush on a large canvas, this colorful splash of life teeming all around me.

As a child, I was always mesmerized by the herculean force of brouettiers (cart men) who, for a modest fee, fended their way through congested streets, dragging bags of charcoal or rice on locally crafted wheel carts made of wooden planks and recycled car tires. One day, I watched in disbelief a shirtless man, his back shiny with sweat and his muscles ready to burst, load concrete blocks and cement bags on his wheel cart. Inch by inch on the pavement, the man maneuvered through unruly pedestrians and impatient vehicles. With each step, he affirmed his resilience to life's challenges, his defiance in the face of adversity.

Retailers say "Nan Bòdmè," when they refer to the Bord-de-Mer commercial zone. Downtown is also the center of life, in Port-au-Prince: it is where fortunes are won and lost, where rich and poor mingle, shoulder to shoulder, in a symbiotic association indispensable to their respective survival.

My great-grandparents Habdoul, who, like others who had emigrated from the Middle East, lived on the second floor of their shop, managed their commerce until their death. With Leilah married, and Farid in the United States, they had no children to ensure continuity of the business. The sale of their store in Grand-Rue, Port-au-Prince's Main Street, closed a chapter in the Habdoul book and signaled the end of an era for our family.

Fortunately, I remember...

~19~

Present in France without an official host family, I am today a frequent guest at classmates' homes on weekends. Miles away from the terrorizing gaze of the Macoutes and the tense political climate of Haiti, an intoxicating taste of freedom is feeding my desire for new discoveries. Paris fascinates me. Gisèle invites me to the Tutankhamen Exhibition. Her father, a doctor and antiques collector, teaches us how to find deals at the flea market, the Marché aux Puces, and discover hidden treasures in piles of dusty junk. I got to taste the famous ice cream at the Drug Store of the Champs-Elysées and visit the Palace of Versailles with Annabelle. Frequent weekends with Agnès always unfold in the same peaceful pattern: Sunday mass followed by lunches in the family's courtyard, when the weather allows. The Renauds have become my unofficial correspondents—my host family.

Sister Marie Laurence never objects to my weekends at the Renauds' but always frowns at queries from other classmates. Unbeknownst to me, my parents wrote in a letter to the school: "In her letters, Myriam recounts, with a bit too much enthusiasm, her outings with friends. She is in France, first and foremost, for her studies." At their request, I will remain within school premises every two weekends and concentrate on academic work. Saint Joseph becomes the golden cage I begin to loathe. I'm its unwilling prisoner, a caged bird with one obsession: to escape. Since an escape is not in the picture for me, a silent desire for revolt and provocation starts to germinate. Like a brainless butterfly that will burn its wings by flying too close to the light, I begin to gravitate around Astrid, the leggy blonde troublemaker who nicknamed our teacher "Mary, the eternal virgin," and who smokes behind the foliage in the park, at recess. Unconsciously perhaps, I try to provoke the teacher who is too severe with me and whose authority I am starting to resent.

Astrid locates her regular smoking spot on a tree trunk, as I follow her like a puppet. From the depth of her pocket, she pulls a Gitane (a strong cigarette brand), lights it, takes a deep puff and exhales. Small, clear circles of smoke ascend into the air. She hands me a Gauloise (a lighter brand cigarette, also called a blonde) and declares with caustic humor, "Myriam, since you are a novice, you will take the blonde."

A violent coughing spell shakes my entire body. My classmate calls me a clumsy idiot as she offers me a gulp from the tiny mouthwash bottle she carries with her to conceal the cigarette odor. But Ishtar, who, I found out, also smokes at the home of her correspondents in Paris, and whose sense of smell must be sharp, is not fooled at study hall. Our desks are adjacent. "Be careful," she whispers, when the bell rings for dinner.

Lea, from Guadeloupe, secretly shares her fotonovelas magazines with me, attentive to protect us from the mockery of other students, should our scheme unravel. The news of famous singer Dalida's attempted suicide has hit us hard. My Caribbean classmate also worships the Italian-Egyptian-French performer. Heartbreak is said to have inspired the diva's desperate gesture. The idea makes me sad. Love should not hurt. I write feverishly during the weekends when I remain cloistered at Saint Joseph. Solitude has awakened a fickle muse. I imagine myself an aspiring writer, isolated on a desert island.

Enrico Macias embodies, for me, the face and voice of Love. Physical beauty moves me deeply, as does the breathtaking majesty of sunsets. My portable record player broadcasts Enrico's amazing voice, on weekends when I am alone in the dorm. Tonight, Ishtar keeps me company. Her correspondents are traveling. We spend the entire Saturday evening eating nougat and strumming notes on the guitar, humming with Enrico, *Adieu, mon pays*. Sister Angèle, amused, agrees to join us before returning to her room at the entrance of the dorm. After hot chocolate and croissants, followed by Sunday Mass the next day, Sister Marie Laurence invites us for a walk in the park. The big bare trees will soon wear the foliage of resurrection again. Spring is in the air. The nun evokes God, and we listen silently. "My daughters, never lose your quest for beauty and higher grounds. You will return to your countries someday. Share generously what France and Saint Joseph have offered you."

~ * ~

My father wrote, "Mother confronts a difficult pregnancy…." The idea of Yvette being pregnant again seems ridiculous. While women in Haiti see motherhood as a full-time career, none of my classmates in France lives such an old-fashioned family situation. They will think I am a true hillbilly, I think, embarrassed.

~ * ~

A witness of my recent disobedience to Saint Joseph's non-smoking rule, Astrid decides, impulsively, to invite me for the weekend. I hate the idea of another confrontation with Sister Marie Laurence regarding my outings. Caught between a rock and a hard place, I wonder who to fear the most: my legal guardian, favorite victim of my classmate's sarcasms, or Astrid herself, the forked tongue of our class.

"Myriam, if you let me down, I will tell our goody-two-shoes Marie Laurence, and your twins Agnès and Ishtar, that you begged me to teach you to smoke."

Astrid's evil genius, like a destructive poison, has inspired this blackmail. Her parents have contacted Reverend Mother, a long-standing family friend, who authorizes my weekend outing. Sister Marie Laurence, upset but obedient to hierarchy, signs the release form which symbolizes freedom for her student this weekend.

~20~

Since birth, Leilah Habdoul had been promised in marriage to her second cousin Foaz in Lebanon. This custom allowed families to remain together. The same blood flowed in their veins. There would be no bad surprises in a path already laid out by their elders. Children submitted obediently to their parents' decisions. These arranged marriages seemed to work. Unions lasted, and were cemented by the offspring these young couples brought into the world. Family fortunes, modest or big, would not disseminate among strangers but would be preserved and multiply within family clans.

Kimbram had already placed, with Minieh's best-known jeweler, an order of carved gold bangles that would adorn, someday, the bride's wrists. In line with tradition, Farid, the younger brother, the male heir, would take over the family business of fabrics and imported exotic spices. Leilah would become the perfect homemaker someday, for the husband promised to her.

But fate is unpredictable, and its road full of surprises at every turn. The future is never set in stone. Kimbram and Zahiye, forced to leave Lebanon to escape religious oppression that prevailed at the time against Christians, emigrated to Haiti, on the opposite side of the world. Zahiye sacrificed her precious jewelry to offer her children a new chance at life. However, she kept a treasure: the gold and diamond pendant her mother wore on her wedding day and that Leilah, her daughter, would inherit someday. This tradition, perpetuated from mother to daughter, remained sacred for the woman who had left her country, her culture and her family to follow her husband in the great adventure of exile.

Kimbram and Zahiye woke up at dawn and worked hard until nightfall. Their children were growing up. On the small balcony overlooking the teeming life on Grand-Rue, Leilah played with her dolls, and Farid, his marbles. These young Christian Orthodox discovered Catholicism and the French language at Saint Louis de Gonzague and Sainte Rose de Lima schools. But these notions remained foreign to their parents who, to communicate with their clients at the store, had learned Creole, spoken by the majority. Their business was flourishing. The couple managed the shop on the ground floor and lived with their children on the second.

At the time, these foreigners from the Middle East were frowned upon and patronized by the Haitian bourgeoisie. The public referred to them by the pejorative description of "Arab bwèt nan do" since they were peddlers who had arrived in the country with their meager possessions, did not speak French, and carried their wares on their backs. Settling at the edge of town in the Bord-de-Mer area, these immigrant families lived atop their stores, quickly learned Creole, spoken by all segments of the population, literate as well as illiterate, and carved out a solid customer base for themselves. The bulk of their clientele was composed of travelling merchants who came to the capital city of Port-au-Prince with cash, to stock up on spices, fabrics and miscellaneous hardware goods and resell such merchandise in their respective province towns and villages.

The Levantine community became, over the years, successful in business. Their offspring often attended the best private schools and the new generation, who spoke Arabic at home, was also fluent in Creole and French. Seduced by the prices offered by the "Syriens"(name used in Haiti at the time to refer to Syrian as well as Lebanese and Palestinian immigrants, who formed the bulk of Port-au-Prince's Levantine community), the Bord-de-Mer's clientele also stretched out to the Haitian bourgeoisie. From a very young age, Saturdays meant Leilah and Farid would be at their parents' store, behind a counter next to them, learning the ropes of the business and the secrets to a successful enterprise: roll up your sleeves from dawn to dusk, know how to count money, and last, but not least, treat all your clients as royalty.

Farid, after his studies at St. Louis de Gonzague, abruptly left Haiti to try his luck in New York, at the suggestion of a distant cousin who had emigrated to the United States and had sent him an invitation letter for a visa application. His parents, flabbergasted by the news, were distraught. The immutable order of succession was compromised. In their culture, the future of family businesses rested on the shoulders of the sons. I can only imagine my great-grandparents' pain and sense of loss. But Farid must have wanted to spread his wings, break the traditional mold and journey on a brand-new path of discovery.

~ * ~

Charles Deveaux completed, with high marks, a law degree in Paris. He returned to his country and the ancestral Deveaux home in Bois Verna. Despite the charm of Paris and its Parisian women, his profound love for his family and his birth country had brought him back to his Haitian roots. The youngest siblings to three unmarried sisters, Charles was the only son of the deceased army general Bertrand Deveaux. He fulfilled his role of family head and devoted son to Océanie, his beloved mother, to perfection.

The imposing image of the handsome black officer with a thick, white mustache, displayed on an entire living room wall panel, reminded him daily of his duties toward the four women who depended on him for their survival. General Deveaux had served his country with impassioned patriotism at the end of the nineteenth century, under the reign of President Sam. But he suffered a sudden cardiac arrest prematurely and deprived his children and his grieving widow of his larger-than-life presence. A talented baker, Océanie, who always created wedding cake masterpieces for her customers, stopped the lucrative business after the death of her husband. As tradition expected of her, the heartbroken spouse publicly mourned her dearly departed wearing severe black attire, and clung to Charles, the only son her late husband had given her, for emotional and financial support.

Josephine, the eldest daughter—"Fifine" to her close-knit family—was a pretty griffonne (slightly lighter shade of a black skin complexion), like her mother. Due to a horrible bout with Poliomyelitis as a child, she walked with a limp. Embittered by this unfair setback, she withdrew herself from the world. Reading became her universe, and voice and piano lessons the only luxury she granted herself. She would vocalize all day long in her room. She left only to meet with her music teacher and to attend meals, taken ceremoniously with the family in their spacious dining room, furnished with cupboards made of decorative glass and precious wood.

Eugénie, or "Nini" for relatives, a talented milliner, made elegant women's hats popular amongst the bourgeois of her time. A friend to the First Lady, she had access to the National Palace. But the death of a fiancé, after a stupid car accident on a trip abroad, left her stunned, at the gates of love, without ever entering its world. Her heart would belong to only one man. Ever since the tragedy, she lived in limbo, with the memory of what could have been, but would never be.

Angèle was a seamstress who never made a profit from her talent. She bought retay in town, the small pieces of multicolored cloth sold in bulk at fabric stores, to sew maldyòk (patchwork) dresses; she then tasked the family's housekeeper to sell them at cost on her behalf at the Iron Market.

Their only brother said nothing; he was happy to see them create hobbies for themselves that allowed them to fight boredom. Charles, with a heavy heart, realized that marriage would probably not cross his older sisters' path. All three had reached the age when an unmarried mademoiselle was considered a spinster in those days. He concluded, with philosophy, that he would be the only one to assume the financial stewardship of their home and its occupants in Bois Verna.

Despite crevasses and the overall challenging conditions of the road, Charles traveled to the southern town of Jérémie, the proverbial city of poets. The birthplace of more writers and poets per human capita than any other Haitian city, Jérémie was the Deveaux' ancestral hometown. Charles put up the family lands for sale, and the two-story wooden structure that was rotting over the years, in the heart of the city, abandoned by its owners. He was turning, with nostalgia, a page of the family's storybook. He realized that his family's future would bear only one name: the capital city of Port-au-Prince. His insurance agency, located on Rue Pavée, began to flourish, offering him the financial stability he had hoped and worked hard for. His mother and sisters would not lack for anything.

~ * ~

The union of Charles Deveaux and Leilah Habdoul has enough material for a fascinating novel. Summers would reunite our family in the mountains of Kenscoff, a popular vacation spot among city dwellers. The elders of three generations, gathered under one roof, often traveled down memory lane, during the cool evenings, when everyone sipped hot te ti Bonm, mint tea, after the evening soup. I never got tired of hearing my grandparents' love story, and the marriage of their two cultures.

Leilah, after her brevet, or Junior High, at Saint Rose de Lima, became her parents' right arm at the store to fill Farid' absence. Marriage plans with cousin Foaz were put on hold, as she seemed in no rush to enter into a union with a fiancé she had only met in a photograph. Affable, speaking fluent Arabic, Creole and French, Leilah quickly became the mascot of a diverse clientele who adored her. Following the example of her parents who had an innate sense of trade, the young, slightly plump woman with a long black braid offered the royal treatment to all her customers. The peddlers and resellers called her chérie or doudou, both terms of endearment. Leilah served them coffee, inquired about their children, and placed the best chairs at their disposal, near the fan.

One day, a trim, finely dressed man, escorted by a middle-aged woman in somber attire, entered the store. The young man seemed to dote on his companion. Leilah caught herself contemplating the thin mustache that accentuated the shape of the man's lips. He had nice long hands, with well-trimmed fingernails. A white, immaculate long sleeve shirt with a pair of sterling cufflinks helped confer the air of distinction that emanated from this tall, slender man. His tanned, dark caramel complexion and frizzy hair would describe him as a griffe, since we tend to catalog the many shades of skin tones encountered in Haiti. In any other country, he would simply be called a black man. Leilah, visibly troubled, found it difficult to cater to this customer who spoke French with a Parisian accent. For the first time in her life, a man made her heart race. She was twenty.

~ * ~

It was love at first sight for Charles. The young woman with the long black hair haunted his nights. He had any excuse to go back to Habdoul's store. My ancestors no longer sold fabric, as competition had become fierce in Bord-de-Mer. But they had the monopoly of the best garlic in town and clients found the most exotic spices at their shop.

An unexpected stroke of luck gave Charles the opportunity to confess his love: Leilah's parents, gone to their doctor, had entrusted her to take charge of the store that day. I would have loved to know when they exchanged their first kiss. But how could I formulate such question despite the special bond I shared with my grandmother? Leilah omitted thousands of potentially fascinating details of her story, which left my curious teenager's mind in a vacuum.

"Our respective families did not want this union. In those days, Haitians did not marry Arabs. So, ignoring the rules of social conventions of the time, we eloped in St. Gerard's church where a priest agreed to marry us in the presence of two witnesses, friends of your grandfather. The birth of our children linked our families together and brought

Deveaux and Habdoul to the rank of relatives although, initially, they shared nothing in common. Not even the language."

There was no wedding march for the couple, nor white gown and veil for Leilah. Did St. Gerard's bells ring for the occasion? I wonder. But love that lasts and conquers all obstacles had triumphed over social prejudices of the time. Leilah, suddenly silent, wiped away a tear. Eyes locked into hers, I realized that day that each grey hair bore witness to an exceptional life. Behind each wrinkle hid the memory of a beautiful love story. And every story deserved to be told.

My Habdoul great-grandparents passed away half a century later. Succumbing to a bad flu, Zahiye left first, closely followed by Kimbram, the companion chosen for her at the tender age of sixteen. They had journeyed through life side by side, across oceans and continents. They are resting in peace today, in Port-au-Prince's cemetery, together in death as they were in life.

~**21**~

I closed my suitcase, excited at the idea of discovering Paris through the eyes of nobility. My hosts own large plantations of coffee in Kenya and run their Paris office, explains Astrid. Too busy at managing their wealth, they give free rein to their children for their weekend outings: Christian, eighteen, "classe Terminale" (high school senior) and his younger sister whose philosophy of life boils down to two Latin words: *carpe diem.*

We spent the evening at the theater with Florent and Claude de Panière and their children, followed by a late supper at the Champs-Elysées. Haiti and its dictatorship always fascinate others, and I admit taking pleasure in being an object of curiosity. Friendly and attractive couple: the father has graying temples, a dimpled chin, and long and nervous hands; his wife, slim and elegant, her hair cut very short like her daughter's, would easily pass for her children's older sister. Flanked by Astrid and Christian whose physical beauty captivates me, I focus, with calculated concentration, on my asparagus soufflé, to hide my emotion. Astrid's darting grey eyes have captured the silent waves that spread from my heart to her brother's. I catch her complicit smile. It is obvious she madly enjoys the silent spectacle of our emerging emotions.

Sunday morning, Astrid flatly refuses to accompany me to church for Mass. "Leave me alone, Myriam!" she says, tucked under her covers in her cozy bed. "We are not at Saint Joseph, and I have no intention to become a nun in a convent. Ask Christian to go."

Up early for his daily morning run, Christian dresses promptly and agrees to walk me to the local church. My religious piety seems to move him. He takes my hand silently. Paralyzed by surprise, I leave my trembling palm in his. When I sit by his side on the church pew, our shoulders slightly brush against each other. I am too distracted by the presence of my knight in shining armor to hear, let alone capture the essence of the priest's sermon. On our way back home, Christian stops at a neighborhood bakery. The aroma of fresh bread gives me a gnawing pit in the stomach. He offers me a bite of his brioche, and I share my croissant with him. Such spontaneous complicity delights me.

We talk about our studies, and Haiti. Christian's future has already been mapped out for him: after his baccalauréat, he will attend university; a position has been reserved in the family business for him; he will travel to Kenya. I fancy him, a modern prince charming, shiny riding boots and helmet, crossing, on horseback, their huge coffee plantation.

"Myriam, what are your plans for the future?"

All wrapped up in my reverie, I leave, reluctantly, my beautiful rider in Kenya's coffee plantations to return to the reality of the present moment. I will embrace a medical career, according to my parents' wishes, I confide. As if hiding a shameful sin, I keep total silence on my secret writer's aspirations.

Sunday lunch, chez de Panière is a feast, served by a Portuguese maid in white apron: tournedos with Madeira sauce and chocolate marquise. I am glad to be spared the drudgery of doing dishes, my islander temperament, a bit languid, accommodating fast to the pleasure of being served. Christian makes a point of honor, during the meal, to catch my eye movements. Astrid seems to revel in our confusion.

"Father has agreed to lend me his car!" Christian announces after lunch, with an air of triumph. He waves, like a trophy, the key to his father's vehicle, a victory smile on his lips. Astrid's brother is taking us dancing tonight, at the Tabou, a popular club in Quartier Latin. Saint Joseph, in anticipation of a seminar on Education Reform, has scheduled, for Monday morning, the return of the boarders by the special vans that usually transport the students on Sunday night.

The feverish preparations begin: Astrid helps me choose the pair of earrings that will best suit the outfit I am planning to wear for the occasion. For a Caribbean girl, this piece of jewelry is as indispensable as our clothes and shoes. After what feels like an eternity, we finally emerge from my friend's bedroom, all prettied up. Christian stands on the landing by the door, eyes fixed on us with silent approval. Gallant, he opens the door to the front passenger seat for me and takes the wheel. In the back seat, Astrid mutters, "Ooh la la! My brother is totally mesmerized."

Embarrassed, I dare not answer.

~ * ~

In the smoky atmosphere of the Tabou, Christian de Panière, with casual elegance, cuts through the crowd of young dancers, trying to locate a free table. He takes my hand with gentle authority. With an anxious gaze, Astrid anticipates her boyfriend Jacques's arrival. I am wearing a black miniskirt for the occasion, stylish suede boots, and a flame color silk blouse, which highlights my dark hair, brushed loose on my shoulders. Round creole earrings dangle from my ears, reflecting, no doubt, the psychedelic lighting of a huge metal globe suspended from the ceiling.

I stare, fascinated, at the crowd and the strange décor that surround me. For the first time, I have stepped foot into the world of Parisian discos. Music escapes from countless loud speakers, making all conversation difficult. I sip, silently, the tonic water Christian has ordered for us, eyes riveted on this live masterpiece painted on an invisible canvas, moved beyond measure by his physical beauty. Astrid, with growing impatience and nervousness, consults her wristwatch every few minutes. With close-cropped hair, like her brother's, she is also wearing a black turtleneck sweater that enhances their extreme blondness. Christian fixes his gaze on me, and I can feel my cheeks burn. How embarrassing to be unable to conceal one's emotion.

Jacques' arrival at the Tabou breaks the quiet magic of this surreal moment. He leads Astrid, with the possessive gesture of the official boyfriend, on the dance floor. Left alone at the small bistro table, Christian approaches his seat and we shyly smile at each other. I am grateful to him not to invite me to the dance floor, fearing, by my ignorance of the latest Parisian rhythmic dance moves, to appear ridiculous. Suddenly consumed with nostalgia, my heart and thoughts turn to Haiti and reminiscences of Youth Night at the Rond-Point, where the youth also danced, Saturdays in the summer months, to the sound of the Shleu-Shleu musical group, under a metallic globe in a disco atmosphere.

A trip to the bathroom to check my makeup becomes a challenge in the dark lighting, as I have to cut through a dense and noisy crowd. On my way back, I bump, head-on, into a tall young man who spills his drink in the collision. We offer reciprocal apologies and formal introduction, which leads to an incredible revelation: we both come from Haiti! By an extraordinary coincidence, the Tabou starts to vibrate to the sound of a Caribbean merengue; the dance has become increasingly popular on the Parisian scene in recent weeks, Gerard reveals. My compatriot gallantly escorts me to the dance floor.

~22~

When nostalgia hit me the hardest, all I needed was to close my eyes, to feel transported in the heart of Haiti and find the birthplace of my childhood all over again. Alone in France, I realized we do not escape our past; we carry it with us in our hearts. Even when my host country greeted me with open arms, the foreigner that I was often created a sort of personal, nostalgic exile for herself...

The sounds, colors and smells of Port-au-Prince would become landmarks on my journey down memory lane: the fresko (shaved ice) merchants, surrounded by a rush of buzzing bees that led a dance around the grenadine syrup bottles, who carried a huge block of ice covered by salt crystals and a large, coarse, empty bag of sugar in their makeshift wooden cart on wheels; the street vendors, always claiming their patties were hot in their wicker basket; the shoeshine boys, who signaled their presence through the chime of a little bell; the cry of peddling pharmacists who sold antibiotic pills or painkillers to a public who had mastered the art of self-medicating.

Public transport vehicles called tap-taps, carrying crowded passengers and live chickens or pigs sometimes, crisscrossed the congested streets of the capital city, scattering pedestrians with their noisy horns. Their colorful chassis was the canvas of artists with unbridled imagination, picturing a thriving jungle inhabited by lions and tigers, or depicting religious and mystical images of Catholic saints and intricate Vaudou symbols called Vèvè. Sometimes, these vehicles' windshields harbored love messages, posted in large letters by the tap-tap owner: "Rita Darling," or the driver's proclamation of faith: "God is good."

"Men bèl twal, bèl dantèl!" Buy beautiful cloth and lace, the fabrics vendors offered. They sourced among the Bord-de-Mer's Arab store owners, and peddled their wares, shimmering colorful fabrics, for resale in the streets of Port-au-Prince.

"*Men bèl mango, bèl zaboka, bèl fig mi,*" *the fruit vendors echoed, anxious to sell their perishable mangoes, avocadoes and ripe bananas.*

Merchants of fresh produce from the villages of Kenscoff and Furcy woke before sunrise and carried wicker baskets full of vegetables on their heads. With the dim light of a tèt gridap, a small kerosene lamp coarsely made of tin and cotton wick, they prepared for the long journey on foot to the capital city, where they hoped to sell the products of their gardens. Their courage, in the daily struggle for survival, was unreal.

Vierge, with muscular legs and cambered torso, dressed in jeans cloth material and a red canvas belt tightly wrapped around her waist, a pair of sandals slung over her shoulders to protect them from the filth of the road, was my grandmother's official "vegetable lady." Vierge sold us fresh produce every summer at our Kenscoff mountain cottage, and, Tuesdays and Fridays on market days, supplied us with her vegetables in Bois Verna, offering us, throughout the year, the health and freshness of Kenscoff. Leilah always paid her two orders, hers and Yvette's, who relished the opportunity to share a cup of coffee and a hug with her mother in Bois Verna, before returning to Bourdon with her bag of fresh produce. Vierge carried her heavy load in a huge hand-woven wicker basket sitting on top of her head on a snake-like rolled up cloth called twokèt, for cushioning support.

~ * ~

Every year, on November 2, Yvette and Marguerite had a fight. Their different views on the Day of the Dead celebration would become a war of attrition, where there would be no winners or losers. My younger brothers paid little attention to the theatrical scene that would unfold in the kitchen, between the gas stove and refrigerator. Besides, everything would get back to normal the next day. Yvette would pretend to forget, and Marguerite would return to her old habits of devoted housekeeper, pampered by the family.

Faithful to her mother Charité's traditions, Marguerite, who never missed her Sunday masses, would leave at dawn on November 2, date dedicated to the memory of the deceased, and go to Port-au-Prince's main cemetery, with a huge coffeepot wrapped in a delicate white, starched and ironed fabric. Coffee would be generously poured on the ground at each kafou of the cemetery, strategic corners at the four cardinal points, to please the Loas—the Vaudou gods—and Baron Samedi, the Vaudou god guardian of the cemetery.

A devout Catholic, Yvette attributed this practice to the cult of Vaudou Loas, inconsistent with her Christian beliefs. But Marguerite blithely combined both religious cultures without an ounce of hesitation or scruple. That day, she would stand her ground and defy Madame Jim, whose birth she had witnessed in Bois Verna and who would always remain her "little Vivi." Marguerite used public transport to the cemetery that day, as Yvette would drive off, furious, to join her parents for their annual visit to the family mausoleum, a large bouquet of yellow marigold in the back of the vehicle.

Defeated by the elderly woman's stubbornness, my aunt usually surrendered, by day's end, to the one who used to cradle her as a baby. Life would resume its normal course the next day as Yvette and Marguerite would pretend nothing ever happened.

My father chose to pay his respects privately, on Claire's grave. The hustle and bustle of mourners in the cemetery on November 2 bothered him. I had turned ten when the family decided I was old enough to visit my mother's grave. Nothing is more powerful than to see two dates follow a name on a marble headstone: the beginning and the end of a life. "A time to be born, and a time to die," Ecclesiastes reminds. The painful sense of finality takes you by the throat...the engraved evidence, on the stone, that your loved one will never return... But there is also a comforting feeling to know that my mother is not just the smiling face, frozen in a frame, on Grandfather's piano. Claire existed, was made of flesh and bone, and knew laughter and tears.

She is resting today, in eternal sleep, under the marble. I will see her again someday, affirms my Christian faith.

We always said a prayer for my Deveaux ancestors, my great-grandfather General Bertrand, his wife Océanie, and my great-aunts Fifine, Nini and Angèle. Under the truncated marble column, I hope they are all getting along together, watching over my beloved mother, Claire, and her older sibling, Robert, whose life was cut short, before age one.

My great-grandparents Habdoul also have their vault in Port-au-Prince's cemetery: a modest, painted cement structure surrounded by a wrought-iron fence, located near the main alley and more accessible to the family than the large marble mausoleum of the Deveaux. I always helped my grandmother lay flowers on the graves. A concern troubled my mind, as a child: what would become of the deceased, when the crowded cemetery could no longer accommodate new occupants?

~ * ~

In the heart of Bel Air, Port-au-Prince's oldest neighborhood, at the top of a sloping street, where one can see, from a distance, the bay of Port-au- Prince, stands the statue of Madan Colo. I know little about the origin of this statue which haunted my childhood: some say it was built centuries ago to symbolize one of the first women in colonial era, known for her protective love of children. If historical facts were lacking, Madan Colo held, according to family legend, a special place in my little girl's heart.

Leilah, fond of car rides, would become an adorable ingénue on Saturday afternoons and Charles, my grandfather, could never resist his wife's charms, when she approached him, with a smile, upon his arrival from the office. "Darling!" she'd say. "A little drive?"

I would climb in the back seat, giggling with pleasure at the idea of riding with my grandparents in the heart of my birth city. The Ford strolled around Champ de Mars, where the statues of our forefathers, heroes of Haiti's independence, towered under the clear, blue sky. Cautious, Grandfather always slowed down in front of the national palace and government buildings, before taking Rue Pavée, which would lead us to Port-au-Prince's commercial zone, closed for business on Saturday afternoons. We would park the car on the sidewalk in deserted Grand-Rue and pay a short visit to my Habdoul great-grandparents.

The Bord-de-Mer area was delightfully calm, after store hours on Saturday afternoon. We passed through a narrow alley behind my great-grandparents' store, that led to an inner courtyard, and climbed the cement steps up to their apartment, on the second floor. Leilah often brought them a present, cookies and cigarettes for Kimbram, and cologne water for Zahiye.

I usually sat on Charles's lap, one of those rare snapshots engraved in memory, of a close physical contact with my grandfather, to listen to Leilah speak Arabic with her parents. After coffee, we would head to the Bicentennial boardwalk and reach the wharf of Port-au-Prince, where majestic cruise ships docked. Painters and sculptors had displayed their works of art on the pavement, a colorful feast of the eyes for tourists. I pictured Haiti as a vast tapestry upon which art burst everywhere.

Sometimes we made a detour to Bel Air, before reaching the business section of town. As a four-year-old girl, I was stunned, and had clapped with excitement the first time Madan Colo's statue had come into view. It was love at first sight. This pilgrimage to Madan Colo subsequently became a ritual, weekends when I stayed at my grandparents' house.

~ * ~

Every year, my grandfather's cousin invited the family to watch the Carnival festivities unfold from his dental clinic overlooking Champ de Mars, the perfect vantage point to view the three-day Mardi-Gras parade. Yvette took pleasure in dressing up her brood: I was, *alternately, an Indian princess with my long dark braids, a Chinese girl in silk kimono, a Spanish dancer with red flowers in her hair. My younger brothers would be transformed, by the magic of the costume, into cowboys, pirates, and heroes of mythological legends, Hercules and Spartacus.*

The parade began with the Native Indians dance, in their folkloric attire, followed by oxen flapping their whip in the air, the big heads in papier-mâché, the wooden-legged giants and the legendary Choucoune, who proudly paraded her generous derriere. Padded silk floats housed the King of Carnival and his Queens, who blew kisses at the audience. Loud music blasted from rival orchestral groups, competing for the best musical creation.

On Ash Wednesday, we received, on our forehead, the gray mark of the cross, to remind us that we are dust.

~**23**~

Driven by a magnetic force, I dive with delight into Caribbean music, following Gerard's lead, in a rhythmic tempo unique to islanders. Fully immersed in the pleasure of music and dance, I did not realize a circle had formed around us. All eyes are on Gérard and me. A second merengue succeeds the first, offering my dancing partner and me the opportunity to move on the dance floor under the bright spotlights of a crowded disco.

"What would my parents say if they caught me showing off dance moves with a stranger in public?" I ponder, for a fraction of a second. But I am in Paris, free as a bird and life is full of promise. Astrid and Jacques, won over by the rhythm and the excitement of the moment, have joined us on the dance floor. Other dancers, caught in everyone's contagious hilarity and good humor, follow suit.

When a slow dance follows the fast-paced merengue, I come back to reality, to take leave of Gerard and return to my table. But my compatriot holds me prisoner in his arms, sending a clear signal he intends to keep me on the dance floor. He has fulfilled "the call of the blood," as our common Haitian heritage revels in the shared enjoyment of merengue. But, this moment of euphoria gone, I realize I have no intention to devote my entire evening to Gérard at the Tabou.

Christian, whose gaze had been glued to the dance floor during our impromptu show, must have guessed my distress. Rising swiftly from our table where, glass in hand, he followed our dance number, he invites my compatriot to step aside and give him way. Christian's tall, trim stature and calm assurance are imposing.

Gérard, flabbergasted, hesitates a second then quickly disappears in the crowd, convinced Christian is my boyfriend. Stunned, I stare at my Prince Charming, who, with infinite tenderness, wraps me in his arms as we get lost in the magic of the slow dance. Our eyes lock, our gazes melt. My knees shake furiously as I feel my heart vibrate to the wobbling of his heart under his black turtleneck sweater. My head on his shoulder, Christian gently runs his fingers through my hair and whispers in my ear, "I am crazy about you."

Electric shocks travel through my body. What is happening to me? I have never felt that way before. I close my eyes, deeply stirred by his presence, losing all reason. Christian did not leave the dance floor tonight. At the heart of the loudest disco music, we remain glued to one another, transcending space and time, alone in our own enchanted sphere, blocking the world and its noise all around us, as we listen to love's symphony played only for two.

And what I feared and wished all at once takes place: with a deeply moving gesture, he cups my face between his hands and slowly, inexorably, approaches his lips against mine. The earth stops. Eyes closed, heart in turmoil, I kiss him back passionately. His profound caress reveals new horizons, where no one before him has ever led me to. We are the sole living creatures on a deserted island. Christian tightens his embrace, his body welded to mine, for eternity.

I feel so lost. Ruth's immortal words, the Moabite of the Old Testament, capriciously fill my mind: "*Wherever you go, I will go! Your people will be my people.*"

In a last-ditch effort, I manage to open my eyes. This brutal return to reality hits me head-on. Frightened by the emotional storm taking over my senses, I implore, to save myself, "We should leave."

On the way back, we're in total silence. Astrid smiles conspiratorially. Sitting on the back seat, she and Jacques exchange caresses without restraint. I dare not look back, feeling quite uncomfortable by the scene. Christian at the wheel drives without saying a word, but his fingers imprison my trembling hand. The vehicle finally stops at the entrance to the plush building where my hosts reside. Jacques and Astrid, entwined under the portico, share a goodbye kiss that lasts forever.

With a firm gesture of the hand, Christian holds me back by his side on the front seat. My heart is pounding. I seek refuge against the door of the vehicle, overwhelmed by the growing agitation that has taken over me. My companion approaches and is now leaning over me. His lips skillfully seek mine. They open slightly under his, offering a delightful path to a luminous sky and myriads of stars. His tender mouth ventures toward my ear, neck, and I hear, from the depths of the earth, from the confines of my soul, moaning sounds, rising in crescendo. When his nervous fingers feverishly undo the buttonholes of my silk blouse, I return abruptly to reality, offended by my own behavior. "Please, stop. I beg of you!"

Although my plea is a whisper, Christian abruptly stops and moves away, trembling and breathless. Not a word is spoken, as we get out of the vehicle. Astrid is no longer under the portico. Ashamed of my weakness, tormented by remorse, I feverishly button my blouse. I will never dare to look Christian in the eyes again.

~ * ~

Bundled up under the thick blanket in the next bed, Astrid whispers, in her smoothest voice, her full support for her brother's idyll: "I shall make every effort to help Christian see you again. My mother will send you an invitation letter for next weekend."

I keep a cautious silence. Everything is happening so fast! The wise world of my adolescence has been turned upside-down, tonight. In the morning, the de Panière family gathers around the breakfast table for a hasty meal. The smell of black coffee brings me back me to a calmer, clearer vision of things. Christian quietly butters his toast, Astrid sips her hot chocolate, and their parents are planning their day at the office. They will drop us at the Val-de-Seine bus station on their way to work. Christian will take the metro.

My classmate and I, in navy woolen berets and knee-high socks, must be the exact replicas of the young female characters in the Countess of Ségur's classic novel *Les Petites Filles Modèles*. I have the unpleasant feeling of having desecrated Saint Joseph's uniform last night.

Christian offers his sister a quick peck on the forehead and comes towards me, smiling, for a brotherly kiss on the cheek. How does he manage to exhibit such ease and nonchalant behavior? His parents seem clueless and suspect nothing. When everyone heads for the exit door, Christian grabs my suitcase. He is the last one to cross the landing, where he dares hold my hand with desperate strength. Taken aback, my eyes cling to his, imploring him to keep quiet. Christian, in a slow, calculated gesture, locks the door behind him.

"I love you," says boldly my Prince Charming. Embarrassed, I do not answer, avoiding his gaze. Christian follows in my footsteps, as I feel his warm breath behind me and can hear the pounding jolts of my heart.

~24~

My baptism and legal names are Marie Claire Myriam Tyler. Myriam also means Marie, in the Hebraic language. By these names, the Virgin Mary, Mother amongst all mothers, and the one who gave me life, are honored. It never occurred to anyone the idea of gracing me with a nickname, unlike my younger brothers. I was Myriam, no more, no less. The first possession of every human being, in life, is his name. Without a name, the very existence of that individual is being questioned.

The misuse and abuse of the "ti" word (means "little" in Creole) always made me laugh in Haiti. James Junior almost became "Ti Jim," had it not been for Yvette's fortunate intervention. His mother saved him from a cacophonic disaster that would have plagued him his entire life, if Marguerite had had the last word. I chuckled as I imagined "Ti Jim" having a "ti kafe" (a small coffee) and planning a "ti sòti" (a stroll) when my younger brother became of age to try his own wings.

~ * ~

Every month I was entitled to a weekend at my grandparents' house, as a reward for my good grades. With great fanfare, monthly report cards were presented to Sainte Thérèse's student body by Mother Agathe, the French-born director of studies, who inspired a mixture of fear and admiration to all. Her severity encouraged self-transcendence and hundreds of students understood, without the shadow of a doubt, that the only path to excellence was the one of righteousness and Christianity. Gaze focused on Mother Agathe, immobile like a statue, hands sweaty and nervous, heart racing and forming a lump in my throat, the tense atmosphere of the study hall felt unbearable. The name of the top student of each grade would be announced last, amplifying everyone's overall suspense and nervousness. I always forced myself to strive for academic excellence by late night studies in my bedroom and my successes at school had become cause for celebration at home. My father never failed to offer praise about my report card, hoping to inspire my brothers to follow suit. He would drive me to Bois Verna afterwards, where Leilah, unable to contain her excitement, would greet me at the gate. A copy of Tout l'Univers, *bought by Grandfather at the Rue Pavée bookstore, was waiting for me on my night stand. He was a man of few words, so this gesture was enough to convey my grandfather's pride. An avid reader, I devoured my favorite magazine, cover to cover, overnight.*

Awake at dawn on Saturday, I opened wide the wooden shutters and invite daylight into the room. In the distance, the busy street of Petit Four, at the intersection of a five crossroads point marked by a round cement structure, was always packed with cars. I could hear the familiar noises of a town that comes to life again, after the night's uncertainties. Impatient taxi drivers competed for the loudest horn, as they terrorized pedestrians along their way. Vendors on foot, wicker baskets on their heads, offered their hot patties with a strident cry: "Pâtés chauds!" I loved to feel Life that swarmed in the streets of Port-au-Prince, from my window view. One day I picked up bits and pieces of a lively conversation between Dieudonne and André, about the mystical crossroad.

"Things are not that simple, friend!" noted André, dogmatic.

He knew that strange objects would mysteriously appear at the crossroad during the night: a brown wax candle, a laced shoe, a boutèy monte—a bottle filled with tree barks and roots. The Loas, or Vaudou gods, attributed mystical powers to the crossroad and manifested themselves. This story, heard in broad daylight near Dieudonne's bungalow, did not scare me. But at nightfall the landscape would change and inspire nightmares.

Nature greeted the dawn of a brand-new day around me. The surrounding hills, watching over Port-au-Prince stretched at their feet, traded their night blue evening mantle for a soft, green, veil attire. Some mountain flanks exposed, without modesty, their sad, raw nakedness, the deep scars left by excessive plowing of the land. Finding quiet pleasure in the familiar sights around me, I smiled at the neighbor's palm tree, stiff and majestic like its owner, Mr. Lambert. Next to the royal palm, a huge trunked calabash tree bent its spine, the large, round calabash shells dangling like heavy earrings from the leafy branches,

~ * ~

The cycle of life continued also, in my grandparents' backyard, with the rooster's crow. Sometimes I joined Charité under the mango tree. She was an elderly washwoman with white, frizzy hair like small cotton balls under her silk scarf. Sitting by her side on a smooth, flat stone, leaning against the trunk of the mango tree, I would watch, fascinated, this pèsonaj, as the elderly are often called, dip her bread, with her deformed arthritis laden fingers, in her enamel cup filled with piping hot coffee. Charité tilted her head to gulp the last sip of the beverage that would give her the strength to tackle the day. Then, methodically, she packed her clay pipe with tobacco, watching me with piercing eyes.

"Pitit mwen," she started invariably, as she prepared to share one of her wonderful stories.

I listened, mesmerized, to the old woman with the toothless grin unveil another chapter of Jacmel's (Southern coastal town) cave, and Mèt Dlo, its revered spirit: a beautiful mermaid with long, wavy hair, fiercely guarding the entrance to the aquatic cave. Those who found grace in the eyes of the mermaid mysteriously disappeared and, according to legend, went on to live forever in the water depths with Mèt Dlo. Charité's tired eyes, creased forehead and callused hands reflected the struggles of a laborious life. At sixteen, she started her own laundry business. Financial independence was a bold concept for women her age in those days. Charité would walk every morning to Rivière Froide, a long riverbed located in the heart of Carrefour, on the outskirts of Port-au-Prince. She carried a huge bundle of clothes on her head, her clients' laundry, her pratik as she liked to refer to them. The following week, clothing items and linen, impeccably folded, bleached with indigo and starched to perfection, were delivered to their owners in exchange for money.

My great-grandmother Océanie Deveaux, her most important client, held Charité's eldest daughter at the baptismal font and became her godmother. Marguerite later joined the Deveaux household, where she would comfortably spend the rest of her days surrounded and pampered by those she helped nurture since birth. Charité had other children. The men in her life would abandon her, at the news of her pregnancies. At the price of enormous sacrifices, her two sons were able to attend primary school. She hoped they would be her support in her old age.

The eldest of the sons, Joseph, learned to drive, became a tap-tap driver and built for his mother a modest house in concrete blocks and galvanized roof in Carrefour, Port-au-Prince's crowded suburb. She spoke with pride of kay mwen—her house. The father of Jean, the younger son, owned a boutik—a small retail shop where he sold basic staples: rice, soft drinks, cement, school supplies, candy and even aspirin tablets kept in a large glass jar. Ti Jean pursued his secondary education, with the financial support of this man who, after years of indifference, agreed to play a role in his son's life. Jean became a primary school teacher in Port-au-Prince, was called Master, and cut off all ties with his mother, whose status of washwoman in service to others embarrassed him totally.

Dieudonne, furious by such conduct, shocked by the ingratitude of a son whose mother had made so many sacrifices, shared her friend's drama with every indulgent ear who would listen. Her daughter Ti Sò and I were a curious and hungry audience longing for details.

Jean got married to anchor his reputation as a respectable man. His dreams would be commensurate with his ambitions: someday his sons would be doctors or lawyers. They might get a scholarship for France or Canada. If luck was on their side, they would find a wife abroad, and buy a fancy car. And every year, Master Jean would host his pale skinned daughters-in-law's visit. Charity would learn from her eldest son, Ti Jo, that she was the ancestor of little biracial children who lived across the oceans.

Charité kept her way of life, despite a modest annuity provided faithfully by Joseph, her true support in old age. The devoted son's wish was that his mother could finally rest, after so many years of hard work and quiet heroism raising her children. In the long run, Ti Jo understood total inactivity would slowly kill the spirit of the courageous woman he was proud to call mother. The precious gift he offered her was total freedom of mind and heart, the serenity of knowing that she worked because she wanted to, and not because she had to. When, riddled with arthritis, she wisely decided to retire, Charité continued to find room and board in Bois Verna, when it pleased her to leave her routine and her home for a friendly visit and share Dieudonne's bedroom. Marguerite, informed that her mother was in town, would catch public transport, a tap-tap from Bourdon to go visit her in Bois Verna.

Charité died of old age, in her sleep, in her own bed, and her own house—a special grace, granted to a fortunate few. When Charité passed away, I lost a wonderful storyteller, a little-known historian, a link between two parallel worlds, two cultures that often coexist in Haiti without truly knowing one another, unfortunately.

~25~

Thursday morning's chemistry lab session has finally ended. I was finding no pleasure in the manipulation of sulfuric acid. Sister Marie Laurence, an irate look in her eyes, inspects the students' work benches. As she approaches toward my vials and flasks, she whispers I will be excused from swimming lessons tonight and must meet her, instead, at her office.

Convinced she has bad news to report about my family, I panic in silence. Yvette has fallen ill, perhaps? She is confronting a difficult pregnancy, my father shared. After the swimmers left with Sister Jean, I knock, anxious, at our teacher's door. I detect metallic sparks behind the silver-rimmed glasses. Her furious gaze is the color of the raging seas, when menacing storms loom over the waves.

"You might have guessed why I asked you in my office? Exiled from your family at such a young age, I made it my duty, as your elder and teacher, to support and guide you in France. I thought I knew you well, Myriam: a tad emotional perhaps, but with great depth and originality. I never pegged you for a hypocrite."

I open my mouth in disbelief, but no sound comes out. My teacher picks up an envelope from her desk. With trembling hands, she pulls out a letter and starts reading, in a broken voice. "My dear Myriam, since our evening at the Tabou, I cannot get you off my mind. I see our entwined bodies on the dance floor, I dream of your perfume, the softness of your skin, your heart trembling against mine. We vibrated in unison, and made love Sunday. I must see you again next week. Remember: Astrid is our ally. I love you! Christian."

I remain still, speechless, frozen in time, overwhelmed by emotion, convinced I will wake up from a horrible nightmare. Furious, I feel sudden hatred for Astrid's brother whose compromising words are causing me such humiliation. Sister Marie Laurence pulls out a copy of Saint Joseph's Code of Ethics, signed by Yvette, and which clearly states, "Censorship is allowed in the best interest of students subject to our custody."

My teacher explains, "A letter from Astrid's mother, addressed to you, arrived yesterday. I assumed she had written you a kind note after your weekend at their home. But today a second letter came from Paris with the same return address. Such epistolary enthusiasm seemed excessive. My duty commanded me vigilance. I used my right of censorship for the sole purpose of protecting you. Yesterday's letter must have, undoubtedly, been from this foolish young man as well. But your ploy has been discovered."

I'm denied the chance to defend myself tonight and will remain cloistered at Saint Joseph this weekend; my teacher will be expecting a confession while I am hoping for the opportunity to clear the air with my correct version of the distorted facts. In the heat of teenage emotion, stunned by the sensuality exuding from crowded bodies on the dance floor, Christian wrote this compromising letter whose twisted words have condemned me. My naiveté caused this. My parents will be devastated if I get expelled from school. This thought makes me sick. Tonight, I feel like a slain lamb, at the altar of misunderstanding.

On Saturday's noon release, laughter always explodes from everywhere, in a joyous contagion, as students prepare to return home to their families. As the packed shuttle buses disappear toward Paris, I whisper to Astrid, whose eyes are open wide in disbelief, "I will explain everything when you get back on Sunday. I cannot accept your parents' invitation. Sister Marie Laurence intercepted a compromising love letter written by your brother Christian."

Feeling the heavy weight of loneliness upon my shoulders, I return to the empty dormitory, and swap my blue uniform skirt for jeans and a thick, woolen sweater. But it is my heart that feels cold today.

I follow our teacher to the park, grateful for her suggestion of the great outdoors, rather than the restricted space of her office, to meet with me. Crude daylight will clear all mysteries and reveal its dark corners. In my pocket: Madame de Panière's invitation letter that will absolve me. It will prove I might have been a bit naïve but was never a hypocrite. On Chateaubriand's bench, in late winter on Saturday, alone with a strict disciplinarian, the spoken truth will lighten my load and free me of a heavy burden.

The order is simple: "Tell me *all* about your weekend at de Panières."

Tall and trim in his black velvet jacket, Christian sprang straight from the pages of a childhood fairy book. An enchanting evening unfolded in the City of Light: the theater and a plush restaurant. Miniature crystal pins were sparkling in my hair, like stars in the night. Christian's dreamy grey eyes kept trying to catch mine, as I timidly lowered my gaze. He became a prince of light as I felt a strange affiliation with King Solomon's Shulamite. A few inflamed stanzas of the biblical "Song of Songs," read in secret like a forbidden fruit, emerged from the depths of memory: *"I am black, but beautiful, daughters of Jerusalem."*

At the mention of this religious text, a laugh bubbles up. The ice, finally, has broken. Chateaubriand's park wraps us in its quiet majesty. The air is cold, but the sun shines. The cracked, antique bench must have witnessed other confessions and confidences, through the years: distant echoes of burning human dramas, or passionate oaths of love.

With courage, I describe the dance floor at the Tabou and my growing emotions in Christian's arms. I evoke my trembling knees and confess the strange sensations felt throughout body and soul. I reveal the mesmerizing magic of his caressing gaze and our first kiss, on the crowded dance floor. In the complicity of the padded car, my reserve eroded, and an inexorable attraction pushed me towards the unknown shores of sensuality. But, in a burst of foresight, I asked my prince charming to stop.

"I regret the incident of the letter. I am ashamed of what happened. But, I swear, *no* guilty act took place between Christian and me. You must believe me."

Tears pour down freely. Confession liberates me. At this very moment, facing the judge who has authority over my future as a boarder, it matters less to be expelled from Saint Joseph as to be trusted on my word and good conscience. I want to hear three simple, yet powerful words. I am offered this precious gift: "I believe you."

Relieved, I pull out of my pocket Madame de Panière's letter, proof of my innocence in the illicit correspondence. Handing me back the crumpled paper, Sister Marie Laurence admits, "No one should ever feel above a humbling act of apology. I deeply regret my incorrect assumption about the first letter."

The teacher, who keeps an aspirin bottle on her desk as an indication of her humanity, stops being the condemning judge. She apologizes to her student, who forgives her for her accusation of hypocrisy. This word pierced, like a burning arrow, the deepest corners of my soul and hurt me so much. In the heart of Saint Joseph's park and the pure light of a late winter day, I experience, with new intensity, the power of words. One word can destroy. It can also bring joy and liberation. This life lesson, I will never forget it. I look furtively at Sister Marie Laurence whose eyes evoke a clear summer sky. Our class of twenty incorrigibly romantic adolescents cannot fathom why she renounced forever the love of a man, by taking the veil.

"Heartbreak, no doubt," Astrid concluded, dogmatic.

The epitome of happiness to us is the glorious encounter with Prince Charming, in an apotheosis of sounds and colors. At fifteen, the curve of a forehead or oval of a face can sway our emotions.

The world is this vast, colorful fairground, where silhouettes, dark and pale, seek one another in an eternal waltz. Her students have fabricated, thanks to their wild imagination, the love story of the century, starring Sister Marie Laurence, who has become the heroine of a Greek tragedy or starlet of a fotonovela. The option of voluntary celibacy does not even cross our minds.

The tall, proud trees are watching us, impassive. Our presence in the park seems insignificant, and our problems a tiny particle in this vast universe. With frank and surprising ease, my teacher begins this course that our class missed through Astrid's fault: "Sexuality and The Youth." I will be that attentive audience who has the privilege to hear the master. It all starts with a simple question, which shines a light on any shadowy corner, any misconception fed, in secret, by ignorance:

"What do you know of the facts of life?"

~26~

The little book offered by Yvette, the day of my first period at age eleven, described human reproduction through illustrations of a strange creature, the appearance of a tadpole, embarked on a journey to penetrate the female ovule: the male spermatozoid. This exciting story was missing one minor detail: books devoured secretly did not help either. The "gesture of love" these illustrated pages were discreetly referring to, remained shrouded in mystery. Cathy, my best friend and confidante, shared her theory of the "spermatozoid-meets-ovule" riddle: a man gifts his seed to his wife with a kiss on the mouth.

What an epiphany! Suddenly, it all became crystal clear. I figured out why our Catechism teacher urged us not to kiss boys. This revelation granted us an aura of wisdom. At recess, Cathy and I would gravitate toward the "sophisticated girls," a tight-knit circle who found our chuckles, giggles and sly looks during animated boy-meets-girl story tales amusing. Were our comrades swimming in a sea of errors and misconceptions too?

As Cathy was approaching thirteen, she had blossomed into a beautiful teenager, graceful, pensive with a touch of elusive mystery. She manifested deep, pious behavior that started to intimidate me. My elder by one year, we had never felt our age difference before. Cathy's metamorphosis caught me off-guard, and I did not pay attention to mine, which had started to emerge.

At the threshold of adolescence, our childhood friendship entered another, more complex phase. We discovered the joy of hearts-to-hearts, under the shady mahogany branches, sharing a school bench at recess. Issues that triggered our curiosity a few months before were no longer a topic of our conversations. Reserve and modesty had become the new normal in our friendship. Cathy joined the group "Daughters of Marie," and I followed suit. Unbeknownst to me, I was creating a fictitious image of my childhood friend. I paired her with sainthood and holiness the day she confessed her religious aspirations to take the veil some day and become a nun. Sheer panic engulfed me at her earth-shattering revelation. How would I bare my soul to her chaste ears?

~ * ~

Nature, through an innocuous event, the year of my twelfth birthday, had revealed the truth about the spermatozoid and ovule saga. André, Leilah's gardener, had gifted me with an adorable, mixed-breed puppy. It was love at first sight for the new dog owner. Months later, we caught her with the neighbor's dog. André who, standing next to me by the mango tree, was watching Cookie and Baron's antics in the yard, concluded with a funny shrug of the shoulders, after the dogs' live performance: "Mademoiselle Myriam, you will have puppies in a few months."

How ironic and silly! My dog had just showcased, in broad daylight, one of life's most profound mysteries, under the awkward gaze of a naïve twelve-year-old and her grandparents' sexagenarian employee. I burst into tears, feeling like an idiot, caught off guard by the raw, uncensored display of animal kingdom's primal instincts, orchestrated for survival of the species. That day, I mourned the loss of my childhood innocence gone forever; thoughts of the "conjugal act" became a secret obsession, inspiring a mixture of fascination and disgust all at once. It was hard to fathom Yvette, so poised and reserved, engaging in such intimate acts with James, my father, behind closed doors, at nightfall.

~ * ~

Sergo, a heartthrob with a ripe, peach complexion and amber-colored eyes, enjoyed a discreet flirtation with me while pursuing other conquests. "Be careful!" Cathy warned, wise beyond her fifteen years. I must admit Sergo attracted and intimidated me all at once. His mother and Yvette had been classmates, in their youth. Our path would cross *at private dance parties and on Fridays' Youth Night at the trendy Rond-Point. I found great pleasure following his clever moves on the dance floor, our steps perfectly synchronized in the catchy merengue rhythms as well as romantic slow dances that kept us engulfed in each other's arms. Transported by the magic of the dance, Sergo would play with the fire of my emerging sensuality.*

One evening, at a party, he tried to kiss me. Flustered by his caressing eyes, his heart trembling against mine, I dodged his lips that were heading dangerously close toward mine. Taken aback, Sergo left me standing on the dance floor, and chose to ignore me the rest of the evening. An older sibling to three younger brothers and a student at an all-girl congregational school, boys my age were a mysterious breed, an elusive species that occasionally crossed my path on private dance floors. I had no clue to help me decipher the wiring of their brains, or their behavior.

My greatest fear, in those days, was to sit, unescorted, on the sidelines, and watch, from a lonely chair, happy pairs on a crowded dance floor. Disco nights at the Rond-Point, in the summer months, was the meeting ground for the youth, the place where young hearts embarked on new discoveries, as music blended with moving shadows.

Patrick jumped at the opportunity to fill the vacancy left by my favorite dance partner and became my knight in shining armor that evening. Tall and muscular, Cathy's cousin was, at first glance, more attractive than Sergo. But Patrick's shyness ruined everything. He stumbled over my feet as we danced. Torn between pity and anger, my toes in agony, I pretended not to notice his clumsiness. But how could I sustain Cathy's disapproval look and confess to her my stubborn attraction for the exuberant Sergo?

The summer Patrick turned sixteen, his parents threw a lavish birthday party in his honor. The young man was beaming as he greeted me at the door and I felt myself blush under his admiring gaze.

"Myriam, will you be my date tonight? You look so pretty."

Older schoolmates had praised the delight of kisses on the mouth with boys. Some described the experience as an explosion of shooting stars. Others felt dizzy and weak at the knees.

At the threshold of my fifteenth birthday, the smell of jasmine and my voracious curiosity triumphed over scruples and any hesitation. I was wearing a spaghetti-stripes red dress at Patrick's birthday party. My hair was dangling loose, covering my bare shoulders. We had stepped out on the terrace, away from the noisy party atmosphere. The evening breeze felt cool on my skin. A captivating scent of jasmine, rising from the garden below, filled the air. My companion risked a timid arm around my shoulders. Surprise paralyzed me on the spot.

Patrick locked his trembling lips against mine. The contact of his nervous fingers tangled in my hair, his sweaty palms on my bare shoulders broke the fragile spell of the sweet-smelling night. A new force in me longed to discover the magic of "first kiss," but confusion had prevailed. Patrick finally let go of his embrace, basking in the glow of the hour. So, I had just experienced my first kiss! I struggled to convince myself of its reality, surprise and disappointment claiming the best of my emotions.

A few weeks later, I left for France.

~27~

Sister Marie Laurence does not take offense, or appear amused by my revelations. She agrees to answer all the questions I had kept buried in my heart up to that point:

Q: "A kiss is just a kiss?"

A: "It should be an act shared by couples involved in an exclusive relationship on their journey of mutual discovery. But to let curiosity take over, and practice kissing before the right moment, is to miss out on its deeper meaning."

Patrick's kiss was the disappointing culmination of my curious adolescent nature. Romeo stole a kiss from me. I felt robbed. Christian's gesture had finally ignited shooting stars in my brain.

Q: "Adolescence: the age of torment and confusion?"

A: "I would define it as the age of tough choices and conflicting thoughts. The slightest misstep can carry serious consequences. Teenagers' physical transformations enable them to procreate, although they have not reached adulthood maturity. Keeping the youth in total ignorance of their bodies' metamorphosis and its impact on their emotions can be dangerous. The ideal parents should practice a policy of openness with their children. Beyond their role as providers and authority figures, parents should reach out as guides, as friends. The 'facts of life' should be a topic discussed, first and foremost, in the home."

Q: "Physical attraction: a force to be reckoned with?"

A: "Hormonal discharges related to adolescence exacerbate desire: the close proximity of two bodies on a dance floor, a furtive glance, a silhouette moving through one's visual field, a lingering fragrance in the air, can trigger all the senses into spiraling motion. It is especially the case with teenage boys, who, at this stage of their lives, are often guided by the visual. Well-informed girls will practice self-control and avoid the potentially disastrous consequences of a moment of intense emotion."

With Christian, I glanced, dazzled, at new lands of voluptuous fragrances, and skies full of sparkling diamonds.

Q: "Self-control: a gift or an apprenticeship?"

 A: "It is an act of intelligence and wisdom. The freedom of choice is given to all. Humans possess a force greater than their physical urges and emotions: their reason."

Q: "Friendship with the opposite sex: fact or fiction?"

A: "Comradeship is desirable. Friends will rise above the issues of lust and desire. The young man who made one's heart jump in the shadows of a dance floor will lose his aura and mystery in the bright midday sun."

Q: "Marriage: the only path to happiness for couples in love?"

 A: "The union between husband and wife is approved by God, and marriage lifted to the rank of sacrament. These couples, who made their commitment public and exchanged vows before God and man, have in turn, a better chance at lasting happiness."

I want to live a burning union of love and passion. For my husband, I will write poems that will make us blush. We will share gestures that engulf our shadows and become complicit of our nights full of stars.

Q: "Celibacy: a fate of destiny or a deliberate choice?"

A: "It is preferable that it be a choice. For those who have chosen this path, the key is not to deny their own humanity but channel it differently than couples, who seek fulfillment from their physical and emotional association with their partner."

In Haiti, as she bends over her infant girl's pink cradle, the new mother already dreams of the charming prince who will marry her daughter someday. Becoming an old spinster is most unmarried ladies' nightmare and unattached young men are eyed as potential catches, a quest that will only stop at the altar of a beautiful church. Nuns and priests are comparable, I imagine, to pure spirits who fly in ethereal spheres.

Q: "Physical beauty: indispensable in the pursuit of happiness?"

A: "In the Creator's garden, are planted endless fields of flowers of limitless shapes and shades. We are God's beautiful garden masterpieces. The young too often see the superficial, the physical envelope, the flesh. But our souls harbor our true fragrance, the one that lasts and will not be wilted."

~ * ~

Sister Marie Laurence has shared, today, the wealth of wisdom accumulated over the years, through her life of service. Behind the silver rims of her glasses, I notice the thin wrinkles, around the corner of her eyes, the undeniable proof of age but also how fragile life is.

Winter suns set early. Night's shadow will soon engulf Chateaubriand's bench. We abandon the tall, naked trees of the park for the familiar towers of Saint Joseph, where steaming hot soup and a warm, cozy bed await. Keeping pace with her brisk, rapid steps, I listen attentively as my teacher offers, through prophetic words directed at me, her legacy: the treasures of her heart. Her indulgent smile seems to absolve me of my missteps.

"God's designs have allowed our path to cross, in your parents' absence. Remember, we are pilgrims on earth, en route to our eternal home. During our brief, earthly passage, we should aspire to perfection, albeit our imperfect humanity will not achieve it."

She pauses, her gaze intense. "Never forget that life is a gift. Do not stain it in your pursuit of happiness. Your desires will flourish one day alongside the one who will meet your deepest expectations. The purity of your heart will honor the Lord and sacredness of your marriage vows. Finally, remain in tune with your life's calling. Be true to yourself and the aspirations of your soul. You cannot achieve total harmony with another unless you have first achieved it with yourself."

A strange premonition fills my heart—of a pending farewell, of an abrupt end to things. An angel has visited my young life, to resume her solitary journey of total service on a straight and narrow path. Life's powerful moments do not last. They reach their zenith, followed by unavoidable free falls. Like lightning bolts, their brightness quickly disappears from our skies.

~28~

For financial reasons, Charité had placed her daughters in service with her best customers in Port-au-Prince. Welcomed since adolescence by her godmother "Ninninne," General Bertrand Deveaux's widow, Marguerite always enjoyed a privileged status amongst the household staff. She attended night school, learned to read and write, and spoke French impeccably. Her sunken cheeks quickly filled up. There were no more somber nights, of sleeping on a sisal floor mat, seeking refuge from the harrowing pain of an empty stomach.

Despite her young age, Marguerite would prepare a list for the market and one for the laundry that her mother would deliver the following week, washed, starched and ironed. The young woman oversaw the polishing of the silverware and stored all embroidered tablecloths and fine linen in a cedar chest of drawers. She supervised the ritual of the morning coffee, served in bed to her mistress, and would come out of her room with the day's directives, which she applied to the letter. The daily purchase of bread was made, under her direction, by André, a young house boy newly arrived from the southern town of Jérémie, where the deceased General Deveaux and his widow Océanie were originally from. André faithfully handed the bread to Miss Marguerite for inspection, and she made sure, by a light pressure of the index finger, that the baguette was fresh. The young man would grin from ear to ear, happy to have accomplished his mission. He had not allowed the baker to sneak a stale baguette by him.

Ninninne, who was getting older and relied more and more on her goddaughter, revealed her culinary secrets to her so that she would, in turn, share them with Mister Charles' wife, someday. Leilah, whose knowledge in this domain was limited to the typical dishes of her Lebanese culture, learned the basics of Haitian and French gastronomy, to entice her husband's appetite. Marguerite soon became her only ally, in this huge gingerbread house in Bois Verna, where her mother-in-law, Veuve Deveaux, a stern and stiff widow, intimidated her. Her sisters-in-law did not even hide their hostility toward the "foreigner" who had stolen their only brother from them.

A nice reception was held, in Océanie Deveaux's formal living room, when Marguerite married Boss Etienne, the carpenter with steel muscles who had refurbished the stairway leading to the second floor. Mrs. Etienne, flaunting her wedding ring, was beaming with pride. Her godmother had orchestrated her special day with a touch of class. Nothing was missing: the portrait at the photographer's studio; the snow-white wedding dress; the three-decker frosted cake decorated with small silver balls, and a bottle of champagne for the couple. On her husband's arm, Marguerite left Bois Verna that evening to start her married life in Bel Air, Port-au-Prince's oldest neighborhood. Widow Deveaux lost her goddaughter and the skilled governess of her home. Leilah lost an ally, a trusted friend.

Three years later, at Océanie Deveaux's funeral, a grieving Marguerite returned back home. Boss Etienne had started to drink, desperate by his wife's inability to conceive and enraged at being a target of relentless mockery by his peers. He would put up with almost anything, but he would not tolerate infringements on his privacy or verbal attacks on his manhood. His wife was a mule, unable to give him a child. He came to loathe their expensive conjugal bed. Etienne would come home late from work, and bring less and less money, seeking, in other women's arms, the affirmation of his shattered masculinity. The day he raised his hand at Marguerite, in a fit of rage, she understood that their union was doomed to failure. Only her pride stopped her from confiding in her godmother.

Marguerite fooled everyone, until the funeral of the woman who had torn her away from the clutches of poverty and affirmed her right to pursue dreams and write her page of history.

Leilah understood everything. Since she sometimes helped her parents at their store on Grand-Rue, the young Madame Deveaux decided to embark on a delicate mission. Charles was a generous provider and their unborn child would lack for nothing. His proud nature would never allow his wife to turn to Kimbram and Zahiye Habdoul for a financial need. But Leilah could, at times, be stubborn. The Habdoul business would be hers, and her younger brother Farid's, one day. She saw no harm in knocking, for the first time in her married life, at her parents' door.

After Océanie Deveaux's death, Mrs. Charles had become the new, undisputed mistress of the house in Bois Verna. Leilah would not dare to admit it, but she had felt a great weight lifted off her shoulders. Respectful however of her husband's grief and attentive to hearsay and gossip, she wore, as expected, traditional black mourning clothes for an entire year, in memory of her mother-in-law. Leilah had concocted a clever plan: to build and furnish, with Habdoul money, a comfortable bungalow for Marguerite in the huge backyard. It was her project. No one could dissuade her, not even her husband. Leilah needed her ally by her side, in anticipation of her pending delivery date. She relied heavily on her wise counsel, common sense and street smarts, for support.

This arrangement had pleased Marguerite, who deserved, after her marital setbacks, the comfort of a quiet and serene life, free from all financial worries. Leilah secretly covered all legal fees for her divorce, but Marguerite chose to keep her married name and be addressed as "Madame Etienne" by the household staff.

A terrible loss, the untimely death of baby Robert, clouded the picture of happiness for Leilah, who could never give her husband another son. The arrival of two precious little girls, in the following years, helped mend her broken heart. Charles would say, of his daughters, "They are the apples of my eyes."

"I was present at your birth," Marguerite often reminded the Deveaux girls. Yvette and Claire's unwavering attachment to her knew no boundaries. For the love of Claire, Marguerite agreed, years later, to leave the comfort of her spacious bungalow for a room in Bourdon. Her "little one" needed her, at the dawn of her new life as a young wife. Leilah deprived herself of her ally, for her younger child's sake. Dieudonne and her daughter Ti Sò became the new occupants of Marguerite's bungalow.

~ * ~

"We must think of Myriam's welfare."

Yvette, the second Mrs. Tyler by an unpredictable turn of event, begged Marguerite to stay by her side in Bourdon. Marguerite realized that her place was where life flourished, where babies were born. And Charité's daughter, with the barren womb, basked in the indescribable joy to feel, day after day, year after year, the soothing beats of little hearts, asleep against hers. Marguerite became my official nanny and, later on, of every baby Yvette gave birth to, in the following years.

Called Vivi at birth, then Mademoiselle Vivi at eighteen, Yvette became Madame Jim for her old nanny, on her wedding day. Madame Etienne, in line with a culture where her own mother, like so many, had been a common-law wife, offered the respect and validation granted to married women in our island. At key moments of the day, in fact, in every circumstance of life, Marguerite would prepare an herbal concoction, a rafrechi leti—or lettuce tisane—to keep an unblemished complexion; verbena tea for strong emotions; hibiscus and lemon infusion for colds; soursop to calm one's moods; and ginger tea, on key dates of the month when Yvette would lie on the veranda's lounge chair. At nightfall, a steaming cup of mint tea, the "te ti bòm," sent the entire family to bed with peace in their hearts, as Marguerite, their rock, ensured the intricate synchronization of their lives.

"Krik?" Marguerite would say when I was a little girl, as she tucked me into bed.

"Krak!" the eager child would reply, with great anticipation at the prospect of another kont kreyòl—folk tale—or riddle.

"Ti won san fon?"

"Bag!" I would shout, clapping hands, and giggling with delight.

One evening, Yvette, furious, caught my old nanny by my bedside, telling a curious, yet terrified little girl a scary story about the lougawou—a mystical shapeshifter, half-human, half-beast that rummaged the night, spotting disobedient children to devour.

One could not escape the influence of Vaudou in my beloved island where the fear of the supernatural was as powerful as the reign of terror dictatorship was already demonstrating. On full moon nights, on our deserted veranda, I would listen to Marguerite chant a melodious song, dedicated to the bright silver disc shining in the sky: "Beautiful Moon, fill my pockets." I would be scolded by my nanny for having missed my chance at a nice present. Fingernails were cut Mondays through Wednesdays. A day with the letter 'r' signified a bad omen, when one had a pair of scissors in hands. Marguerite forbade us to evoke the future, or talk about the next day, without adding: "Si Bondye vle..." If God wants. A powerful reminder that life is fragile, and its course, uncertain.

~29~

After our weekend in Paris, Ishtar promised, "One day, I will tell you everything, because you are special."

The week before the long-awaited Easter break, I am summoned to Sister Marie Laurence's office. My anxiety is short lived when I find out the incredible nature of the meeting. Several classmates wished to invite me for the holidays and, to paraphrase the French poet du Bellay, I would proclaim, "Happy is he, who, like Ulysses, went on a long journey." My teacher wears a happy smile. She informs me, a touch of excitement in her voice, "Myriam, guess who just left my office? Princess Najlah, King Omar's sister and your friend Ishtar's mother. Her Majesty has requested the school's permission to invite you, all expenses paid, to their palace for the Easter truce. Ishtar told her you both share a special friendship. You are now the only student at Saint Joseph to know a secret fiercely guarded by the staff."

I'm so surprised I can't speak. Blown away by the extraordinary revelation I just heard, I am propelled into the world of fairy tales: a palace in the heart of the mysterious Orient! Aladdin and his magical lamp, childhood tales of a Thousand and One Nights begin a whirlwind dance in my brain, filled with bearded men in tunic and veiled women, flying carpets and gold palaces. Everything becomes suddenly clear: Ishtar's extravaganza at La Coupe d'Or, the black limousine with tinted windows, and the exotic driver with a foreign accent. My friend, my accomplice at Saint Joseph is a princess of the Orient. This dazzling revelation transports me beyond my wildest adolescent dreams: on the mysterious shores of royalty.

"For political and security reasons, you must not, under any circumstances, reveal Ishtar's true identity to your classmates."

The familiar voice of my teacher snaps me out of my reverie. Ishtar, a princess! All the parts of the puzzle perfectly fit: the need for incognito, the faded jeans and oversized raincoat, the bodyguards following, impassive, the black limousine, Ishtar's concern for her brother's safety and the threat of death, present like a sword of Damocles over his head. Ishtar lives, trapped in a gilded cage, the complicated existence of royalty. I will be my friend's guest, in her sovereign uncle's palace!

Must I learn to curtsy? What clothes shall I wear? Is the veil mandatory for women? Will they speak French? A total struggle has begun between my romantic side that wishes to experience royalty and my timid nature, in sheer panic at the prospect of such exciting challenge. I fear that at King Omar's palace, I will be a clumsy fish out of water and Ishtar will regret my presence by her side. My teacher, clueless about the drama unfolding inside my brain, continues, "Discreet security measures will be implemented and you will fly out of Paris with Ishtar, who will travel incognito. Saint Joseph will require a written authorization from your parents. You need to reach out to them by phone, as soon as possible."

I believe that, in my heart, I have already turned down the incredible invitation offered to me on a gold and silver platter. The fear of the unknown will triumph! My father, consulted, refuses the idea of sending his daughter "in search of adventure in the deserted sands of the Orient." Relieved, I get the parental refusal I secretly wished for. But I am certain my father would have said yes, had it been my wish...Sister Marie Laurence invited me to seize the chance of a lifetime But I opted for the comfort of familiar zones. I have a poignant dream that night: Ishtar, splendid in her red evening dress, wearing a sparkling tiara of precious stones, walks toward me, eyes drowned in tears, dragging a chain at her feet. In the morning, head down in shame, I am about to betray a beautiful friendship.

"Ishtar, I cannot believe Sister Marie Laurence's revelation and your mother's incredible invitation."

"Myriam, you are my best friend at Saint Joseph. I am thrilled to make you discover my beautiful country."

"I am so sorry, Ishtar, but Gisèle had already invited me to her grandparents' house in Auvergne, for Easter."

I am consumed with remorse. My classmate says nothing. But I can read, in her dark velvet eyes, all the pain of the world. Her face harbors the mask of sadness. I bite my trembling lips and try to fight the tears. Ishtar, proud and strong, does not say a word. She shows total self-control, offering a stony face at the news. Finally, shrugging her shoulders, she turns around and disappears with her gangly, elastic gait.

By turning down the opportunity of an extraordinary journey to the land of a Thousand and One Nights, I've lost the gift of a lifetime. But the worst part is to disappoint Ishtar who, out of pure, trusting friendship, unveiled the mask of her royal status to me. I swear to pick up the shattering pieces of our broken friendship. "In life, we can never turn back," Sr. Marie Laurence reminds her students. But we can forgive! Today, a hole has been dug between Ishtar and me. Will I ever deserve her forgiveness?

~30~

On the school grounds at Sainte Thérèse, there was a majestic tree where, for a brief period of the year, delicate pink flowers with hundreds of small tentacles would blossom. The early-arrival students would collect the "mimi" which littered the ground and formed a pink carpet at their feet, under the jealous gaze of latecomers like me. As with everything of value, the rarity of the seasonal flower made it more precious. I learned, years later, the scientific name of the "mimi tree," also known as the "shaving brush tree": Pseudobombax ellipticum. To this day, I envy those fortunate enough to have, in their backyard, the tree that symbolizes the magic of childhood wonder, for me.

~ * ~

With summer just around the corner, sudden afternoon showers would bring life to my grandmother's grass, hidden in the large backyard. In fragrant waves, the smell of green stems mingled with the pungent scent of humid soil. Raindrops twinkled in the wet grass, under the caress of a teasing sun, happy to play hide and seek with the clouds. The birth of a pretty flower, the waltz of butterflies draped in their colorful wings, filled me with delight.

In the garden of childhood happiness, I loved to seek refuge on the large roots under the shadow of the old mango tree and sit near Dieudonne's bungalow, surrounded by the green carpet of grass. Books like Sylvain & Sylvette, Tintin & Milou, *and* Tout l'Univers *were my faithful companions. Later,* Le Club des Cinq *and* Le Clan des Sept *set my imagination on fire. I traveled through the Swiss Alps alongside* Heidi, *and journeyed, overwhelmed, with* Anne Frank, *at adolescence's doorstep. Purple and yellow bougainvillea shared the space with pink and white laurel hedges, cut in shape of spheres and cones.*

André, wearing his eternal straw hat, shears in hands, carved works of art in the garden. Grandmother gave him free rein in the yard.

The gardener's gray temples betrayed his age, not the muscular torso he loved to bare, shiny with sweat, under the sun. The bountiful red hibiscus, in bloom all year long, symbolized for me a happy childhood, a bright and cheerful note in the album of memories. Its tender petals, crushed in the palm of the hand, could bring shine to the dullest leather shoes. The te choublak, or hot, sweet herbal hibiscus tea, combined with lime juice and honey, became this deep red infusion that could heal a recalcitrant flu and warm the soul all at once.

But the hibiscus flower symbolized, first and foremost, these irresistible red blood hearts where the butterflies of la Saint Jean (feast of St John, June 24) came foraging. June signified for me the launch of butterfly hunting season. Grandfather, born on June 24, would remind us that butterflies, adorned in their finest attires, came in multicolored swarms to visit our garden in honor of his birthday. They gravitated from hibiscus to hibiscus, and would land gently in their deep, sensually red corolla. Yellow and speckled-brown butterflies, delicate ones sprinkled with fine turquoise dust or majestic orange and black travelers would seek refuge in the hibiscus' heart to be picked, gently, by the wings and imprisoned in a clear jar.

After a short stay in the glass cage, the girl with the long dark braids would offer, to the stunned butterfly, the gift of freedom, her pleasure residing in the catch rather than the possession. Will I ever see, again, the graceful butterflies of "la Saint Jean"?

~31~

Final exams for the third quarter are fast approaching. Summer was at our doorstep. The excitement of returning home to my family is mixed with a touch of melancholy. My first school year in France! I get attached to people and places that shape my daily life. Agnès and Ishtar have been my accomplices, and Sister Marie Laurence has become the compass that leads to the right path. Saint Joseph, nestled in the heart of Chateaubriand's park, has sheltered me from the vast unknown, under its protective shadow. An obscure premonition settles inside me, casting a doubt on the future: will I ever return to these familiar walls and century-old trees?

Agnès whispers, puzzled, "Strange…Astrid stopped tormenting Sister Marie Laurence."

Astrid avoids her classmates at recess these days, opting for solitude, a study book held like a shield on her chest, to protect her against an invisible enemy. I detect a distress signal in her strange attitude. My loyalty will float like a banner over the one who suffers. After lunch, I sneak behind her and follow her trail, deep into the park, to the undergrowth where my smoking lesson took place. Defiant, Astrid stares at me from the superior realms of her seventeen years, and, with a harsh, cold, piercing look, shouts, "Leave me alone, Myriam! My problems are not for your chaste ears. Go back to Agnès, the unblemished lamb, and to Marie Laurence, the goody-goody nun."

Like a sheepish dog, its tail between its legs, I leave Astrid on her tree trunk in the park, powerless to help her. At mealtimes, she dumps her meat behind the heating radiator, dubbed Astrid's personal trash station. The ploy is eventually unmasked but, bound by the unwritten solidarity code of students against faculty, the entire class keeps silence. With steely eyes, our teacher urges the guilty student to come forward and confess. "Show courage for your actions or the entire class will suffer a collective punishment. Such cowardice is shameful."

Sister Marie Laurence preaches in the desert that day, before the stony wall of our collective muteness. A series of events, the following week, produces a surprising grand finale: Astrid, who disappeared into the bathroom after meals, is found, unconscious, on the floor, the sink bearing nauseating traces of her indisposition. Our classmate fails to appear in class Saturday. By Monday we learn, flabbergasted, that Astrid left Saint Joseph for health reasons. Inflexible, Sister Marie Laurence offers no details to ease our concern, or satisfy our curiosity. She simply states, "Astrid's life is not in danger, but a long rest has been ordered."

I am the only student to know the nature of Astrid's drama. After the last school bus left for Paris Saturday with a happy and noisy crowd, my classmate joined me in the dorm, deserted for the weekend and conducive to secrets. Astrid's revelations gushed like a stream: the delay in her menstruation; the bouts of nausea and vomiting; her fainting episode on the bathroom floor, which alerted her scapegoat, Sister Marie Laurence; Dr. Leroux summoned at her bedside; her refusal to be examined; the decision to urgently call her parents and finally the one-on-one with our teacher, whose calm resolve and solicitude moved Astrid to reveal her fear of being pregnant.

Despite her aggressiveness, Astrid is just a vulnerable teenage girl, lost in the gravity of the moment. Sitting on my comforter on Saturday, she confessed, "Sister Marie Laurence forgave my constant wickedness toward her. I cried on her shoulder, tormented by remorse. I begged her to hide the truth from my parents, because I wanted an abortion. With her brutal frankness, she reminded me that, by destroying a fetus, I would destroy a life."

The delicate subject of abortion was thrown right in my face. My classmate just shattered my adolescent's naivety. The wonderful world of innocence and fairy tale love fell apart. The future has now taken a dramatic turn for Astrid. The insolent girl with the scornful glance is far. I realize the magnitude of her drama.

"My parents said I brought shame into their lives. Where were they when I would come home in the wee hours of morning? My father roared, 'What will our friends think?' Sister Marie Laurence replied, 'Sir, worry about your daughter first.' Reverend Mother found me a home for single mothers. Sister Marie Laurence will administer my final exams there."

Our teacher extended a helping hand to the student who, without remorse, inflicted the deepest wounds to her. Her prophetic words still echo in my memory, since the fateful day of the botched discussion on Sexuality and the Youth: "I hope for you, that at times of big decisions, you will still have a choice."

"It must be hard to believe, but I will actually miss this place."

Astrid, in her hour of truth, no longer had a choice. Her luggage closed, she took one last look at the double row of cubicles, then abruptly turned around and disappeared, carrying, for her bumpy journey ahead, her personal drama and her suitcase. My classmate, I imagine, must be shedding tears.

~32~

Montinar, my family's summer cottage, clung to a slope on Morne Kenscoff, between Bon Repos Hotel and a steep ravine that led to a gorgeous waterfall. This mountain village of Kenscoff, perched at five thousand feet, a forty-five-minute drive from the capital city, inherited its name from colonial times. In the summer, the village became a holiday resort for some city dwellers fleeing Port-au-Prince's heat for cooler temperatures.

July brought the launching of summer holidays for my parents and grandparents, who would share the same roof during the hottest months. A wave of excitement filled the air. My senses, in high alert, soaked everything in: the narrow, curved road after Pétion-Ville; the open-air marketplace, teeming with people: local vegetables growers and livestock merchants selling swine and goats for slaughter; the pungent smell of wet soil suspended in the air; the red-clay mud that lined the narrow street; the ambient air that made us shiver under our sweaters.

Ti Kout, the guardian of our property, always waited at the gate for our arrival, with a basket of freshly picked peaches and plums, our welcome gift from his garden. A broad grin brightened the usually somber face of the man who, wearing an old woolen hat and a jacket too long for his short, stocky build, held the keys to Montinar and insured its stewardship. A damp, earthy scent floated in his presence. His house was hiding behind a hedge of flè klòch, a white corolla flower held upside down by its rod, said to be used by Vaudou sorcerers to "zombify" their victims. Ti Kout took pleasure in scaring us when, unbeknownst to our parents, we would venture to his house, careful not to brush against the mysterious flower's hedge.

One night, his son, Tonton, swore he saw a zombie awakened from his grave, draped in a white sheet, being dragged, by his chains, to his new life of perpetual servitude. Beware! Should one inadvertently give the zombie salt to taste, he might regain his cognitive skills and his spirit could reclaim his body. Our fondness for Ti Kout was a strange mix of affection for the elderly man who watched over us in the summer and a hefty dose of fear he inspired us, with the aura of mystery hovering over him.

The division of tasks and responsibilities was simple at Montinar: Grandmother, assisted by Marguerite, was in charge of the kitchen and meal planning, whereas Yvette, helped by Celia, her mother's housekeeper in Bois Verna, supervised the smooth running of the household: the cleaning, the laundry and the children's many activities. Leilah's cook, Dieudonne, spent summers in her hometown of Jérémie with her daughter, until school resumed in October. Bobby and I made our beds in the large bedroom we shared with our younger siblings. My father and grandfather, the breadwinners, drove down to Port-au-Prince together, to save on fuel. We ate supper when they returned from town on late afternoons. Grandfather's task was to bring fresh, crusty baguettes from the bakery. The two men presided over meals, at each end of the long mahogany table. Grandmother's specialty was her delicious vegetable soup and the daily appetizer we all looked forward to, at dinner.

Leilah's fresh produce vendors, her pratik, brought their merchandise on our porch for display on market days. Grandmother always exchanged confidences with her "vegetable ladies" as she loved to call them. Vierge, her favorite, would reserve, for our evening soup, the most beautiful carrots of her garden, big bunches of spinach, long stemmed leeks and firm, green cabbage heads. Potatoes were stacked in a large, dented tin pot that had probably seen better days. Vierge would always add a few potatoes to the pyramid, kindness reserved for Leilah, her son Ti Jacques's godmother.

An artist lived year-round at Le Château (The Castle), an impressive dwelling overlooking our modest country home. His reputation as a hermit was known. He never came out of his ivory tower, leaving his shopping to his household staff. No one ever noticed a feminine presence, or any children. Everyone called him blan (white), a designation reserved for foreigners, regardless of their skin color. The painter drew his inspiration from the vivid Kenscoff Mountains' colors, but sold his work overseas to be paid in dollars. The thought of an artist living in our midst filled my heart with delight. At ten, I fell in love with this puzzling character without ever laying eyes on him, seduced by the romantic appeal of his art, and the fairy-tale name of his home. One day, consumed by curiosity, I climbed the slope leading to Le Château, as the family was taking a nap. I sneaked toward the only window that was not hidden by curtains and allowed light to penetrate: the artist's workshop, perhaps?

Face glued to the glass, I found myself nose against nose with a white bearded figure, like a patriarch from the Old Testament, eyes throwing daggers at me, angered by this invasion of his privacy. Terrified, I tumbled down the steep hill, risking breaking my bones, my heart pounding. My infatuation for the artist instantly vanished, like snow in the sun. I never shared this story with anyone. My journal kept my embarrassing secret.

I knew every trail and mound that led to the waterfall, my favorite excursion spot. Armed with a cane and a sweater, I loved to be in the presence of this force of nature, this icy cold, crystal-clear water, which crashed furiously on the rocks during the rainy season and turned small stones into smooth pebbles. Bobby, obedient and tempered, often joined me. He followed my steps with caution, down the slopes, and accepted with great wisdom the helping hand stretched out to him. We improvised a picnic by the water, with the sandwich and juice grandmother had packed for our hike. Freddy and Junior, unruly, were allowed by the cascade only if Ti Kout accompanied them. For a few gourdes, our parents sometimes rented a docile horse for the day. We took turns riding on the grounds of Montinar, Ti Kout holding the reins hooked to the horse's bridle. Our father had bought a brand-new saddle with the strong smell of coarse leather, for our equestrian promenades.

At a short distance from the waterfall, our property stopped at the foot of a large flat rock overlooking a valley planted with rows of cabbages and carrots. Those who dared to venture too close to Pè Lucien's garden faced his wrath. Respectful of others' territory, I often sought refuge on this rock, tucked in between both properties, and named it "my" turf, to read and dream, away from my younger brothers' incessant babbling. Lying on my back to invite the caress of a timid sun on my skin, I became one with the rock's smooth surface, which turned cold at dusk. By the whims of my imagination, clouds formed scary monsters or smiling cherubs in the sky. When my eyes caught menacing signs of rain on the horizon, I rushed to the refuge of the family cottage and a hot cup of mint tea.

~ * ~

The summer of my eleventh birthday in Kenscoff, armed with pen and paper, I started an ambitious project: to write my first novel. I went down the steep slope to "my" rock, while my brothers played soccer with Tonton, the guardian's son. Putting ink to paper, I filled, with an exalted and passionate tone, over two hundred pages of spiral notebooks about the mishaps of Domino, a motherless adolescent, who lived, barefoot and fancy free, with her father on a deserted island... until the day a stepmother's arrival challenged the heroine's status quo. Too young to devote myself to psychoanalysis, I did not realize, at the time, the influence of my personal drama as source of inspiration. These pages slept for years in a secret drawer. Cathy, my soul sister, was the only one to read certain passages. She offered to prepare a typewritten version of my handwritten manuscript, full of ink spots and erasures—a project that never materialized.

~ * ~

I made an exciting discovery at the foot of my "writing rock," one day: a brilliant, crystal clear little stone, half buried in the rich, reddish mountain soil, was blinking its eye at me. Convinced I had just unearthed a diamond in the rough, I ran to the house to reveal my newfound treasure. Smiling indulgently, Grandfather explained that my diamond was, in fact, a fine specimen of quartz. This lesson of geology did not damper my excitement that peaked to high levels that summer. My brothers and I spent our vacation digging for "diamond" mines. Pink and white quartzes would surface, and Ti Kout, amused by our collective excitement, cleaned each piece as precious stone. The joy we experienced, this year, was priceless. Through the magic of childhood, we were explorers on a treasure hunt.

Sitting on the grassy front lawn, on summer evenings when nature spared us the rain, I basked in the sheer delight of nightfall around me. Its light veil wrapped my body in a cool caress. The rich perfume of eucalyptus mingled with the smell of wet grass and lingered over me. The scent of earth clung to me, as if to swallow me…Earth, trees, winds and grass were celebrating the essence of life that pulsates around us, in the foliage that sings in the breeze, the flowers that exude their sweet fragrance, and the mysterious fireflies that light up, with the stars.

~33~

Gisèle's grandparents, my hosts, greet me with open arms, at Easter. I discover the charms of their corner of paradise, Auvergne's countryside, its quaint little dirt roads and one-story homes, the warm, cozy kitchen with the blackened hearth and pungent scent of firewood, where a perpetual soup simmers in a huge kettle. My friend's jovial and chubby grandmother reminds me of Leilah. The neighboring village of Collonges-la-Rouge sleeps under the protective shadow of painters, poets and artists like famous writer André Maurois. I daydream: Montinar will be a haven of peace and inspiration for artists who will flock to my beloved island from all corners of the globe, in search of their Muse. I will publish books, alongside my sculptor husband. If he happened to be a doctor, poetry will be his secret passion.

In May, Saint Joseph's high school students visit the Floralies Internationales d'Orléans during a class trip on the south of France's longest river, the Loire. Strolling through the botanical garden, I am mesmerized by such display of beauty and colors. Another key attraction: a life-size reproduction of the Gallic village of Astérix. My brothers would have loved this plunge in the fantasy world of Astérix and Obélix. Back at school, I delve into my textbooks to prepare for our class's end of year exams. My eyes are set on the Award of Excellence. Summer is in the air and excitement stirs among students at the prospect of returning home to their families. We exchange addresses, and promises of epistolary exchanges. Bonds have been forged. We have written a page of history together, at the crossroads of our young lives.

Reverend Mother surprises me with a dream gift: to take my final exams before my classmates, in secrecy, and join the "Terminales" (senior class) on their end-of-the-year trip chaperoned by Sister Jean. Our itinerary: The Grand Duchy of Luxembourg, Switzerland,

Belgium and border towns in Germany. Europe flaunts her treasures. I fall under the spell of the "old" continent's captivating beauty and historical richness: In Verdun, northern France, where the longest battle in history during World War I took place, our group reflects at the Douaumont's ossuary, a memorial where fallen soldiers' skeletal remains rest in a chest. In Luxembourg, the picturesque little village of Esche-sur-Sure, by the river Sauer, captures my imagination. Beaufort's castle, in the East, reveals its famous torture chamber to curious, yet horrified visitors. Troubling nightmares keep me awake, as medieval warriors wearing armors and armed with javelins chase after me the entire night.

Near the Luxembourg border, in German wine country, the town of Trier (Trèves), on the banks of the Moselle River, greets us with a meal of sauerkraut and sausages, served by our hosts in a restored little castle, turned guest house. A sightseeing tour and group portrait at the foot of the Porta Nigra, built by the Romans during César Auguste's reign, are on the menu the next day. In Switzerland, seduced by the postcard perfection and beauty of its landscapes, I lose all faculties. "I will marry a Swiss, and live in the most gorgeous country on Earth," I think, dreaming with eyes wide open. The seniors are pampering their young Haitian comrade, and stuffing her with delicious Swiss chocolate. Europe just offered me her dazzling magnificence, I marvel, in the tour bus back to France.

My wonderful fairy tale ends when Saint Joseph's walls arise on the horizon. A vast, empty dorm waits. I realize, stunned, that the students have all returned home to their families. Summer recess has officially begun. Agnès, Ishtar, Sophie and Gisèle have collectively signed a touching farewell note and put it on my pillow. They expressed their regret at "missing the chance to say good-bye" but rejoiced at the prospect of being reunited again in September. "Write to us from Haiti," concluded the message. The silence weighs heavy on my heart. The abrupt and unexpected absence of my classmates throws a blanket of sadness around me. I furtively step inside their small cubicles, hoping to catch a shadow, searching for the slightest indication of their presence.

By joining the seniors on their class trip, I opted, unaware, for a brutal separation with those who shared my daily reality as boarders for an entire school year. We have become friends. We are accomplices. How will I bear their absence tonight, lost and alone in this double row of empty beds? Will we even meet again? Who knows, really? Life has a way of surprising us, always. A quiet footstep in the hallway brings me back to reality. Relieved, I recognize the familiar silhouette of my teacher.

"I am so happy to see you. Did you have a pleasant trip?" She approaches and grabs both of my hands. Sincere joy is on her face.

I quietly stare at the one whose existence I practically forgot, in the euphoria of my European trip. Sister Marie Laurence is a haven of peace. I secretly pray she does not abandon me to my solitude tonight. "Thank you for allowing me to go on this unforgettable trip. I would like to express my gratitude to Reverend Mother as well, before I fly back to Haiti."

"You will have this opportunity tomorrow night, Myriam, as the senior class will officially bid farewell to their teachers before returning home to their families."

My legal guardian took care of all travel formalities and hands me my passport and plane ticket for Haiti. The only task left for me to do is to pack my suitcase and offer my goodbyes. Sister Angèle, our angel in disguise for details of daily living, briefly joins us to confirm Saint Joseph's approval to store my winter clothes until my return in September. I will travel back with my guitar, determined to practice my musical notes this summer. Sister Marie Laurence will be on dormitory duty this evening, as she was on the first day of school, to welcome students to their new lives as boarders. I suspect

it is her discreet way of making herself available, on the eve of my
return to Haiti.

My teacher hands me my end-of-year report card with a total
grade point average beyond my expectations. She also wrote
words of praise on my behalf in the comments' column. I can
already imagine my family's pride when I hand them this trophy.
The moment is ripe for a final exchange and a chance, perhaps, to
thank the nun for her support and guidance throughout the year.
But, the contradictory feelings of joy and sorrow struggling within
me paralyze all expression of gratitude from me. A simple "thank
you" can be so hard to voice, sometimes. Lost for words, I whisper,
anxious to hide my emotions in the folds of my pillow, "Good night,
Sister Marie Laurence."

"Good night, Myriam," she simply echoes. A placid look on her face
and her voice serene, Sister Marie Laurence returns to her room
at the end of the hallway, accustomed, for so many years, to give
rather than receive, and sow the seed of service to collect, in return,
baffling silence.

The "Terminales" farewell evening the next day allows me to
measure the senior class' commitment to their alma mater and
to the teachers who traveled, by their side, the complicated road
to maturity. After the appetizers and refreshments, Beatrice, the
eloquent speaker of their group, thanks Saint Joseph's community in
an improvised speech that prompts discreet tears. Reverend Mother,
as she hands them their report card, offers words of wisdom to the
graduating class ready to embark on their new journey. Careful to
not disturb the charged emotion in the room, I stay in my corner,
quiet as a church mouse. In two years, it will be my class's turn to
graduate. I can already imagine Agnès and Ishtar in the fever of our
final goodbyes. Such is life. Links form, to be broken later.

The highlight of the evening is the touching farewell scene between students and professors who share embraces to the sound of muffled sobs. By such display of emotions, the seniors teach me a profound lesson: Life sometimes offers us, in a flash of light, the chance to let our heart speak. The page, once turned, no longer belongs to us. I timidly approach Sister Marie Laurence. Silence speaks volume. She understands the hidden message and simply opens her arms. I am finally able to whisper, "Sister Marie Laurence, thank you. For everything!"

Then she collects, against her shoulder, the sobs of her fifteen-year-old pupil who, strangely, recalls her poignant arrival night at Saint Joseph. The next day, I leave for Haiti, carrying in my heart the treasures France bestowed upon me, during this unforgettable first year.

PART II

The Journey

~34~

Paris: Notre-Dame – September 1967

Fall promises to be chilly, as I return from Haiti. Parisians are already wearing their trench coats. Notre-Dame, nestled at the entrance of Paris, offers a splendid setting with its modern buildings and large, luminous glass windows. To my surprise and delight, all boarders are entitled to their very own private room, albeit small. No partial partition with open tops any more, where the least sound can be heard across the thin divider wall. I am ecstatic after the visit to the laboratory, equipped with state-of-the-art instruments. Reverend Mother Pascale is in charge of orientation for our group of newcomers. The Mariale Order has approved the modernization of the religious habit, and their Parisian school is the first to adopt it. The short veil that stops at the height of the shoulder becomes the symbol of the nuns' commitment to God and to their congregational order.

At sixteen today, I am a "Première," a Junior who bravely faces her new life. Yvette is notably absent for the launching of my second school year in France. Saint Joseph has planned, to the minute detail, my transfer to Notre-Dame, where I am now enrolled in the Section D: Biological Sciences. I am relieved to find my winter clothes trunk stored under my bed, thanks to Sister Angèle. A letter from Agnès, who is pursuing a literary branch at Saint Joseph, is waiting on the narrow desk of my sparsely furnished room. I learn that Ishtar, enrolled in Section B (Political Sciences) has been transferred to The Mariale Order's Colombes School on the other side of Paris. A choice that perfectly suits her personality, I smile to myself. Besides, the revelation of my friend's royal status and my subsequent refusal following her invitation last Easter has eroded our friendship. Time and distance will heal our wounds, I hope. I realize that emotional ties have the potential to affect the smooth course of our studies, the main reason for my presence in France.

Perhaps it is all for the best? I already dread the famous BAC, this challenging national exam I must assiduously study for, pass with flying colors and offer as a trophy to my family next year.

Contrary to my predictions, I adapt, in the blink of an eye, to my new life at Notre-Dame. The fear of the unknown that haunted me at the end of summer has vanished. I had no choice but to confront this fear, like a brave soldier. Life is good again. Karie, seventeen, quickly adopts me. Her goal: medical school after her BAC. Her parents, of Lebanese descent, invite me to their Parisian home on weekends. This common link in our origins has created a bond with Nassim and Yamile Assam. They offer to play the role of official correspondents, and refuse any financial reimbursement they would be entitled to as host family to a foreign student.

"You will, instead, host our daughter Karie in Haiti this summer."

This perfect arrangement provides me with a weekly escapade to an upscale Parisian apartment, a beneficial change of pace after our strenuous weeks as boarders at Notre-Dame. My classmate's studious influence is contagious. An only child, she devotes her time exclusively to her studies, her eyes set on a very special prize: to pass her BAC with honors next year. Her parents, successful professionals, nourish high career ambitions for their daughter. Karie will not disappoint them.

"After medical school, I will think about marriage and family," she announces with conviction.

I do not doubt her prophetic words for a second, her quiet determination becoming rule of law. Karie, with her round-rimmed glasses and her hair pulled back in a messy bun, is reserved. Her strong will, academic ambitions and tenacity are guaranteed assets to her future success. Under her loose-fitting clothes, one can still guess a slim figure. She attracts the studious type, young men who visit museums or public libraries on Saturday afternoons. But Karie always discourages their timid advances. "No time, Myriam!" she explains. "A steady boyfriend would complicate matters. We will consider it *after* the BAC."

But my island roots claim the best of me, sometimes, when I long for the magic of dance floors. Evangeline, a regular guest at a Caribbean flavor Parisian disco, invites me one day. Eve is Notre-Dame's moderate version of Astrid de Panière. She has mastered the art of balancing school work and pleasure on the weekends and reminds me, a twinkle in her eyes, "Moderation is key, my dear Myriam."

Notre-Dame and my Parisian hosts grant me their seal of approval to accept Evangeline's mother's invitation. Karie politely declines to join us on that Saturday night. "Go ahead! I do not dance. I would rather study."

I leave the Assam's household, feeling guilty that evening, to join Eve and her family. Karie whispers, "Be good!" as she shuts the door behind me. I remain, once again, the young exotic friend that one protects and showers with good advice. "*Who are you, Myriam?*" the inner voice of reason asks. A confusing mix of Karie and Eve. At what age do we fully embrace our individual personality? When do we take full ownership of who we were always destined to be? Do we get an epiphany, a dazzling revelation, when all becomes suddenly clear to us? Or will we finally recognize, without pomp or fanfare, the road that will lead us to our own truth?

~ * ~

We are living a key moment in show business history: singer Dalida's return on the stage of the famous Olympia in October 1967, after her recent attempted suicide. In the packed concert hall, her fans are throwing bouquets of flowers at the singer's feet, homage to their idol who narrowly escaped death. Raw emotion fills the air. Dalida's voice is charged with moving gratitude toward her large audience. Karie, amused by my fanaticism, stands by my side for two hours, under an umbrella in the drizzling rain, hoping for an autograph from the star. When my idol finally approaches and puts her signature on my album cover, Dalida briefly stares at me. "Where are you from?"

I'm about to faint. I whisper, "Haiti."

"Ah, the island of eternal sun!"

The star disappears shortly after, leaving behind a trail of mesmerizing light.

~ * ~

The prospect of weekends in Paris with the Assam family gives me wings on Friday. Their guest room is now referred to as *my* room by my hosts. What have I done to deserve the warm hospitality of their Parisian home after our studious weeks at Notre Dame? Karie, punctual as a clock, is always in bed by nine o'clock, and I allow myself the great pleasure of solitude in the company of my Muse. My black notebook and my Parker pen are always at the rendezvous, discreet, ready to emerge from the bottom of my bag. I never make a move without them.

They are the faithful instruments of the aspiring writer who walks through life, her secret dream buried in her heart. Someday, my grandchildren will read the chronicles of my years in France. In the solitude of my Parisian bedroom, a fickle muse occasionally carries me home to the sunny shores of Haiti. By the magic of the written word, I recreate the illusion of their presence. When the blues settle in and refuse to let go, I hide my mood in the privacy of my room, not to hurt my hosts. Eve picks me up sometimes. Chaperoned by her cousin and his fiancée, we delve in the pleasure of dancing in the heart of a disco atmosphere. Cautious, I always reject any offer of lasting friendship with my casual dance partners. "I am a boarder at a religious school with strict rules."

I have chosen to bask, unattached, in the French culture, enjoying the delights of this intoxicating freedom of the heart. Myriam, citizen of the world, opens up to life and its wonderful surprises. I love our Parisian strolls, where Karie gently mocks the gentlemen who tag along sometimes. My dark hair and olive skin inspire their bold curiosity, I presume: "Where are you from? Egypt? Greece? Italy?"

I just smile, letting a cloud of mystery float in the air. The City of Light has literally captivated me. Everything is a sheer delight: old buildings that hide a piece of history; narrow neighborhood streets; men in berets, walking home from the bakery, a crusty baguette under their arm; overstuffed shelves of wines and cheeses. I love the friendly, unpretentious cafés where, in front of two steaming cups, Karie and I are "building castles in Spain." I imagine sometimes, a bit envious, Jean Paul Sartre and Simone de Beauvoir, writing, side by side, literary masterpieces at a Parisian café.

~35~

My father and younger brothers were expecting me by the exit gate at François Duvalier Airport. Grandfather proudly welcomed his young "Parisian". Leilah whispered under her breath that it was imperative to spare Yvette any stress. As I approached the lounge chair, I noticed my aunt's tired look as she anxiously waited for her baby to arrive. Two days later, James and Leilah took Yvette to Canapé-Vert Hospital where her obstetrician had preceded her, on this torrid night of June. Childbirth would be difficult, the doctor had warned. Luckily, no political storm showed any dark clouds on the horizon. I kept a cautious optimism, worried a cruel repeat of the drama that left me motherless could reoccur. I learned, in the morning, that my fourth brother had come into the world by caesarean section.

Mark's arrival led to medical complications and a tubal ligation. Something mysterious was in the air. Yvette's friends came to visit, worried looks on their faces. My aunt had difficulties recovering from her surgery. I surprised her in tears, one day. She was mourning the loss of her fertility. In our Caribbean culture, a woman of forty is still considered in her prime, on the topic of procreation. That summer, Yvette suffered in her flesh, and in her heart.

Mark seemed a miniature portrait of Grandfather: brown complexion, curly hair, eloquent testimony to our African roots. I loved the baby brother that Yvette, exhausted, entrusted to me in the morning. Her dark, sunken eyes revealed the stresses of the night. Mark and I would chat for hours, eyes locked, swinging on the dodine—a rocking chair. In this silent language, close to this small heart that beat in unison with mine, I was in bliss. Yvette had shared the stark news and intimate nature of her recent surgery, in the solitude of her bedroom where I helped her change Mark's diapers: "Myriam, you will be our only daughter."

Her sadness pained me. I wished I could find words of comfort, which would put a soothing balm on her wound. But my voice remained stuck down my throat. I found the strength, finally, to say, "I will always be there for you." She then hugged me, holding me close to her heart, sobbing. But her display of emotion would be brief: a calm, collected individual, Yvette did not usually show her feelings. By a strange premonition, I predicted the summer following my first year of study in France would not be like any other.

Never before had I felt the mystery of life and its fragility so deeply. We had all feared for Yvette's life. I rediscovered the exceptional woman she was. Her fertile womb had produced a fourth son, and today she was suffering at her core, after a difficult birth. I would have loved to open up to her and ask about my own childhood. Had I been a sweet and happy child, easy to care for, or a restless and greedy baby like Mark? And the big question that still haunted me, leaving in my heart an unquenched thirst for human tenderness: "Did you love me as much as you loved your own?"

Alas, in answer to a question I will never ask, my reason offered the logical answer: how can we love, with the same intensity, another's child and our own flesh and blood? I will forever be the daughter of Claire, the sister who left too soon.

My best friend Cathy would come to visit at nap time. The sun's heat was like a caress on the open terrace. A slow feeling of laziness engulfed us. Yvette welcomed a bit of sleep as we played with my baby brother. We took turns rocking Mark, our real-life doll, dreaming already of the day we would become mothers. But we had to first meet Prince Charming! "All the interesting boys left Port-au-Prince," my friend would lament. "They are all abroad for their studies."

Cathy no longer spoke of joining a convent's religious order. I ventured a stealthy glance at my childhood friend, secretly relieved. My first year in France had changed me. Inspired by a newfound reserve, I kept quiet about Christian and Romeo. But I shared with energy details of my new life as a boarder at Saint Joseph. I saw Sergo and Patrick at parties we were invited to. As usual, they tried to flirt during slow dances, while all I sought was the sheer pleasure of the dance floor, the joy of perfectly synchronized merengue steps, happy to just be a girl from the Islands again with no secret agenda of romantic conquest.

Sergo, disappointed, concluded I had a boyfriend in France. That evening, we argued. The young man with the peach complexion proceeded to taunt me, holding his new partner tightly on the dance floor. Humiliated, I pretended to be indifferent and carefree, but my feminine pride took a blow. I imagined, furious with myself, my summer wasted away without my favorite dance partner. Was that the life of the privileged youth in the Caribbean, until marriage? I longed for more than the stark reminder of dictatorship and poverty amidst the joys of music and dancing.

~36~

One Saturday afternoon, Michel comes up to me as we are perusing the dusty shelves of the Quai de la Seine's booksellers. The tall, skinny young man with the gentle gaze touches my heartstrings. I can feel a special friendship is about to bloom, in the depth of my soul. Michel directs my steps toward his paintings an old friend is trying to sell for him, next to his display of second-hand books.

I contemplate, fascinated, the artist and his creations. My artistic temperament recognizes a soulmate. We stroll amidst the booksellers napping on their chairs and graven images of Notre Dame de Paris that litter the sidewalks. Karie finds me in the next row of books and throws a suspicious look at the guy who cordially offers a polite handshake: "Michel Dalcourt, student at the Sorbonne."

On our way back home, I share my secret with Karie: Michel will be expecting me, next Saturday, by his friend's book display. She urges me to be cautious. I know I can count on her reserved character and total discretion with her parents. Our weekly Parisian strolls become a nice routine with the tacit, if not approving, complicity of Karie.

I join Michel. Hand in hand, we discuss painting and literature. One day, without preamble, Karie decides we must space our Saturday strolls near the Seine. Head down, respectful of the wishes of my host, the lanky young man holds my hand tightly. His silence speaks volume. I appreciate his reserve: unlike casual dance partners always anxious to forge links beyond borders of disco walls, Michel will not force, nor claim anything. The artist has learned to appreciate every gift life has to offer, with no strings attached: the blessings of each new day, the beauty of each new face met randomly but never forgotten.

"Come when you can, Myriam. I will be there, waiting for you."

The school year runs at breakneck speed. Stripped of any emotional tie that can sometimes hamper its course, I am learning to balance school and leisure. With Karie, I become a familiar face at museums and public libraries. Sometimes, we join her parents at scientific conferences where Mr. Assam is a guest speaker. His wife, a senior executive in a foreign firm, is his rock, a discreet presence in the audience. My schoolmate is moving in a circle where the intellect, rather than public display of affection, holds priority.

This period of my life suits me perfectly, giving me the lure of intellectual challenge. Agnès was an attentive older sister at Saint Joseph. Karie forces me to break into the hidden corners of my intelligence. The shy teen in long tube socks and blue beret is part of another time, another place, another décor long gone. Influenced by Karie, whose future as a doctor is already mapped out, I firmly believe I will, one day, choose a career in the field of medical research. Notre-Dame's state of the art laboratory offers the perfect setting for those resolutions of the mind.

My diary enters a phase of quasi silence.

~37~

July was coming to an end when an unexpected twist of fate suddenly took Grandfather away. He collapsed at his desk, struck, just like his father General Deveaux, by a massive heart attack, days shy of the two months arrival of his miniature replica of a grandson. Grandmother, his faithful companion for over forty years, plunged into deep mourning. Leilah, whose trademark was her inexhaustible verve, numb with pain, became unusually quiet. Yvette, who had barely recovered from her surgery, gathered what was left of her strength to help her mother. In the weakness of the one who gave her life, she would muster courage for them both.

Grandmother, distraught, lost in a world that had abruptly changed, followed her daughter to Bourdon in the evenings. Embroidered sheets, fresh flowers and a photograph of Grandfather were placed in the guest room in Leilah's honor. But she remained oblivious to her surroundings.

My father, with philosophy and resignation, watched the foundation of his quiet family life collapse. All of Port-au-Prince appeared to have landed in Bois Verna: the city notables; the grieving friends; Grandfather's faithful agency employees. Everyone praised Charles Deveaux, "a good and decent man." Marguerite tirelessly served strong coffee to friends and acquaintances who had invaded the premises to offer their condolences.

Yvette who, despite her recent surgery, had remained strong after the death of her father, planning the multiple details with the funeral home, snapped the day of the ceremony. The view of Grandfather's corpse, lying in the coffin of precious wood and upholstered silk, made her unravel. In this profusion of fragrant flowers that surrounded the deceased and would, later, head to the cemetery, the slim figure, dressed in black, knelt.

Shaken with convulsive sobs, Yvette repeated tirelessly, her forehead leaning against the open coffin, "Father! Oh, Father!"

Drama suddenly unfolded before our eyes: Yvette, her face pale, lost her balance and fainted. My father, a tall and vigorous man, carried his wife outdoor, trusting the fresh air would help her recover. Dismayed relatives and friends gathered to support our grieving family in the viewing room. A misty veil clouded my memory of the religious ceremony afterwards. But I remembered the pungent smell of incense. Grandfather was laid to rest beside his children Robert and Claire.

~ * ~

"I understand. I understand."

Lying on the bed next to mine, Cathy repeated over and over, with a big sister's patience and affection, that she understood my conflicting emotions but I was NOT responsible for my mother's death. I had never before discussed my motherless status with my friend. Cathy's parents had invited me to spend the night with her, after the funeral. The sight of my grandfather lying, rigid, in the coffin, had deeply affected me. For the first time in my life, I had come face-to-face with death.

Cathy, kept in the loop by her mother about Claire, played naive, for years. I myself was foolish to believe that in Haiti, family secrets could be safely tucked away in an undisclosed, mysterious chest. I ventured to ask if she thought Grandfather held me responsible for Claire's death. Cathy was cautiously silent. I put her friendship to the test that night, seeking answers to metaphysical questions her age and life inexperience were unable to offer.

~ * ~

Leilah had watched, like an automaton, her world collapse, without warning, around her. Charles had been the center of her life, the chief, the man with hands of an artist, who had shaped her body and soul, to mold her into the woman she had become. Over forty years of happiness by her husband's side! How would she survive solitude and loneliness?

Grandmother offered our family to come and live with her in the spacious six bedrooms of the Bois Verna house, too empty since Grandfather's departure. Leilah had blossomed in her married life within these walls: from blushing bride to timid daughter-in-law, from young, inexperienced spouse to savvy hostess, mother and life partner. Her children had grown up in Bois Verna. Yvette knew each crack of the wooden floors, every garden scent and caress of the afternoon breeze.

Leilah had known unfathomable pain too, with the loss of her son and daughter in Bois Verna. How could she abandon a home so rich in memories, where destiny had woven happiness and sorrow, intertwined to make the great tapestry of her life?

My parents had a heated argument. James had categorically rejected Grandmother's proposal. Leilah having lost the center of her life since her widowhood, needed to cling to the only daughter she had left. Defeated, resigned, she accepted my father's suggestion to rent out the spacious gingerbread family home, which had housed several Deveaux generations, to trustworthy clients. Grandmother would move to the guest room in Bourdon. Proceeds from the rental would, in the future, finance the construction of a bungalow adjacent to our house, where she would maintain a measure of independence while enjoying the proximity to her daughter, son-in-law and grandchildren.

My heart bled, contemplating the silver-haired grandmother who felt, in painful silence, the collapse of a huge part of her life. The absence of my grandfather had transformed our existences and plunged us into total disarray. I wanted to go back to yesterday, turn back the clock to when the family basked in peace and happiness. Any change to the immutable order of things always upset me.

~ * ~

I left every morning with Leilah and Yvette, carrying, like a fragile porcelain doll, my baby brother. Grandmother and her daughter were packing memorabilia—photographs, letters, trinkets, these eloquent witnesses of an era that was now part of a past that would never return. Yvette offered a consoling shoulder to Leilah's frequent tears. She patiently helped her mother choose which memento to keep or toss, and carefully wrapped each keepsake, precious but fragile like life itself.

Mark also claimed his rights: Yvette would stop and discreetly prepare to feed her son. With the outmost care, I would hand her the fussy infant boy, who would latch on to his mother's breast and magically calm down.

Leilah resigned herself to the sacrilegious invasion of strangers into her home. A non-profit Canadian organization moved their local headquarters within our walls. The client accepted Grandmother's terms: Dieudonne would keep the bungalow which had become mother and daughter's abode; with Charles gone, Leilah would take on Ti Sò's school tuition; André would retain his post as gardener of the property, his fiefdom for so many years, and keep his room in the servant's quarters.

Relieved, Leilah felt emotionally released from Bois Verna, knowing that her faithful employees would keep vigil.

~38~

After the stress of Grandfather's funeral, the family sought solace in Kenscoff. Our rustic mountain home was a haven, away from the torrid heat and stress of Port-au-Prince. Yvette closed her late father's agency for reshuffling of the staff. Mr. Landry, Charles Deveaux's right-hand man, was entrusted with the office keys and the task to handle all pending matters until the official re-opening of the agency in October. Grandfather's absence had added another task on his daughter's overloaded shoulders: Yvette, convalescing and nursing an infant, also held the reins of her household, the stewardship of a husband, five children and her newly widowed mother. I promised myself to assist her in the care of my baby brother, Mark.

I basked with delight in the coolness of the crisp mountain air and the lingering scent of earth and foliage. The close contact with nature woke up in me a quest for beauty. This change of scenery, after an emotionally tough month of July, would be beneficial to us all. On "my" rock, under the shade of a large pine tree, I kept my journal. I often lay on the flat surface, to gaze at the sky. When a soft breeze caressed my face, I closed my eyes, lost in primitive happiness and unspeakable joy, incompatible with our recent loss.

The aroma of vegetable soup, simmering from the kitchen, signaled it was time for me to put pen and paper away and climb the slope back to the house that held so many memories for Leilah: her honeymoon with her husband; their two girls who picked wild flowers for manman—mommy—during their afternoon strolls. Yvette's cheek colors slowly came back in Montinar, the home that symbolized past summer bliss. My father's cup of tea always greeted him at his arrival from town. He would rock Mark, who disappeared into his arms on the enclosed porch's mahogany rocker. My younger brothers, amateur explorers, crisscrossed the hills and surrounding valleys with Tonton, our guardian Tikout's son.

No grey cloud on the horizon would tarnish the serenity of our bereaved family, together for a much-needed respite, a halt before September's inevitable stress and forced return to normalcy.

However, a letter from France addressed to my parents, brought another upheaval in our quiet Montinar haven. In clear and accurate terms, the leadership team at Saint Joseph informed us of the school's strict literary orientation in September, and the need for me to transfer to their sister school, Institution Notre-Dame, better equipped for the scientific branch I had chosen.

Why *this change to the immutable order of things? The heartbreaking memory of my first night in the freezing dormitory of Saint Joseph, and Sister Marie Laurence witnessing my desperate sobs of young exile, came back to life. Adaptation had not been without pain or tears. Friendships had also sprouted to become, over time, beautiful blooming flowers. My thoughts turned to Agnès and Ishtar. I did not want to cultivate new friendships, nor adapt to another life, another school, another decor. Saint Joseph's majestic park, Chateaubriand's old bench that had defied the centuries, had become my turf. In sheer panic, I begged my father to enroll me in Saint Joseph's literary program. He replied curtly, "Literature will not pay the bills."*

Yvette, who had traveled to France with me on my maiden voyage last year, understood better than James, my father, the emotional challenges of adaptation to new surroundings and felt caught between a rock and a hard place. They argued. My father, in a tone that left no room for compromise, voiced, loud and clear, his final decision: I would follow the path of science. It had been his plan for me all along. The die had been cast, and my fate decided by others. The message of the letter was, in fact, crystal clear: "Notre-Dame will offer Myriam the ideal setting for the pursuit of a scientific studies branch. Formalities are underway for her transfer to our Parisian establishment." My vacations in Montinar were ruined. Only Mark found favor in my eyes: he would just gaze at me, mesmerized, thrilled to find refuge in my arms. I caught myself envying my baby brother, wishing the simplicity of his young life, his only tasks limited to eating and sleeping.

A letter from Agnès, who had enrolled in Saint Joseph's literary program, gave the last, earth-shattering blow: "Sister Marie Laurence was transferred to Africa and will be leaving, in the next few days, for Congo."

Fate was to blame for my forced move to Notre-Dame. But by leaving France without breathing a word to her student, Sister Marie Laurence opted for a final break with all that Saint Joseph represented for the young foreigner from Haiti. I realized I would not forgive my former teacher her departure without warning. Rancor settled in, like a destructive poison, fueling the secret feelings I already harbored against Yvette, on the nights when I cried in silence Claire's absence.

September: I had blown sixteen candles and packed my suitcase. Taking the plane, alone, to Paris, I had dried my tears. The emotional strings that had tied me to this old castle were officially cut: Saint Joseph had turned its back at me. The vision of the shy student, blue blazer and long tube socks, climbing the brick staircase alongside Yvette, came, in a flash, to memory. Then it disappeared, like a small dark spot on the horizon.

Today, Myriam Tyler, straight skirt and nylon stockings, would travel alone, with courage, to the future that would finally reveal, beyond anxieties and doubts, her true self.

~39~

Michel has become the friend my heart craved. A connection, an unseen energy, is transmitted from one to the other, in a shared silence, a complicit smile, a timid confidence on a public bench. We meet at intermittent intervals, in the same location, near his paintings. But, he is always there waiting for me, eyes lit with sincere joy, his frail, lanky body leaning against the parapet overlooking the river Seine. My status as a guest of the Assam family, and cautious prudence on my part, will not allow him to initiate encounters elsewhere. I become, with Karie's support as my chaperone, the deciding factor of our rendezvous, at the controls of an emotional relationship that is emerging.

We have slipped, unaware, in a grey area, a sort of romantic friendship, where conflicting feelings intertwine with each new encounter. Karie, discreet, takes refuge at the library, and I meet the young painter for a walk by the Seine. Artists have always fascinated me. Hand in hand, we exchange our dreams, and our aspirations. I bask in the sweetness of this friendship where everything stands between us: our lives, so different, our social condition and our cultures. However, our souls vibrate in unison. Michel becomes the secret that flourishes in Karie's shadow.

One night however, she joins me in the room I occupy at her parents' apartment on weekends. Karie found us, my head on Michel's shoulder and his arm around mine, cozy on a bench, as if alone in the world in the heart of Paris. Not a word was spoken during our short metro ride home. Dinner was unusually quiet. I took leave of my hosts early, evoking a headache.

I notice my classmate's look of concern directed at me. "Myriam, I hope your friendship with Michel will not become a romantic attachment. We know nothing about him. Be careful that your heart does not play a trick on you."

I feel my face turn red. Karie, tactful, offers me an elder's advice, a sister's plea to be cautious. I would like to reassure her and reveal my attraction for the broad-shouldered types, those who will shield me from the pains of the world. Michel's frail and skinny frame inspires feelings at a whole new level, foreign to me, and takes me to a place where our souls converge. Is it pure friendship or fragile love, about to bloom?

"Studies take up all my time. We need to space our meetings."

My companion, resigned to the crumbs I will grant him now, bends his head down. Prudent, I decline his offer to pose for a portrait in his modest studio. He wanted to capture on canvas, the candor and passion of adolescence. Oh, the beautiful rhetoric that moves, to the core, the artist's soul lurking inside of me. *"Be careful,"* reminds the voice of wisdom.

The end of spring brings *May '68*, the total paralysis of Paris and disruption of the student world. The Students' Revolution has been launched. High school and university students, angry with an imperfect status quo, concerned for their future, are throwing stones, refusing the established order and dream of rebuilding a better world. Michel embraces the cause with passion. In a crowd of angry youth, he voices his pain and sings his hopes.

June 68. The airports are running again. Our plane finally lands in Haiti. My family is relieved we left Paris's hot bed of students' unrest for a well-deserved change of scenery. Karie is about to discover the irresistible charms of my magical island.

~40~

We landed in Haiti in June, under a scorching sun, during a truce of the students' revolution in Paris and the fortunate reopening of the airport. An only child, unaccustomed to physical affection by young children, Karie became subject of intense curiosity for my younger brothers. They monopolized her attention without remorse, giving her little respite. Her sober character loosened a bit, overwhelmed by the spontaneity of childhood. Mark and my French classmate became great friends. I caught Karie more than once, sitting on the flowery veranda, cradling my baby brother with the eternal gestures of love. She had blushed, as if she felt a need to apologize for her moment of weakness, for her touch of humanity. I watched, stunned, the closed petals of a timid flower about to bloom.

Karie received the royal treatment from everyone. My family was grateful to hers for offering me a home in Paris. They extended the red carpet of hospitality in her honor. Mountain excursions in Kenscoff were followed by sunny beach days, where Karie worked on a perfect tan, to her delight. We sipped herbal tea in the evenings, a nightly ritual that gathered everyone in the living-room. I would share anecdotes of our lives in France, as my younger siblings listened, mesmerized by my words.

Karie rocked Mark. Junior, my godson, loved to snuggle against me, thumb in mouth, always asleep before the end of the story, hypnotized by the sound of our voices. My father would take advantage of "story time" to grab Yvette's hand and quietly slip into their bedroom, leaving Marguerite in charge to turn off the lights later on and tuck the younger ones to bed. These children's faces, nudged against ours, reflected happiness—the pure, genuine kind, that envelops us every day, unpretentious, so ordinary, yet so precious.

Their favorite story: my stay in Troyes during All Saints recess, my first year in France, with my friend Sophie de Maisonrouge. Troyes— an ancient-style city made of picturesque, dark and narrow streets, and old buildings hiding a piece of history—stood in stark contrast to the countless, modern hosiery plants that abound in that town. In a quiet neighborhood of Troyes, the ancestral de Maisonrouge home offered the allure of a small castle straight out of my childhood picture books: the emblems and family coat of arms, incrusted in the wall; the hideous, sculpted gargoyles; the stained-glass windows with chivalrous designs; an imposing bronze armor that stood, straight and proud, at the entrance to the vestibule and scared me upon arrival. This image always got a laugh from my brothers.

Cathy, escorted by her cousin Patrick, would invite us to parties and youth gatherings that abounded with the arrival of summer and the students' return from overseas. My best friend was almost eighteen years old. Would she marry Paul, in the near future, and continue the Caribbean tradition of numerous offspring in her elders' shadow? Karie developed a taste for Caribbean music, danced with Paul and Patrick, changed her hairstyle and fell in love with her newly acquired golden tan. Sergo and Patrick competed for our dances. Summer remained this eternal merengue, under enchanting Caribbean nights. Patrick refused to believe my heart was free. This tall young man, with whom I'd exchanged my first kiss one jasmine-scented evening, moved me, nothing more.

Michel's image, the gentle young man who shared with me a fragile emotion, appeared in a flash. Sergo and Patrick were my "brothers" and our lives too similar to ignite a romance. I longed for exotic lands and new discoveries, shores unknown and fragrances, captivating...

~41~

Karie, tanned by our powerful Caribbean sun, is fetching our luggage. At the dawn of my third year in France, I feel like I am returning home, to familiar land. My heavy Islander's accent has given way to that of an accomplished Parisian. In a curious reversal of circumstances, my classmate, seduced by the contagious spell of Haitian merengue, wants to go out to clubs now. But it is the year of the BAC, this climax of our secondary academic cycle, for which we have labored so hard, and I am determined to avoid anything that would hinder my success. Karie bursts out in laughter, amused that I would use her favorite quote to paraphrase her: "No time, Karie. We will consider it *after* the BAC."

I see Michel again, however, after our return from Haiti. Autumn is already knocking at our doors. He smiles…His back leans against a parapet, the Seine in the background and his canvases at his feet. My artist friend is wearing a large red sweater, too big for his frail shoulders. I want to run into his arms, but Karie's presence holds me back. Our Saturday strolls by the Seine will come to a halt after November. Winter will soon return in full force. Everything is ephemeral in life: the seasons, people and things, I say to myself, in a nostalgic mood.

"I wake up every day, anxious to see emerge, under my fingers, the spark of creation," my friend confides. "May '68 revived hope for us, young people. I cling to my brushes, to my dreams, even if I would be the only one to believe in my talent. Myriam, never give up your dream of writing. Pursue it with all your might. Believe in yourself. Against all odds, persevere!"

~ * ~

Preparations for the BAC consume me. As predicted, Michel is on the back-burner all winter long, the cold and the stress of keeping our noses in the books claiming the best of me. Confined in our respective rooms on weekends, Karie and I close our review books only at mealtimes, under the watchful eye of her parents, who support our total devotion to our studies. But, at springtime, nature wakes up from its long slumber. The buds burst open, and proclaim new birth in the land. Birds are flying back from their exotic exile, with the return of spring.

And I return to the booksellers of Quai de la Seine, escorted by Karie, whose summer glow has given way to the pale complexion of the overworked student. Michel comes to greet me, smiling, as if we had parted only yesterday. A woolen shawl is wrapped around his neck and his frailty, once more, moves me. I arrive early, anxious to see him, but pained to have to bid him farewell. Paul Mauriat's song "Love Is Blue," that I have listened to, for months, on my portable record player at the risk of scratching the disc, taunts me. I feel a knot in my heart. Events will move at a fast pace: the BAC followed by my final departure from France. At this thought, a node tightens my throat.

Karie will wait at the library to allow us a private moment. Michel takes me by the hand as we walk, both of us silent. His hand pressure gets stronger. How can I tell him the time has come to say *Adieu?* Farewell, friend…. Our paths will not cross again. In the sad look of his deep, sunken eyes, I read the shocking resignation of the weakest one, who faces destiny's inevitable course. France was a passage, the unforgettable stage of a long journey yet to cover. I met travelers along the road, who reached out, and walked, by my side, for a season, before we parted our separate ways. Michel finally breaks his silence. "I have a present for you."

From our bench, we can spot the tired-looking building which houses his studio on the sixth floor. Torn between my conscience, which warrants caution, and the desire to please my friend, I enter, my heart pounding, in his sanctuary: a tiny lounge, where sunlight pierces its way through the wide bay window flanked by an easel and brushes. Countless unfinished canvases litter the floor. From the kitchen corner, sparsely furnished with a hot plate and a huge espresso coffee pot, the divine aroma of coffee fills the air. A sofa, that has seen better days, seems the only piece of furniture evoking a degree of comfort in this modest studio. Strangled by emotion, I should not hurt my friend's pride.

I feel ecstatic by the view of Paris. But this note of gaiety rings false. The silent display of his poverty hits me full force. Michel is not fooled. I sense it, in the sadness written in his eyes, under his silent gaze fixed on me with poignant eloquence. He brings two cups of coffee that we sip slowly, like precious liquor. I can guess, by a circular look, that a hot meal symbolizes luxury for him. A poignant sense of helplessness crushes me.

The one who would make overtures of affection on our bench, in the heart of Paris, shows extreme reserve in the privacy of his home. Michel finally rises from the couch where we had taken refuge, each lost in our own thoughts. He approaches, timid, and, with trembling hands, unveils, with calculated slowness, one of his paintings to offer me. "I will never forget you. You symbolize an impossible dream, an exotic land to conquer. I have painted, from memory, this portrait I always wanted to create of you, and want to offer it to you. *Remember me from time to time, Myriam. Promise?*"

I witness, overwhelmed by surprise, the unveiling of a masterpiece: a deserted island, in the heart of a huge ocean; a feminine portrait, like a rising sun on the horizon, reflecting the passion and innocence of adolescence. I stare, stunned, eyes blurred by tears, at this reflection of myself, forever captured under the skilled brush of a talented artist. Head buried against his shoulder, the intensity of the moment unbearable, I cry my heart out. A young woman, with newly felt emotions, is emerging today from the warm ashes of adolescence.

As I open the entry door to the dimly lit, shabby stairway, driven by a sudden impulse, I lay my precious canvas at my feet. Slowly, with tenderness and certitude, I cup my hands around the bony face brushing against mine...Closing my eyes, my lips seek his, in a profound and tender gesture, a moving parting gift which echoes Michel's precious last words. *"Remember me from time to time, Michel. Promise?"*

I leave quickly, without looking back, with a brisk and hurried step, toward life, where the BAC, Notre-Dame, Karie, my cozy comfort, and the straight road to the future awaited.

~ * ~

The fateful date for the BAC national exam approaches. I lose my appetite as well as sleep, reviewing study material late into the night with a flashlight hidden under my covers, in the silence of the sleepy dormitory. Illogical panic totally consumes me. Mother Superior got wind of my repeated absences in gym class and decides to stop my weekends at the Assam's. Karie has also showed signs of erratic behavior in light of the pending June exam. Our combined stress could become detrimental to our individual performances for the BAC. Notre-Dame remains the supreme authority in France in major decisions concerning their foreign students.

I will have no choice but to remain cloistered at Notre-Dame on weekends, during May. The boarders gone to their respective families at the end of the week, I find myself alone again in a big empty dormitory. Flashbacks of similar moments at Saint Joseph crowd my mind and bring emotions to the brink. Reverend Mother Pascale, in a show of solicitude and concern, pays me a friendly visit during my first solitary weekend at Notre-Dame. "Myriam, what is going on, my daughter?"

I confess my growing fear of failure, the absurd terror I could lose the entire school year's achievements and especially my nightmare of the potential disaster I would create if I disappointed my parents. Frazzled, I burst into tears. Reverend Mother, in a reassuring tone, brings to focus the fact that a nervous panic is commonplace in decisive upcoming exams, but totally unjustifiable, considering the caliber of students Karie and I are.

Notre-Dame's director concludes, in a firm tone, it is imperative for me to regain my physical and mental equilibrium. Doctor Michaud prescribes, after a complete physical evaluation, capsules of vitamin extracts, phosphorus for memory, and a mild sedative which will be dispensed to me at the infirmary. Diagnosis: exhaustion, complicated by a nervous disposition. Treatment: rest. My flashlight and the instant coffee powder I've attempted to dissolve in warm tap water, in a desperate move for a cup of coffee, are confiscated. Mother Superior requires my participation in gym class, "even at the time of menstruation," she adds, thus rejecting my favorite excuse.

Reverend Mother encourages long walks in the perfectly tended garden of Notre-Dame, "to enjoy the fresh air," she likes to say. She orders the kitchen staff to serve me gourmet dishes with island flair, on Saturdays and Sundays, in the deserted dining room. Colors slowly come back to my cheeks. I rediscover, in the big empty dorm, the regenerating power of long weekend slumber.

Balance and serenity have reclaimed their rightful place into my life. I spend one last weekend with Karie's parents, who have been mine too for a season. Sadness prevails in their Parisian apartment as I gather my belongings, with the anguish that precedes a looming separation. As for Agnès at Saint Joseph, I am about to lose another adopted sister with Karie. Departures often leave a taste of bitterness behind. Yet, at the heart of grief, a newfound maturity takes shape inside of me. Our paths cross the souls we meet along the way, throughout our journey, but separation will inevitably be at the rendezvous…Such is life.

I pass, with honors, the national BAC exam, Section D: Math and Biological Sciences. The country of France and the religious Mariale Order fulfilled their mission on my behalf. Three years after leaving my birthplace of Haiti, I am ready to turn a new page in my life, as I pack my heavy suitcases. I will carry with me, forever, the imprint of France.

Reverend Mother holds me close to her heart. Nassim, Yamile and Karie Assam sadly wave goodbye when, drying a tear, I turn around for the last farewell. Then I take, bravely, the travel corridor crowded with passengers on their way to locate their seats for the long plane ride across the Atlantic... *Adieu,* Europe! I feel, to the core, the poet Edmond Haraucourt's famous verse: *"Partir, c'est mourir un peu..."* To leave, is to die a little.

~42~

New York, USA - June 1969

Wearing a halo of victory over my head, I landed on a beautiful late June morning in New York, where my family had preceded me, at Uncle Farid Habdoul's apartment: James, Yvette, Leilah, Bobby, Freddy, Junior and Mark, who would not keep his agitated little body still, even for a fraction of a second. Grandmother kept an adoring gaze on her only brother who, breaking with age-old traditions in their Middle Eastern culture, had left the family business to carve his own future in the great American metropolis of immigrants. Aunt Doris, a New Yorker by birth, had welcomed us with open arms and offered us her heart, and her apartment.

Laughing and crying at the same time, I get bounced in the moving wave of hugs. Stuck like sardines on the seventh floor of their building in Queens, I conclude, pensively: this is the true meaning of life...Family! My grandfather, who never lost his elegant Parisian accent from his years of law studies in France, would have been so proud of his young Parisian.

Yvette observes with emotion this masculine replica of her mother: the same nose, strong, generous, carved from the same mold; the thick hair, jet black in their youth, more salt than pepper today; the dark, sunken eyes, mysterious as the Orient of their ancestors. A tiny cup of coffee in their hands, they are whispering in Arabic, this language of One Thousand and One Nights which pulls, I imagine, their parents Kimbram and Zahiye out of the depths of memory.

My father, happy to hear his native tongue, casually chatters with Doris, who speaks English only. We exchange one of these winks which he, alone, holds the secret: the silent pact between father and daughter that will eternally link us to Claire. My younger brothers, motionless in front of the TV and sipping Coca-Cola, forget their usual bickering. Fine whiskers line Bobby's upper lips. The eldest of my siblings is fifteen years old. A girlfriend awaits his return to Haiti, perhaps? Freddy's voice changes involuntarily at different moments. Junior mocks him royally, to Yvette's dismay, as she fears a fight will start and cause drinks to spill on the beige living room carpet.

I rock Mark silently. He agrees to leave Yvette's arms and nestle into mine. He just celebrated his second birthday. His mother smiles, surprised. Few are those who find grace in Mark's eyes. On the usually unchanging face of the one who raised me, I learned to capture, over the years, the fleeting emotion that passes quietly. I saw Yvette cry twice, after the loss of her fertility, and overwhelmed before Grandfather's coffin. Her tears moved me, as much as the sight of Grandfather's lifeless body resting in the eternal rigidity of death.

With his heart full of hope and adventure, Uncle Farid left Haiti in his youth, to conquer America and its promises. He married Doris, who gave him two beautiful children and petitioned for his U.S citizenship. Will we ever meet our cousins, someday? My uncle's fabric store, in a commercial zone of Queens Borough, paid for cousins Diane and Dennis' university years. Thanks to Dennis, the male heir, the name Habdoul will live on. These cousins have settled in Chicago and Los Angeles respectively, with their spouses and their offspring.

A proud Doris pulls out photo albums: a happy family, gathered around the traditional feast of turkey and pumpkin pie, smiles at the flash of a photographer. They are celebrating Thanksgiving, this holiday when America gives thanks to God for its new homeland and brings families together, even from the farthest parts of the country.

My uncle, who attended Claire's funeral, followed by Kimbram and Zahiye's a few years later, talks about his only visit to Haiti that had not focused around a coffin. Life and its long list of responsibilities were the culprits: the fabric store; the children, still too young for the adventure of an overseas trip. And time had passed in the blink of an eye. Farid can hardly believe it. Leilah forgives the only sibling she has. Their bond is solid and has defied time and distances. In truth, she did not travel either, to visit her brother. Although she never officially admitted it, my grandmother's fear of flying was obvious in her comments. "I feel fine **only** when my feet are on solid ground."

"I can still visualize the following scene, as if it were yesterday," Uncle Farid reminisces. "Yvette and Claire, long, jet black braids dangling above their hips, intimidated by the tall gentleman with the foreign accent, hold hands. Yvette looks straight at this uncle who fell from the sky into their lives, for a brief encounter. She already shows, at the tender age of ten, signs of the serious, a tad melancholic, woman she will become. Claire, eight, hand locked in her sister's grip, offers me a prudent smile. Then, mustering enormous courage, she frees herself from Yvette, approaches the male replica of her own mother and raises her little arms toward me. Moments later, she is swiftly picked from the ground and kept at eye level by me. Our gazes lock and she starts to stroke my thick head of hair, amused perhaps by the striking resemblance I share with my sister Leilah."

Farid left Haiti, conquered by his nieces. He would never get to know the radiant, vivacious brunette in the red evening gown, who stole the heart of *a* handsome stranger in a dark suit, one day. The timid little girl, clutching the hand of her older sister, is Farid's fondest memory of Claire, preserved in the depths of his souvenirs. I capture this image of my mother, a priceless treasure I will safely tuck away in the folds of my heart, in a vain attempt to quench a thirst that will never stop. All my life, I will carry the unfulfilled longing of an impossible presence, the burning wish to grasp, touch, or simply feel, for a brief moment in a waking dream, the fleeting shadow of the one who lost her life to give me mine.

But Leilah, Farid and Yvette, creatures of flesh and bone, proclaim, by their presence by my side, that the bonds of blood and family will always survive Death. They will transcend eternity. Love also conquers Death. James reminds me of this truth, with his conspiratorial wink. Claire's spirit floats, a sweet, light fragrance amongst us.

~ * ~

July 21, 1969: Man walks on the moon! We are all glued to the TV screen: astronaut Neil Armstrong of Apollo 11 has taken his historical first step on the lunar surface. His message: *"One small step for a man; one giant leap for mankind."* Our family is living an unforgettable moment of history.

~ * ~

Grandmother, whose arthritis is slowing her down, has opted for the comfort of Uncle Farid's apartment and the pleasures of television. Meticulous tourists, we climb the narrow steps to the torch of Lady Liberty, enthroned as Liberty Island's queen. The gigantic bronze statue, France's gift to a young America, covered in verdigris, seems to defy eternity. Lady Liberty symbolizes freedom and hope, the gifts of the modern Promised Land: the assertion that anything is possible in this new country.

Two days later, in the heart of Manhattan, the Empire State Building's elevator propels us to the 102nd floor. Trapped in the flying cage, I am convinced my eardrums will burst. Bobby, Freddy and Junior find it pure torture to control their excitement. Perched on the observatory deck, over one thousand feet high, we watch, fascinated by the moving vehicles below; they look like busy ants or Matchbox cars crisscrossing New York's congested avenues. Mark, excitedly sitting on Father's broad shoulders, tries to grab a cloud. Yvette, cautious, envelops her two-year old in a touching maternal embrace and moves away from the parapet. Mark's head is nestled against her chest, and she whispers soothing words to her son. They make me think of the painting "The Virgin and The Child." Against his mother's heart, a serene calm gives way to Mark's dangerous trampling on his father's shoulders. His darker complexion and curly hair attract the attention of curious passers-by who, unfamiliar perhaps with the surprising complexity of genetics, might assume my baby brother is adopted.

Every morning, Uncle Farid, punctual like a Swiss watch, drops us off at the nearest subway station and heads to the store with Doris as we journey to conquer Manhattan, this fascinating, multicultural metropolis bursting with energy and people. We grab lunch on the go: hamburgers and hot dogs, a delight for my siblings' taste buds. In the evening, Aunt Doris greets us with the roast beef or the meat loaf that have earned her a solid reputation as an excellent cook.

Yvette and I take charge of the dishes, and my aunt confides, in the intimacy of the small kitchen where we stand side by side over the sink, that I should learn to take over some household chores. The spoiled daughter from the Islands is about to write a new page in the personal adventure of her life. At bedtime, the living room turns into a make-shift dormitory for my siblings.

Mark, who initially shared cousin Dennis's athletic trophies laden bedroom with his parents, agrees to join my grandmother and me in cousin Diana's quarters. My father has never seemed so in love, away from their Haitian life. He often puts his arm around Yvette's shoulder or caresses her hair silently. I am mesmerized by their unusual display of affection. My aunt blushes like an adolescent. It took a change of scenery, for the couple to discover each other again.

~ * ~

After supper, James, my father, and Doris help me fill out lengthy applications to several universities across the country. The United States is better equipped for the pursuit of scientific studies, reminds Father. He decided on the career path I will take and never gave me a choice. Docile, I will follow suit. I *will* graduate with a degree in the field of Health Sciences. James carved this mantra in stone, and, over the years, his desires became rule of law.

In the footsteps of my hero Albert Schweitzer, I will target a suffering humanity. We are all called to leave our mark on earth, I think philosophically to myself. I will fight diseases, through the lens of my microscope in a medical laboratory, and offer concrete proof of my passage in this world. Patients, who return home, grateful for their newfound health, will not know that, in the shadows, behind my test tubes, I played a part in their healing. Here I am, carried away on the wings of a vision full of altruism. I pour out my soul, in my letter of intent attached to the application forms: my deepest aspirations and the unshakeable determination that will lead me to the final goal. Doris corrects a few misspelled words and notes, as she hands me back the letter, "Well said! This letter and your transcripts from Haiti and France will open every door."

At the threshold of my university years, James and Yvette surround me. I measure their love by the concrete act of their presence by my side, not emotional outbursts. The main purpose of their trip was my physical and emotional support as I enter this new phase of my life. The young and naïve Haitian school girl, the Bachelière—high school graduate—from France is about to face a new challenge: her entrance to an American university and adaptation to a new language of studies. Uncle Farid and Aunt Doris offer the hospitality of their home until the academic year's second semester starts in January. It is too late for a September enrollment. My aunt points out, "She will perfect her English."

My family accepts the offer, providing, notes Yvette, "that they contribute financially to the household expenses." Despite strong protests from Farid and Doris Habdoul, Yvette insists, with her legendary pride, inherited from Charles Deveaux. A debate follows between stubborn family members. Tyler and Deveaux come out victorious. I admire their sense of honor. After their departure, at the threshold of my eighteenth birthday, a terrible sense of loss engulfs me.

~ * ~

I drag myself idly, in Uncle Farid's apartment, between my bedroom, the TV, and the refrigerator. Sadness consumes me. As in France, the actors of my childhood have left me to my solitude. Their absence weighs heavily on my heart. This month of July by their side helped me rediscover, albeit for only a brief halt, the joy of *family*. But life remains this moving force that requires me to pack up as soon as I slip into the comfort of a sweet routine, and to adapt to new places and the new faces who cross my path. My Parker pen begins a frantic race on the blank pages of my diary. I use the red pen today. The black one sleeps in its case. I pour my soul on paper, the outlet that will save me from depression.

A week later, Doris and Farid take on a situation that will eventually deteriorate. With their sales associate on maternity leave, they need my help at the store. It must be a pretext to chase away my gloomy thoughts. Alongside Uncle Farid, I learn the ropes of the business, the trade of my merchant ancestors. I watch, fascinated, from a front row, his tremendous power of persuasion with his female clients. He will drape one, in front of the mirror, with the shimmering cloth she selected, flattering her complexion or her figure, or approving with his expert opinion the choice of another hopeful client. I observe how Uncle Farid's dexterous fingers seem to caress the cloth. No buyer will resist this sexagenarian's charm. He has trade in his blood.

Doris, methodically, piles dollar bills in the cash register. They are the epitome of partners for life, in business and in love.

Standing at the sales counter, scissors in hand, I measure yard after yard of fabric for the customers, a shy smile planted on my face as I hand them their purchase. Regular clients, as at my ancestors' store in Bord-de-Mer, are entitled to the tiny cup of strong coffee prepared by Doris. In the heart of New York's dense humanity, she brings the exotic flavor of the Middle East. On Friday, my aunt hands me a hefty check at the close of business, after my first week of work. I open my eyes in disbelief; the amount offered exceeds all expectations. They insisted on giving me this "job," the salary of a salesperson was in their budget, they had assured me, despite my offer to help them on a voluntary basis. I suspect that in their own quiet way, they want to help me financially, while sparing my parents' pride.

During this memorable weekend where I taste, for the first time in my life, the fruits of my labor, I offer Uncle Farid a silk tie, and Aunt Doris a bottle of French perfume. They scold me as they kindly accept my gifts. Planning my next trip to Haiti already, my entire paycheck is spent, the following week, in a shopping frenzy for my family, searching, I guess, the illusion of their presence. My third check will be deposited, in its entirety, at the bank. I have never managed a bank account before. Doris introduces me to the art of balancing a checkbook. I promise myself to be frugal, in anticipation of a new wardrobe for my first semester at university.

~ * ~

The hippie style has flourished in the streets of New York. I swap sweaters and classic skirts for jeans and long peasant blouses. The 60's fashion and trends have seduced me. Change is in the air and is felt across America. Dr. Martin Luther King Jr. has shaken the status quo in the United States. The Civil Rights movement is born.

Heroism is punished but a hero never dies. His legacy lives on in people's hearts, by the resonance of his immortal words.

Gloria Steinem and Angela Davis, activist orators, question the immutable order of things. Bob Dylan's "Blowin' in the Wind" becomes the anthem of the times. Joan Baez protests the Vietnam War with her voice and her guitar. She sings "Where Have All the Flowers Gone?" and "We Shall Overcome."

From August 15 to 18, in Bethel, NY, the Woodstock Festival brings together, in a unique musical celebration of the '60s counterculture, a crowd of half a million youth, thirsty for peace, change, hope and love. Joplin, Baez, Hendrix give them a voice and a platform. Nostalgic, I remember France during the student revolution in May '68.

~43~

A newspaper ad catches my attention one evening: "Qualified teacher is offering affordable guitar lessons, on Saturdays in Greenwich Village."

"Absolutely *not*," Uncle Farid fumes. "Greenwich is a reservoir of losers, drug addicts and lazy hippies."

Aunt Doris, more malleable than my stubborn uncle, points out, "New York, like any large metropolis, has its quota of misfits. Greenwich simply holds a higher percentage. One must be vigilant everywhere."

I enroll, at the end of August, for the Saturday music class at Greenwich Village. I have dragged my guitar from place to place since Haiti but the opportunity to formally attend a class never presented itself before. I buy *The Village Voice,* the neighborhood newspaper that reports artistic activities and intellectual forums. As I browse through the Village's square, I reminisce, with a touch of nostalgia, about Michel and the booksellers on the banks of the River Seine. Autumn is fast approaching. The local artists, busy at their easels and paintbrushes, want to capture the last colors of summer on their canvases, before leaves turn gold and wilt to the ground. Giving free reins to my wild imagination, I mentally picture them with colored stains splashed on their white smocks and berets tilted on their foreheads, befitting the classic artist look evoked in novels and movies.

Mario, our teacher, runs dexterous fingers on the string instrument, drawing melodious sounds or rhythmic beats from his guitar. I am in awe at his talent and the elegance of his gestures. The slim, dark, curly haired Italian with the huge moustache seeks the obvious pleasure of his captivating audience composed of a dozen students, with shoulder-length hair, or large afros, heads towering over their ponchos or multi colored shawls. From the back of the room, it must be difficult to distinguish the men from the women. One Saturday after class, Mario invites me for a Coke. Trusting, guitar strapped on my shoulder, hair blowing in the wind, I follow our young teacher to the local café, convinced we will talk music. He grabs a hand that shyness does not let me remove. Is my passivity construed for encouragement? At the entrance of the coffee shop, deserted at this hour of the day, Mario pulls me close in a brusque gesture, and tries to kiss me. Flabbergasted, I muster a few seconds to react. His strong breath and thick mustache suffocate me. Above all, his boldness and audacity shock me. I push away the arms that are closing in on me, and throw a four-letter insult at him that would make my father blush, before running to the closest subway station.

I will not go back to Greenwich and cross paths with its colorful hippies again. To my uncle, puzzled by the abrupt end of my guitar lessons, I offer a silly pretext, reluctant to reveal the real reason for my decision and spare myself the embarrassment of his potential comments. However, Aunt Doris, aided by the legendary "feminine intuition" perhaps, is not fooled. I eventually confess my mishap to her, upon her insistence—a rather trivial incident, I admit, but nonetheless troubling for the naïve young woman learning to fend her way as a New Yorker. I foresee Doris will be more understanding than Uncle Farid. She might be the one who will help me navigate the complicated waters of American life. By mutual agreement, we decide that my uncle will be spared the uncomfortable truth…

My life as a young salesgirl is unfolding into a familiar routine, with no surprises or highlights. I am told I will keep my job until I start university in January, despite the return of their sales associate. I am not fooled: it is their way to help me financially while teaching me the value of work and discipline. I take over Doris's duties as barista for our special clients, and master the art of making great espresso coffee. I enjoy the fruit of my labor every Friday and my little nest egg is growing at the bank. I will turn eighteen next week. This country, whose nationality I inherited through my father, has yet to conquer my heart, in which Haiti still holds a special place. I am homesick for the land of my birth, and the family I am exiled from. New York, with its grey high-rises and its rainy days, feels like a heavy cloud hovering over my head. Engulfed by nostalgia, my sunny island becomes this paradise lost much too soon in my young life. Some nights, in the privacy of Cousin Diana's room, I cry myself to sleep.

~ * ~

From the first glance I exchange with David Rosenberg, at the counter of the delicatessen that supplies me with fresh bagels on Sundays, I fall for his radiant smile and congeniality. Enrolled in the Pre-Law program of the prestigious NYU, he is earning pocket money at his father's store on weekends. He assumes I am Jewish too, the first time we meet. Later on, he laughs his heart out, when he learns I am living with an uncle whose last name is Habdoul. I love pumpernickel bagels, which I serve with cream cheese, fruit and coffee for Sunday breakfast. In the footsteps of Leilah and Yvette, I set a pretty table with linen tablecloth and fresh flowers. This weekly ritual offers me the chance to thank Farid and Doris for their kindness toward me. I proudly tell them, as I keep my promise, "Aunt Doris, Uncle Farid, enjoy your rest on Sunday mornings. I will take charge of breakfast."

David, who has brown curly hair and broad shoulders, a sparkling smile on a clean-shaven face, calls me every evening on the telephone. We chat for hours, on topics ranging from the weather, to our future as students, and the great debates of the century. An extension line, conveniently installed in my room, offers me the intimacy I crave for my calls. Lying on Cousin Diana's big double bed, immersed in the pleasure of our nightly chats, I do not realize how fast time flies.

It feels as if we have always known each other. One day, he invites me to the movies.

"What will your parents say if they find out their son is going out with a Catholic of Lebanese descent?"

"What will your uncle say if he learns a Jewish man is courting his niece?" David replies, in echo to my question.

I realize, from the outset, that this budding relationship will lead nowhere. The ancient rivalries of our two cultures have been cultivated over the centuries and will continue for generations to come. But my emotional solitude weighs heavily on my heart, at this juncture of my life. I am so young, and so alone! Is it terribly wrong to have a friend, across cultural barriers? David has broad shoulders that would perfectly suit a friend's head to snuggle against. Friday night, I dress with the outmost care. Thanks to a successful blow-dry, my hair falls in light waves on my shoulders. Doris is accustomed to the familiar tone of David's voice on the phone. When he rings the bell at seven o'clock, he offers her a bouquet of roses and instantly wins her heart. David, freshly shaven, is sporting a white shirt under a khaki sport jacket of elegant cut. My little feminine vanity is pleased. As I expected, heart trembling with anxiety, my uncle keeps his distances and offers the cold shoulder to my date.

Farid sternly reminds me, the next morning, "Jews do not marry Arabs."

"But he is *just* a friend," I reply, in a defensive mode.

Ishmael, the ancestor of the Arabs, and Isaac, the father of the Jews, were both sons of Abraham, the Bible teaches us. This irony of life makes me smile. We also often share similar features and physical attributes, like the protruding nose. In the complicity of the movie theater's darkness, David seeks my hand. Dustin Hoffman's performance in *The Graduate* is extraordinary. Dinner at Antonio's

Place, his favorite Italian restaurant, follows. I have gained a few pounds since my arrival in the United States. Foods are said to be fortified with hormones in this country. Fable or not, I opt for a salad and grilled salmon in this irresistible Italian pasta sanctuary. At the corner of my street, David turns the engine off and leans over to kiss me. As our lips meet, I conclude that he will be more than a friend... even when the outcome will be inevitable and the barriers of culture and faith will prevail. On the landing in front of the apartment, I'm engulfed in David's arms; his fingers run through my hair as I close my eyes. My aunt and uncle, discreet, did not wait for my return to retire to their bedroom. I am relieved to seek the refuge of my bed without the glare of their inquisitive gaze. "Thank you, Aunt Doris," I murmur, eyes wide open fixed on the dark ceiling, David's shadow hovers over me. Sweet dreams follow and carry me away on their wings. David quickly becomes an integral part of my life.

I celebrate my eighteenth birthday, separated from my family by an ocean. No fireworks are launched in my honor. We talk every night, David and I, when Farid and Doris have gone to bed, and I can monopolize the telephone in the privacy of my bedroom. We go out on weekends. I did not dare inquire if his parents observe Shabbat. He surprises me with theater tickets to the musical performance *Fiddler on the Roof*. I emerge enchanted from my dive into the life of Tevye, his Jewish traditions, and the adventures of his daughters in their quest for marriage. David invites me to his younger brother Samuel's bar mitzvah one day and proudly displays his exotic Haitian friend around, offering colorful anecdotes on Caribbean life to the curious uncles and aunts from the Rosenberg and Levy clans. Lost in their Jewish human tide, I experience, for the first time in my sheltered existence, the uncomfortable feeling of an outsider. Prudent, David does not bring up the name Habdoul. Too many eyebrows would rise. Already his parents, whom I had met early in our friendship, had frowned in disbelief.

Sarah, David's older sister, is marrying Joshua at the end of November and invites me to be part of her bridal party. David will be my official escort, and I measure the depth of his feelings toward me. Marriage in the Jewish culture seems to represent the focal point of a young woman's existence, the realization of the wish formulated by some matrons, as they place the tiny "Jewish princess" in her pretty cradle: "May God grant me the joy to dance at your wedding."

Radiant under the canopy, the traditional ceremonial tent, Sarah and Joshua are about to bind their future together. The officiating rabbi, in his sixties, answers by the name of Moses. David stands by my side; biblical names of the Old Testament are coming to life all around me. The bridegroom, in line with tradition, kicks, with a swift thump of the heel, the crystal cup placed at his feet. The couple is reminded, through this symbolic gesture, of the fragility of life. The guests, hyper excited, shout in unison: "Mazel Tov!" Raw emotion fills the air. David leans toward me to plant a kiss on my cheek. Our lips brush by accident. He presses my hand in his. Wine flows in abundance and young and old toast to life: "L'Chaim!" On the first musical notes of "Hava Naguila," groups of men and women, in general euphoria and a segregation of genders, face off to dance to the tune of the popular song that runs through their veins and tighten their ancestral roots. Good wishes echo from everywhere and follow in our footsteps as we take our leave.

"Who are you, Myriam?" murmurs the little voice of my conscience, nagging. An electrifying desire consumes me, to go on a mission of self-discovery and claim my true identity. In this eclectic mix I am the product of, in the meandering journey that has been my life, I might have lost myself along the way. Head buried against his shoulder, in his car that evening, I catch myself dreaming of a future with David.

His heart seems to beat in unison with mine. He says, "We could perhaps get married, someday? Like Sarah and Josh, under a canopy?"

At the sound of these words, the tender magic of the moment instantly vanishes. I stare at David's profile. With his kippah sitting atop his curly hair, he displays the inevitable obstacle that will forever separate us. We could perhaps have married someday…if connections of the heart were all that mattered; if we had walked the aisles of a Catholic church and a priest in a white vestment had blessed our union. Our mutual silence spoke volumes on a sacrifice neither one could expect of the other.

~ * ~

I witnessed Farid and Leilah's touching reunion, siblings separated for years by life, and an ocean. In each other's arms, they abolished time and distances. That day I grasped the extraordinary scope of the phrase, "blood is thicker than water." These links bind families scattered around the world, who reunite as if they only parted yesterday, to toast at a marriage, share Christmas and Thanksgiving dinner, or cry their pain around a coffin.

I miss David terribly. I realize that blood supersedes desires of the heart sometimes. So many couples surrender, powerless to fight taboos and prejudices that make up the vast tapestry of this world. Love, often, is not enough.

~44~

Dressed in jeans and a poncho, I walk the streets of Manhattan, indifferent to the eager crowd bursting out of department stores. The post-Thanksgiving week symbolizes the official opening of Christmas shopping, this period of frenzy where the consumer society forgets the true meaning of Christmas. I am shivering and winter is at our doorstep. A hippie couple smiles at me as we cross paths on the crowded pavement. They recognize in me a soulmate, probably. The burning desire to belong to a group, a cause, or simply someone, consumes me.

I do not share this joy that floats in the air. Lost in a human tide of busy New Yorkers, a poignant feeling of loneliness engulfs me. My heart goes back to my first night at Saint Joseph, when I felt I had reached the deep abyss of despair. I am cold today, like I was on that unforgettable night, a young Caribbean girl distraught and lost in a frigid dormitory.

Alone in the midst of an agitated crowd, I let my tears flow, disconnected from the buzzing life teeming around me. I am a foreigner, an orphan, unattached, and without friends. Would it be so terrible after all, to marry David Rosenberg under the canopy? David, with his dark curly hair and broad shoulders, has crossed my path to leave a bitter void and my heart broke into a thousand pieces. Suddenly a perfect stranger approaches me out of nowhere and puts a knitted-gloved hand on my arm. "Why cry, Miss? You are so young. Life belongs to you!"

The white-haired gentleman quickly disappears in the crowd. Frozen by surprise, I do not attempt to hold him back. An angel has just visited me to remind me that life goes on, even without David. I dry my tears and catch the subway that will bring back me to Queens. I will join Farid and Doris, who will have kept my supper warm. The colorful graffiti on this old train suddenly look like a work of art.

~ * ~

From a dark corner of my brain, sprouts the crazy, absurd idea to meet, for the first time, my father's family. Inspired by Farid and Leilah's touching reunion, the Rosenbergs' display of strong family ties, frustrated by the absence of a mother I will never get to know and feeling the blues around Christmas time, this desire to locate the Tyler branch of my family has become an obsession. Strange, the total trust and blind faith of childhood... A child accepts the evidence spread before his eyes, of people and things, without challenge or hesitation. I do not recall, as a little girl, ever asking my father the question troubling my heart today: "Why don't you *ever* talk about your family?"

The obsession to know my paternal ancestors is growing day after day. I have inquired about the cost of a trip to Georgia. Seeking the refuge of my room after dinner, I dial the numbers provided by regional telephonic operators. Strangers' voices, visibly annoyed by my call, usually reply in a dry tone, that they do not know James Tyler and I certainly have the wrong number. One day, a broken voice whispers, "**Who** *are you*?" The female voice sounds laden with anxiety. I hang up, in sheer panic. That night, I heard the voice of "blood."

I have landed in Brunswick, a city located in the southeast coast of Georgia with its main street flanked by old lampposts, its historic district, and its port deserted at the end of the day. The quiet residential neighborhoods and mansions seem to come right out of the pages of Margaret Mitchell's *Gone with the Wind*. My taxi drops me back at the hotel and I pay the astronomical sum that has cost me this ride around town. Tomorrow, I will knock at Louise O'Brien

Tyler's door. Alone in an impersonal hotel tonight, I cannot sleep. The scenario of the last few days comes to mind:

Aunt Doris, discreet, joined me in my room. "The telephone bill lists several calls to Georgia."

I sensed the concern she was awkwardly trying to hide. Out of respect for this amazing couple who provides a roof over my head, I agreed to a heart-to-heart in the living room. In the spirit of total honesty, I unveiled my bold project: my salesgirl position at their fabric store allowed me the savings that will finance a Georgia trip to discover my Tyler roots.

Uncle Farid frowned. "Your father must be informed, Myriam."

"No, Uncle Farid. I am eighteen years old. For the first time in my life, I will take an adult decision."

I rode alone to the airport, to launch a very personal journey, a pilgrimage to my Tyler roots.

~ * ~

The taxi has come to a halt. Tall, naked trees line both sides of the road and likely create a thick, shady hedge in the summer. Hidden in a cul-de-sac at the end of the street, an old-fashioned red-brick structure appears. A staircase, built with lighter shade of bricks, welcomes visitors. Garlands of lights are hung on the closed shutters. Christmas will soon be upon us. I adjust my wool shawl. Overwhelmed by emotion, I hesitate, a fraction of a second, to ring the entry bell. There is still time to run, my tail between my legs, and disappear. The occupants of the house will never know. They ignore that, frozen with fear at the top of the stairs, her heart pounding, a young woman is desperate to come to her senses and get a grip on her composure. A long and frail silhouette emerges through the crack, a puzzling look on her face as she discovers my odd presence at her front door. "*Yes?*"

I instantly recognize the broken voice heard over the phone in NY. The timbre of her voice, the short, snow-white hair and discreet wrinkles around her eyes and lips betray her advanced age. Elegant and classy in her cashmere sweater, her universe is about to collapse.

"Allow me to introduce myself: I'm Myriam Tyler, James's daughter."

At these words, the elderly woman puts a hand to her chest. I am afraid, a fraction of a second, that she will pass out. We chat for a long time, seated side by side on the leather couch, near the fireplace. A steaming teapot has been placed on a small marble table. I politely accept a cup. Louise and Myriam Tyler, mother and daughter of James, gathered under one roof, through extraordinary circumstances, worthy of a novel.

Louise confesses the extent of her pain as a mother, and her powerlessness in the face of her late husband' intransigence. I must look perplexed, confused. Louise O'Brien Tyler, my paternal grandmother, sees fit to stop talking in parables and comes straight to the point: "Our ancestors were slave owners, before the Civil War. James, by marrying a woman of color, denied the ties of blood, and became an outcast for our family."

For the first time in my sheltered life, color prejudice hits me head-on, like a humiliating slap in the face. With eyes open to the crude light of my grandmother's revelations, the painful mystery connected to my Tyler roots is finally solved. I say nothing. Not yet. On the console, ancient and modern picture frames keep each other company. I locate Ross, the deceased grandfather, a bald gentleman who disowned his son without even knowing my mother, Claire. Have they met, beyond the grave? Does the family even know Yvette exists?

Louise examines the family picture of James and Yvette, flanked by Myriam, Freddy and Bobby that showcases Junior, their newborn. This color photograph, taken in a professional studio several years ago, never leaves me. The picture, dented in all four corners, has been my faithful companion, my tangible reality, my anchor, during my years in boarding school. The opportunity simply has not presented itself to pause again for the flash of a photographer with Mark, the newest member of the family.

My surprise will be dramatic for Louise Tyler. A silent desire for revenge is brewing in me. She offered me tea. I will serve her, piping hot, the naked truth about us. This truth must penetrate every fiber of her heart and expose the painful absurdity of this human tragedy. I remain on the defensive, a tigress ready to fight for those who are dear to her. Louise scrutinizes, with fascinated curiosity, each smiling face on the color photograph.

"Why did you hide the truth from us? Your mother does *not* look black."

This spontaneous cry from the heart, the relief Louise feels at the pallor of Yvette's skin complexion digs a profound wound in my soul. Louise cuts the thin line, the fragile connection that briefly linked me to my Tyler roots. Grief and rage engulf me and claim a deep corner of my heart. For twenty years, the Tyler family banished James from their lives. It is my turn now to bury Louise and Ross and relegate them to total oblivion.

"Claire, my mother, died in childbirth. My widowed father married my aunt Yvette after."

Grandmother, stupefied, opens her eyes wide in disbelief. I wave, in calculated slow motion, the other picture that never leaves me: my mother, smiling, in a red evening gown. Louise Tyler stares, silent, at the photograph, looking perhaps for a clue, a revealing sign of this black blood flowing in my mother's veins. Determined to preserve the element of surprise for my grand finale, I get up to leave. So many questions will be left unanswered for Louise. Her emotional hunger will remain unfulfilled. My hand on the door handle, ready to go, I pretend to suddenly remember I had another photograph to share with Louise. Stone-faced, I approach my grandmother for the final act, the twist before the curtain falls on the drama. "Oh, I forgot! I have a picture of Mark, the youngest sibling. He is the exact replica of my grandfather Charles."

With an unflinching gaze, I observe Louise who refuses, after two decades, the unconditional acceptance of her son's choice, who found his soulmate in Haiti. With life smiling on him and offering the promises of tomorrow, Mark exemplifies the innocence of childhood, in the face of an adult world laden with bigotry and prejudices. The elderly woman's wrinkled hands tremble. If his brothers and sister can fool the vigilance of those whose untrained eye does not detect the trace of mixed blood, Mark's looks, on the other hand, clearly proclaim our African roots, in the color photo. With an aggressive gesture, I retrieve my younger brother's photograph and slam out of the door. Halfway down the brick staircase, I turn my head, one last time: Louise Tyler, bent in half on the landing, sobs uncontrollably.

I left Pillar Street in a rush, looking for a phone booth. A taxi will soon arrive and sweep me away to my hotel. My only focus: flee, as fast as I can, a home where my family has no place, and where my father's photograph has been removed from the console. I am anxious to leave Brunswick, where all my illusions shattered in one thousand pieces.

~ * ~

The plane trip back feels painfully long. I cannot contain my joy to return to New York, the city of immigrants. Hugging Farid and Doris, I prolong the embrace to hide my emotions and the tears clouding my eyes. Our silence speaks volumes. The myth of the prodigal child's homecoming to claim her roots self-destructed with Louise's cry from the heart: *"Your mother does not look black."*

With the crumbling of my illusions, came the relief of liberation. Louise did not kill the fatted calf upon my arrival. She did not seek to hold me back when I left. Her tears were just a weak moment, the manifestation of her maternal cord and mother's instinct, in the presence of James's daughter who, unmistakably harbored in her veins the Tyler blood too. Louise Tyler, sobbing, mumbled, "I am *so* sorry." These words still resonate in my wounded granddaughter's heart. A silent remorse is ruining my peace of mind. I write her a letter, to free my conscience, but mail it without a return address. I've changed, a hundred times, the content of the letter. Finally, the words came gushing out in powerful jets:

"How does one forgive the person who betrayed her son and grandchildren? Yet, you have shed tears, when I left. On behalf of these tears, I offer you the hope that someday, I will forgive. James has learned to be happy without you. He built a life in our beautiful island of Haiti, the foreigner whose host country adopted him with open arms. He shares with his wife a relationship where the heart, not the nuances of the skin, defines their love. We cherish our father, and Leilah, my grandmother, shows her son-in-law the tenderness of a mother. You have deprived yourself of the joy of watching your grandchildren grow and flourish. You will never know their dreams and aspirations. And, I will have been deprived of the love and affection of a grandmother, which should have been my birthright. I understand your weakness. But on behalf of this weakness, I will vow to be strong; to partake of the happiness life has in store for me. The halo of mystery that surrounded you has vanished. I can finally make peace with my heart, as I also wish for you. Our meeting in Brunswick was ordained by destiny. Nothing in life is ever mere coincidence."

~ * ~

Christmas 1969. I cry my heart out tonight, when I regain the solitude of my bedroom. In eighteen years of existence, this is the second Christmas I spend away from my family. I have not traveled to Haiti, as my aunt advised, to handle the complicated formalities of a January first semester college entrance. Earlier, Farid and Doris placed a beautifully wrapped package under the tree for me: an elegant suede winter coat, lined with sheep's wool; a very generous gift in anticipation of harsh winters. We exchanged hugs and gifts at midnight. My aunt served hot chocolate. New York's temperatures are frigid. Doris and Farid did not intend to brave a cold winter night to go to midnight Mass. With young children, such an adventure proved difficult in the past. And over the years, habits settled in: the anniversary of the Savior's birth celebrated in slippers and a cushy robe, with the TV on, the Christmas tree lit, and a cup of hot cocoa warming the palms of our hands. Hot steam enveloped my face, and I closed my eyes to fight the tears, my heart sinking in deep melancholy.

Last year's Christmas away from home comes to mind: Notre Dame had organized a field trip to Megève, the famous winter sports resort village located in the French Alps at the foot of the Mont Blanc region. We traveled by train with our classmates, Karie and I, the day after Christmas, spent with her parents. A trip to Haiti, long and costly, was out of the question over the Christmas holidays if I also wanted to go on a ski adventure. My journey, this unforgettable Christmas recess, was marked by a series of "firsts": excited at the idea of my first train trip and the prospect of skiing on snowy slopes, I could not keep it together. The anticipation of these new pleasures supplanted the grief that was already brewing in my heart. We went on a shopping spree in Paris with Karie's mother: I selected a sky-blue ski jacket and thick matching gloves.

On the ski slopes of Megève, I experienced the exhilaration of my first launch on the white carpet that sparkled in the sun. I also endured the embarrassment of my first fall, buttocks on the cold blanket of snow, and skis pointing to the sky, under the gaze of a young, gorgeous ski instructor with the face of an Adonis. In the evening, gathered around the crackling wood fire with my classmates and Notre Dame's chaperones, we sampled the delights of the fondue savoyarde. By opting for our Megève's ski trip, I chose to be far from Haiti and my loved ones during Christmas holidays. These precious moments with my family can never be relived. The times lost cannot be replaced.

Diary and Parker pen in hand, shivering under the quilt, I become my own philosopher, in the solitude of my bed, on Christmas Eve in New York. I note: the path of life is a straight and narrow road that rarely offers the chance of a comeback. At every turn, we have choices to make. And each choice comes with its baggage of gains and losses, its amazing joys and profound regrets.

~45~

Boston - January 1970

This winter, acceptance letters from several universities begin to arrive. I receive partial scholarship offers, due to my academic performances in Haiti and France. But the most extraordinary news come from Bradford University in Boston. A full scholarship will be granted as long as I maintain a grade point average of 3.6 out of 4. Farid and Doris are thrilled at the news. I remain silent, paralyzed by emotion at the prospect of such financial relief this offer will represent for my family.

Bradford University. My aunt and uncle drive me from New York to Boston. Farid carries my bags, and Doris inspects the space I will share with Deborah, my roommate. My aunt's silent gaze poorly hides her obvious disappointment: my roommate's corner hints of a staggering mess. Bundled up in our winter clothing, we exchange farewell hugs. "Do not hesitate to call us," Farid recalls after one last embrace. Moments later, from the glass window pane, I watch their grey sedan disappear behind the naked trees, scattered around the campus in winter outfit. My eyes take in the new landscape that will surround my university years.

My guardian angels' departure brings a deep sadness upon me. I must, once again, adapt to a new life, new surroundings, meet new faces, and, if lucky, build new friendships along the way. Deborah, harboring faded jeans, a shell necklace and rings on all fingers of both hands, watches, with obvious curiosity, the preppy "bon chic bon genre" girl in a suede coat who just stands, like a muted idiot, in the middle of the room, feeling like a lost soul. My roommate has the great advantage of attending Bradford since September. I proceed, methodically, to put my clothes away, under Deborah's piercing gaze. She feels no need to grant me some privacy and finds it perfectly normal to just stare at me as I lay out my folded underwear in the drawers. Sitting cross-legged, like a Buddha, on her narrow bed littered with miscellaneous objects, she finally decides to break the ice. "Deborah Bernstein, first year art student."

Life and fate's irony will allow our opposite cultures to blend well together and get along just fine, over the months. This young Jewish woman with the disheveled hair, vegetarian by moral choice, will open my eyes and heart to a fascinating world: the hippies of the Sixties at the dawn of the Seventies.

~ * ~

I have enrolled in the Health Sciences program. Bearded professors in corduroy jackets welcome their new students—future doctors, researchers, physical therapists and laboratory technologists. My classmates harbor a studious look. My English proficiency, although respectable at the conversational level, might not fare well with the arduous classes in store for me as a pre-med student: anatomy, physiology, biology and organic chemistry looming on the horizon later on. Dog-tired, I always find Deborah in the evening, in her favorite position, sitting cross-legged on an unmade bed, strumming the guitar, just as I left her in the morning. I wonder if she even attends classes. The only child of a jeweler father, she exerts the minimum effort required to pass her courses and earn the famous Bachelor of Art degree her parents seem focused on. But Deborah confesses that this "piece of paper" is the least of her worries. Not when the world around her is deteriorating, when young people die in the war, and the speakers of the Civil Rights movement are losing their lives for the cause, in the hands of fanatics.

"I refuse to miss the extraordinary experience that is offered to today's youth to mark our passage in this world, to make a difference.

We live in times of protests, the world is changing before our eyes, and I want to be part of this change."

Deb is loquacious. I quickly realize that my study sessions will be held at the library rather than the comfort of my bedroom. My roommate intrigues me more and more. Her passion and non-conformism are contagious. One night, as I am feeling a tad melancholic, I agree to tag along with her to one of her meetings. All my suppressed desires for human justice and universal solidarity find an outlet, that evening. A group of long-haired students offer me, with their index and middle finger, the hippies' popular peace symbol and welcome, with open arms, the new recruit. At the dawn of the most decisive years of my life, an intoxicating freedom is unfolding before my eyes. Young, naïve and inexperienced, I suddenly must confront the temptations of sex, drugs, and atheism and face, head on, the gleaming lure of pleasures in all their surprising forms.

Noble causes always hold the power to thrill me. Influenced by Deborah and her friend Dany, tall, bearded Political Sciences major with dark, shoulder-length hair, I officially join their movement, the Anti-Vietnam War Rally. Am I looking for the emotional comfort of belonging to a group, and blend in the anonymity of a crowd? During my first college campus march, held on the grounds of a twenty thousand students' institution, flanked by Deb and Dany, I think of Michel, and the protests of May 68 in Paris. This time, I am free like the wind, unattached and unsupervised. Our group burns to change the world and brandishes signs with powerful slogans: *Flower Power! Peace Now!   Stop the Vietnam War! Make Love, not War!*

~ * ~

Deb and I talk for hours, at night, dreaming of a utopian world where we would live free and without constraints, in the huge garden of a brotherly community of young bearded men, wearing seashell necklaces and ponchos. Women, long peasant dresses and flowers in their hair would bake fresh rye bread. We would name our children Sky, Rainbow, River and Forest and raise them free to roam around fields of flowers, eating nuts and vegetables harvested from the land, and dance to the sound of guitars or the crackle of wood fires. Evenings, hands clasped together, we would form a chain of love, brothers and sisters singing in unison hymns to the moon, the stars, and to Mother Earth's generous bounty.

Deb invites me to travel with her this summer to a kibbutz near Jerusalem, where she plans to join forces with pioneers of Israel's vast reconstruction projects. My Lebanese ancestors would cringe in their coffins, at the thought of what they would consider an absurd adventure. Fierce advocate of a vegetarian way of life, Deb condemns the murderers who slaughter animals for human consumption and their accomplices who, like me, feed on their flesh. She will not even eat an egg, comparing it to the abortion of a fetus and the destruction of Life, which is sacred. Her narrow frame and slender body reflect her dietary lifestyle. Mine will flirt with obesity, if I give it the slightest opportunity. My plump grandmother Leilah's blood runs through my veins.

"We do not need to consume animal products for our health. Nature provides other sources of proteins to sustain our bodies," the wise oracle reminds. "Soybeans, nuts, green leafy vegetables, etc."

Sometimes, I enjoy the sadistic pleasure of frustrating my roommate, reminding her that plants, too, are living entities and deserve our protection. That day, taken aback and unable to offer a clever answer, she sulks. My corner of the room displays a large poster of the peace sign, popular symbol of the anti-war movement. Next to it and creating a visual cacophony, a life size image of Paul Newman in a T-shirt is also hanging on my wall. I find him gorgeous with his rippled muscles and sky-blue eyes.

"Yuck, Myriam!" Deb's mocking tone pierces me like an arrow. "Newman is so conventional."

"Who are you, Myriam?" whispers the voice of my conscience...

This mixture of the conventional and the New Wave perfectly define me. I am still at the age of self-discovery, in search of my true purpose in life, through the years, people and places I crossed on my journey. Deb, without the shadow of a doubt, proclaims her radical views on every rooftop and stands firm in her truth. Her politically charged posters, displayed above her bed, are a testament to her beliefs. A self-described chatterbox, Deb often leads me to the shores of a utopian world where peace and universal love would prevail. Happiness for her is an eternal dance, under the complicit stars, in harmony with the cosmos. Her great passion is the "cause." All her efforts converge toward one single goal: total peace on earth and the brotherhood of mankind, freedom of mind and body, perfect connection with the universe. The brutal return to reality is always painful.

Afterward, I must catch up on the hours of study time lost because of my great complacency and Deb's constant conversation. Bound by my scholarship's requirements, I begin to panic, wondering how I will maintain academic excellence while taking full advantage of college life and quench my thirst of new discoveries. The strong coffee swallowed in the late hours of the night fails to keep me awake. Dany, Deb's faithful friend, proposes amphetamines, with energizing and appetite curbing properties, a little pill loved by students, assures the tall, dark, long haired hippie. "Don't worry. Doctors even prescribe them sometimes."

Desperate at the prospect of failure on the eve of a biology exam, I let myself be tempted by Dany's pill, which keeps me awake all night, with strong palpitations and an anxious fear of death. I conclude that I will never be so naively adventurous again. Dany pokes fun at me. I despise this hippie whose ego is bigger than his brain, and who thinks, erroneously, that he is all-knowing. After that fateful night, Deb and I have a frank talk. My roommate agrees to respect my study time and to turn down her stereo. Fortunately, we share some common taste in music; otherwise I would take steps toward drastic measures. I miss moments of solitude and purchase a bookshelf, to help offer a semblance of privacy between our two spaces.

~ * ~

I fall in love with Daniel Mitropoulos, grandson of Greek immigrants, because he writes poetry. That is the truth, in its pure simplicity. I am surprised myself. This hippie goes against everything that symbolizes my universe. Dany embodies the male version and deep beliefs of my roommate Deb. Driven by my secret writing dreams and aspirations, I enrolled in an elective creative writing course. At the start of the second semester, I find myself sitting next to Dany, Deborah's faithful shadow. I always assumed the insolent, hairy hippie was romantically involved with my roommate.

"Myriam! What are you doing here, future scientist?"

I blush stupidly, like a teenager caught in a mischievous act. On this huge campus, it is my luck to find this career rebel, who finds pleasure in the unveiling and mocking of human nature's profound weaknesses, or secret aspirations. I retort, annoyed, "And you, Dany, you dropped your political science courses?"

He bursts out laughing, and I notice, under the thickness of the beard, a perfectly aligned set of sparkling white teeth. Over the months, I learn that Deborah is strictly a soul sister. When he is not discussing politics with his peers, or launching campus marches, Dany writes poetry! The mystery of his presence in Doctor Pat Cummings's Creative Writing class is now solved.

The persona intrigues me: this elusive figure made of contrasts, this Hercules with a sharp tongue and a poet's soul forces me, like Karie in Paris, into the hidden recesses of my intelligence. I enjoy talking to him, and picking his brain, while sipping strong coffee. Dany opts for plain water at the cafeteria, saving himself for the delights of exotic infusions in his studio. When he invites me to join him for chamomile tea at his place where we would burn aromatic incenses, I decline his offer, ever prudent.

After class, Dr. Cummings turns back her students' creative writing homework pieces. Mine bears the following annotation: "Good descriptions; strong images; a bit too romantic, perhaps."

Sensitive to criticism, it matters less to me that my grade is excellent. In my text, I invested my soul. Dany takes me by the hand and we sit on the aging grass. The fallen leaves around us indicate autumn's imminent arrival. The ambient air has become cool, already. My friend puts his arm around my shoulder and I feel safe against his chest as he says, "Myriam, romance is part of your charm. It defines who you are. Learn to love yourself as you are."

From now on, I will reply to the small voice of my conscience— the one that has taunted me over the years, with self-doubt and confusion: "Who are you?"

With newfound assurance and self-affirmation, I will reply, "I am Myriam, the romantic."

~46~

Deb, my roommate, always writes "human" in the official forms inquiring about race and ethnicity. A redhead with green emerald eyes, her ancestors emigrated from Eastern Europe. She knows too well the subtle stigma plaguing some Jews, who choose to remain on the defensive. I do not have my roommate's guts. But the question still bothers me. Born to a mixed union, I find it difficult to be cataloged. The choices listed limit me: Caucasian; Black; Asian; American Indian; Hispanic. Inspired by Deb and her ironic contempt for these forms, I made the decision to note "Unknown" in the race column. A little innocent pleasure on my part, to be taken at the expense of the statisticians who will have to decipher these forms and perhaps raise an eyebrow.

I undertake a theoretical exercise; the mental calculation of my maternal lineage and statistics: Claire and Yvette are fifty percent black by their Deveaux father and fifty percent Levantine on their mother Habdoul's side. Based on their physical attributes, it would be easy to imagine the sisters doing a belly dance and wearing the veil of Middle Eastern women. But for the United States, they would belong to the black race. What percentage of the dominant race defines its affiliation? Should we rely on the mathematical formula, or the physical characteristics of the person?

In Haiti, a country with a predominantly black population since their historical struggle for independence in 1804 and the victory of the slaves over the colonists, subgroups were established to physically differentiate ourselves from one another. Hair texture, coarse or soft, curly or straight, and the different shades of skin tones offer an elaborate classification that labels dark skinned Haitians as nwa (black, the majority), grimo (lighter skin with coarse hair), grif (a darker shade of grimo), marabou (dark skin, with soft, straight or wavy hair) and milat (mulatto). This category encompasses a segment of the population with skin tone of varying shades of light beige to brown, and soft, straight or wavy hair. They view themselves as descendants of distant ancestors, sons and daughters of colonists and their pretty slaves, when their shadows mingled in the haunting sensuality of tropical nights, or clashed when the master used his strength against weakness.

 In reality, the Haitian mulatto is the product of generations of men and women who, over the years and their passions, have mixed all types of hair and skin colors. The clever game of genes and chromosomes did the rest. Outside Haiti's borders, exposed to a world often divided over ethnicities, these mixed-race individuals, viewed as light-skin in the land of their birth, suddenly face an identity crisis as they feel, for the first time perhaps, the crushing blow and sting of color prejudice.

Sometimes a white visitor decides to plant his roots in Haiti, and bring "a touch of milk to the coffee" of our race, as some locals comment with caustic humor. The word blan (white) often implies a "foreigner" in our Creole vocabulary rather than a skin color. So, we have invented a composite new word with a fascinating etymology, making reference to black visitors called blan-nwa (white-black). My conclusion: the human race moves and changes in an eternal waltz called Life. Wanting to catalogue races is a daunting task that will become more and more complicated, in a world increasingly complex, with more and more subgroups.

~ * ~

Sitting cross-legged on the bare floor, twenty of us are gathered at Dany's place: bandana around the forehead, colorful ponchos, shoulder length hair or wide afros, the group listens to Bob Dylan. Cloudy marijuana smoke escapes toward the ceiling. We dream of a new world, where universal love would replace war. Wearing faded jeans and a long peasant blouse, I quietly pass the "joint" around.

The heavy smell that floats in the air seems to lift me from earth and take me up to another sphere. I close my eyes, lulled by the music, and a strange, overwhelming feeling of well-being.

Dany whispers, "Come on, Myriam, try it at least once. You are depriving yourself of a super experience."

I shake my head from side to side, and gently let it fall on his shoulder. Marches and slogans? Yes! Marijuana? Deborah glares at Dany and advises, with an irritated tone, "Leave her alone."

My roommate tries to hide her disappointment at Dany, for whom she harbors secret romantic feelings, I suspect. I told her we are dating. Surprised at first, Deb thanked me for my honesty. "Be careful, Myriam. He may claim from you what you are not prepared to give."

She is not referring to sexual freedom which, for her, is not an issue, provided feelings are mutual, but to Dany's overbearing personality and revolutionary character. He might require perhaps that I make a clean slate of the principles and beliefs which, so far, have governed my life. Dany, with his fiery eyes, dark hair floating on his broad shoulders, dressed in an eternal poncho and leather sandals, reminds me of a prophet of biblical times. This hippie exerts a strange fascination over me. Known for his non-conformism, he goes against all my principles in his virulent stands. But when we are alone, the poet finds the perfect words to melt my heart.

~ * ~

We shout peace slogans, emotions at the height of passion, around Bradford's large campus, calling for immediate troop withdrawal from Vietnam. Then, exhausted, we meet at Dany's. We dine on alfalfa, sesame seeds, bread and crudités. In a corner of the studio where a strong smell of incense burns, is a large bed covered by a bright, Mexican patchwork quilt. Protesters have calmed down.

Some are asleep on the bed, in a mingling of the genders. Others are kissing, lying on the carpeted floor, and exchange intimate gestures without an ounce of self-control. Are they going to make love, under everyone's gaze? Dany watches me silently and gets too close. His glassy look troubles me. I turn my head, confused. On the wall painted with strange colors, a huge poster of the peace sign hovers over us.

Dany placed on my wrist a P.O.W. bracelet bearing the name of a prisoner of war, symbol of my new adherence to the cause. His name: George. Somewhere in this vast U.S.A, a mother is mourning the absence of her son. Is he married, and a father? What were his dreams and aspirations? Will he return some day, and get a hero's welcome? Did his captors kill him and hide his corpse in the muddy rice paddies of Vietnam? Will he be flown home, asleep in a coffin wrapped in the star-spangled flag? Posthumous honor will never replace a life lost at war. I will always keep this bracelet, talisman of an unforgettable era when, as youths full of dreams and illusions, we hoped, in a contagious excitement, to change the world. Inspired by Dany and Deborah, I embraced the hippie movement with enthusiasm. To be conquered by Dany was easy. Under the influence of the "flower power" ideology and the peace slogans, I have become one of Dany's faithful shadows.

The day he invites the Island girl to join him at Bradford's artificially heated pool, I freeze, awestruck: Dany greets me at the foot of the wet stairs. I remain motionless, breathless: the bearded giant has emerged from the water and towers over me, like an ancient Greek statue, a valiant warrior of mythological times, a sculpture of muscles and harmonious curves, exposing, like translucent pearls, small drops of water on his broad, naked chest. Moved by this living illustration of the canon of beauty, I can't help but gulp. Dany slides with me into the warm pool, holding me close in the shelter of his arms. Our eyes lock. He takes my lips in a deep embrace that leaves me stunned.

Eyes closed, weak at the knees, I am convinced I will faint and may even drown. *You are lost, my daughter.* The small voice of my conscience takes pleasure in taunting me. The proximity of his body, hard as steel, puts me in a state of turmoil. Dany reads my silent panic like an open book and seems to madly enjoy it. He whispers, in the hollow of my ear, "Myriam, your inexperience drives me crazy," and I feel all weight leave my body, to become fluid as the water that caresses us in its reassuring warmth. Under his bold lips and prying fingers, all notion of time capitulates.

Over the months, this reserve eventually discourages Dany, strong proponent of sexual freedom. During the Christmas holidays recess, I fly back to seek the refuge of my island and reassuring comfort of my family. When I return, Dany breaks up with me, because I refuse to partake of the intoxicating experience of marijuana and of a sexual relationship with him. My inexperience moved a chord in him at the start of our romance. He finds it unacceptable today and calls me a hypocrite because, during our marches, I have chanted, alongside him, the slogan: "*Make love, not war!*" His departure leaves a poignant void in my emotional life. My studies begin to suffer.

Deb is watching me with piercing eyes. Did she guess my dilemma? There comes a time in life when one must express their choice by a concrete act, reminds my roommate…. Dany returns one day, and presents an ultimatum on a silver platter of reconciliation. At the height of despair, his kisses mixed with the salt of my tears, I almost say *yes*…Daniel Mitropoulos, my Greek statue carved in the perfection of the human stone, disappears from my life, without even looking back. Deb, whose acute radar has captured the drama I tried hard to conceal, brings me some chicken soup from the cafeteria: "comfort food," as they call here this magic soup able to warm the heart or heal the flu. My roommate has violated her vegetarian principles, out of pity for me. For the first time since my arrival at Bradford, I skip class and stay in bed the entire day.

~ * ~

Time, the great healer, does its work. The demands of my arduous paramedical classes force me to regain control of my life. Deb no longer invites me to her group's meetings, whose headquarter is Dany's studio. She does not breathe a word when she returns—to salvage the fragile balance of my heart. I've agreed however to attend, with the anatomy class, a "mixer" organized by Cornell University's medical students in New York—a providential opportunity for a quick visit to Farid and Doris. I finally can let go of the crushing weight of the Vietnam War, and delve in the pleasure of a dark and noisy dance floor.

Dany's image arises in my mind at times, when I see a hairy hippy crossing campus. With the objectivity of hindsight, I am now able to see, in a whole new light, the one who made my heart race: this controversial figure who favored the purity of water and infusions over coffee, did not hesitate to damage his body in the abusive use of marijuana. In the name of peace, he declared war on the driving principles of society. He made a point to challenge the established system, because it is always easier to destroy than to build. Dany was searching, in the company of gurus, for answers to his metaphysical questions and hoped, with words, to change the world, rather than confront life. His stunning arrogance was perhaps a mask for his weakness?

My P.O.W. bracelet is put away in a drawer. George, prisoner of war, will always have a special place in my heart. But I am ready to continue the journey today, to add another chapter to my story. Deborah and I no longer have much to share, each lost in our own closed universe. At the crossroads of our lives, the time has come to part our separate ways. We silently wish that cohabitation ceases. I cling to my books to forget Dany. For my second year at Bradford, resolved to remove any obstacle that might hinder my studies, I promise myself to dodge a potential failure for the toughest class of the pre-medical branch: Organic Chemistry. It is vital for me to pass the course and salvage my scholarship. As for the BAC in France, panic engulfs me. But there are no guardian angels to watch over me today. I am utterly alone, in an increasingly competitive world totally indifferent to my academic failure or success.

Dr. Shapiro, in his eternal tweed jacket, bears a striking resemblance to Professor Calculus in Hergé's *Tintin* series. He is perhaps a genius of the Nomenclature of Elements but he lacks empathy. At the beginning of the semester, his unforgettable words caused me to shiver: "Eighty percent of you will fail Organic Chemistry. If you want to be of the twenty percent that succeed, focus on nothing else, except passing my class this semester."

~47~

On October 12, 1954, Hurricane Hazel struck Haiti, causing more than a thousand deaths, the destruction of vital food staples, entire crops, cattle, and infrastructures.

As a result of this horrific natural disaster, foreign aid poured in, and food programs, dubbed "sinistre" by the population, made its appearance in the country.

A scene arises from memory: a three-year-old girl, standing by the wrought iron bay window of her grandmother' dining room in Bois Verna, watches, eyes widened in horror, the furious wind gushes attack the backyard trees. Coconut trunks bend down, in a terrifying genuflection toward the ground, at the sound of a mournful whistle.

Her grandmother, visibly agitated, repeats over and over again, like a robot, "And the Word was made flesh, and dwelt among us."

The little girl learns, years later, that one of those atmospheric monsters was on a path of destruction when her mother died.

Since then, she has developed a phobia of hurricanes and air turbulences which prove that Man is only a small, obscure, insignificant and helpless dot in the grand theater of Life.

The Creator of heaven and earth is also the master of wind and thunder, volcanoes and earthquakes. The girl understands, at a very young age, that life is precious, but so fragile also.

~ * ~

In the heart of Bourdon, a house with beige and brown trim hangs on a steep, wooded hill away from the hustle and bustle of the busy road that links Port-au-Prince and its fancy suburb Pétion-Ville. The large, cement structure's roof is built of reinforced concrete, to defy the strongest hurricanes of the Tropics. Gutters discretely hang along the *concrete roof, to catch rain water and feed an underground reservoir. Water is a precious commodity.*

Intricate wrought iron bars surround every window and wrap around what was once an open porch. Climbing ivy has mingled with the metal's design to give the flowery veranda the illusion of an indoor garden. Occupants can admire the splendid Bay of Port- au-Prince, and the most glorious sunsets of the firmament.

A tanned, dark-haired woman in a yellow floral dress is resting on a rattan lounge chair. The tall, male silhouette approaches and leans over to kiss her. They smile. Their black and golden hairs intertwine a short time. The woman with the ripe, peach complexion evokes a pretty garden flower, whose fragile stem may break. But the handsome man will sweep her off her feet, engulf her in his arms, and carry her in an eternal waltz.

I am six years old and in my child's eyes, James and Yvette form the most beautiful couple in the world. They will later achieve the tour de force of harmonious living in the heart of a dangerous dictatorship. The picture of happiness is this scene, suspended in time and space, of a man and woman in love.

This perfect happiness, I want to live too, one day, when my Prince Charming will come knocking at my door. As in any respectable fairy tale, the prince of my heart will be young and handsome, and we will have many children.

I run to take refuge in the couple's arms, and I shout, smiling at life, "Mommy! Daddy!"

This scene that portrays happiness in soft, pastel colors is the last picture I keep, tucked away in my heart, of a perfect childhood memory. I do not know it yet, but the very foundation of my own origins will be shattered, a year later.

Everything can be taken away from us, at the speed of light. Nothing is ever the same, after. I would also learn a painful truth that will haunt me my whole life: the past cannot be changed; the future is fragile; only the present is palpable.

But this image of happiness, this moment frozen in the perfection of the present minute, has been, the time of a flash, mine to behold.

PART III

Arrival

~48~

Dr. Michael Roye, tall, with brown wavy hair, a trimmed, short beard and John Lennon-style glasses, has a pleasant face. He is replacing Dr. Shapiro, on medical leave, he informs a stunned audience. The students can hardly believe their good fortune. The new teacher, classic suit and tie, becomes the lifeline of the students who surround his desk like a swarm of bees. Once class is empty, I timidly approach the platform. Dr. Roye offers a sparkling smile and a perfect row of teeth which push me to conclude silently that he is not a coffee drinker. Such a personal thought makes me blush.

Armed with courage, I expose my dilemma: my shortfalls for a subject matter that has given me, since France, a huge challenge; my struggles to keep up with Dr. Shapiro's class without hope of rescue. The language barrier is evoked as well, a fact that cannot be ignored. Dr. Roye shows a keen interest in this latest revelation. I expect the logical question that follows: "Where are you from?"

In France, my Haitian origins never failed to raise people's curiosity. They wanted to learn more. They would evoke Papa Doc. I spoke of our beaches and eternal sun. I clarified for some, whose notions of geography were rusty, that I was from *Haiti*, not the Pacific island of Tahiti. In the United States, it is the French language that always fascinates, and gives a kind of aura to the French speakers, regardless of their country of origin.

"Parlez-vous français?"…the favorite question to escape the lips of those Americans who took high school French.

"Oui, oui," I always respond, knowing it will delight them.

I'm happy to play the francophone foreigner card with my teacher. We leave a deserted class. Dr. Roye agreed to help me bridge the gaps for Organic Chemistry. We will meet the next day for a tutoring session in the empty conference room adjacent to our chemistry class. For the first time since Dany's departure, I dream of flowery landscapes and sun. I wake up, a smile on my face, under Deborah's suspicious gaze.

Dr. Roye's passage at Bradford will be a short one. An alumni member of Bradford, he has kept close links with the school. Dr. Shapiro's best student agreed to fill an urgent vacancy for his bed-ridden teacher. An intern of OB/GYN at Boston Memorial, affiliated with Bradford's school of Medicine, these few hours teaching chemistry outside hospital walls offer him a welcome change of pace. With patience, Michael Roye manages to reconcile me with organic chemistry. And the miracle I was praying for happens. My fear gradually evaporates.

But as final exams approach, I swallow my pride and beg our young teacher to grant me additional tutoring sessions for another few days. I confess the need for me to keep my scholarship, and the obligation, incumbent upon me, to maintain academic excellence. He accepts with good grace.

~ * ~

Final exams will soon begin. Hours of stress and anguish are waiting on the horizon. On the menu: Anatomy II, Physiology II, Microbiology I, Genetics, my favorite course, and the last exam of the semester, Organic Chemistry. Review sessions are scheduled in class, a wise initiative of Michael Roye. Dr. Shapiro will return to his post the following week to administer the final exam. At this thought, my heart is consumed with sadness.

Dr. Roye will resume his internship at Boston Memorial. The week before the chemistry exam, he says his goodbyes to a class saddened to see him leave the post we knew was temporary. His words of encouragement feel like a balm upon our hearts. Hope shines on the horizon. My classmates surround our young teacher, as they did on the first day. A student with an angelic smile approaches so close to him, her hair touches Dr. Roye's shoulder. Annoyed by this image, I remain quietly in my corner, brooding over my disappointment.

"Myriam, my daughter, would you, by any chance, be jealous of your handsome teacher?" whispers the small voice of my conscience, taunting. Michael Roye has been my lifeline for the past several weeks. During our tutoring sessions in the conference room, we shared confidences about our families, our mutual tastes and aspirations. He expressed great interest in everything affecting my person, my country, my travels, and my family. I could not help but think about Dany who never inquired about these details. Dany's great passion was the "cause," and the satisfaction of desires, his apparent birthright.

Flabbergasted, I came face to face with him last week. As he used to do at the start of Dr. Shapiro's class, Dany had come to wait for me at the entrance of chemistry class. He seemed sure of himself, resolved, as if we had only parted yesterday, with plans to meet again the next day. I had not seen him in months, but the wound in my heart had not completely healed.

"Myriam, I must talk to you." The authoritative tone admitted no rebuttal.

"Leave me alone, Dany."

Just as he tried to grab my hand and pull me toward him, Dr. Roye arrived for his class. Surprised by the scene unfolding between his student and this bearded hippie in a ponytail, he stopped a second to inquire with concern, "Is everything all right, Miss Tyler?"

I nodded "yes," embarrassed. Class was about to begin. I resigned myself to listen to Dany, so he would quickly disappear.

Not being able to drag me into his bed probably still frustrates him. Yet he's never lacked women followers from his group, too happy perhaps to satisfy his desires. I imagine the forbidden fruit must have a strong power of attraction, for the hunter. But I have turned the page. My wardrobe has changed: a classic look had replaced my peasant blouses. I no longer wear bandanas on my forehead, just a few flowers in my hair occasionally.

Yes, Dany, I have changed. If you interpret it as a betrayal to the cause, it is your choice. I will never forget our shared emotions when we marched for peace. I learned a lot by your side. But you asked too much of me: what I was not ready to offer any man.

In the face of disappointment, last week, Dany swore to have the last word. He turned toward me with a sultry look and condescending tone. "Look at you," he said. His fiery eyes could hypnotize. "You are no longer one of us. I do not know you anymore."

As he turned away to disappear from my life, I entered the classroom under the curious gaze of the students.

~ * ~

Michael Roye invites me to join him for a cool drink at the cafeteria, in lieu of our tutoring session. It is not uncommon for students and teachers to sit together in small groups at lunch, but this is the first time I am in Dr. Roye's presence outside chemistry class, or the conference room. He wants to offer some words of wisdom before the final exam. I have become his project, I presume: the student who, against all odds, will pass her test, and surprise Dr. Shapiro. To fail is no longer be an option. Dr. Roye generously offered his help. My show of gratitude will be my success.

"Stop your reviews and sleep early, the night before the test. Above all, keep calm and do not panic."

Dr. Roye leans over toward me. What secret is he going to share? At close range, his narrow, silver rimmed glasses accentuate the emerald transparency of his eyes. He asks, "Do you know it is forbidden for faculty members to socialize with students?"

Taken aback, I pull my head away, furious with him, and especially with myself. The sting of Charles Deveaux's pride is rushing to my face, like a raging sea. I am about to explode. "I hope you do not believe we are socializing, Dr. Roye," I say. "I have every intention to cover your tutoring fees. I only have one goal: to pass my test. Afterwards, I wish never to see you again."

"Yet, for my part, I would love to see you again."

Michael Roye, with a twinkle in his eyes, bursts out laughing. Bewildered, my anger evaporates in smoke. Totally confused by his laughter, I wonder if I am the victim of a joke but cannot grasp its humor. A contagious sparkle lights his eyes. I am not sure to have heard right. The ambient noise, certainly. Did he truly say he would love to see me again?

Suddenly serious, Michael reminds me he is not a member of the teaching staff at Bradford, and therefore, totally free to socialize with whomever he pleases. He wants the opportunity to get to know me better. This time, I hear correctly, unequivocally. Sitting across from me at the table, our juice glasses empty, he seems to delight in the display of my emotions, which have gone from anger, to confusion, to total surprise. The young professor, who finds chemical formulas fun to juggle with, loses his comfortable assurance when he confessed, in a solemn tone, "I noticed you since my first day as substitute teacher. You looked different, exotic: a quiet demeanor, in your 'flower child' outfits; your adorable accent; your concentration in class and furious note-taking, a desire to absorb everything; your silent panic written in a melancholic gaze; your jet-black hair, adorned with tiny daisies, which surely cause men to turn around in your footstep."

The cat has gotten my tongue. I sit still, speechless, dumbfounded.

Michael Roye continues, visibly agitated, "The long-haired gentleman who waited for you before class, is he just a friend? Myriam, is your heart free?"

Dany was the involuntary instrument of Fate. His presence by my side, his proprietary gestures triggered, in Michael Roye, a feeling that has shaped our humanity since the beginning of times: the pangs of jealousy.

Should I view that day as an accidental encounter, or the universe's master plan at work? Would Michael Roye's newfound boldness have come to pass, had he not witnessed my last heated exchange with Dany? Michael has asked the key question that will require me to probe the deep abyss of my soul. Is my heart free? Through my journey, and with the people I have met along the way, I have favored honesty of feelings and clarity of truth, over grey areas of secrecy and ambiguity. Nothing is simple, however. My heart is free but still carries fresh traces of Dany.

"Can we forget the past?" Sister Marie Laurence's students asked, in religion class, one day. And the answer, full of wisdom, surprised us all: "No. But the past helps us shape the future."

Dany is part of a past that I will never forget. He has helped shape the human being I am today. His passage in my life has left traces. I will never be indifferent to peace in the world, and to mankind's cruelty toward animals. But, we parted ways, at this juncture of our lives. It will take a little time to start on another course.

~ * ~

My first official date with Michael, outside of Bradford, will follow my chemistry exam. It's a symbolic choice: Chemistry, once more, will bring us closer. My jeans with the flowery patches will be traded for stylish black pants and a silk blouse will replace the long flared ones with cross-stitches. My blow-dried hair will float, loose, on my shoulders, and I will revive my make-up bag's treasures: mascara, blush and nail polish, futile items Deb convinced me to retire from circulation. Beyond all expectations, I pass Chemistry with flying colors! Dr. Shapiro, who resumed his post, is overjoyed.

As a token of my appreciation, the architect of my victory is invited out by his pupil. Michael picks me up, and we drive to the fanciest restaurant in town. I can finally fulfill my desire to enjoy a juicy steak again, free of guilt, under the amused gaze of my companion, who hears every detail of my vegetarian phase. Other confidences naturally follow. Michael is charming, serious, yet humorous too. The kiss we share, as we part for the evening, seals what our hearts already guessed.

During one of his rare weekends of freedom from hospital duties, Mike drives me to New York and surprises me with two Broadway tickets for *Hair*, a musical tribute to the hippie movement and its deep emotions. I am able to enjoy the show, this celebration of a bygone era of my life. My aunt and uncle, impressed by Dr. Roye, welcome him with open arms. We are officially dating now. The memory of Dany, like turbid marijuana smoke, has faded. Over time, Michael symbolizes the breath of fresh air, the solid rock, the calm waters my heart has been yearning after.

I am afraid to wake up from a dream too wonderful to be true. But Mike is right here, next to me. When I'm engulfed in his arms, our hearts beat in unison. No, I am not dreaming! I have simply reached the finish line at this stage of my journey.

~ * ~

"Good luck, Myriam!"

"Good luck, Deb. I hope you find what Life has in store for you."

We hug as we part ways. I will never forget Deborah, and our endless discussions on Life. Some people, met along our path, will leave traces of their passage. Michael found me a place, strategically located at walking distance of the university and the hospital, to share with two of his female colleagues. A studious atmosphere prevails in this apartment where we each have our own bedroom. My own sanctuary, at last, that will be a reflection of my soul.

We go out on weekends when Mike is free, a pleasure all the more valuable as it is rare. My studious temperament adjusts, with serenity, to the demands of our respective schedules. We both aim at excellence. I hope to graduate, with honors, in the field of Health Sciences.

Fate has been kind to me. It took me by the hand, and led me to still waters, where Life was waiting, to offer me my share of happiness that had been, all along, reserved for me. I believe in the Creator, Lord of the stars and the universe, the orchestra conductor who ensures the intricate balance of His creation and offers, in His complacency, the display of His marvelous wonders. If, like these hippies, the "flower children," I dreamed of a world where pollution, hard concrete, selfishness and hate would give way to the beauty of flowers and universal, unselfish love, I am fed up with stars-gods and gurus. I long for the comforting shadows of childhood churches and the unapologetic simplicity of religious faith.

The trivial side of my human nature stakes its claim also, I must confess: I am happy to be able to enjoy a steak, away from Dany and Deborah's accusing glares. I aspire to find, on a crowded dance floor and at the heart of loud music, the magic of dance, and forget, one brief moment, the horrors of the Vietnam War.

I think of you sometimes, long-haired companions of a bygone era for me. Will you go to Kathmandu, Dany, like so many brothers, looking for Universal Truth? And you, Deborah, with whom I celebrated, at your parents' home, the feast of Passover, tasting the bitter herbs and unleavened bread, will you raise your children, Sky and Rainbow, naked and free, flowers among fields of colors, in communion with Mother Earth?

Who knows? Dany might finally realize that you are his soul mate. I will then share, with all my heart, your joy. Through the "cause", the drugs, nature and your gurus, it is God, perhaps, that you've been seeking. When Destiny came knocking at my door, enlightened by our shared experiences, I recognized its face.

~ * ~

The perspective of meeting Mike's parents, I confess, intimidates me at first. Mike, whose teasing ways have the gift to annoy me at times, comments with a wink, "If we get married one day, our mixed children will speak English, French, Creole and Arabic and have the colors of the rainbow."

Never before has the word "marriage" escaped his lips. Confused, I wonder if I should take him seriously. And why the mischievous smile? Is he laughing at me? The wound in my heart, caused by Louise Tyler, still hurts. Brunswick is a dark cloud over me. I could never bear a second rejection. Mike realizes that his tone should be a solemn one. He holds my hands and locks his eyes into mine, to make amends and voice his unconditional love.

"Do your parents approve of our relationship? I am nervous about our meeting. Their opinion matters to me."

"Darling, I plan to spend my life with a fascinating, mixed background young woman from the Caribbean islands. My father and mother are not as close minded as you think. Their only concern is my happiness."

The exotic Haitian is greeted with open arms. Dr. Stephen Roye and his wife, Kathryn, are a charming, refined couple. Everything around them exudes good taste and measure: a nice home, warm and inviting, a library with rows of thick, medical books. Michael, an only child, will follow in his father's footsteps. A beautiful yellow cat purrs near the fireplace. Photographs of a mischievous-looking little boy surrounded by a younger version of Stephen and Kathryn abound on the mantel. Peaceful happiness reigns between these welcoming walls. As Mike and I sit by Kathryn at dessert, the albums of a happy childhood come to life for a little boy with a mischievous face and disarming smile. With each page, a flurry of anecdotes follow—a priceless look into Mike's past.

Late that night, I remain curled up against him, in the privacy of his Volkswagen Beetle. My entire being already belongs to the man who's won my heart. He is the one who's always been waiting for me at the end of the road. The mood, tonight, is light, as he murmurs sweet nothings in my ear. In an intentionally angelic voice, I ask him, with a coy smile, "Must I conclude I received a marriage proposal today? I am not so sure."

Mike burst out laughing. "Patience, Myriam, is a virtue."

~49~

I could never conceive of Christmas celebrated outside of Haiti's borders. The previous year, I had been happy to return to my family, far from Dany, Deborah, and the Vietnam War protests. I had not breathed a word about my controversial, long-haired boyfriend to protect my family's emotions and spare them a collective heart attack. Marguerite, without a doubt, would have died at the sight of Dany flaunting his pony tail in the December breeze, his long shadow against the flame-colored sunset skies on the hills of Bourdon.

To my dear nanny's favorite question, on each of my trips, as she held me tight in her arms and whispered, "Ou gen yon ti menaj?" I would invariably reply, leaving her great curiosity in a vacuum, "No, I have no romantic attachment or special someone. My studies take up all my time."

To keep up with tradition on Christmas Eve, the entire family, dressed in festive clothing, drove to Midnight Mass at St. Louis de Gonzague. Dr. Toussaint, Grandfather's longtime friend and former student of St. Louis, provided, year after year, the tickets that would ensure us a seat inside the crowded place of worship. At the stroke of midnight, the faithful of the church rose to their feet to sing "O Holy Night." Overwhelmed with emotion, I pretended to have a speck in the eye, my poor attempt to hide my tears from my younger siblings. Bobby, seventeen, a high school senior, threw a half-amused, half-ironic look at me.

His love life was surrounded by mystery. Tall like our father and grandfather, he made ladies' heads turn. Marguerite had divulged his secret to me: One night, Bobby did not return home. Knowing all too well the constant dangers of living under a dictatorial regime, Yvette and Leilah's emotions and sheer panic got out of control. The next morning my six feet tall brother had received a humiliating spanking from our father.

I glanced at James from the other end of the church pew. Over the years, my father had put on a significant amount of weight. Of the three women in his life, who was the guiltiest? Yvette, Leilah and Marguerite showered him with attentions and flattered his food indulgences. I was away from my father now. Life had separated us, I thought, with a grain of melancholy. At the end of the mass, hugs were passed round, followed by the traditional dinner at Le Rond Point, whose menu carried my favorite dish of snails in garlic butter.

Gift exchanges took place the next day around the colorful Christmas tree. We had all grown over the years. Except for five-year-old Mark, Santa Claus no longer left beautifully wrapped presents under the bed by our slippers: the toys we, as children, had hoped for and lusted after, the entire year. Baby Jesus' stable, and the village of Bethlehem, at the foot of the tree, was an award-winning artistic production, created with starched papier-mâché, hardened to imitate the hills and crevasses of an entire village. In an isolated corner overlooking the flickering village lights, stood the humble stable with the thatched roof, where the divine infant laid, in a manger, in a bed of hay. Wooden figurines of Mary, Joseph, the shepherds and the Three Wise Men on their camels, surrounded the newborn. In Bourdon, Yvette had maintained her mother's village tradition in Bois Verna. Leilah always reminded her daughters, "Children, never forget the true meaning of Christmas: the humble birth, in a stable, of our Savior."

The men of the family were tasked with decorating the tree. Marguerite's job was to season the traditional turkey the day before Christmas dinner. Leilah prepared the chocolate Christmas log. Yvette, the wise orchestra conductor, planned every detail of our elaborate Christmas dinner, which would unfold with total perfection. Despite the dark, menacing clouds of dictatorship, the lucky families who were not grieving a loss by the brutal regime forgot politics one brief moment, to partake of the joy of Christmas with their loved ones.

~ * ~

I clung to Mike for an eternity before handing him my winter coat at the airport. This year's Christmas celebrations would be different: I was leaving my heart behind, with the man who was frantically waving goodbye behind the glass partition. The plane carried me to my sunny island for Christmas vacation with my family. My summer months were booked by laboratory internships in several Boston hospitals. December recess was my only official break for the year. I was literally exhausted.

"You need rest, darling. Go enjoy your family."

As I was about to board the plane, Mike had handed me fifteen letters, dated and sealed, with instruction to read one every day and help fill the void of his absence. I had followed his directives "to the letter," no pun intended. In the privacy of my former bedroom, untouched since I left for France, I would delight in the letter of the day, written on pastel blue paper, and keep it safely tucked under my pillow afterwards. I was searching, by this gesture, the illusion of his presence, perhaps. Mike, a teaser, often caught in the hustle and bustle of hospital life, had revealed, through his words, the tenderness of his heart: It was my face he saw, at night, before closing his eyes. He already imagined "our" little girl, who would look like me. My family was anticipating some big news announcement: Farid and Doris had already informed them of Michael Roye's visit in New York. Blushing, I finally told them I had found my soulmate.

On New Year's Day, as I had begun packing for my return trip to Boston, Mike landed in Haiti to officially ask my father for my hand in marriage. Flabbergasted, I burst into tears. Laughing and crying all at once, I buried my face on his shoulder, moved beyond measure by his thoughtfulness: in these days and ages, when parents had no voice in their children's lives, Mike honored the world I was raised in, with its customs, traditions and old-fashioned values.

An engagement ring sparkled in a dark velvet case. In the presence of my entire family, Dr. Michael Allen Roye officially became my fiancé, placing the diamond ring on my left hand.

Marguerite, moved beyond measure, burst into tears. "I can die now. My baby has found a husband."

"No," I advised laughingly. "Wait till I get married first."

My father was thrilled. Mike seemed the perfect son-in-law. Yvette, usually cool, calm and collected, could hardly contain her joy. Taking my hand, she walked me to the porch after our champagne glasses were empty, leaving the men chatting in the living room. Blushing, she offered me some sound advice. "Be wise, until the wedding. Show some interest also in the kitchen. It is important in the running of a home."

Yvette's words left me pensive. The first piece of advice implied her great insight on the undeniable force of passion; the second did not surprise me, as my father had always been pampered by his wife, an accomplished hostess. My thoughts turned to Mike: What were his tastes and preferences? Would he require a spotless home, or would he leave room for my whims and caprices? How would I live without a younger version of Marguerite?

We flew back together. Boston was waiting for us. His parents would welcome us at the airport with our winter coats.

~50~

We landed in Miami for our connection flight and now fly over Boston, where my last semester of College is waiting and Mike, his first year at the post of OB-GYN hospital resident. The city welcomes us, covered in a white blanket of snow. Freezing temperatures prevail. Mike's parents greet us with open arms and insist I address them as "Steve and Kate." They have prepared a candlelight dinner to celebrate our official engagement. A bottle of champagne is served in our honor. Kathryn insists, "You should not brave the cold tonight. The guest room is ready."

I will be their daughter soon they tactfully remind me as they wish us goodnight. Mike will always be "Mousy" for his mother—her little mouse. I was able to contain my hysterical laugh and settle for a discreet giggle. He owes his nickname to his childhood love for the most famous mouse in the world, Mickey Mouse. This couple will share secrets about the little boy they had the joy to raise. Leilah will tell my future husband the story of my life, if I will be her interpreter. They felt an instant connection without exchanging a single word. Mike wants to learn a bit of French before our next trip to Haiti. Bobby taught him an important sentence in Creole:

"Mwen renmen w..." I love you.

Cuddled on the couch, Mike and I are dreaming out loud and making wedding plans: I wish we could marry in the country of my birth, under the starry December skies, to the sound of Sacred Heart's bells.

Eyes wide open in disbelief, I wake up in the pale light of a January winter morning. Mike at my side, all scrunched up, stretches and smiles at me. We fell asleep last night, exhausted after our long overseas trip, huddled in each other's arms, on the living room sofa. Hair disheveled and clothes wrinkled, I quickly sneak to the bathroom. Kate knocks on the bedroom door and invites me to join them. They drink tea. My cup of coffee is waiting for me, steaming. Mike has also emerged in fresh clothes after a long shower. I wink and smile at the man of my life.

I want to wake up in his arms, under the soft caress of his kisses, every day, for the rest of my life.

We talked, till the wee hours of the night and set our wedding date for December, in Haiti. My dream will come true. I will be twenty-two and Mike, twenty-eight. An acceptable difference, which gives him, as my elder, an aura of wisdom. Dany was trying to control my soul and my body. I will freely trust Michael with my life, my dreams and my aspirations and hand him the rudder, knowing, without the shadow of a doubt, that he will lead us to safely. He has the face of Destiny.

~ * ~

I am determined to complete my course of study and graduate in June rather than December, thanks to the "credit system" which allows students to carry a heavier than usual academic load. I have other plans for December. Mike started his first year of residency. We will rarely get to socialize, but our respective schedules' demands will allow the months to fly faster. Mandatory internships in hospitals, which have been an integral part of my curriculum for the past two years, including summer months, offer us the chance to get a glimpse of one another in hospital hallways: a discreet smile, a complicit wink exchanged.

Assigned to the Clinical Microbiology lab, dressed in my student white coat, I note in my diary the highlights of my life as a medical technologist intern. Sometimes, it is a comical situation that amuses me: the Russian microbiologist, a disheveled, gray-haired woman who strangely reminds me of Einstein's famous photograph, masked and gloved to protect herself from contaminating spores in the Mycology Section, who repeats, every day, like a mantra, in her heavy accent, "There are pathogenic fungus spores everywhere here. In the air. Everywhere. *Everywhere.* Everyyyywhere!"

I often meditate on the dangerous power of a cloudy bacterial culture broth, or an agar Petri dish where bacterial growth can be seen by the naked eye. I have the privilege to observe, through the glass tube, colonies of the pathogenic tuberculosis agent on a green, Löwenstein-Jenson medium. Through fluorescence dark field microscopy, I watch, fascinated, the moving brilliance of the Syphilis spirochete, Treponema pallidum. Preparing antibiograms to select the most appropriate antibiotic treatment for a patient, I imagine working alongside Fleming, the father of penicillin. I am sold on a specialty in microbiology.

But genetics also fascinates me. Mendel's experiments on pea plants have revolutionized the concepts of heredity. Mendel's Law will help predict whether our children will be bald, like Charles Deveaux, or inherit their father's emerald eyes. With my brown eyes as the dominant gene, the percentage of such scenario is low. Each of our children will arrive with their unique surprise baggage.

After two semesters flirting with creative writing courses, I, unfortunately, gave up this secret pursuit. The academic requirements of a scientific branch are merciless. Creative writing is the regret I will always carry in my heart, just like the unfulfilled dream to meet Claire, my mother, someday.

~51~

Papa Doc Duvalier, the architect of so much grief in Haitian families, died of natural causes on April 21, 1971. I tried to imagine what went through the minds of these bereaved families who had lost a loved one to the brutal regime, at the news announcement? Even at death, François Duvalier had managed to have the last word. He did not die at the hands of executors seeking to ease their pain by revenge.

The dictator planned his last act by appointing his successor while alive. Baby Doc, his nineteen-year-old son, grabbed the torch and launched, in turn, a revised and renewed version of Duvalier dictatorship, adding to the mix the breath of youth and inexperience.

A strong gush of wind blew on the day of the dictator's funeral; skies darkened too, according to a rumor that had reached all the way to Boston. I'll share a funny anecdote: My grandmother, who, escorted by Marguerite, and without Yvette's knowledge or consent, had joined the horde of curious spectators on the Champ de Mars, lost her purse and one of her shoes, in the midst of a restless crowd that had filled the streets of Port-au-Prince to watch the somber convoy pass by.

Leaning on Marguerite, Leilah limped on one foot the entire Petit Four Avenue, until she reached her home in Bois Verna. Her tenants, the Canadian Non-Profit organization, surprised and perhaps amused, offered a chair and a glass of water to the their landlord, who wore only one shoe, and to her companion, faithful in the hilarious and crazy life's moments as well as the serious ones. Leilah, resigned to the admonitions she would endure from her daughter to have launched such an adventure, waited sheepishly for Yvette's arrival and anger.

Deschapelles. July 1973.

On the former land of the Standard Fruit Co, in the Artibonite Valley, is located Hospital Albert Schweitzer of Deschapelles. The founders, Dr. Larimer Mellon and his wife, Gwendolyn Grant Mellon, a lab specialist in tropical diseases, had welcomed local and foreign volunteers freshly landed in their midst. My room, sparsely furnished, was waiting for me. I would take the hospital bus to Port-au-Prince on Fridays and spend weekends with family. This chaotic journey, several hours long on poorly maintained roads, would be repeated on Sundays.

I had left Boston, with my degree in Health Sciences as a proud trophy. I had not deviated from the final goal, despite the distractions of the road. Mike and my parents shed tears, at the graduation ceremony. James and Yvette, Steve and Kate had formally met and, in preparation for the pending nuptials, had broken the ice of mutual reserve. Mike kept me close to his heart, before flying in the sky. He was leaving for a six-month internship program in Germany. His plan had been kept secret, not to spoil the euphoria of my graduation. I was inconsolable in his arms as the man who had become the center of my life swore to me we would never part again after our marriage.

A week later, it was my turn to fly to my island. I had decided to volunteer my services to Haiti's vulnerable segment. I owed a debt of gratitude to the country of my birth. The desire to honor my hero, Albert Schweitzer, and his philosophy of "Reverence for life" had guided my steps to Hospital Schweitzer of Deschapelles. Absence makes the heart grow fonder, as the saying goes. Distance would allow Mike and I to anticipate wedding bells with newfound excitement. I was already dreaming of his return. Fireworks would explode in my heart! In the austere sanctuary of my room, at night, I wrote my fiancé letters full of love and passion that would certainly make my father blush. Mike's precious love letters slept under my pillow.

I walked to the lab every morning, past the long line of patients who had arrived at dawn, to wait their turn in the shady courtyard. Suffering and pain were present everywhere, contemptuous of bodies bent by age, blind to childhood innocence. The knowledge I was gaining on tropical diseases weighed more than my contribution to the cause of service: malaria and other parasitic diseases, rare in the U.S., abounded. At dinner, the large refectory would become a classroom for missionaries and foreign volunteers, anxious to learn Creole.

Hannakah, a Dutch retired volunteer nurse, shared the following story with me: "In the African village of Lambaréné, I worked, long ago, with Dr. Schweitzer. He enjoyed long walks, alone, hands behind his back, dressed in an often-crumpled white suit, on his rare moments of leisure. In his refuge, away from the sick, he loved to play Bach, on the organ." ... Listening to Hannakah's story, I could almost feel the great doctor's presence.

~ * ~

A memory of a camp hosted by les "Enfants de Marie," Mary's Children, at Belle-Fontaine, came back to mind, as I lay on the narrow metal bed, in the solitude of my room at Schweitzer Hospital: a group of adolescent girls, aiming for the high peaks of altruism under the direction of Sister Nicole, had embarked on a journey by Jeep, mule and foot to the remote village of Belle-Fontaine, alias Trou Coucou. During two life-changing emotional weeks, we extended a hand to fight poverty and suffering. The priest of the tiny, destitute village opened his cottage to us. His powerful, unforgettable welcome prayer was: "Lord, give bread to those who are hungry, and hunger to those who have bread."

~52~

Port-au-Prince – December 1973

On a cool December evening, the Sacred Heart church bells were ringing, under starry skies for Mr. and Mrs. Michael Roye. In white veil and gown, radiant on my husband's arm, I left the church courtyard, floating in a sphere where dream and reality collided. Deaf to the feverish agitation swarming around us, I asked God what I had done to deserve such happiness. My younger brothers, so handsome in their dark suits, had fulfilled, to perfection, their role as groomsmen, escorted by three lovely ladies in turquoise blue. Mark, six, in his white shirt and bow tie, was a very proud ring bearer.

With my heart ready to burst, I had made my entrance on my father's arm, to the sound of Pachelbel's Canon in D. Beaming with pride, James had led me to the altar to take place alongside Mike, who had arrived escorted by Kathryn, his mother. Taking to heart her role as maid of honor, she adjusted my veil before I sat down. Yvette, the epitome of self-control and measure, had wiped a discreet tear. I had stopped at the first bench, reserved for immediate family, to offer them a smile.

Elegant in her long, navy blue gown and fancy bun, my aunt exuded grace and good taste. Grandmother and Marguerite, dressed to the nines, could hardly contain their excitement. These three women, who had marked my life and claimed, from fate's unexpected blow, my right to life, surrounded me, today. An inner struggle was taking place, between the tears at the corner of my eyes, and the haunting fear to spoil my light make-up. Jean-Claude Duvalier's dictatorship had not discouraged travelers who had crossed my path outside Haiti's borders: Farid and Doris, who, during a brief stop in New York, had been surrogate parents, to me. Their children, Diana and Dennis who, for the first time of their lives, had set foot on Haiti soil and would discover their paternal roots. Steve and Kathryn, Mike's parents; Alex, his best friend and future partner, someday... Karie, a student now at the Faculté de Médecine, had flown from Paris to share the joy of her high school friend. My father had selected the best hotel in Pétion-Ville to insure our foreign visitors a pleasant stay on our island.

Vows were exchanged in English, for Mike's sake. My new spouse spoke with ease, professing, before God and guests, his love and fidelity to me. Convinced that shyness and the solemnity of the hour would consume me whole and instantly make me mute, great was my surprise to be able to voice, in the presence of friends and family gathered to share our happiness, my commitment to be a faithful and loving wife.

Figures from the past, present and future surrounded me. Cathy, escorted by her parents, her cousin Patrick, and her friend Paul, shared in the joy and happiness of her childhood friend. Two nuns from Sainte Thérèse, ambassadors of my former school, attended the wedding ceremony. Karie represented France. Hannakah made the trip from Deschapelles to the capital city, inviting Dr. Schweitzer's presence with her. Ti Sò, who had become Mrs. Yanick Tremblay, Canadian citizen, had traveled from Montreal for the wedding. Her Afro hairstyle suited her perfectly. Her mother had joined her and helped care for her daughter's children. A providential visa granted through the Canadian organization that rented the house in Bois Verna, had changed the course of destiny for Dieudonne and her daughter.

The year of my marriage also marked, by official decree from President Richard Nixon on January 27, 1973, the end of the Vietnam War. Every step of our lives keeps track of the passage, and captures the faces of those we have met on our journey. Each era brings back significant dates, raises emotions and revives memories. Some fleeting shadows were not part of the celebrations, today: Dany and Deb, who might have lost their sense of purpose, with the end of the war; David;

Agnès, Ishtar, and Sister Marie Laurence relegated, by my fault, in the cloudy mist of Saint Joseph's memories...Louise Tyler, who died without seeing her son.

My father had received, by General Delivery post at his embassy, a mysterious package, a few months ago. It contained photographs, yellowed by time, of his childhood; a lock of hair; a bank transfer check, representing his share of inheritance: a hefty sum that will help cover university costs for my younger siblings.

In a velvet box, a pair of diamond earrings held a short message, scribbled by a shaky hand: "To the granddaughter my son might have given me..."

Grandmother Tyler is gone, taking our secret to the grave. In a message to her son, Louise Tyler repeated the words of my letter. She hoped James would forgive her, one day. She grieved for the family she would never know. Louise was trying to repair, from beyond the grave, the pain caused to her son. My regret: leaving Brunswick without hugging, albeit for a brief moment, the one who rocked James in her arms, as a child.

Leilah engulfed me in a loving embrace: her gold bangles adorned my wrist. Grandfather would have been so proud, today! Charles was keeping company to Claire—the mother I never had the privilege to know, and who would have been happy tonight, to marry her daughter. But she left me her sister, the guardian angel who watches over me, in her place. Yvette adjusted my veil and held me for a long time against her heart, after the ceremony. The Habdoul family heirloom, the gold and diamond pendant, sparkled around my neck. As tradition required, Yvette had gifted me the precious jewelry on my wedding day, and I will be the steward of the pendant until my future daughter marries.

~ * ~

His Excellency Mr. U.S. Ambassador to Haiti, my father's colleagues, Grandfather's agency employees, friends and family of Deveaux, Habdoul and Tyler—all surrounded us in Bourdon to toast to our happiness. Champagne flowed. Mike's parents, lost in the crowd of Haitian guests, had been taken under Uncle Farid's wing, a foreigner also in the land of his childhood. Cathy and Karie were happy to renew their acquaintance after seven years. Sergo and Patrick, glass in hand, had joined them. I winked in my friends' direction.

Under the pergola decorated by a profusion of white baby's breath, I smiled at my brand-new husband. Mike cheerfully submitted to the inspection of Yvette's curious friends, middle-aged, retired ladies present at every wedding and every funeral in Port-au-Prince and Pétion-Ville. They had come to share in our joy and shake the groom's hand.

My father had outdone himself these last months, in anticipation of his daughter's nuptials: a deck had been built over the pool to become a dance floor at the reception. The walls had undergone a makeover with a fresh coat of paint. Huge bouquets of flowers were placed at strategic corners of the open terrace. To justify his extravagances, James would repeat, clutching hands with the guests who were raving about the décor and the scrumptious food laden tables, "I only have one daughter to marry." A gracious host, my father had stopped at every table, thanking everyone for their presence on this special day. Later that evening, after the last guest had departed and the projector lights had been turned off, James held his wife close to his chest, in a silent dance of bodies and souls, on the deserted deck, reported my faithful chronicler of family news, Marguerite.

Love is a work of art, created anew through each couple, and partners become the artists of their own creation. Mike and I embarked on a precious journey of mutual discoveries in the cradle of my birthplace, this island of hidden mysteries and provocative appeal, just like a young bride. To our cold nights at Montinar, where, nestled against each other, we sought the other's warmth, succeeded glorious sunsets on the sand of Kalico Beach; stopover in the southern town of Jacmel, at Pension Alexandra; picnic at Cyvadier Beach, where my husband baked in the sun, and ate fresh conch.

Precarious road conditions made us unable to reach Jérémie, dubbed the city of poets, birth place of my Deveaux ancestors. We headed north toward Cap Haitian. Love is an exhilarating, sometimes dangerous journey: we climbed, by mule, to the top of Bonnet à l'Evêque, where stood, strong and proud, touching the clouds, the Citadelle Laferrière fortress. In awe before this eighth wonder of the world and symbol of Man's courage, hand locked in Mike's grip, my Haitian pride reached its peak.

James and Yvette were outstanding hosts. Swimming days at the beach and mountain excursions were orchestrated to perfection. Visitors flew back home, delighted with their trip. Briefcases full of memorabilia will help them recall their unforgettable visit to Haiti. Karie held me in a long embrace after the wedding reception. She was flying back to France, the next day. Bidding me farewell, she said, "You will also come to my wedding, someday."

I will keep my promise.

The fairytale continued for us. I fulfilled my dream of a night's stay at Habitation Leclerc—a luxurious hotel with marble sinks and golden brass finish, built on Napoleon's sister' estate, Pauline Bonaparte. According to legend, during French Colonial times, Pauline would fill her pool with goat milk for her ablutions, to preserve the smooth texture of her skin. On the dance floor of the Hippopotamus disco, Mike favored romantic slow songs. He held me still, heart against heart, as his hips and legs could not follow the fast beat of merengue music.

A bittersweet moment wrapped up our final evening in Bourdon, alongside the actors of my youth. Myriam Tyler had landed in Haiti from Boston a few months ago...Today, Mrs. Michael Roye would be departing, leaving her family behind, to launch a new chapter in her life. I had officially cut the cord with those who had shaped who I was, today. In fact, my umbilical cord is buried in Bois Verna's backyard, my grandparents' property, where I was born. How would I ever survive the sale of a home that has always symbolized my happy childhood?

Yvette whispered to my husband, "Take care of my daughter."

Mike engulfed her in his arms, affirming his devotion to me. Since the loss of her husband Charles, Leilah has enjoyed the peace of her own living quarters in Bourdon: a spacious bungalow designed by James, next to the main house. She shares it with Marguerite, who, like a guardian angel, watches over her. These two women will age side by side. They have come such a long way together. Bobby, who inherited his mother's moderation, will be Grandfather's successor, under Yvette's wise guidance. My father always wanted a simple and uneventful life. His wife has been his rock, his firm assurance.

Hugging the actors of my childhood before catching our plane back to the U.S., I did not even try to hide my tears.

~53~

Happy people have no story, the saying goes. I am basking in a state of pure joy, my heart suspended between a marvelous dream and the disbelief of my good fortune. Michael has fulfilled all the desires a bride could ever imagine. I will never stop loving him…We will grow old together. But at the dawn of our conjugal lives, I still have a sunny future stretched in front of me, before old age creeps in and claims our youth. I have not yet discovered a flaw in my spouse. Ah! Yes! One: Mike cannot dance. I made the stunning discovery during our honeymoon. In due course, I will help him remedy the situation. But this time I will be the teacher, and him, the student, I conclude with a smile.

Mike found a small apartment in a residential area, with parking for his Volkswagen Beetle but far from public transport. I do not drive; my travels will be limited. We decide, by mutual agreement, that I will take a respite year before launching a paramedical career. If we lead a frugal life, his salary as a medical resident should suffice for our simple needs. He wants me available, to share with him his few hours of rest, away from the hospital. I am offered, for the first time in my existence, a vast savannah of free time, without navigation map, structure or safeguard. My only mission: transform our tiny love nest into a haven of peace and harmony and offer Mike the soldier's welcome at each return from the hospital, his battlefield. Diving with delight into my new role as a housewife, I strive to keep a spotless home, evoking, in my mind, Yvette and my mother-in-law Kathryn, the epitomes of grace in their perfect interior space. Sometimes we dine with his limited circle of friends, colleagues from the hospital. Mike, a twinkle in his eyes, likes to call me his "French girl," in their presence.

I sometimes think about France, its cultural wealth and traditions, a touch of nostalgia in my heart. I have kept a slight Parisian accent, inherited from my years of study on French soil. Sometimes, the islander arises on the surface, a bout of languid laziness in her behavior that would perfectly suit the persona: elders so often seen in my childhood, dressed in loose, colorful muumuu, rocking in a dodine (rocking chair), on a flower-filled veranda and gossiping with friends of the season's latest wedding, while furiously moving their hand fan to dissipate the rising tropical heat. I discover the charms of culinary art. Giving free rein to my imagination, I invent dishes that I concoct with love for my husband, and delight in my kitchen creations.

When Mike leaves for the hospital, a serious apathy begins to settle in, without warning, over the months. To fill the void caused by my husband's absence and the total lack of structure of my days unfolding before me, I lose myself in the fictional life of soap opera characters, plunging in the heart of their romantic stories, while stuffing sweets. I blissfully swim in blind contentment, unaware of the pounds piling up with the growing apathy that has claimed the best of me. My precious journal is forgotten at the bottom of a drawer. My universe spins around TV shows, my pots and pans, and, thankfully, intimacy at night. The love that binds us remains vivid. Except for the threshold of our bedroom, life is passing me by, under my nose and I do not know how to fully bite into it. I feel trapped in a gilded cage.

Another cloud disturbs the perfect image of happiness: After his medical residency, Mike, the wise oracle of our couple, plans to establish a strong private practice before bringing a child into this world. He wishes also to enjoy our life together as a couple, before having to share it with another, however small. Already, Marguerite had asked on the phone if I was expecting a happy event. She does not conceive of marriage without baby.

That evening, we had argued. I called Michael selfish, and he blamed me for my great naivety. By morning, I realized my husband would win the battle. My body swiftly adapts to birth control pills. When remorse assails me, I sweep it away, in the intoxication of marital bliss and freedom without constraint, bought in a pharmacy. Michael, fulfilled in his emotional and professional life, laments the spark that left my eyes. Equal partners in the great adventure of marriage, my husband suggests to put an end to my sabbatical, after just eight months. I land a part-time job in the Clinical Microbiology section of the hospital. The image of the scientist bent over his microscope and relieving the misery of the world, comes to life, fruit of years of study and effort. The sun shines again. At evening time, Mike and I celebrate our homecoming together.

The opportunity to write a new page to our story takes us by surprise, one day: Mike's former classmate Alexander extends an invitation to join him in Florida. His uncle, Dr. John B., is getting old and looking for two young partners to help him run his OB-GYN, state-of-the art clinic. John, Alex and Mike would share the heavy client load at the clinic, and take turns with on-call duties. The young wife finds it hard to contain her joy at the prospect of more time with her husband. The Caribbean-born exults at the chance to escape winter, and be geographically closer to her family. Mike's parents, after their initial shock at seeing their only son move away, bend to this ever-changing and unpredictable force that is Life…

Mike leaves on a fact-finding trip. Excitement is written all over his face, when he returns: a charming home is waiting for us, at the edge of an artificial lake with an abundant duck population, and coconut trees line our backyard fence. He signs a purchase contract, with a thirty years mortgage. The die is cast. We are packing and heading south to Florida.

~54~

Florida - Summer 1976

Ducks have spotted, from afar, bread crumbs flying in the direction of the lake, and they fight for the choice morsels. My favorite, a male with white plumage, baptized Elvis, wears an odd crown of feathers on its head. Elvis visits us every morning in our garden planted with yellow hibiscus, and then proceeds with daily ablutions in the lake. Mike, on the screened porch, sips his tea and smiles at me, before heading for the clinic. I love this quiet morning ritual, prelude of a brand-new day unfolding before us. It is hard to believe, but at this phase of my life, I feel total peace and contentment in my role as a housewife. Mike gives me free rein on the direction my life will take.

I studied the option of a clinical lab post at nearby Presbyterian Hospital, accessible by public transport. But today, my heart and mind long for the sabbatical I had cut short the first time, in Boston… I feel like a bird consumed with the desire to build its nest and create a comfortable, welcoming abode for my spouse. I crave serenity. My décor of bamboo furniture and fresh palms reflects this harmony to which I aspire, in communion with nature and the universe.

~ * ~

To celebrate our three-year anniversary, Mike surprises me with a romantic Bahamas cruise. We enjoy a scrumptious supper on the ship, in the enchanting glow of the dining-room. For dessert, my husband takes me tenderly by the hand, and heads for the desk. The night is cool off the Florida coast on this beautiful December month. I tighten the shawl around my shoulders. We have spotted a few stars hanging on the dark velvet of the night sky and formulate the wish to live an everlasting love story. My companion pulls out a flat velvet box from his jacket's inner pocket: a delicate gold bracelet emerges and is lovingly placed on my wrist. Mike bends his head toward me. The wind, playing in our hair, has a salty taste. Pressed tightly against one another, I imagine us alone on the cruise ship. Our lips are locked. Emotion are so intense, they hurt.

~ * ~

Mike resumes his daily schedule at the clinic, and I return to my haven of peace and solitude, in our home by the lake. But a curious shift has taken place in me: an awakening of the soul, so to speak. Flashes of our two shadows, glued together on the "deck of love" play back in the creative part of my mind. I taste again the salt of the sea breeze, and Mike's burning kisses on my lips. Myriam, eternal closet writer, an obscure dot on the horizon, shyly emerges from her blissful slumber.

Parker pen in hand, I want to recapture, through the power of creative writing, these emotions, fragile yet powerful, fugitive yet lingering, when I felt Life vibrate in the depths of my soul. And a miracle occurs: I experience exhilarating joy again, when pen meets paper, in the fever of inspiration. Sitting by the resin table under the parasol, in our little patch of grass overlooking the lake, a flow of words emerge from an inexhaustible source. Our magical anniversary celebration, under starry skies in the middle of the ocean woke up my muse, the capricious visitor I thought I had lost forever. On the lined pages of a student spiral notebook, "Une Nuit au paradis" is born: "A Night in Paradise."

Mike's sudden arrival startles me in my refuge under the parasol. This man, whose life can be defined as a race with the watch, and for whom every precious second is construed as a valuable asset, managed to break free, early, from the clinic, to surprise me with the gift of an afternoon together. "Just the two of us…" The message is laden with undertones. He hands me a bouquet of roses and grabs a resin chair next to mine. Cheek to cheek under the shady parasol, we yield to the afternoon heat that slowly engulfs us. Removing his silver-rimmed glasses, I cup Mike's face in the palms of my hands: tiny yellow sequins shine in his emerald colored eyes, like miniature suns. This lazy afternoon is ours. There is no rush. We taste, in silence, the flavor of the moment.

His gaze suddenly falls on the written pages of my notebook. "What are you writing, darling?"

Like an awkward teenager taken at fault, my face burns with embarrassment. Sooner or later, such a scenario was bound to occur: my well-guarded, life-long secret, exposed to the world, naked, raw, under the sunny noon glare. Facing the man who won my heart but not yet penetrated my secret garden, I turn into an ice sculpture, in its cold, muted rigidity. My soul has been exposed. Time freezes. Mike symbolizes the mocking public, ready to devour and laugh at the aspiring writer. I realize, at that very moment, how much harder it is to achieve intimacy of the souls, than of the bodies. Being scrutinized by others is to offer our vulnerability to their criticism and misunderstanding. To pursue a dream, is to risk failure and ridicule all too often.

But, I underestimated the man who has joined, for better or worse, his life to mine. Upon his insistence, I offer Mike a sight translation of my composition. I suffer the ordeal of the unveiling of the soul, exposed through each line, each inspired word written in the heat of passion and emotion. He listens ardently, arm around my shoulder, to my short story's conclusion: the main character meets the love of her life and they share a passionate kiss on a cruise ship deck, sealing the theatrical ending of a romantic love story.

I discover, in Mike, a captivated audience. "Beautiful!" he says. "You must translate your text, and get it published."

The idea of a possible publication never occurred to me. Pages written, over the years, always ended, forgotten in an eternal sleep, at the bottom of a drawer. We spend the afternoon poking around yellowed papers, notes and unfinished stories from my creatively fertile adolescent years. Michael purchases a portable typewriter, dubbed my faithful companion in the garden or on the porch, according to the day's mood, and Muse's inspiration or fantasy. Mike has made it his mission to revive the spark of creativity in me.

My typewritten text, titled *A Night in Paradise* is revised for typos. I give my husband complete freedom to dispose of it as he sees fit. Out of fear and superstition, I refuse, the following months, to even mention the manuscript. Exhilarated by the Muse's return in my life, consumed by the fire of inspiration, I feverishly work on a second short story, where the hero's tragic death brings tears to my eyes, as words are born on paper.

Yes, the old spark is back. My life-long dream has been unveiled in broad daylight. New breath has been infused into my heart. This sabbatical has become instrumental for me to appreciate total freedom of the mind. It fed and inspired my soul to create again, through the magic of the written word. Mike returns from the clinic one day, an air of triumph painted on his face, as he holds a mysterious yellow envelope, out of my reach, above his head.

"You will get the envelope on one condition: You must first grant me a long, passionate kiss."

Eyes closed, lips offered, I approach. The flame remains alive between us and sets the sails that will lead the vessel of our emotions on its journey… In this melting of the hearts, the envelope is forgotten on the tiled floor.

~ * ~

"We are pleased to inform you...your short story "A Night in Paradise" has been selected by *Whispers Magazine* for publication. Please find, enclosed a contract agreement, etc. Copyright, etc. Payment, etc. We will also be interested in other submissions from you in the future. Please receive, etc. "

My eyes are misty with tears, and words from the letter are drowning in one gray, shapeless smear. A magazine editor has judged my text worthy to appear in print. The monetary gain matters little, compared to the official validation of publication. My dream, always kept secret, is now legitimate.

Mike, the incorrigible optimist, dared what I could never do: a text submission. With a self-addressed stamped envelope to his clinic, armed with patience and perseverance, he had sent a copy of my newly translated text to several women's magazines. He kept under silence the rejection letters that piled up at his office, to protect my extreme vulnerability. He had grasped a truth that, so far, totally eluded me: in the long list of "**No, No, No,**" all it takes for the aspiring writer to join the mysterious realm of published authors is a single "**Yes!**" And the world will never be the same.

~55~

The Bahamas cruise was our anniversary present, the celebration of three happy years of marriage. With his delicacy of heart, Mike offered me, a couple of weeks later, a wonderful Christmas gift: two tickets for Haiti. Despite my best efforts to conceal the sadness that was creeping in my island girl's heart with the approach of the holidays, Mike had sensed the vital need I felt to return to my family and the country of my birth.

At the twelfth stroke of midnight, the family rose and joined their voices in unison with the crowd to sing "Oh, Holy Night." Hand locked in Mike's grip, I did not try to hide my tears; they flowed freely, uncontained, liberated. A horde of mixed emotions was claiming the best of me... Bobby did not laugh at me this year. He understood, perhaps, the solemnity of the moment for the sister he was now towering over by several inches. Fresh out of business school, my younger sibling was about to celebrate his twenty-third birthday and spoke of a possible future with his girlfriend. Freddy smoked in secret. He was enrolled in an architecture program and dreamed of going abroad for advance studies, someday... Would he join me in Florida in the future? Junior, my godson, more interested in games and girls than school, might fail his BAC, to his parents' dismay. Marguerite continued to be my faithful chronicler of family gossip.

At eleven, Mark was already as tall as I was. There had not been, since my youngest sibling, any more babies in Bourdon. Marguerite held me tight against her heart and whispered, upon arrival, to keep the faith... I would, one day, conceive a child. She would die, if she learned that my apparent barrenness was only a deceptive mask. Yvette and Leilah kept silent, but were sending puzzled looks my way. I pretended to be blind and clueless. Mike and I sunbathed at the beach, drank coconut water from the same fruit and exchanged, under starry December skies, passionate kisses, snuggled on a blanket on Montinar's wet grass in the cool, crisp Kenscoff air. In the euphoria of my return to the sources and the shelter of my childhood home, surrounded by people of my past, I failed to take the pill my heart and body had been accustomed to. We returned to Florida after the New Year, relaxed and happy, more than ever in love. Mike, enthralled by the captivating charm of Haiti, decided, "We will retire in Kenscoff, someday."

When I understood that I was pregnant, the light, all of a sudden, blinded me. This compulsion to build our nest in harmony and serenity, this emptiness that gnawed at a silent corner of my heart, were none other than the call for motherhood, a topic that Mike and I avoided for three years. I ardently wanted a baby. Nothing was clearer or more obvious. My entire being aspired to this flesh of my flesh, living consecration of the strong love we shared. This miracle happened without warning and would forever change the course of our lives.

Would Michael be angered by my negligence? He approached to engulf me in his arms. He said something incredible to my ears. For some time, he too had wanted a child, the tangible fruit of our love. He dared not tell me, sure that I was fulfilled, at this stage of my life, with the realization of my dream of always: writing! A child would upset the harmony of the present. However, fate stepped in, because two right-minded people, faced with the mystery of life, were losing their objectivity.

~56~

The paper exudes a sweet smell of light perfume. But the words resonate, like a death knell, in my head. I re-read Agnès Renaud's letter that has crossed the Atlantic from France to Haiti. Yvette forwarded it to my Florida address. Adorned with splendid postage stamps, the pink envelope landed in our mailbox today, buried under a stack of bills.

Grey clouds announce one of these brutal summer showers, fleeing Floridian skies as quickly as they appear. I dragged myself, idle, from the living-room sofa to the porch this morning. My source of inspiration has dried up: I've stopped writing. I blame fatigue, but it is fear that lives in me. Like her mother, my baby will be born in September. How ironic! Claire's drama silently haunts me, to remind me of life's unpredictable fragility. Mike, eternal optimist, discourages all negative thought, to ensure I carry a serene pregnancy.

Back from the clinic, he discovers a chapter of my life I buried and almost forgot. For my husband, I evoke the images of a splendid park, and a famous bench, that withstood centuries of age. Through my emotional words, my boarding-school friends and the teacher who left without warning to serve Africa's suffering humanity arise from the past. I can never accept the seeming abandonment of those dear to me. It is the price they pay when their route crosses my path. Claire's death forever left this haunting, gnawing fear in me.

At Mike's request, I read out loud Agnès's translated words: "Sister Marie Laurence had to leave Africa for medical reasons. Back at Saint Joseph, her health has been declining. I had the opportunity to visit her on a trip from Nantes, where I now reside, to Paris. Bedridden at Saint Ann Hospital today, our teacher has been diagnosed with terminal liver cancer. She will not survive the season. Sister Marie Laurence often made reference to you, in her correspondence with me, over the years. I confessed to her that you never answered any of my letters."

Agnès did not deserve my stubborn silence. When I cut ties with Saint Joseph, my loyal friend became the innocent victim of an old grudge, in the process. Life sometimes throws these unexpected turns of events our way, and their apparent irony is matched only by their painful outcome: In the same Parisian hospital where she was an angel at my bedside, Sister Marie Laurence is fighting her last battle. The obvious is crystal clear as water from a mountain source: I must make amends with my former teacher and ask her for forgiveness.

Fate, through Agnès, is reminding me of this debt of love I must repay. It is time to break my ten-year-long stubborn silence. I will write to Sister Marie Laurence... Mike, who just accomplished, by my side, a difficult journey through time and space, offers, with his boundless impulsivity and generosity, "We must go to France, Myriam."

Suddenly dizzy, I close my eyes. Everything is happening so fast. Will I have the courage to cross into the depths of the past? I might not know it yet, but this trip will save me from myself. Turning to the suffering of another, I shall silence my superstitious fears of another September drama. As Haiti, Florida is on the course of atmospheric monsters that leave the coast of Africa, to become these hurricanes and tropical storms that bring death and destruction in their path.

My belly looks like one of those huge, heavy clouds clinging to the dark sky and about to burst today. This child was conceived in Haiti. Nostalgic, my thoughts linger on my family, who would love to pamper me. Yvette has kept her grace and measure, as she approaches middle age. A few gray strands around the temples give her an aura of wisdom. She will join me in Florida, when the time comes for me to give birth. My aunt, who was instrumental to my survival the day I came into the world, took charge of me and raised four sons in the shadows of a dictatorship, will support me with her vast experience. My grandmother anxiously waits for this baby who will provide her a physical legacy of her deceased daughter. Yvette's presence is her anchor to which she clings. James, the future grandfather, simply cannot stay still. At his side, stress would consume me. My child will have four uncles, already eager to play this brand-new role. Bobby will be my infant's godfather. I wonder what herbal infusions Marguerite would make me drink? I will always remain her "little one."

~ * ~

Doctors affiliated with Presbyterian Hospital are invited to their annual barbecue, held on the hospital grounds, to celebrate the Fourth of July. Hamburgers and hot dogs cook on charcoal barbecues. Coca-Cola, mini star-spangled flags and star-studded plastic hats abound. We mingle with Mike's partners and their spouses. Men are discussing work, and the ladies compare notes on the latest diet fad, around baskets of cupcakes. With the rounded belly I exhibit, the scene seems hilariously funny. We take our leave after a spectacular fireworks show that illuminated the skies with all the colors of the rainbow.

Tomorrow, Mike and I are flying to France. My husband was granted a two-week leave of absence by his colleagues. Our neighbor will keep the keys to our house and water our plants. As I lock the door, silent anxiety washes over me. Who will win this race against Death? Will we get there on time? A taxi drops us off at Miami International Airport. The dice have been cast.

~57~

Paris - July 1977

Sitting by the window, eyes riveted on the vast Atlantic waters we have spent hours flying over, my thoughts are meandering on the banks of the past. I remember my return trip to France when I fell ill from typhoid fever a decade ago. The blurry image of Jean Pierre, a casual travel companion, comes to mind. Memory sometimes plays these ironic tricks, capturing an insignificant moment to bring it back, years later, to the surface.

Images are rich in fond memories: Chateaubriand's park in autumn clothing; students giggling and walking arm in arm, blue berets tilted on their foreheads and long woolen socks stretched up their legs. They smile at life and its promises. Myriam, a little dot on the horizon, exchanges pleasantries, surrounded by Ishtar and Agnès. Painful memories too. Struck down by typhoid and glued to a hospital bed in Saint Ann, I reach the deep abyss of despair. An angel holds my hand in my delirium.

There are troubling adolescent memories. Strong, intense emotions were exposed, naked and raw, amplified, and wisely channeled with a mentor's help. Christian de Panière's image emerges and sends a flush to my cheeks. Michel also arises from the mists of the past: a gentle gaze and smile, but a heart burning with artistic passion. A distant past, yet still so close. Just at that moment, the child I carry inside of me does a somersault. I put a hand on this round belly that brings me back to reality, to the present, to the man resting in the quiet abandonment of sleep. He gave me his name when he gave me his heart. My eyes linger, full of love, on my travel companion sleeping next to me.

Michael has set a time machine in motion, out of love, and orchestrated this pilgrimage to the sources of the past. I finally doze off, my head against my husband's shoulder. When I open my eyes, our plane has just landed in Paris. Tired from jet lag, aching limbs and overall discomfort associated with an advanced pregnancy, I follow, docile, Mike's lead. He planned every minute detail with his travel agent. The taxi drops us off at the entrance of a charming hotel. To talk of a second honeymoon in magical Paris in my current physical condition would border on the ridiculous. Besides, this return to the sources, inspired by painful circumstances, would hardly be the time or place.

But we will return to France, I promise myself, cozy under the duvet. We will visit the Louvre and the Eiffel Tower. We will walk on the Champs-Elysees, after ice cream at their famous drugstore. In Montmartre, near the Sacré-Coeur, we will pose, cheek against cheek, for a charcoal drawing portrait. On the banks of the Seine, watching the bateaux-mouches, the river boats, we will exchange long, amorous kisses under the soft gaze of bearded booksellers. Evenings will catch us in glamorous attire, as we head to the opera and the Folies Bergères. I will dress to the nines for my husband. We will drink champagne at our midnight supper, bathed in the glow of the City of Light. My neck resting in the hollow of his shoulder, I take refuge close to his heart. Mike is my rock, the anchor that holds the vessel of our lives. He is the shore where the great waves of love come crashing, when all emotions converge at the source.

Eyes open in the comforting darkness, sleep is slow in coming. Setting foot, after so many years, on French soil I left as a teenager, to return with a woman's heart, has stirred complex feelings, and set in motion so many conflicting emotions. Flash-backs bombard my brain, on this strange, silent night. We will visit Versailles Castle and its splendors. I will teach my husband French history, with its pomp and pageantry in their time of glory. At the Trianon, Queen

Marie Antoinette's refuge, we will meditate on the tragic end of French royalty. We will stroll, hand in hand, under shady alleys at the Bois de Boulogne, when the park is clothed in golden fall attire. The birds will share the crumbs we drop at their feet, and spread their wings toward infinity. I will envy the thrill they must feel to fly, free as the wind, in the sky. I wake up the next day to a room service delivery of a scrumptious French breakfast: fluffy croissants and crispy baguettes; the sweet scent of fruity jams; the divine aroma of café au lait, steaming hot coffee and milk, served in large crystal bowls. Mike, used to his morning tea mug, is amused: "Bonn-djourr, Myriam," he shouts, with good humor.

The present scene, with its flavor of novelty, enchants me. We savor the delights of breakfast in bed. I wish I could stop time and forever capture that moment, on the canvas of memory: the tender image of a man with dark, copper-colored locks, ready to taste his brioche like he bites into life. His eyes cling to mine. Silence is worth its weight in gold. Our faces lightly brush. His lips are seeking mine. The moment is filled with tenderness. There is no rush. Behind the closed door of our hotel room, the world, with its sorrows, will wait till tomorrow. Today belongs to Michael, and to the love we share.

~ * ~

Mike has rented a Renault for our visit to Val-de-Seine. The summer breeze sings in the foliage. We ride in silence through the undergrowth that leads to Saint Joseph's main entrance. Chateaubriand's park offers the warm caress of a sunny July month. A profusion of green flows in abundance from the park's centuries-old trees, silent witnesses of my past... Rich, new sap, symbol of life's rebirth, must crawl under their wrinkled bark. In a navy blue blazer and dark tie, Mike takes my hand as we climb, with calculated slowness, the large brick staircase leading to the parlor. This pilgrimage to the sources of the past brings up a range of strong emotions to the surface. Saint Joseph, a lofty facade with its towers stretching high in the sky and its heavy carved doors, seems to defy time and space. But Myriam, adolescent in blue beret and knee-high socks, is not part of the decor today. A young brunette, heavy with child, a serious look painted on her face, has taken her place. Heart consumed with grief, she finds it painful to walk up the steps.

Reverend Mother was waiting at the parlor. She opens her arms and holds me against her heart. The years have passed, immutable: her face does not carry the slightest wrinkle. Hand stretched out to Mike, she welcomes him in her impeccable English. In a flash, I see Yvette, mustard-tailored suit and stilettos, by my side. The past seems to taunt me: the same décor; Reverend Mother, faithful to her image. But the graceful silhouette in long black veils, who welcomed us in France ten years ago, remains absent. Reverend Mother confirms Agnès's letter: the days are numbered for her convent companion, bedridden at Saint Ann Hospital. Sister Marie Laurence left Africa at the threshold of her tenth year of missionary service. Her health, shaken after her bout with hepatitis, malaria and other tropical fevers, steadily declined. She is fighting end-stage liver cancer today. Saint Joseph's Superior reminds me, "Time and distance do not alter the bonds of affection."

Mike is offered a grand tour of the premises: study hall, refectory, chapel. A flood of memories assail me, at the doorway of my former classroom. Time has stopped. Agnès, Ishtar, Astrid and Sophie emerge from a misty past. Chalk in hand at the blackboard, our teacher instills arid chemistry formulas in her students' minds. Reverend Mother snaps me out of my reverie with unexpected news: dorms will soon turn into research libraries.

"The Mariale Order will no longer take boarders in a few years. Saint Joseph will become exclusively a day school. Vocations to join the Order are declining and our sisters are getting old. Our religious congregation has significantly been reduced."

Saint Joseph belongs, in my mind, to the immutable order of things. Its walls defy eternity. But they also harbor Life's surprising changes and people who age and die. Heavy silence follows. How can I explain the panic I feel at the idea of change, even when it no longer touches my life? I always return to the seven-year-old girl who sees her universe crumble around her, when the tragedy of her birth is brutally revealed to her. Reverend Mother hesitates, and then agrees to lead us to the cramped office, witness of so many adolescent confidences. I fondly recall my teacher and all those who came knocking, confused, at the door of her heart. Science and religion textbooks, countless student copies creating a startling mess in this austere shelter, have vanished. The image of a welcoming Christ, arms stretched open to greet visitors, is no longer hanging on the wall. Cold, perfect, bone-chilling order prevails.

With no regrets, I aim for the door. Sister Marie Laurence's spirit has left. The space houses a new occupant. Sister Angèle, House Mother for the boarders, riddled with arthritis, now lives in a convent in the South of France, with milder climate. Mike is pulled into a chapter of my adolescence. Imbued with images of my past, captivated by the charm of the place and the friendliness of the nuns, he holds on tightly to my hand. Reverend Mother will alert the medical staff of our surprise visit at Saint Ann. Tactfully, she prepares me for the grueling encounter waiting for me. "You will find Sister Marie Laurence changed," she explains. "Her body is worn out from the cancer, but her spirit remains strong. She has not ceased, over the years, to hope for news of you and remains deeply attached to you. We learned of your marriage through the formal announcement your parents mailed to our Saint Joseph community. But we did not have your address in America to offer our congratulations."

We take our leave in guilty silence. The towers of Saint Joseph disappear forever, at the turn of the clearing.

~ * ~

With a map of Paris spread out on our table, Mike locates the best route to Saint Ann Hospital. We have lunch in an unassuming little neighborhood café. Cigarette smoke rises from nearby tables and bothers me. I would like to turn back, and postpone the painful encounter that awaits us. The Renault stops at the corner of an austere, grey building with an imposing perimeter: Saint Ann Hospital. Mike takes my hand with the authority of the elder, of the confident guide.

We walk along corridors permeated by the strong odor of bleach, in search of Room 24. A flood of memories assails me, a brutal assault on my senses already on high alert: the caustic smell that burns one's throat; long, empty hallways, impersonal, depressing as death itself. Each door displays a number; behind each wood panel, a human drama unfolding at the heart of *Life*: successive waves of hope and despair, intertwined, tearing each other apart in the bitter struggle of health versus disease, of life versus death…

Between these silent walls, Sister Marie Laurence must also fight her obscure but heroic battle. In a few seconds, I will be propelled to the heart of her drama, overwhelmed by the prospect of a painful return to the source. Mike tightens his grip on my trembling hand. He stops in front of the last closed door at the end of the hall and grabs the metal handle. I must control my emotions for the sake of my unborn child, and for the soul about to bid farewell to Life.

A nun rises at our approach and we exchange a discreet smile. She was waiting for our arrival and disappears in hushed little steps. In the face of obvious, yet silent display of suffering, we remain idle, frozen in a moment that seems to last a hundred years. I approach the edge of the bed: an emaciated face I do not recognize, with oxygen tubes connected at the base of the nose, lies motionless, on a large pillow. Two bony arms rest on each side of a narrow, child-like body covered by a white sheet. The patient's chest moves at a steady pace: shallow, but rhythmic breaths, indicators of life. I have been thrown in the eye of the storm with its terrifying tranquility. I wish I could hear Sister Marie Laurence's familiar voice again: "*Myriam, it is just a nightmare.*" Yet, the implacable reality is right before my eyes, displayed in this bed of sorrow, encrusted in a shrunken body ravaged by cancer and holding on to life by a fragile string.

Mike has quietly slipped a chair under me. I grab, without a word, the hand inert on the sheet, and hold it in mine, not letting go. The patient suddenly emerges from her lethargic sleep in response to my touch. Her sky-blue gaze lingers, puzzled, on the tall, bearded masculine figure, then follows the outline of the feminine shoulders where the man's large palms rest. Eyes widened by surprise, she stares, in disbelief, at the woman's face leaning toward her, transformed by pregnancy weight gain and hair pulled back in a classic bun.

~58~

Sister Marie Laurence, stirred, attempts to raise her neck and a barely audible cry escapes from her lips: "*Myriam*!" Then the weary head falls back on the pillow and two big tears leave the quivering eyelids to get lost in her sunken cheeks. By the eloquence of her silence and quiet tears, the one who, throughout her life as a teacher, always promoted meaningful conversation over empty talk, expresses the depth of her emotion without uttering a single word. Time remains frozen in space, suspended between past and present. A young nurse enters the room, a medications tray in her hands. As I prepare to leave, I lean toward the patient and whisper, "Sister Marie Laurence, meet Mike, my husband."

Solemnity has no place, in life's decisive moments. Michael approaches and seizes, in his own, the hand that had remained trapped in mine, to gently place it on my belly, where new life pulsates: "Meet Laurence, our baby."

Mike offers, by his moving gesture, an unexpected tribute to my dying teacher. Love that becomes flesh reaches another dimension: whether a boy or a girl, Laurence will forever alter the course of our lives.

My husband remains this impulsive force, the man who forges through life and propels me along in its dazzling trail. Alongside him, the sky will be bluer, and our nights full of stars. In the cozy darkness of our hotel room tonight, head against his shoulder, I listen to Mike's gentle breaths. I cannot sleep, reminiscing about the past. As dawn timidly appears at our hotel room window, I'm in the throes of a splitting headache and swollen ankles. Nausea flares at the sight of breakfast and the smell of coffee. Mike, puzzled, puts down his stethoscope. With a worried look on his face, he reveals, "Your blood pressure is dangerously high."

At the Emergency entrance of Saint Ann Hospital, admission procedures are complicated for foreigners. Fortunately, our travel insurance will be honored. I am finally settled in a room with a bay window in the newly equipped wing of the hospital complex. My eyes linger on my rounded abdomen: new life has filled my womb, taken possession of my body and decided, today, of this unexpected turn of event: In France to be at Sister Marie Laurence's bedside, I find myself, once again, a patient at the same Parisian hospital. All the tests confirm that baby is clinging to life. But, cautious, doctors want to keep me in observation for a few days and rule out risks of pre-eclampsia. Mike holds my hand.

The idea of an emergency return to Florida crosses our minds. But air travel would be contraindicated before blood pressure stabilization. Immediate lifestyle changes are ordered: coffee is banished until I give birth; a salt-free diet is imposed, dashing my plans to feast on Camembert and Brie cheese while in France. Reverend Mother, worried about my health, hopes, nonetheless, to spare her convent sister the medical reasons of my presence at the hospital. Will I be given the chance to be by Sister Marie Laurence's side, during the last moments of her life?

A genius idea crosses my husband's mind. My soulmate has not forgotten the primary motive of our pilgrimage in France. Medicine can no longer help the one who's arrived at the end of her journey. Palliative care, meant to keep the patient comfortable while the body finishes its last race, can continue in the new wing of the hospital, where a room with bay window will be reserved for Sister Marie Laurence. Her new space will bathe in the bright summer light. Reverend Mother gets approval for a transfer from the oncology ward to the new hospital pavilion, and my former teacher becomes my adjacent neighbor.

Mike has not left my side and falls asleep on a chair, his hand locked in mine the entire night. I find myself staring at this tall, masculine shape twisted uncomfortably on the chair next to my bed. I listen to his rhythmic breaths. His presence soothes all fear, silences all anxiety. He leaves at dawn to catch up on some sleep. He will change hotels and sacrifice comfort for proximity in order to avoid long travel times through Paris. The physician comes out of my room. Short therapeutic walks are prescribed to me, which will end in brief visits to my "neighbor." Sister Marie Laurence has clearly expressed her last wishes: to die with dignity, without artificial prolongation of a life whose inevitable course will soon come to an end.

The Martin siblings, her childhood companions, surround her this morning. A slender man with silver temples offers me his seat. My former teacher, by her prolonged hand pressure, confirms she is aware of my health condition and the reason for my odd presence as patient of the hospital. The nurse's aide agreed to stop for a visit after our walk. The story of my pilgrimage in France with Mike has stirred the medical personnel who discreetly tolerate our twists to their rules and regulations. Jean looks like his sister, silver streaks running through his light-colored hair. Marie is dark-haired like Paul. Sister Marie Laurence helped her younger sister with homework and ironed her brothers' shirts, my teacher revealed, one evening of shared confidences at Saint Joseph.

I motion to take my leave, anxious to respect the privacy of their family, in these difficult times when the certainty of an impending departure leaves no doubt, and no room for hope. But the patient's grip holds me prisoner by her side. "Death is only a necessary passage to the *true* life," she reminds her devastated audience. "In Heaven, all suffering will be abolished. Dry your tears. My time on earth in the Lord's service has simply been fulfilled."

The one we should support in her final hours becomes the comforter that day. As farewells approach, the patient shares the treasures of her heart. Life is fragile, and its special moments can be compared to precious comets that briefly illuminate our sky with their ephemeral trajectory. Chemotherapy has been suspended at Sister Marie Laurence's request, six weeks prior to my arrival in France. Medicine is, once again, losing its battle with cancer. The teacher, the missionary, driven by her unwavering religious faith, has reached peace and serenity with the inevitable. What would have been my reaction at the sight of her bald skull last month? Today, a light fuzz has grown back, indicator of life's fragility, but tenacity too.

We are alone on the hospital's sun deck. Reverend Mother granted her friend an ardent wish: to feel, for the last time, the caress of a bright summer sun on her skin. I traded my hospital gown for a cozy bathrobe and, escorted by Mike, joined Sister Marie Laurence on the terrace. She is seated on a wheelchair, and supported by pillows. Mike fetches me a chair, and takes his leave to allow us a private moment.

Fate, by an unexpected twist of events, has offered me a precious gift: A few hours of intense sharing to reconnect with the past and erase the years of silence. I cling to the essential. Death, already knocking at Sister Marie Laurence's door, warrants a return to basics…to what truly matters. We have ten years to catch up on. Will we have time? Every precious second must count, as if it will be the last….

~**59**~

One memorable Saturday at Saint Joseph, Sister Marie Laurence had gifted me a treasure in words: "Your desires will flourish one day alongside a Christian husband, who will meet all your expectations." With poetry from the heart, I share the story of my encounter with destiny, at the crossroad of life. On the artist's canvas, I paint the face of love. The man who has met my expectations? A name escapes from my lips: Michael! At the hour of confidences, pastel-colored snapshots of my Florida existence come to life: An artificial lake stretches across our backyard. On Sunday, ducks leave their aquatic world to share crumbs from our breakfast table in the garden. I planted pink and yellow hibiscus that remind me of my childhood in Bourdon.

I always wished to marry a man who can capture the message of this vast universe by my side. I evoke our December escapades when Mike and I headed for Floridian countryside in the heart of the night, away from light pollution, stretch a blanket on a grassy patch and feast on celestial displays of meteor showers. Every moment is a precious gift. When we approach the sublime, we must quickly reach out, before its free fall. If the waves of nostalgia come knocking at my door, I always look for familiar landscapes by Mike's side. Profound happiness unites us, renewed day after day, on the shores of our lives.

In a country called the melting pot of cultures and ethnicities, the southeastern state of Florida, the port of entry for the Caribbean and South America, is a striking example. Blessed with a mild climate and geographically close to the tropics, Florida enchants my island girl's heart. In my adopted city, more Cuban than American, Spanish often supersedes English. People offer warm welcomes. I am often greeted with words like "mi vida" and "mi amor" by perfect strangers: clerks at department stores, or baristas in coffee shops, a familiar sight at practically every street corner. I need, for my survival, the strong, dark cafecito served in miniature paper cups and swallowed in one gulp, head tilted backward, and throat on fire afterwards. Mike gave up his fight against the influence of coffee on me. "It's in my blood," I remind him. Yes, in this Habdoul blood flowing in my veins.

Sister Marie Laurence breaks out in a light-hearted laugh, and for a brief second, I feel I have my former teacher back in my life. She, in turn, recalls the scene Saint Joseph's dormitory supervisors so often caught a glimpse of: the young Haitian boarder concocting, with hot water from the sink and instant black powder, a tasteless brew, which was an insult to the word *coffee*. The patient seems to find pleasure in these minute details that paint a rosy picture today. I have transported her, by the magic of words and the colors of imagination, to America.

I describe our trips to the Everglades, this vast swamp land where water lilies and alligators abound and cohabit in harmony. A few Indian reservations are planted there, relegated in the shadows—a sad reminder that America, once, belonged to their ancestors. Mike loves to travel to Florida's West Coast, to capture the most beautiful sunsets of the Gulf of Mexico on his camera. I mention our weekends in Key West, Ernest Hemingway's town, located on a narrow strip of land at the extreme southern tip of the United States. When, on a deserted beach, we contemplate a majestic sunset on the horizon and watch the orange star plunge into the ocean, unforgettable words always come back to mind: *"Nature sings the wonders of the Creator."*

My meeting with Louise Tyler is examined with a fine-tooth comb. Will I ever heal from the wound I carry at the bottom of my heart? Color prejudice, officially banished, remains dormant in my adopted country. I also confess the influence of the hippie movement during my university years. The blurry image of Dany, my long-haired bearded friend, with his leather sandals and dark poncho, rises slowly to the surface. He had dangled dazzling sparkles on murky waters to attract me. I become silent, suddenly: the child I carry might cross path with other "Danys" along the way, but, unlike me, will not leave the nest at fifteen.

"Like you, Myriam, your child will rely on personal values of the heart," recalls, in a whisper, the teacher full of wisdom and measure at my side. With unsurprising humility, she fails to acknowledge that God places angels like her on the path of lucky travelers who might have lost their way on the journey. My former classmates emerge from the past: after Sister Marie Laurence's return from Africa, Reverend Mother shared accounts of her students' lives with their former teacher. My old friends obviously kept ties with Saint Joseph, our alma mater.

Agnès, my adopted sister at Saint Joseph, the instrument of my return to France, immersed in quiet happiness, has settled in Nantes with her son and her husband, a civil engineer. She always looked after the student from Haiti, who had felt, by her faltering steps and obvious accent, totally lost upon her arrival on French soil. They have been exchanging letters for a decade, reveals Sister Marie Laurence. I do not comment. I want to keep, intact, the memory of this sunny morning on Saint Ann's terrace.

My dear Ishtar, accomplice of our attempted fugue, one night of madness at Saint Joseph where the generosity of adolescence collided with our extreme naivety, returned to her homeland to live in the shadow of her country's Islamic culture. A graduate in Political Sciences at the Sorbonne, she will perform, without a doubt, ground-breaking work for the emancipation of women and their access to higher education back home.

Astrid de Panière gave birth to a son, fell in love with him and refused the idea of adoption as initially planned. Sister Marie

Laurence's tormentor had murmured: *"It is hard to believe, Myriam, but I will miss this place."* Those were Astrid's unforgettable words, as she left Saint Joseph's dormitory forever. The name of her brother, who managed to stir all my senses into a state of turmoil and make my adolescent's heart race furiously, is kept in discreet silence. Christian belongs to the yellowed pages of a faded past.

Gisèle, whose grandparents hosted us in Auvergne, studied medicine and now works at her father's practice. She is single, according to Saint Joseph's latest news. Annabelle, my academic rival, holds tenure in the math department of a prestigious university. Sophie, who invited me to the de Maisonrouge's ancestral home during All-Saints holidays, married Charles de Boncourt, her childhood friend. His name also bears a nobiliary particle, and the couple will head the family hosiery business, typical of Troyes, the picturesque town with its narrow, cobbled streets and Middle-Ages structures. Noah, guided by Reverend Mother, has joined the Mariale Order to devote a life of total service to God. She will transfer to a convent in her native Vietnam. Sister Marie-Laurence notes, a teasing spark in her eyes, "Myriam married Dr. Michael Roye. They live in Florida and await the birth of their first child."

I say nothing, savoring this moment I know is ephemeral. Mike approaches and leans towards me. His yellow pullover brushes against the yellow scarf that holds my dark hair. My cheek lightly touches the hand that lingers on my shoulder. My teacher is offered the vision of a double sun shining bright, by her side: this profusion of yellow, which radiated the joy of shared love.

"Motherhood suits you well. Welcome all the young lives God will bless you with, in the free sharing of your mutual affection."

Suddenly the fetus executes a somersault. I reach for the patient's bony hand and lay it on me, to share with her these instants of extreme emotion where Life manifests itself in the womb: a precious moment in time, to end ten years of silence. But the dark corners of my soul must be exposed before the final curtain falls.

~ * ~

Mike has gone back to the hotel, late afternoon, to enjoy the comfort of a soft mattress after a steaming, long shower he reminds me, a teasing wink painted on his face. My husband knows how much I love these hot showers where I transform our bathroom into a virtual sauna and my skin undergoes a vigorous exfoliation with a massage glove. My afternoon walk completed, I stop for a brief visit: Sister Marie Laurence, miraculously, is alone in her room. The stars of the universe have converged to offer us another chance for a heart-to-heart. The nurse's aide has agreed to fetch me back before the evening nurse's shift begins. I quickly realize the patient, with help from Mike and Reverend Mother, gone to rest at Saint Joseph, has obviously orchestrated this meeting. She will finally clear up all misunderstandings. The Saint Joseph student, in her blue beret and knee-highs, emerges from the past. The vindictive soul blurs out a question stifled for ten years:

"Why your unexpected departure for Africa?"

At the tender age of seven, I learned, flabbergasted, that Yvette was not my mother, and the world collapsed around me. I cling since, to places and people that shape my existence, lest they disappear without warning and abandon me.

The patient's unexpected, simple response leaves me stunned: "God had called me, at sixteen, to a missionary life of service. I waited, patient, for His time. Saint Joseph was a transit stop."

Bewildered, I try to find, from the depth of my soul, the appropriate comment, in light of such revelation. But I am unable to... It is a bitter reproach that escapes my lips instead:

"Why such long silence?"

Sister Marie Laurence remains pensive a moment. Like she used to do during Sciences class, she concentrates to dig for the exact word, stripped, simple, all encompassing, which will leave no room for doubt or misunderstanding:

"In the heart of silence, we listen to the voice of God. I heard it while cloistered in prayer and meditation, the summer after your departure. Myriam, you had to overcome the challenges of change, alone. There was a force lurking in the depths of your soul. But you had to tap into it! No one could do it for you. I took a backseat after the news of your mandatory transfer to Notre-Dame, which coincided with mine to the Congo, to allow you to stand on your own two feet when you would return to France. You had to navigate, yourself, the formalities of new school enrollment, adapt to new surrounding and new classmates. It never was an abandonment of my part."

She paused briefly and spoke again, her tone suddenly maternal. "At Saint Joseph, your young age, coupled with your status of foreigner, far from home and family, made you vulnerable. I took you under my wing, to arm you with sage advice, inculcate in you wise principles of life. I shared with you the only possession I had: my experience as an elder. I guided you in your complex journey of self-discovery, revealing, unsuspected to you, the extent of your strength. But you were reluctant to seize life's exciting challenges!"

Ishtar's invitation to her uncle's palace, declined by cowardice, comes to mind. The patient continues, "Hiding in the comfort of a reassuring routine, effort and self-transcendence would not have their raison d'être. Your transfer to Notre Dame, where you had to adapt, alone, to a new school and cultivate new friendships, made you strong! You had all the assets to succeed and you learned to rely on your own resources in France."

Sister Marie Laurence concludes, in a broken voice, "You could have reached out through Saint Joseph, as did Agnès, Ishtar, and even Astrid, who sent me a picture of her son. They learned of my transfer to Africa by their faithful contacts with the school, not by a personal letter from me. But you had cut ties with the past, and I chose to respect your silence. You were not alone, however, on your journey. God was watching, every step of the way, over you. I have never stopped praying for you."

I look down, with a contrite and humble heart. Everything becomes crystal clear: my fear of abandonment, of the unknown, and my panic over life's unavoidable changes, have been the major culprits of a long and foolish silence. Holes and cracks settled in. The echo of a painful truth, so often voiced by our teacher, emerges from Saint Joseph's buried past: *"We can never go back."* Would redemption be possible?

Mike returns late from the hotel. Night has already settled in. As he approaches my sleepy face, he notices traces of tears…I apologized to my teacher for my ten-year stubborn silence and asked for forgiveness, before taking leave…She pressed her hand into mine without a word and she gave it to me wholeheartedly.

~60~

Florence de Val, a boarder at the Mariale Order's Parisian school, developed a solid friendship with Laurence Martin, a day student of the same Parisian all-girl institution renowned for the excellence of its curriculum and education. The wise child with long dark braids, spoiled by life and a privileged upbringing, admired the thin, blonde classmate who reaped all the awards.

They would visit each other's home on weekends. Florence enjoyed, at the Martins, the simple joys of family life, united in the sharing of a modest existence. Domestic work was performed with contagious good humor by Laurence and her siblings. After the soup, evenings came to a close with prayer. A pretty girl's bedroom always waited for Florence's friend, at the de Val, and the maid, with deference, spoke of "Miss Laurence".

After a particularly moving religious retreat, the two adolescents, overwhelmed beyond measure, received their life changing calling to take the veil: *"I will be a missionary in Africa,"* proclaimed Laurence with conviction. Florence opted for the quiet, regulated convent life in France. The two friends graduated from École Normale to become teachers and both pursued a degree in the field of sciences. Laurence also earned a certificate in psychology and Florence, management. The frail-looking child had become an attractive young woman, who, out of vanity, only wore her glasses during her long study sessions in the evenings. An up-and-coming Normalien (a graduate from École Normale) nearly won Laurence's heart; she even imagined their future as a secular missionary couple, on the African continent.

But the young man did not share her noble aspirations. Laurence, unflinching, ended their romance. She realized that God alone would fulfill her high expectations. Through meditation, prayer and in-depth study of the scriptures, the two young postulants were training for austere religious life: Sisters Marie Laurence of Charity and Elizabeth of the Annunciation, prostrated on the ground by the chapel's altar, arms stretched out in a cross, joined the Mariale Order to pronounce their perpetual vows: obedience, poverty and chastity. The moving ceremony, which made them brides of Christ, proclaimed the total gift of their life to God.

The Mariale Order's main apostolate was to establish and lead, throughout France and beyond borders in former French colonies, all-girls Christian schools with a solid academic curriculum. Sister Marie Laurence's educational background made her a prime candidate for a post in the Parisian region, as a physical sciences teacher at Notre Dame. She set up a state-of-the-art laboratory facility that became the envy of other schools. Her young age and inexperience of missionary life were evoked as grounds to deny her transfer request for Africa, to which she ardently aspired. Obedient to hierarchy, Sister Marie Laurence stoically launched her long teaching career in France.

By a twist of fate, the two childhood friends reunited, years later, on the same path of service. Saint Joseph's director suddenly passed away, creating an urgent vacancy. The Superior of the Mariale Order wanted to rejuvenate their aging institutions. She selected Sister Elizabeth, known for her administrative talents, to head the school.

The new director approached her childhood friend. "Would you agree to lend me a hand?"

With the young staff, new life was infused within the walls of a centuries-old décor. Enrollments began to pour in. Yet her missionary aspirations remained alive in Sister Marie Laurence's heart. Africa, inexorably, was calling her. A suffering humanity troubled her spirit at the core. She was anxious to serve the destitute of the world, in areas where hunger, disease and death are the daily lot of the "forgotten" of this world. These fragile souls who, too, have their story to tell, their message to share.

The summer right before my arrival in France, unable to tame her impatience any longer, Sister Marie Laurence went to her Superior's office. In public she owed Reverend Mother Elizabeth obedience and respect. But when the two friends were alone, they could drop the hierarchy protocol.

Sister Marie Laurence's tone was poignant. "Flo, I am forty. I beg you to use your influence to facilitate my transfer to Africa, while I still have the strength to serve."

The following year, the post of Superior of Saint Mary's convent in the Congo was offered to her. She had waited, in obedience and submission, twenty-four years for the fulfillment of a calling she received at sixteen. Setting foot on the African continent, Sister Marie Laurence had finally met her destiny.

~ * ~

Mike has returned to our hotel to place calls to his clinic and our respective families. He is already implementing the logistical details of our return to Florida. I cling to the present moment, a fragile gift, and want to keep it, intact, in its treasure chest. But the present is also my unborn child asleep in my womb, this precious life that palpitates in symbiosis, with me.

Reverend Mother concludes, with sadness in her eyes, her story and offers me these words that will always resonate in my heart:

"The best friendship proof I could offer was to facilitate my friend and spiritual sister's departure to Africa. Myriam, love sometimes means to, bravely, agree to say goodbye."

Africa was her destiny, concluded Reverend Mother, offering a window into the soul of Sister Marie Laurence, the missionary. A pilgrim briefly crossed my path, to disappear at a crossroad and follow the inexorable course of her own story. She waited a quarter of a century, in faithful obedience, and the perfecting of her innermost self, to finally be allowed to fulfill the great calling of her life.

~ * ~

Mike is next to me, our chairs stuck together by the patient's bed, his arm around my shoulder. The language of Shakespeare does not understand Molière's words but those of love are universal. Reverend Mother, by the window, recites her rosary in silence. She remains discreetly available, near her friend.

Sister Marie Laurence smiles at my husband. She whispers, *"Thank You,"* with her Parisian accent, and Mike returns her smile. He perfectly understands the profound scope of these two little words: our pilgrimage to France, which lifted the veil of silent misunderstanding, and offered the soothing balm of forgiveness.

Egyptian murals show the souls of the deceased surrounded by familiar objects and precious riches, on their journey through the underworld, toward the afterlife. Christians, on the contrary, aim to be free from the chains of material possessions and complex emotions that will hinder their ultimate voyage and encounter with their Maker. Sister Marie Laurence chooses to unburden her heart and make a clean slate of the past before saying goodbye...

Through her own words, snapshots of her busy African life parade: the refectory with the thatched roof, exposed to the elements, where hundreds of children receive their daily ration of wheat; Ahmed, three years, rounded belly and hair reddened from malnutrition, who likes to snuggle in her arms at nap time; visits to neighboring villages with the nurse, to heal wounds and hearts; hygiene classes with the locals to avoid infections and parasitic diseases; the village chief's son marriage, a victory against cohabitation.

Sister Marie Laurence describes, with poetic imageries, the breathtaking sunsets she witnessed every night under the cool shade of the gazebo, where splashes of red and inflamed orange tones in the African skies proclaim the Creator's artistic majesty.

But this strong soul inhabits a frail and vulnerable body. The patient confesses, with resignation, her health challenges: the malaria attack, despite preventive quinine; the bout with hepatitis following six years of missionary service, and her convalescence in France, by orders of her superiors. In the shadow of Saint Joseph's community, surrounded by her convent sisters and spoiled by Reverend Mother's solicitude, Sister Marie Laurence slowly recovers: she puts on weight and regains her color during a sabbatical year of rest and prayer.

Several former students visit her. She writes *In the Shadow of His Footsteps*, a small collection of personal reflections and exhortations aimed at young candidates for religious life, these postulants who, in their untamed enthusiasm and fiery desire to serve, risk missing God's silent presence.

She motions for Reverend Mother to approach and hand me a mysterious envelope, a bit wrinkled and discolored, bearing a simple name: Myriam. I instantly recognize my former teacher's handwriting. A little book emerges, with a dedication by the author: "To my spiritual daughter Myriam. May you always live in the shadow of His footsteps."

Discreetly hidden in the pages of the booklet, an amateur photograph reveals, to my stunned contemplation, Sister Marie Laurence, dressed in the white robe and veil of missionary sisters in tropical regions. She smiles at life, radiant joy painted in her face, with an adorable, shirtless little boy in her arms.

I exclaim, "*Ahmed!*"

She nods. "*Yes.*"

I hold, between fingers, the obscure testimony, the blurred snapshot of a consecrated life. It summarizes, more vividly than any word, the story of Sister Marie Laurence, the missionary. The Mariale Order grants her ardent wish: to regain her post at Saint Mary. Sister Marie Laurence agrees to stop active ministry and embrace an advisory position; her congregation of sisters, the village elders, the impetuous youth full of dreams and hopes come to seek from her, words of comfort and wisdom. But the ravages of past illnesses left scars on her liver. Two years after her return to Zaire (former Congo), Sister Marie Laurence's failing health warrants her immediate repatriation to France. She realizes, with tears in her eyes, that she will not go back to Africa.

The farewells to Saint Mary are heartbreaking: the village men and women, wrapped in eloquent silence, are determined to follow on foot, the all-terrain vehicle covered in dust, to the tiny airport of the area; little Ahmed sobs and screams, as his white "mama" disappears forever; the missionary sisters mourn their beloved Superior's departure. At the airport, Reverend Mother bravely smiles, as she welcomes her ailing friend back to France. The frail silhouette emerged from the plane, escorted by one of Saint Mary's nuns who journeyed back to Europe with her to be of assistance. A few months later, an advanced liver cancer diagnosis is pronounced.

My pilgrimage into the past is coming to a close. Sister Marie Laurence and her former student revisited the past, and reclaimed peace along the way. The missionary took us to the land of Africa to get a glimpse of her journey…She met Mike, my marvelous present, in real time. The circle is closing . I feel it in the deepest corners of my soul. As I motion to leave, my teacher beckons me to approach and, extending her frail arms, holds me close to her heart. Such a rare gesture, from the epitome of restraint and measure, symbolizes her goodbyes, the prelude to the inevitable.

Africa claimed Sister Marie Laurence's health by its tropical fevers and infectious diseases; but the vast continent was also the land where profound joy was felt, and lifelong dreams, fulfilled. In my hands, a precious talisman—the yellowed envelope with its modest, yet symbolic content: the story of a missionary life. I will cherish these relics, the humble treasure of a valiant pilgrim who has arrived at the end of her journey.

~ * ~

The nurse quietly leaves the room. My blood pressure is stable. Silent darkness engulfs us…Mike, without a word, slips his long body by my side to offer me the shelter of his arms. Comforted in the warmth of his familiar presence, I close my eyes; I am at peace.

~ * ~

Ten years of silence have been abolished in a few hours of intense sharing with my former teacher. No more cloud will obscure the fragile sky of our emotions. The dark corners of resentment and misunderstanding have disappeared, bathed by the light of forgiveness and reconciliation.

The view of her closed eyelids and oxygen nasal canula shock me when, arm in arm, Mike and I approach Sister Marie Laurence's bed the next day. Her last mission completed, she is declining rapidly. It is hard to fathom she was enjoying sunshine in my company, two days earlier, on Saint Ann's terrace. A priest visited her this morning to administer the anointing of the sick…The Last Rites, before the ultimate journey.

"The night was challenging," reveals the nurse, as she adjusts her morphine drip. Sister Marie Laurence smiles weakly, to the pressure of my hand on hers. I am resolute not to shed tears and upset our patient, but my stoic composure crumbles as Mike puts his arm around my shoulder. The inevitable is fast approaching. Pretending anything else would be absolute foolishness.

A barely audible whisper escapes from her lips. "Myriam. We are pilgrims on earth; travelers, on our way to our eternal home. When the moment arrives to part, we must accept, bravely, to say goodbye."

I do not realize it yet, but the mentor has just pronounced her last coherent words. This is her final gift to her student, the last life lesson of a dying teacher. Morphine alleviates suffering, but obscures the brain with a murky veil.

Can we ever affirm to have voiced all we needed to share with our loved ones before we part? Will we let shyness or denial claim the best of us in life's painful circumstances? If we could predict the exact moment of the last, conscious farewell to those who are leaving us, would we change our words and our gestures? Will we carry remorse or regret to the grave, should we fail to speak from the heart when there was still "time"?

Sister Marie Laurence, eyes closed, is slowly fading away. Her shallow breath remains the only indicator of life that clings to her emaciated body. Reverend Mother, her face reflecting all the sorrows of the world, keeps vigil by her friend's bed. It is a matter of days, or hours, perhaps? Lying in the hospital bed, the patient is already unaware of her constant presence.

~ * ~

Dr. Bastien concludes his physical exam. My blood pressure has stabilized, my ankles are no longer swollen, and he is signing the papers for my discharge, which is scheduled for tomorrow. The men exchange a cordial handshake, as Mike will work to enforce my doctor's orders: no salt; no spices; no stimulants (like caffeine); no stress. Daily walks and frequent rest are advised.

That is the price to pay for having a doctor as a husband: no deviation, no rule-bending will be allowed for me. Mike will be my parole officer and my conscience. I thank the young Dr. Bastien for his understanding. The medical staff, I have no doubt, will long remember our visit to Saint Ann and the minor rules and regulations they bent, to allow us precious moments with a very special patient, at the end of her earthly journey.

This life that pulsates in the closed universe of my distended body will, once again, guide our steps. I carry, in my womb, the most profound mystery of the world, the result of a dance between two bodies and the merging of intense emotions. I'm confronted with both joy and grief: a life is about to leave us; another will soon enter our world. Life has come full circle, to form a perfect sphere.

Mike, aware of my highly charged emotions, urges me to rest. He will not leave my room tonight, he promises. Curtains are drawn. The dim nightlight allows us to recognize the nurse's silent shadow; she is making her evening rounds. Foregoing the hotel's comfortable room, my husband prepares for the night on a stiff chair by my bed. My hand secured in his grip, I have no recollection of drifting off to sleep.

Reverend Mother, with a stealthy step, enters the room in the heart of the night. "Myriam, come quickly," she says. "You must be brave." Mike jumps to his feet and, in a flash, I understand.

Sister Marie Laurence, extremely agitated, is uttering bizarre sounds. The death rattle, I conclude, as a nervous tremor runs down my spine. In the subtly translucent light of the night lamp, I watch the face of agony bravely lead the final battle.

Brushing against this life about to leave us, I will watch weakness turn into strength: as she takes her last breath, our brave pilgrim will communicate the resilience of her spirit to us.

To respect the dignity of the hour and the need for privacy, Mike waits behind closed doors. I grab the poor fingers clenched on the white sheet.

Reverend Mother has clutched Sister Marie Laurence's other hand and wraps her emaciated fingers with the rosary she carried throughout her religious life. Mustering all her strength to keep a firm, steady voice, Saint Joseph's Superior recites Psalm 23: "Though I walk through the valley of the shadow of death, I will fear no evil; for though art with me."

In these poignant moments, the friend whispers, "Go in peace, Laurence, you have accomplished your earthly mission."

At the sound of these words, Sister Marie Laurence breathes calmly for a few seconds. She offers us a poignant look. A glassy gaze follows. She exclaims:

"Oh, so much light!"

Laurence Martin takes her last breath with a smile. Maybe I will wake up and Mike will hold me in his arms and say, "This is just a bad dream." No. This rigid body, motionless in the bed, says otherwise. Death's reality hits me head-on. Reverend Mother tenderly closes her eyelids. We remain silent, next to the one who just left us. By her bent forehead, I assume Saint Joseph's Mother Superior is in prayer for the repose of her friend's soul. At the heart of grief, she worries, nonetheless, for my welfare and invites my husband to join us in the deceased's room. Mike silently approaches and wraps his arms around me. My tears can no longer be contained. I start sobbing uncontrollably against Michael's shoulder.

A pale, dull day emerges at dawn. Eyes still red from our night of sorrow, Reverend Mother will remain, until the end, the Superior. She allows medical personnel to come and fulfill their last duties for the deceased. The Martin family has also been notified. My mission in France has ended. Sister Marie Laurence is no longer with us. God granted me the grace to hold her hand, on her last breath. Her soul has already crossed the gates of heaven. I am convinced I heard her voice, in a whisper:

"Have peace, Myriam, I am happy."

Reverend Mother Elizabeth holds me close to her heart. At the door, escorted by Mike, I turn around one last time:

"Farewell, Reverend Mother. Thank you for having loved her so. She was a mother to me."

"Goodbye, Myriam," Saint Joseph's Superior replies in an echo. "Thank you for having loved her so. She was my friend, my sister in battle."

Epilogue

Israel planted six million trees, in memory of six million Jews whose lives, broken, served as Holocaust to the Absurd. Each planted tree, watered by tears, symbolizes the renewal of life, which must continue. Life goes on, indeed. The planted tree is symbolic: it is my daughter Laurence Claire's name, chosen out of love by Michael. I stare, in disbelief, at this fragile, miniature human asleep in my arms, and I'm overwhelmed by life's wonderful gift.

We left France abruptly. "It is better this way, my daughter," Reverend Mother said with a reassuring tone on the phone. I will be spared the sight of Sister Marie Laurence lying in a coffin. Thinking about her, I will envision Africa's vast, open landscape, Handel's "Hallelujah" playing in the background. She flew toward the infinite blue sky. "Go in peace, Myriam," I believe I heard. And my heart made peace with fate that, once again, deprived me of a mother.

I will go back to France one day and pay Agnès a debt of gratitude. She was the instrument of my return to Europe. At Saint Joseph, I will stroll through Chateaubriand's park, holding Laurence's hand, to gain control of my emotions. And my daughter will marvel at the earth's carpet of gold autumn leaves under our feet.

Mike fulfilled his dream of a private practice with Alex and John, his partners. They established, on a rotation system, a work schedule compatible with family life. Thanksgiving holidays will take us to Mike's parents in Boston. Our children' youth will be the antidote to their old age, slowly creeping up in their lives. We will travel to Haiti during December's cooler season, when the sky is adorned with millions of stars. Deschapelle's Hospital Albert Schweitzer has welcomed my husband's annual offer to volunteer, and Mike plans to rally his colleagues and their resources to the cause of service. I will return, with delight, to the island and the family I have carried in my heart on every journey and every frontier life has taken me. *My roots are planted in Haiti.* If I ventured to distant boundaries and reaped emotional discoveries, the story began in the land of my birth.

Following my father's example, Mike also married my Haitian family the day we celebrated our union. Christmas will gather us, under one roof, in my childhood home. Summer rallies will bring the clan to Florida. James, Yvette, Leilah, Bobby, Freddy, Junior and Mark symbolize my home port, my base, this mosaic of loved ones who, in their divergences and imperfections, are essential to my survival. Grandmother is determined to see all her grandsons marry. And Yvette, quietly turning grey over the years, will always be the mother who helps welcome the birth of our children. My husband is my Rock of Gibraltar, the captain of our lives. He will be the anchor I will hold on to, when life's storms come crashing on our shores.

Someday, after the birth of our son, we will embark on a journey… We will discover the vast African landscapes under Zaire's skies. My children will hear the painful story of my ancestors from the Dark Continent. We will accomplish a moving pilgrimage to Saint Mary. I will share with Laurence and her brother the true account of a missionary calling: Sister Marie Laurence's, whose life and death were a valiant quest for the highest summits.

Our ambition for our children will be simple: *"Find your truth! Accomplish your full potential."* The spark of creation will flourish freely in their young lives. They will discover the magic of gardens, and the grace of butterflies. We will share the legend of the pot of gold at the end of the rainbow and read, at bedtime, tales of *One Thousand and One Nights* before our good-night kiss. Our children will sleep in peace, knowing their guardian angel watches over them, in the still of the night.

I will seek a post in the paramedical field, when we become empty-nesters, and our children have spread their wings. The sunset of our lives will surprise us gently, on the flower-filled veranda of a small chalet in the heart of Kenscoff. Mike has promised a return to my native land, when the time comes for us to retire. Sitting side by side on a two-seat swing, we will tenderly hold hands as we watch our grandchildren blossom before our eyes.

At Sister Marie Laurence's bedside, I learned to face and accept Death, which, ultimately, is just an extension of Life, in another dimension. Through the years, I felt fulfilled in my role as wife and mother. What is missing in my life for perfect happiness?

Mike steps in, once again, to alter the course of destiny. "Harness your creative energy. Revive the magic of pen and paper. Recapture your adolescence years, in their strong and weak moments. Your words will be your testament."

Author's Note

Myriam rediscovered her journal in her treasure chest of memories. Encouraged by her husband, she avoided routine's dangerous pitfalls, which erode the soul. Writing became the spark that renewed her spirit and brought her back the joy of literary creation.

About the Author

Born in Port-au-Prince, Yamile Stitt studied abroad, in Europe and the United States, in the sixties and seventies. She returned to the islands for a while—Haiti and the Dominican Republic—but Florida has been "home" to her and her family for decades. Today, with her children grown and raising families of their own, she balances life as an interpreter and a writer.

Writing has been her childhood dream and lifelong passion: "I was always an avid reader. My fondest childhood memories in Haiti take me back to blissful times of solitude with my favorite books. The summer of my eleventh birthday, with my special Parker fountain pen, I wrote my first 'novel' on a student notebook, full of ink stains and erasures."

A closet writer for years, with stacks of poems and short stories in her personal files, **Yamile Stitt** is the author of *Memories in Technicolor*, a coming-of-age novel set against the colorful backdrop of tumultuous and profound times on the world stage.

*A French version of her novel, *Les Chemins de Lumière* was published in 2016 by Educa Vision.